Jasper County Public Library System

Overdue notices are a courtesy of
the library system.
Failure to receive an overdue notice
does not absolve the borrower of the
obligation to return materials on time.

Nov '08

THE ACTRESS

Also by Elizabeth Sims

Easy Street

Lucky Stiff

Damn Straight

Holy Hell

THE ACTRESS

Elizabeth Sims

St. Martin's Minotaur

New York

This is a work of fiction. All of the characters, organizations, and events portrayed in this novel are either products of the author's imagination or are used fictitiously.

www.minotaurbooks.com

ISBN-13: 978-0-312-37727-4
ISBN-10: 0-312-37727-4

First Edition: June 2008

10 9 8 7 6 5 4 3 2 1

THE ACTRESS

ONE

I screamed.

I filled my lungs with the stale, coffee-smelling air of the dungeon and let out a ragged howl that ricocheted off the cold walls. I closed my eyes and screamed again as every cell in my body writhed in a futile attempt to deny the horror that was being inflicted on me by the guy in glasses holding a small cardboard box that said DEATH.

The guy, who had introduced himself as Ned, stood to the side and brandished the box in his freckled hands. I decided to scream once more, this one a sharp, convulsive type of cry.

"OK," said the casting director, a thin black woman named M'kenge, with expressive hands. "OK, Rita, please do it again, only"—she cupped her hands as if to suppress a flower growing—"this time don't shrink down. Get all taut and tall, like you're going to break out of your skin." Upward release of hands.

I did so. I stood at attention, remembering I was supposed to be tied to a pole, put my hands behind my back—behind my butt, actually, which looks more like natural bondage because your shoulders aren't all hiked up—and arched my neck like Joan of Arc at the stake. Ned shook the box at me and I screamed.

When you take a breath to do a scream, you don't just grab a gulp of air and let go. You need to take the time to load your lungs all the way to the bottom. You need to pull all the slack from your diaphragm like you'd pull a bowstring in archery, and then and only then do you unleash that scream to its target, which is the red beating heart of every human within four miles.

I screamed, and it felt good. I was screaming well today. I ululated in the middle of this one—nothing fancy, just another jolt of emotion, just another ripple in the violent fabric of my horror. I'd warmed up carefully.

This was a job I wanted. A job I needed. This was Evan Granger Jackson's new teensploitation movie, *Fingershredder II,* sequel to *Fingershredder,* the low-budget instant-cult terror film you've doubtless heard about or seen. If you're a male age thirteen through seventeen, you've seen it three times.

The role I was trying for was Student Teacher Who Gets Her Fingers Shredded Halfway Through the Script by the Evil But Understandably So Because of Childhood Abuse Sadistic Killer. The fingershredder.

So I screamed. I screamed my ass off, discharging the screams through relaxed vocal cords but tight external throat muscles as Sam Wojczyk had taught me in his acting class at UCLA.

I was lucky to have Ned standing there holding the cardboard box, because at least he was human. In case you've never auditioned for pictures like this in Hollywood, you often don't have anybody playing opposite you. You're just there all alone in front of the casting director, maybe possibly a producer, an assistant with a clipboard who might also be running the video camera, and the empty coffee cups and scone wrappers of the day.

The cardboard box was a stand-in for the fingershredder device audiences came to know and love so well in the original. See, the fingershredding guy figures out pretty early in his career that paper shredders don't work well on fingers: they jam quickly, even the heavy-duty, government models. Plus he likes to shred other body parts too, then eventually the victim bleeds to death in terrible pain. So he invents this gadget using parts from a vacuum cleaner, a Cuisinart, and a walkie-talkie. Works great on the screen. A fiendish device, of course you've seen stills of it in *People* and *Teen* and such. I'm surprised they didn't license miniatures of it for inclusion in Happy Meals.

"OK, stop," said M'kenge. I had not met M'kenge before today's audition, but I'd carefully learned her name because that's what a professional actress does. I feel unusual names are more critical to remember than ordinary names, because people with unusual names have a bigger burden in life than the rest of us, in a small but important to them way.

An unusual name practically *invites* you to forget it. M'kenge pronounced her name *Em-ken-gay*. On the page M'kenge looks as if it might be pronounced *Ma-keng-ee*, which would make it sound Scots, which her parents surely could not have intended.

So M'kenge said stop. I looked at her attentively. She blew a breath down at the tabletop, then ran two fingers along the side of her skull as if trying to unzip a headache and let it out. Her head was one of those beautiful short-cropped African heritage ones, large smooth cranium, narrow jaw. She did not bother to smile. She was looking at me with intensity and thrilling dissatisfaction. Thrilling because she clearly wanted to help me get it right.

I so wanted to get it right.

"Rita, can you do it again, this time full-face to me. I know in this scene you're supposed to be watching your student Melissa's fingers getting shredded, and then her tongue and all that, but now I'd like you to scream as if *your* fingers were getting shredded. You were given pages for that scene, so let's try it, just the screaming part." She clenched one hand on her stomach and reached skyward with the other. "Bring it up from your gut, but not totally from there. Give me some highness, I guess what I'm trying to say is can you make it more piercing?"

Piercing.

"Yes," I said, my heart singing because she didn't say, *Thank you, next!* If they ask you to do it different ways, they think you might be able to deliver exactly what they want.

"Make the hair on the back of my neck stand up."

"Yes."

I thought of the most horrifying thing in the world to me right then, which was getting my credit card declined again at the grocery store, which would mean I would have to sell Gramma Gladys's diamond brooch to buy cereal and juice boxes for Petey and to prevent the landlord from evicting us.

So I imagined walking into Adil's Pawn America with that diamond-and-sapphire brooch, and all that it meant, and I felt not only frightened but angry, and I set my heels into the carpet of the soundproof audition room which was doubling today as a bloody dungeon, and I screamed and screamed again.

Plus usually for a film role you're doing it in somebody's office, not a casting studio, the studios being the cattle chutes between the herd of actors out there and the yearned-for slaughterhouse of TV commercials. The company that made the *Fingershredder* movies, Half Fast Pictures, however, rented studio space for these auditions because everybody in the offices would have gone insane listening to people screaming for days on end. Evan Granger Jackson liked to have lots of first audition tapes to look at.

We had already done an earlier scene with dialogue in it, not that there was lots in those movies. Which is what makes horror movies so much like pornos. There's not that much difference between "Please don't! Stop!" and "Please don't stop!" The scripts are interchangeable, it's only the action that's different. Really, just listen sometime.

"Thank you," said M'kenge with finality in her voice, and I could tell she was disappointed. She crunched up one cheek wistfully. To me, an acting professional, it was the worst kind of disappointment, that tone that says, Man, this one *just missed*. Missed by *that much*. Next!

Of course they rarely say anything at the moment, they leave that for your agent. But I was experienced enough to know that tone; I'd heard it so often.

Was my life's ambition to play supporting roles in teen horror flicks? No. But give me credit for not having stooped to doing porn, not that I have the body porn requires anyway—the Macy's parade tits, the lion's-mane hair. I'd had breast augmentation, but only one cup size, up to C from my God-given B, which I felt was necessary for the movies, but no way could I ever compete in porn.

I was a serious actress, and I'd long known acting was the best path in life for me. But time had become my enemy: at this point I was twenty-nine and grimly fighting the concept of thirty. Thirty is what you never want to turn in Hollywood, let alone forty or worse. Time, frankly, was running out. My agent was getting me lots of auditions, because she still believed in me. But if you could convert auditions into car payments what a butt-sassy world Los Angeles would be.

I thanked Ned, I thanked M'kenge, I thanked Ellen the coffee-stained assistant. Thank you, thank you, they thanked me back and Ellen flipped my head shot to the bottom of the stack. I caught a glimpse of my face, spritely and wholesome above the collar of my crisp white blouse, then—flip—there was the next actress's face, spritely and wholesome, possibly just what they were looking for.

I passed her on the way out. Her head was high, shoulders back, confident smile ready. We exchanged friendly glances, because you never know who you might be asking for a job someday.

That night Petey and I ate the last can of Campbell's tomato soup and the last of the rice, which came to three-fourths of a cup before cooking. I mixed it all together, put salt and pepper on it, and called it Spider-Man's Mom's Special. God bless my boy, he was so hungry he ate it.

Petey was a Spider-Man maniac. He was four now. When he was three he was a Curious George maniac. When he was two he was a hit-the-rainbow-xylophone-until-Mommy's-ears-pour-blood maniac. I watched him eat and wondered what five would bring.

Precious boy. I saw his father's face in his miniature one: there were Jeff's gorgeous marine-blue eyes, Jeff's touchingly dimpled cheeks, Jeff's contemptuous upper lip. Would he take after his dad? Marry the cute girl next door, move to California for a dull job and start drinking a fifth a day and slapping her around?

I asked Petey that question with my eyes. He looked at me, swallowed a mouthful of the disgusting dinner I had prepared, and answered, "Noah at school? He pooped on the piano."

I hugged him. It was a quiet night.

TWO

The bright sepulchre of Adil's Pawn America was crammed with dead items moldering under a hundred cold fluorescent suns. Petey found the place stimulating.

"Let's buy that guitar."

"No."

"What's that?"

"It's an amplifier."

"What does it do?"

"It makes the guitar sound louder."

"Let's buy it!"

"No!"

"Mommy, I'm still hungry."

"I know, honey."

"I want chips." The boy was only slightly uncomfortable from hunger, but in children a little hunger goes a long way. They teach you that fifteen minutes after they're born.

"No chips."

"Can I have an apple?"

"May I have. As soon as we get back to the Safeway."

"Can I eat it while we're walking around?"

"Honey, be quiet now."

"It smells bad in here."

I held his wrist in my practiced antilock grip against his aimless tugging. The key is to give the wrist some space to twirl, but not enough so it can yank its way out altogether. I achieved this by using my thumb and middle finger for the basic hold, with my index finger poised like a trigger to crank down at any indication of increased pulling force. This took commitment because such a grip hurts your hand after a while. I sacrificed my hand comfort for Petey's almost every day.

The pawnshop not only smelled bad, it was tomb-chilly as well, air-conditioning blasting from an ugly box over the transom. It had been a warm January week. I hated the word *January* because all it meant to me was Christmas bills.

The pawnbroker, whose name I guessed was Adil, Jr., squirted the jeweler's loupe from his eye and neatly caught it in his hand. He laid the brooch on the counter.

I wished Petey hadn't said the word *hungry*, it was too good a bullet for Adil, Jr., who smiled and fired it into my heart. "The sapphires are OK but there's a huge crack in the diamond."

This pawn dude was unstereotypically young, maybe only twenty, and dressed in a white T-shirt with a pink puppy on it. But his eyes were as flat as dimes. Surely you can only get a look like that by growing up in the business. Years of skillful belittling.

I knew enough not to say something pathetic like, But it was my grandmother's. The provenance of the brooch was irrelevant. The meaning of the brooch was irrelevant. The brooch had no meaning anymore. The brooch was going to transmute into sacks of groceries and a rent check. I hoped to God.

"How much?"

"I can give you four hundred."

I further knew enough not to say, But you see my credit card was declined at the grocery store two hours ago and I had to leave all the food and detergent lying there and hustle with Petey to the bank before noon because it's Saturday to get this diamond pin out of the safe-deposit box and it is the last pin. It is the last anything except for my wristwatch, which I need until I get mugged for it some night. The watch anyhow is a knockoff of a Longines, in fact if you look closely and you are the sort of fellow who would look closely, you would see that it says Lon*gunes.* And I'm only one month behind on my rent but I cannot let it become two months because there are Plenty Of People In Los Angeles Who Would Rent My Apartment In A Second, people with pay stubs to show the landlord, pay stubs with regular sequential dates on them, every two weeks, pay stubs, pay stubs.

What I did say was, "That's a two-carat diamond."

"It absolutely is." The pawn dude quirked both eyebrows. "But the setting is the only thing holding that diamond together. If I was to pry open those prongs, the thing would fall apart into a million pieces. I'm buying this on the basis of the sapphires."

It was my cue to fix him with an unflinching gaze, which I did. "There's no crack in that diamond. Four hundred is an insult."

He fixed me back with heartbreaking disinterest. "You don't have to pawn it here."

The reputable jewelers who buy jewels, used jewels, vintage jewels—it's *vintage* to you and *used* to the dealer who's buying it from you—they don't like to do transactions like this. In the first place the appraiser guy only comes in on Tuesdays and Thursdays, and when he does buy something he gives you a receipt for it and then the office person cuts you a check. These reputable jewelers like to buy in lots, they like to buy a boxful of jewelry from an estate. They don't like to deal with people who come in off the street wanting to sell one piece because grocery stores don't give change for two-carat diamond pins.

Petey hung by his shoulder socket, lusting for junk. "Let's buy that fishing pole."

"No, honey."

"Let's buy that saw."

"No."

"Why not?"

"Sh, honey, Mommy's doing business."

He hated to be shushed. "Why not why not why not? Mommy!"

"Honey, please."

"MOMMY! MOMMY! MOMMY!"

"Please stop, Petey," I interrupted, trying for a tough tone but I felt so damn sorry for the little guy. "Because I really don't need a tantrum right now." Which effectively tripped his tantrum circuit. He squeezed his eyes shut and cranked his volume to jet-turbine level and I had to stop him because I needed to sell this fucking brooch. Four hundred dollars was not going to pay our back rent of nine hundred dollars plus nine hundred current, but it would buy us plenty of food, and I would have to think of something else as far as the rent went. I needed to sell the brooch to this T-shirt–clad asshole, so I got down in Petey's face and said, "If you'll stop I'll buy you anything you want from McDonald's as soon as we leave here."

He shut up instantly. Adil, Jr., waited. Another customer came in. Adil, Jr., cleared his throat. I looked at him.

"Four hundred," he repeated.

My eyes slid off his shallow uncaring face and I muttered, "All right."

THINK HAPPY THOUGHTS. Petey had recently passed the milestone of buckling his own car seat harness. Soon he would learn to tie his shoes. But in Los Angeles so many children put in more hours staring at their shoes from the padded shells of their car seats than walking in them. You can buy Velcro shoes for your kid and let him learn to tie a bow when he's fifteen, but the value of car seat competence can hardly be overstated. Your arms are laden with laundry, your purse is slipping off your shoulder, it's raining, you've got cramps, and the kid clambers in and *snappa snappa.* Kid stays put. Yes, that's a downright miracle the first time it happens.

Our Honda Civic had recently celebrated its eighth birthday, bravely holding up under the disappointment of not receiving any new motor oil or wiper fluid. I pulled the car into traffic on Sunset and headed for McDonald's, my mouth watering thinking about a fish sandwich and Diet Coke. The car looked like it had been spit out by a sea monster and shuddered in right turns, but otherwise it was a fine machine. There wasn't time to do groceries before Storytime at two o'clock, so I drove through and we ate in the car on the way to the library where I had the story gig.

Driving and eating while interfacing with L.A. traffic requires no brainwork, just reflexes, so I took the opportunity to mentally beat myself up about my Visa card. My old brain-loop started up: *stupid, stupid, stupid.* Gramma Gladys would no doubt visit me in my sleep tonight and raise a gnarled finger: *That brooch was the most decent thing in the whole family! Where's my brooch? No more cookies for you, ya little turd-butt!*

I am educated, yes, but some people have Nobel prizes and still forget to turn the stove off. I feel kinship with such people. I hated to let down Gramma Gladys. She was dead, but I felt we communed. When I was growing up, everybody—*everybody*—kept calling me pretty. Which was nice, but when Gramma Gladys used to tell me I was smart, I felt special and strong. She was the only one who ever told me I was smart.

My cell phone played "Fame," and I dug it out of my purse.

"I was at cocktails last night with some casting people," said Marly Haynes, my agent. "Fame" was the ring song I'd selected for her incoming number, a little bit of hopeful irony. "You didn't get it, sunshine."

"That's what I thought," I said, palming the wheel onto the ramp to the Hollywood Freeway.

"M'kenge said your screams weren't real enough."

"She did, huh?"

"Yeah, she said you sounded like a coed during a panty raid."

"I didn't think college boys did panty raids anymore."

"Well, she must've read a history book. Look, I think we need to skip horror auditions for a while. It was a faulty strategy for you. My bad."

A cushion flew off a sofa somebody was moving in a pickup

truck. I swerved as it tumbled along the concrete, breaking apart into a thousand beige stuffing chunks. "Thanks, Marly. Uh, well, let's move on, then. Any word from the Oatberger people?"

"Not yet, but I'm working on them. You would be perfect for Oatberger, just perfect."

"I know."

Every man, woman, and child in Hollywood was talking about Serge Oatberger's new project, *Third Chance Mountain*. Based on the hit novel by the same title—I forget the author—the movie reportedly was going to be the most ambitious yet by the legendary director. He dealt with important themes in new, imaginative ways. Like if there was a death scene coming up, he wouldn't do the obvious thing of showing a flower dropping its petals. He'd put in something like a gecko rubbing its nose against a rock, and you would have to work a little to interpret that. All of his images came together so beautifully, and at the end there was never any doubt about right versus wrong. Every man, woman, and child actor in Hollywood wanted roles in his movies.

Oatberger hated working with stars. He liked humble people who took nothing for granted. And he really liked actresses who were youthful but not kidlike, wore bob-style haircuts, and had learned acting from Karen Bell and Sam Wojczyk. At any rate, he tended to put one such actress in the lead or second lead of every one of his movies. Then they'd win an Academy Award and become stars and he wouldn't want to work with them again. Who cared at that point? They were stars.

IT IS A privilege to be chosen to do Storytime by the personnel of the Los Angeles Central Library. Storytime is every Saturday afternoon and there's competition for it. To have a good chance of being selected, you don't just offer to read some story from a book, you must either (a) tell your very own folk story or (b) tell an old story in your own new folk-type way, preferably in costume or with hand shadows or other cultural features.

I demoed how I could give a new spin to Hansel and Gretel, with sock puppets. That was a winner.

Given the events of the morning, I didn't feel much like performing, but the puppets were ready and I was certain my mood would improve once I began. Besides, I was getting paid fifty bucks, which equaled Petey's recent vaccination deductible.

"'WHERE TO TODAY, Hansel?' asked Gretel.

" 'Straight into the heart of the forest!' shouted the boy.

" 'But why?'

" 'Papa says fairies live there.' "

I felt so incredibly glad the children were too young and pure to snicker at *fairies*. My heart swelled with love for them, the whole crowd of fledglings sitting there in the gorgeous glow of the warm wood-paneled children's room. It was the kind of room—big, serious, not junked up with construction-paper daisies—that prompted in kids respectful behavior. They were the lucky little folk of Los Angeles: children whose parents brought them to the library for a spot of free culture on the weekend. Children whose parents gave two shits.

The sock puppets I'd created last night had button eyes and tiny pompon noses, and the Gretel puppet wore a punkish hairstyle of sewn-on Brillo. Hansel sported a tiny cap of Yoplait foil.

The puppets did the dialogue, but my face and voice were the solder that welded my audience to me. The young humans ranged in age from three to seven years today, roughly, plus one girl of about thirteen, hanging humbly in back. It was a multicultural bunch, reflecting today's Los Angeles: much perfect brown clean skin, varying eye shapes. The older girl, I saw, was unwilling to grow into the small breasts nature had seen fit to slap on her one night recently while she was unconscious. I met her gaze with a big-sister look that said, *Don't worry, dear one, you don't have to be a grown-up yet. I kind of wish I hadn't gotten there myself.*

I flung my soul into the story. The sock puppets played and quarreled and then sat side by side on my knees, and their scrunchy faces turned up to listen intently to their parents, whom I portrayed by shifting my shoulders and assuming each persona in turn.

" 'Fool!' growled the stepmother, right in her husband's face." I bared my teeth and spat the words. " 'In that case we will all starve!' "

The children responded to my energy and the story. The startling thing about me to them was I was actual. I was not electronic, I was not a small image on a screen. Their jaded little ears registered the change in air pressure when I dropped to a whisper or cracked a consonant. My body moved three-dimensionally, the sock puppets glided to and fro in space, their little egos bumping around harmlessly and entertainingly.

Petey was having a ball too, completely in the here and now of being four. I caught his eye with a special wink and he blinked back, delighted.

I swapped around parts of the plot, giving Gretel the idea of trailing the bread crumbs. Hansel ought not to be the only initiative-taker in the family. I shocked my audience by cramming

Gretel's head briefly into my mouth, to signify the freestyle dragon I invented, and I imprisoned Hansel in the horrible dark cavern of my armpit.

The parents who'd stuck around appeared to be enjoying themselves. A few exchanged friendly looks. I hoped they were thinking, *What fun! Isn't she amazing?*

At first I didn't notice a man standing off to the side, watching me with particular intensity. But then I did.

He was dressed in a silk polo shirt and knife-creased chinos, nothing imaginative but obviously expensive. His posture was relaxed. He watched my face, and he watched the children watch me. His eyes were quick and smart, I thought, and his eyes were where the intensity came from.

It wasn't a love-at-first-sight type of intensity, nor was it a clinical intensity, though that was closer. No, he was looking at me in the sudden powerful *wham!* way of someone perceiving, all at once, the solution to a problem he'd been stuck cold on for months.

THREE

I pulled down the story with a flourish:

"'O Papa! Now we are rich!' Their papa gathered them to his heart and said, 'We shall feast and dance tonight in our forest home! O Hansel! O Gretel! How I love you!'"

Afterward, as I was excavating a Kleenex from my purse, chino man came up to me.

"Congratulations," he said, smiling.

"Uh, thank you."

"You're very good. You almost made me cry a couple of times."

I laughed. "Well. Thank you." I turned away to dab my nose, then turned back. Seeing no trash basket nearby, I stuffed the tissue in my pocket. "It's just for fun."

Petey, across the room, watched two older boys build a chair fort. A weary-looking librarian nearby was being cool about it.

Chino man said, "You're an actress, aren't you?"

I straightened. "Yes." My confidence was not totally shot, so I answered that way. *Yes, I am.*

Furthermore, I'm OK with the term *actress*. The style these days was to call all of us, male or female, actors, but I like actress. It makes me feel more—oh,—*flowing*.

The man rested his elbow on a bookcase and took a long easy breath. As did I. We stood beneath one of those incredible bronze deco-type lamps that add still more serene gravity to a lovely room. The library's odors were safe and familiar—that unmistakable cocktail of binding glue, paper dust, and rubber bands.

"You had us all eating out of your hand," he said. His diction was precise. He was a multicultural person himself, of Asian descent—Japanese, probably. I noticed his good grooming, lack of obvious nose hair, and Rolexy watch.

"Well, thanks," I answered, "but being great with sock puppets doesn't necessarily translate to the big screen, you know? I mean . . . oh, you know." I tucked a strand of hair behind my ear. He watched me, saying nothing. As I've mentioned, my hair was cut in a bob, as crisp as I could get it, which swam rather upstream against the feathery layers everybody else seemed to wear, but that was the point. Plus it was a darker shade of gold than might be typical of an anxious actress, but Trini, my stylist, told me it looked good on me, and I felt his judgment was sound.

"You're very kind," I said, "but I wish I could make a living at it. That's what I'm supposed to be doing."

The shame of the twin fiascos of the Safeway and the pawnshop came back to me and I felt my mouth set itself against them.

"Oh, I think you can," said the man. "You're very talented. Strikingly so. That's my daughter over there."

In Los Angeles, when you are an unemployed actress and you are approached by a well-dressed stranger who spews compliments, you stick out your hand and say your name.

"I'm Rita Farmer."

He grasped my hand firmly with both of his. "Gary Kwan."

His hands were exactly the same temperature as mine. He moved his left one subtly to my wrist, as if feeling my muscle tone, or pulse. His name had a familiar ring, but at the moment I was coming up blank. He was a handsome son of a gun if you go for exotics, but the look in his eyes wasn't a come-on one.

"I'm an attorney," he told me, "and I think you might be able to help me." He glanced around. "I'm not in the movie business, but I'd like to talk to you about an acting job. Are you working now?" He settled himself more comfortably against the bookcase, one arm hugging himself, shoulder down, making his body language slightly submissive.

That's unusual for a guy to do when he's talking to a woman. I noticed and appreciated it. "Actually," I said, "I'm auditioning all the time. I have a couple of important ones coming up, uh, which means no! No, I'm totally unemployed."

Gary Kwan's laugh was warm, and I realized that didn't fit my image of him, and then I remembered my image of him.

"Oh! Gary Kwan. *Gary Kwan,* oh, my gosh. I'm so sorry I didn't connect your name before. Roscoe Jamison!"

He nodded. "Yes."

I could think of nothing to say except, "Well, uh, how *is* Roscoe?"

He laughed again. "Roscoe's great! Enjoying his freedom."

"Did they ever catch—"

His tone hardened. "No. Not yet."

I couldn't tell whether he was being serious or sarcastic. So I just said, "Right." Then it occurred to me that he was just being professionally neutral. It wasn't his business to wink about Roscoe Jamison, the professional golfer who'd been arrested with his ex-wife's blood all over his shirt but who beat the rap, thanks to Gary Kwan's defense team, which did this incredible jujitsu move against the prosecution by showing how the arresting cop could have gotten there first and sliced apart Mrs. Jamison with her own steak knife, then swabbed blood all over Roscoe while he was asleep, which made perfect sense to that particular jury.

I started feeling somewhat surreal, talking to this famous lawyer whose face was regularly all over the papers, this guy who aggressively, indeed nastily, defended big famous stinkingly rich celebrity people accused of celebrity crimes.

The little girl he'd nodded toward a minute ago came running over and started climbing his leg. He braced himself against the bookcase. "This is Jade," he grunted.

"Hello, Jade."

Jade, about three, had a black haystack of hair and shining eyes. She swung herself athletically on her father's belt.

"Sweetheart, you're going to rip Daddy's pants off. Stop. Go over there for a minute. See those kids over there? I think they need help with that book."

Jade charged off and Gary Kwan adjusted his waistline. It was a trim one, his belt curving nicely over his hipbones.

"She's a dear," I commented, smiling after her. "That's my boy Petey, with the other Y chromosomes over there." The sudden ridiculous thought came to me that if Gary Kwan and I ever got married, that would not preclude Petey and Jade from marrying someday.

Gary Kwan had had enough smiling. With a measure of tense-ness, he asked, "Have you been in any films? Ever had a big part? Or on TV?"

"Just a few commercials—Young Mother—that's the casting designation my agent looks for for me."

"Oh?"

"Yeah, I did a Johnson's Wax one where I'm so happy my twins can't hurt my floor anymore, and I did a Home Depot one where my husband wrecks the hedge but then he goes to Home Depot and everything's OK again. That wasn't a speaking part, so I didn't get full scale. I've done a couple of hosiery ads for magazines. And I'm like in the background on this series of bank ads—B of A, print ads for magazines. I'm at a conference table looking bright."

"Good, good, Rita."

"I mean, I've got my SAG card and everything—Gary. But you know, uh, I am no stranger to the unemployment office. So what kind of non-Screen-Actors-Guild work are we talking about?"

With a pleasant expression, he swiveled his head to scan the room. The kids were deep into their business. He motioned me to follow him to a deserted corner of the expansive room, where we wouldn't be overheard. We remained standing, both of us subcon-sciously remaining spottable by our children.

In a quiet, direct tone, he said, "I've been working on a tough case, and watching you I got an idea and now I'm just plunging ahead with it, even though I haven't thought it through." He gazed at me keenly, his eyes like lustrous black shells. "One more thing before I go further. Have you trained as an actress, or are you self-taught?"

I quieted my voice too. "Oh, I've got training. Only Bubbles the Chimp has more training than me."

"Who have you worked with?"

I searched his face. *Where the hell is this going?* He just maintained his focused, intelligent expression.

"Well," I answered, "after I tried and failed to get acting work without formal training, I bit the bullet and went for my degree from UCLA—and I've got the outstanding student loans to prove it. I studied primarily with Karen Bell and Sam Wojczyk. These days I've been dropping in on an improv class led by Ann Marie Drago, just to keep working on my skills, you know. Do you know them?"

"I've heard of Karen Bell and Sam. Good. This is all very good." Gary Kwan's face broke into a sunshine smile. His teeth were small and multitudinous and he looked increasingly happy.

Lowering his voice even more, he said, "What I want to know is this: would you be willing to serve as a private drama coach to an incarcerated client of mine? She's up for first-degree murder. I'll pay you a thousand dollars a day, and the job would probably last a few weeks, if not months."

Chops of thoughts tumbled through my mind. The main one was, *A thousand dollars a day?* Even though I only had an inkling of what this was about, I felt a huge weight lift from the back of my neck. A thousand dollars a day. I couldn't believe I'd been pitying myself so desperately just an hour ago, and now here's somebody waving a wand at me with dollar signs shooting out of it.

I looked at him, trying to understand the rest of what he'd said, feeling like a dumb ox. He waited, an eyebrow cocked in amusement.

I said, "Drama coach? Is there, like, a theater troupe in the jail? I'd think she'd have other things on her mind than—"

23

He laughed. "No, no. It's not for that. I'm talking about the courtroom."

"The courtroom."

"Yes."

It broke on me. "You want me to help her put on an act in front of the jury."

"That's the cynical way to put it. The compassionate way is, I want you to prepare her so she has the best possible chance of being acquitted."

I hadn't realized I was holding my breath. I let it out. Now, this was interesting.

I think Gary saw that thought on my face, because he took his plunge. "Do you know," he asked, "who Eileen Tenaway is?"

"Oh."

"Do you?"

"Yes, of course."

"Why did you say *oh* like that?"

Because Eileen Tenaway killed her baby. News of the crime, all over the papers for months, had been ugly and dreadful. A little corpse in a crib, a bottle of pills, a rich-bitch mom who had passed out from some intoxicant or other: a rich bitch who was surely lying, a rich bitch who was surely guilty. *Because,* I thought, *I basically despise Eileen Tenaway, as every human being should, but of course you're her lawyer, you're exactly the one she would want to defend her.*

Gary waited.

I answered, "I'm trying to make up something to cover the fact that I'm disgusted by her."

"So you understand my position." He shifted his weight on his feet and shelved his elbow on a bookcase. I stood a little closer to him and paid attention.

He began, "Four months ago today, as it happens, Eileen Tenaway woke up in the morning, went into the baby's room, and found her daughter, Gabriella Tenaway, aged eighteen months, cold and stiff in her crib. She called 911. Paramedics confirmed the baby was dead. The police asked questions. She said she didn't know what happened. She'd heard nothing in the night. The house had been ransacked, and the police found evidence of a possible intruder, but the DA contends that Eileen planted it to cover up her crime. The house had an elaborate alarm system, but Eileen and others say the Tenaways never used it."

"How come?"

"Richard Tenaway felt invulnerable, and Eileen never learned to use it. The autopsy showed the baby died of an overdose of Valium. A bottle of same was found in the medicine cabinet, prescribed for Eileen. Three weeks after the autopsy results, Eileen Tenaway was arrested and charged with first-degree murder in the death of her child." He paused, looking at me frankly. "Do you think she did it?"

The question surprised me. "Why are you asking me?"

He slid his hand along the smooth wood of the bookcase, which held a bonanza of Madeline books, my childhood favorites. Good old intrepid, impulsive Madeline. Many's the time I'd wished to be her. Gary said, "I want to know if you have an opinion."

"My only opinion is that Eileen Tenaway is . . . well, pathetic, to put it nicely, just from seeing her in the party pages with all the bling and that fake smile. I have to say, the incident looks like an upscale version of a hillbilly giving her kid a bottle of Jack Daniel's with a nipple on it."

"Except Eileen Tenaway, with all her advantages, should have known better."

"Right."

"Unless she didn't do it."

"Well, did she?" I thought he would surely know the answer to that.

"She says she didn't."

"Do you believe her?"

"Not my department," said Gary, meeting my eyes calmly. He drew himself tall, feet together. "She's hired me to defend her. Period. It's irrelevant what I think about her guilt or innocence."

"I see."

Petey trotted over to me, patted my thigh in his habitual mom-check, then trotted off again.

"The trial," Gary said, "should start in about a week, we almost have a jury. The main thing is this: a jury trial is a show, with actors and actresses and an audience. The audience watches the show, and then they get to create the ending they want. It's as simple as that. My job is to build a sympathetic plot around my client."

"She was rich and safe and envied, and now she's up against it."

He nodded slowly, smiling.

I said, "Nobody likes Eileen Tenaway."

"They hate her," Gary agreed.

"People love it when the rich and smug go down."

Gary touched the spines of the Madeline books. "They love it more than sex with chocolate sauce."

A shriek split the air. The librarian who had uttered it jumped up. She sprinted from her desk just in time to stop Petey from shinnying up one of the bronze lamps to the inviting stratosphere of the Children's Room. He'd clambered up a bookcase to adult height, and had just hoisted himself aboard the lamp, which swayed but did not topple.

Spouting apologies, I retrieved my boy, who was glorying in the commotion he'd caused. "I went *up*!" he boasted to the world in general. Even the librarian was smiling, now that the danger was over. Petey was so cute and male.

It was time to leave. I turned to Gary, who held Jade on his hip. She and Petey, safe in the grasp of a parent, gazed at each other like chimps in the zoo. Gary said simply, "You're going to help me, right?"

"I don't have the whole picture," I said.

"You will. Meet me in my office tomorrow, and we'll go over everything."

"Tomorrow's Sunday."

"Yes."

"There won't be anyone around your office?"

"Correct. That's the point. We need to be alone; our conversation must be totally confidential."

I looked at him.

"Come on, Rita, you're a big girl. In case you're wondering, I'm married."

"Oh."

"What, now you're disappointed?"

"No!" I laughed.

"You'll come, right?"

"Um. Yes."

"Good." He gave me his card, which showed an address on Wilshire. "Ten o'clock?"

"Ten."

"Come to the front. It'll be locked, but I'll wait for you in the lobby. Remember, don't discuss this with anybody. Don't even tell anyone you met me. All right? This is good." He clenched his fist. "This is so good."

"Gary, uh?"

"Yes?"

"What's so good?"

He shook his head as if he couldn't believe his luck. "You're an unknown."

FOUR

I slid an egg onto Petey's Spider-Man breakfast plate and threw the toast on.

"Spider-Man says oboy an egg! Nature's perfect food! Time to sit down and eat, honey."

Petey jogged to the table and grabbed the piece of toast.

"Sit down, honey, please, and join the grown-ups." I heard the cajoling in my own voice, and as he so often did, he exploited it. He was too little for it to be conscious. Entirely my fault. He bit the toast and remained standing, holding a black helicopter in his other hand.

I'd invited our beloved friend Daniel Clements over for breakfast. After a glance at Petey, he poured three glasses of orange juice. Daniel, a working actor, played the smarter-than-his-boss desk sergeant on the police sitcom *Abilene Cop Shop*. He was towering and gorgeous and big-chested, which made it funnier when the dinky chief ordered him around. He and I had become friends in acting school, and he'd been more or less steadily employed for about the same length of time I'd been struggling, three years.

In a quiet voice, Daniel said, "You heard your mother."

Petey put down the helicopter and climbed into his chair.

"Good fellow," said Daniel with a smile.

I looked at him. You're the good fellow here, but why the hell didn't he obey *me*?

Daniel added, "A man with the same first name as Peter Parker has to take life a little more seriously than others."

"When will I get muscles?" demanded Petey.

"Maybe next week."

I smiled.

"Make a muscle, Daniel!"

"Later. Eat."

The three of us ate and discussed the comics in the Sunday *L.A. Times* Daniel had brought, then Daniel helped me with the dishes.

I knew he was watching me stealthily. He cleared his throat. "So what's this errand upon which you must go alone without your offspring, I ask casually?"

Holding the frying pan over the sink, I looked up. "You must have heard the mystery in my voice."

A wedding gift from one of my aunts back in Wisconsin, the frying pan had started out fully coated with state-of-the-art non-stick material, but now the Teflon was flaking away like scrofulous skin.

Daniel took the pan from my hand. "I should have gotten you a new one of these for Christmas instead of the day at the spa." He clanked the pan into the dishwasher rack.

"Oh God, no. I'd have killed you if you'd given me a frying pan." I wished I could go to the spa once a week. I wished my kitchen were larger so that big cheerful Daniel didn't have to *squirm* his way around it.

My apartment was Manhattanesquely small, which was a disheartening thing because L.A. apartments are almost always bigger than New York ones. That was supposed to be one of the consolations of acting in L.A. instead of New York—you could afford a bigger apartment. But not me, hell no. I managed to get the crummiest (but rent-controlled!) apartment in one of the becoming-thunderously-more-expensive-because-of-all-the-gay-guys-moving-in zones of West Hollywood, on Curson Street off Sunset. The neighborhood was all right. A high percentage of older Russian immigrants still anchored things, in their stone-faced way. And there was a really nice city park just two blocks away. It had been important to get into a decent neighborhood because of Petey. He had the bedroom, a cubic nest with a window to the ugly iron fire escape overlooking the alley, while I made my bed every night on the futon in the quote-unquote living room.

To complete the claustrophobic atmosphere, the kitchen window overlooked a light well, which was worse, in a way, than having no window at all.

I'd known nothing of light wells in rural Wisconsin, where I'd grown up; a light well, I learned when I married Jeff and moved to Torrance, California, where he'd landed an accounting job with a glitzy restaurant chain, is simply an open shaft surrounded by buildings. The buildings' sides make the walls of the shaft. At the bottom of every shaft is always a sorry array of detritus—things dropped or flung from the windows overlooking it: candy wrappers and condoms, *Star Wars* action figures, pearl necklaces (it has happened), rotted auto parts, and lots of pacifiers. It pays to be on good terms with the people in the ground-floor unit, through whose window you can climb to recover anything discarded in heat or haste or both.

The kitchen air smelled greasy. I gave a shove to the warped aluminum window and a spurt of fresh air came in from the light well, pushed down by the square of blue sky.

I did the best I could with thrift-shop furniture I spray-painted in glossy blacks and reds, plus throw pillows and an amazingly OK color-block rug from Target. Fortunately, Daniel painted a little, and he'd given me a few groovy abstract canvases. Their whorls and splashes lent a SoHo-ishness to the place.

Petey was lying on his back on the living room floor about three paces from the kitchen, his feet on the coffee table, his portable ScoreLad perched on his stomach, Spider-Man game in progress. The game made frantic sounds of conflict.

I asked Daniel as we hip-sat on the edge of the kitchen counter, "Didn't you have a date last night?"

"Yes, and it's only because it went like birdshit that I'm here on time and without a hangover."

"I thought he seemed promising."

"He was promising! Fifteen-inch biceps and quads so cut you could see them through army pants. And he was second unit director for *The Emperor of Miami*! I mean my God. But unfortunately he is so in love with himself he couldn't even be bothered to say hi to Sarah Finch—*Bed Head Dead*—when she came over to our table."

I easily followed Daniel's showbiz habit of just saying the name of whatever last film someone was in, as a shorthand ID aid.

"He ogled *all* the guys in the room, of course," Daniel continued, arching a brow to show me, "and he did it so *condescendingly*. He'd check out this guy's butt, then look over at me in this evaluative sort of way, like daring me to compete for his attention. I was his *date*! I should have known it wasn't going to work when he finally asked me to dance and I jumped up and said, 'On a bright cloud of music shall we fly?' and he didn't get it."

"Did you say it in rhythm or anything?"

"Yes! I half sang it, just like that, with the actual rhythm and everything. How can you not know 'Shall We Dance?' from *The King and I*?"

"A-hole."

"A-hole."

"Complete."

"Yeah." Daniel folded the towel over the oven door handle. His high forehead gave him a serious look even when helping with the dishes. Fortunately he hadn't developed a hint of male-pattern baldness yet. Nice thick bitter-cocoa hair, not too wavy.

The two of us tried to be sparing with vulgar language when Petey might hear. *Hell, damn,* and *God* were all OK, I mean let's be real, and Daniel had allowed himself *birdshit* a minute ago, but my current feeling was that *asshole* must be reserved for adult ears.

"So anyway, sweets, you haven't answered my question."

"Daniel, I can't."

"That is very unbestfriendlike."

"I'm sorry—it's true, it's just this—odd thing, you know, this odd opportunity that came up. I don't even know exactly, uh—"

"It's work? Is it Oatberger?"

"Yes. No. But I'm not supposed to say anything about it, and I promised I wouldn't. I don't even know if I'm going to go through with what this . . . person . . . is proposing." *Although I probably will.*

"You probably will. I know how broke you are." Daniel had helped me shop for all the licensed Spider-Man merchandise Petey had wanted for Christmas.

"No, you don't."

"Yes, I do. Why won't you let me give you a little something? Just to—"

"No."

"Rita. I saw you washing your own car when I drove by last week. That pitiful little bucket and sponge."

"So what?"

"I was late for work or I would have stopped. You're not supposed to wash your own car, you're supposed to take it to the car wash."

"I'm broke!"

"Then let me give you—"

"No. Thank. You." I tossed the dishrag. "Please don't make me explain it again."

"All right, sweets," he soothed, "it's all right. You run along and I'll take the boy to the park. We'll show those bad guys how Spider-Man climbs trees."

"Be careful. Yesterday at the library he almost gave me an aneurism when he figured out how to—"

"Stop being such a mom. Petey's almost a better climber than I am now. He's fearless."

"That's what I'm afraid of."

FIVE

M y blood quivered in my ears as I parked the Honda and walked around to the front of Gary Kwan's office building. What was I getting myself into? But I felt fresh and slim and nicely dressed in my black capris and driving moccasins and the sun was out so what the hell's there, really, to be anxious about? Besides, a thousand dollars a day!

Gary was right at the doors, holding one open for me, his face calm and friendly. "I'm so glad to see you, Rita."

As soon as I stepped into the fresh-smelling lobby, I relaxed. The place was deserted, but I didn't get a bad vibe. "Thanks and ditto, Gary." Panels of pink and brown granite lined the lobby, alternating wide stripes like heavy candy.

We took the elevator to the seventh floor. On the ride up I enjoyed the feeling of anticipation that had been gathering inside me since yesterday—an encounter with an interesting stranger, a tantalizing offer. And it appeared Gary was looking forward to doing some vigorous talking. I could tell by the way he bobbed his head ever so slightly, almost invisibly but constantly, which betrays agreeable excitement.

Gary's suite, to my surprise, was small, verging on cramped. Its furniture, meager and cheap, placed it solidly in the start-up tradition. After we passed through the reception foyer, which doubled as a storage closet for supplies, there were doors to three offices. We went into the one with Gary's name on it.

"We work seven days a week during trials and as you know, we've got one coming up. We're in jury selection now. But I told everybody to stay away today."

He indicated a white metal chair for me at a bitsy white plastic conference table. He joined me after retrieving two cold bottles of brand-X drinking water from a small refrigerator. Behind him, the window overlooked downtown and the suburbs beyond.

"I'd have expected you to have an ocean view," I commented.

"Too distracting, too pretty."

"I see."

"You were expecting something posh like in a movie."

"Yes."

"Welcome to my world. I make good money, but when you're a defense lawyer, you never know where your next case will come from. Or when. It's not as if you build much repeat business."

Even so, exuberant California light washed the room. Such direct desert light can be hard and unfriendly outdoors when it's flaring right on you—so unrelenting, so UV—but this way, through the windows, shaded by a sort of cantilever above, it felt benevolent. On my side.

Gary sat opposite me in a college-coach posture, knees spread, elbows down. Very much at ease. On the table was a stack of files in contract-length folders next to a laptop PC, its screen blank.

"All right," he said, smiling eagerly. "What are you wondering about?"

Instantly I understood the harmonious feeling between us: We were both acute observers of other people. Sensitive to the little dishonesties people allow themselves, then eventually adopt as habits. We saw through those things, which was why we were both good at what we did.

"Well," I said, "first I'd like to know more about Eileen Tenaway. What does she say really happened?"

"What she told the police. She figures she must have been drugged somehow while she was sleeping, then somebody robbed the house. She doesn't know how."

"Well, by whom?" I broke the seal of my water and sipped some. The cold flowed down to my belly.

"She's never speculated on that, but I have some ideas."

"*You* have some ideas?"

"I'm working hard here. She is not an easy client."

I thought about that. "Well, when I read about it I wondered why the DA's charging her with murder instead of, like, negligence or something."

"Prosecutors always go for a heavier charge, both for the publicity and to give themselves leeway. They might offer a plea deal, but they also figure, hey, maybe we'll get lucky and the jury'll swallow our case whole. If Eileen had said it was an accident—that she gave the baby a couple of pills just to make her sleep—and thrown herself on the mercy of the court, I doubt they'd have charged her with murder. They did offer us a plea, as a matter of fact, but we're not taking it. She wants to fight."

"But they're not going for the death penalty?"

"No, they think their chances will be better without it."

I was starting to see that my own perception of Eileen Tenaway was based on nothing but shallow sensationalism. Gary talked on, explaining that the evidence against Eileen was strong, albeit circumstantial. "They're going to hammer the implausibility of an intruder," he said, thrusting two fingers at the file folders, "and we're going to hammer back the implausibility of this mother killing her own child. They don't have an eyewitness, but neither do we."

He curled his fingers and jounced an imaginary pebble. "And as you realize, there's a worse problem: Eileen Tenaway doesn't come across well. Increasingly these days, that is significant. Because this is going to jury, the DA is drooling at the prospect of sending this spoiled, complacent society mom to prison forever. Long before Roscoe Jamison, juries made up their minds about defendants partly based on the evidence and partly on the manner and appearance of the defendant."

"But now it's getting worse?" I ventured.

"Depends on your point of view." Gary dropped his invisible pebble and took a pull from his water bottle. I watched the shadow crescent beneath his smooth Adam's apple. "With Roscoe Jamison, I had a charismatic defendant. We picked a good jury, we led them to believe that their preconceptions against the LAPD were the most important thing to take into account, and they did. We won without putting Roscoe on the stand. So for us, it was good."

I got a creepy feeling, and he saw it in my face. "It's irrelevant, Rita. Guilt or innocence is irrelevant."

"You've said that already."

"It's always been this way. Most juries try hard to go by the facts. But they *never* act strictly on principle. I can prove it to you, if you'd like to sit and read historical transcripts and analysis for a few weeks."

That actually sounded like an interesting thing to do, but I just said, "I get it."

"Something tells me you don't yet." He reached for the laptop and touched some keys. His hands were well proportioned and loose, like a piano player's, the fingernails clean and just perceptibly buffed.

A series of video clips started up, and I realized I was seeing jurors emerging from various guilty verdicts.

Gary named a case, a famous national-news-type murder. People with weary expressions stood on the steps of a courthouse talking to the camera.

A guy in a Ford jacket mumbled, "She didn't seem remorseful." Another juror, clutching a suede purse, said, "She didn't seem to feel all that sorry that her parents are dead." Another: "She just seemed guilty."

Gary played half a dozen clips from the aftermaths of different trials, all of them showing jurors explaining their verdicts in the same terms you'd use talking about characters in a TV show:

"She didn't seem to care about her child at all. Poor little fella."

"He just didn't act right. There was something odd about him. I couldn't really follow all the stuff his lawyer said. He just seemed guilty."

"She just seemed guilty."

"He just seemed guilty."

Then Gary punched up another video file, this one of jurors emerging from acquittals saying, "Oh, obviously he was innocent. It was just obvious, you could tell by looking at him." And the like. The last one showed a juror from Roscoe Jamison's trial saying, "We got to guard our own."

My bones revolted under my skin. "Good God."

Gary punched up another movie, this one of a woman sitting cramped on a straight chair at a table in a depressing room. A man in a white shirt asked her questions. Gary froze the image and I studied it. Wearing her customary eye-popping jewelry—she had not yet been placed under arrest—Eileen Tenaway was as beautiful as ever. But Gary was right; her affect was blunted, odd, cold. She looked down at her hands on the table, which lay limp, as if the weight of the gold bangles and rings were too much for them. Gary murmured, with noticeable pain in his voice, "Eileen agreed to let the police question her before she hired me." He turned up the volume.

COP: Couldn't Gabriella have gotten into those pills by herself?

EILEEN: No, I kept them in the medicine cabinet.

COP: Couldn't she have climbed up and opened that cabinet?

EILEEN: No.

COP: Why not?

EILEEN: It has a childproof latch.

COP: Didn't you just give her a few of those sleeping pills to quiet her down?

EILEEN: *No.*

COP: Why would an intruder use *your Valium* to kill your daughter?

EILEEN: I don't know.

Her voice was flat except when she lifted her head at one point, trying for a bit of her habitual arrogance, trying to get the cop to think she was being honest. But I could see how emotionally shut down she was. Pitiable and miserable. As a mother I found myself aching for her, no matter what had really happened that night.

Gary said, "I have a defendant who is totally *unsympathetic* to most everybody in Los Angeles, because she's rich, gorgeous, self-satisfied, she's everything people say they look down on but really envy. If people can't have what they want, they like to destroy it. Never mind that the woman not only lost her daughter, she also lost her husband and her sister before all this happened. Nobody gives a damn about that, and they didn't when it happened."

"Yeah, I remember. Like, a few months before the baby thing? Did they both die, or what?"

"Richard Tenaway disappeared, then turned up dead in Brazil, one of the countries his business imported gems from."

Gary explained how Richard Tenaway had positioned his family as one of the most prominent in Los Angeles by making big money importing raw jewels from exotic places. He'd started the company with his best buddy, Padraig McGower, and built it to impressive size. Everybody in L.A. knew the name Gemini Imports, the world's leading wholesaler of gem-quality emeralds, sapphires, and topazes, and everybody knew the names McGower and Tenaway. The partners specialized in those valuable stones, found in quantity in South America.

"This was Eileen's life," Gary said. "Her husband and his partner started bold, made big mistakes, learned from them, and eventually they became unparalleled experts at judging uncut crystals. They got shrewder every day. She loved the glamour of what they did."

As he talked I understood how the guys' success gave them access to big-shot bureaucrats and diplomats, who helped them breeze through government red tape that bogged down their rivals.

"It was a good life," Gary observed. "Tenaway and McGower collected fancy cars, both of them, and commissioned yachts. Tenaway called his the *Gem and I,* get it? Everywhere they went, they attracted envious attention, their trophy wives on their arms. Richard decked out Eileen in fine jewelry, I'm sure you saw the pictures in the magazines."

"Yeah, and she was Richard's bauble."

"She loved the jewels, she loved the cars and the trips."

"Most women would," I remarked.

"And then it all changed." When Richard Tenaway's body was discovered, Gary told me, the local authorities didn't have much to go on, and neither did anybody else. Eileen could find out little more, even when she went to the interior of Brazil herself with a private investigator and an interpreter to identify the body and look into what had happened. Tenaway's body, with a gash on the head, had been found in a ravine. An accident? If not, there were no suspects anyway.

"Furthermore," Gary continued, "Eileen's sister, Norah Mintz, disappeared the same time Tenaway did. Rumor was they ran off together, but when Richard turned up dead, there was no Norah to be found. That's irrelevant to our case, but you should know it as background."

He paused and rubbed his chin glumly, thinking of something else.

"What is it?" I asked.

"Worse still for me, they've named Tracy Beck-Rubin lead prosecutor." He glanced to see if I recognized the name. When I sort of didn't, he said, "An up-from-blue-collar-land tough girl who knows how to hit all the right buttons of a jury. She was on the DA's team against Roscoe."

"But they lost."

"Yes, but they learned a lot from the experience." He slapped his thigh twice, then stopped, having forced away the negative thought. "Never mind," he said cheerfully. "What did you think of Eileen?"

I knew the power of personality so well, the power of make-believe. I said, "She's in pain, and she's too scared to remember how to manipulate people."

Gary beamed. "Wow! That's cold, Rita, that's cold. Excellent."

"That's what you want from me, isn't it?"

"Can you help her?"

"Yes, I think I can."

"Excellent!" Gary jumped up and paced the small office, snaking his hips around the side chairs and his desk and back around again. Today his trim butt was clothed in a pair of linen slacks, his torso in another silk polo shirt of a rich bronze color. He moved as if he enjoyed it, like a dancer. Nice. Very nice.

"As a team," he said, "we have to make the jury want to do something for her. We have to show her to be an innocent victim of forces beyond her control, beyond anyone's control. Except the jury's. They must understand they have total power, and they must feel free to exercise it."

"On her behalf."

"On her behalf. Now, I've figured out a basic defense, our team's been working together from the beginning, and we've done all our homework. Jury selection's going well." Still pacing, he talked on. "As I said, we're going to pound on the evidence of an intruder. We'll show it was an extraordinary burglary, well planned, perfectly executed, except they didn't find the wall safe with all her jewelry in it. We get Eileen to deny giving her child the Valium. We get her to deny it on the stand. We have to be very brash here, or we could go down. I believe our chances are better now that you're on the team. Needless to say, she's got money for all this. She's paying me to talk to you right now, and as I promised, I'll pay you a thousand of her dollars a day if you'll help her."

"She knows about this already?"

"Not yet." He dropped to one knee next to my chair as if ready to sketch out a play on the rug, and turned the full force of his persuasive brain on me. "Rita, you're perfect for this. You're an appealing woman, you've got a little one of your own, your acting has a special warmth to it, it's palpable. You make people like you. You can show her how you do it. With your help, Eileen could transform her presence in the courtroom."

Before I could say anything, he went on, "The fact that you're so good yet so unknown is very important. Because if you agree to give acting lessons to Eileen Tenaway, you'll have to do it secretly, during visits to the lockup." He smiled excitedly.

"Really? They didn't offer her bail, huh?"

"Not in a case like this. You'll need to pose as a paralegal working for me. And it won't stop there. I'll want you in the courtroom as a silent support for Eileen, so you'd have to play the role there too." He paused. "While it's not illegal to prepare a defendant for trial, what I'm proposing may be considered . . . unethical. If the DA found out, forget it. I don't see it that way, but since this trial will get lots of publicity, I want two things. I want to win, and I want to be very quiet about how I do it."

"What about the people in your office? I mean, the other lawyers on the team and stuff?"

He shook his head, jaw firm. "I don't intend to tell them about your real role. A thousand bucks a day, Rita, and acting for real, not pretending in front of a camera. It'll be hard work, but I have the feeling you're not afraid of that. If you say yes right now, I'll give you money up front to buy some office-type clothes, if you need them, and to tide you over for the next few days. Then I'll pay you in cash once a week. You'll work at least Monday through Friday, probably some weekends too. That's five to seven thousand a week." He rested his arm on the table in front of me, and I stared at his fine black arm hairs and his wristbone. I could feel his eyes on the side of my face.

A thousand a day was a couple hundred over SAG scale, which is toilet paper to a star, but for the likes of me? I closed my eyes and thought of all the months of rent I could save up, all the scrumptious food I could buy, all the beauty treatments I could pay for, all the new toys and clothes for Petey I could splurge on. A zero balance on the credit card.

"I'm up for it," I decided, "but there's just one thing. There's this director named Serge Oatberger." I told Gary how the auditions for the new film were coming up, and how my agent Marly thought I'd be perfect for the second lead, or even the lead. "If I got either part," I explained enthusiastically, "it'd be my dream come true. So if I can just be available for auditions when they're called, and then of course if I actually—"

"No."

The tone of that one *no* gave me a glimpse of the inner Gary Kwan: the icy desire that made him such a good courtroom performer, capable of cheap manipulative sentimentality, cold disgust, and everything in between.

Firmly, he said, "This cannot be a side job for you, Rita. Either you commit fully to this project, or forget it. I can't guarantee you'll be free when that audition comes up."

I stared into space.

I thought about my career.

Gary waited.

I thought some more and drank my water.

He waited some more, patiently, watchfully.

After a minute he added gently, "You'll get a fifty-thousand-dollar bonus if she's acquitted."

"Oh, God." The sun moved in the sky a little bit, pushing a patch of shade over my fingers on the table.

Finally I said, "All right."

"Yes!" In a burst of energy, Gary pumped my hand, clapped me on the shoulder, and strode to the window, as if for a breath of fresh air, though of course the window was fixed in place and the air in the office was perfectly nice and cool. "Good, good, *good*! This is an excellent day, Rita. Trust me. Oh, this is going to be an adventure. A first."

The light from the window shone dazzlingly on Gary's face and charming haircut—short over the ears, thick on top—as he gazed down at the street. I'd wanted to tousle that hair since the library.

He turned and beckoned to me. "Look what's going on down there."

I joined him at the window. Seven stories below, a man in blue jeans lay on the sidewalk, writhing in pain. Dark blood was seeping through his shirt. He appeared to be screaming or moaning, though we couldn't hear it. A bystander had stopped and was crouching next to him, talking on a cell phone.

Gary murmured, "He tripped on that bump in the sidewalk,

fell, and now his arm's broken. See how he's holding it? An open fracture, with that blood. Ten years ago I'd be running down there to sign him up as a client. Sue the city."

The man's suffering made me feel sick. "We should do something."

"If he were unconscious I'd go down and see if he needed CPR. But he's breathing and rolling around, so he'll be OK. And look, there's an EMT truck coming up from Beverly Glen already. They'll take care of him." He watched me watching the man on the pavement. "You need a strong stomach in this world, Rita."

"I have it for some things."

"Yes?"

"Such as I'm not afraid of poop and vomit."

"How about blood?"

"I'm a woman, I know all about blood."

"Touché."

SIX

Beyond the office buildings on Wilshire Boulevard the city seethed and rumbled. It was getting warmer as the day wore on, the temperature edging up to seventy-seven degrees, seventy-eight. A taxi backed over an unopened bottle of Mountain Dew: *poph!* A biplane slalomed overhead, preparing for an air show at Venice Beach. People watered their lawns and thought about cooking out later.

George Rowe, a crew-cut guy who used to wrestle convicts for a living, parked his yellow VW Beetle in front of a house in Rancho Park and got out.

When Volkswagen introduced the cuter Beetle, so many people in Los Angeles bought it that it quickly became an innocuous car, the kind of car people stopped noticing, or if they did notice they thought, *Oh, cute banal car, I suppose a cute banal person is driving it.*

Along with the crew cut, Rowe wore short-sleeved shirts with ties and leather shoes and he didn't care that women thought he was a nerd king because that was just like the car. People flicked their eyes on you and then past, and one second later would not be able to tell anybody what color your hair was if their life depended on it. He was neither tall nor short. He took some pride in having a sturdy build but made sure his shirts didn't show it off too much.

George Rowe walked up to the house and let himself in with the key the owner had lent him.

He was thinking how money is a magic charm. It makes people tell you things. It makes them let you do things to them. It makes people think they're much smarter than they are. Can you buy intelligence with cash? In a way, you can.

The house was empty of people. He went to the laundry room and reached up for the handle to the attic steps. He climbed the steps, hearing the metallic *tinks* of the springs settling under his weight, then scooted over to a miniature video camera he had installed there two days ago. It was very hot in the attic and he felt the slickness of sudden sweat on his face and under his arms. Holding a flashlight in his teeth, he pulled out the camera, looked at it, fiddled with the coat-hanger-wire mount he had made for it, and repositioned it. The lens pointed down through the attic floor. It had worked fine, the camera, but he had not aimed it properly at first, and it had to be just so.

He climbed down and, glancing into the kitchen, noticed a sinkful of breakfast dishes. He washed a glass with a sponge and a squirt of detergent, rinsed it, and took a drink of cold water from the tap. He went ahead and washed the rest of the dishes, setting them to dry on the drainboard.

He left the house, stopped at a grocery store near his apartment in Culver City, and went home and put away the food. He changed into a pair of cutoffs and a T-shirt his boss had brought him from Nantucket. He washed a carrot, cut off the top, and stood chewing it, thinking.

George Rowe's apartment was his nest and workplace. He kept it tidy because he'd discovered that if you're a slob you can never find anything, and then you waste time. His double bed, with its blue-piped coverlet, occupied one corner of the bedroom. Another corner housed his surveillance electronics and his PC. A bank of six file cabinets lined one wall of the living room, and two whiteboards on easels stood in front of them. The boards were covered with Rowe's forward-leaning handwriting in black marker: names, dates, arrows, little sketches, and way too many question marks.

He munched the carrot and looked at one of the boards for a long time. He rubbed out something with the corner of a dry eraser and wrote in something new. Whatever it was didn't please him, because he stood looking at it unhappily, hands on hips, his knotty toes gripping the decks of his house shoes, a pair of cherry rubber flip-flops.

He was working a lot these days. He didn't like downtime and he didn't have a lawn to water.

He looked at his watch. The phone rang.

"We didn't do it last night," a female voice said.

"That's OK," said Rowe. "I had to fix the camera anyway. Try again tonight."

The other voice paused. "Did you do the dishes when you were here?"

"Yes."

"How come?"

Hearing the puzzled smile in her voice gave him a good feeling. People don't expect you to do something nice just for the hell of it.

"I just felt like it. You seem pretty busy."

"Well—thank you!"

He hung up and called the cell number of a urologist who answered while pulling his car into a gas station in Pasadena.

"Doc, we appreciate everything you've done for us. But are you absolutely sure you couldn't testify?"

"Oh, I can testify," said the tennis-tanned doctor, popping his filler door and two-fingering his wallet out of his back pocket, "but it won't be what you want."

"You really can't say if his penis functions sexually or not? I mean, you gave him a complete examination, didn't you?"

"Yes! He was more than willing to urinate for me, but—"

"That was never the issue."

"I know! What did you want me to do, get down on my knees and—"

"OK."

"He said he couldn't give a semen sample, all right? There's no way to actually tell if—oh, he's got some interesting scars on the thing. A ferret attack, for God's sake. I think the bastard probably *does* have sexual function, because I could find nothing organic. But as you know, the sex act—"

"OK, OK."

"—involves more than just—"

"OK. Thank you."

51

Next Rowe called his boss at home. The boss, a supervisor in the claims department at Fenco, the insurance giant, was used to hearing from him anytime, any day of the week.

"I think," Rowe reported, "I'm about to get the video we want in the Crunch & Munch case."

"Yeah? Good."

"You know I hate these porn jobs."

"Yeah, but you do 'em so well."

A few months ago, a bartender from Santa Monica was having sex with another man's wife at her home in Malibu. The woman kept several ferrets as pets, and while the two humans were noodling around in bed after a session of intercourse, one of the ferrets had decided to join them under the covers. The bartender's penis had in some way upset the ferret, which sank its small, needlelike teeth into it and hung on, only to let go and re-grip several times. Finally the bartender managed to part the ferret's jaws. He stanched the blood with a towel and sought medical treatment.

Soon afterward, the woman and her husband received word that the bartender had filed a lawsuit against them for permanent loss of sexual function, for fifty million dollars. The husband was not pleased.

He had, a decade earlier, purchased an umbrella liability policy with Fenco for a maximum of two million dollars. Fenco had begun negotiations with the bartender's lawyer, who insisted that his client would settle for no less than ten million, or go to trial and win Fenco's two million plus everything else the couple owned.

The claims bosses at Fenco decided that the bartender's claim, supported only by an affidavit from an unaccredited cancer specialist in Tijuana, was suspicious. Thus it was that George Rowe got assigned to find out whether the bartender's wounds had robbed him of sexual function or what.

He followed the man, figured out he already had a new girlfriend (a single woman, with no pets, this time), and approached her. After winning her trust with a hundred-dollar bill, he learned the bartender could indeed achieve erection, penetration, and ejaculation. The girlfriend and Rowe decided that in exchange for five thousand dollars now and another five thousand later, she would allow him to install a digital video camera above her bed and leave it in place for one month. He would probably get what he wanted within a few days. All he needed was explicit proof. The girlfriend's testimony could be valuable, should the case get all the way to court, but pictures were always best. Too, pictures were cheaper than lawyers.

The girlfriend wanted to leave Los Angeles anyway, and so she aimed to move up to Portland after receiving the second half of her money. The bartender wouldn't bother her; Rowe knew from experience he wouldn't do anything but drop his lawsuit and hide under a rock for a while, just as soon as his lawyer had a chance to view Rowe's video.

In olden days—that is, five years ago when Rowe left his job as a corrections officer at Folsom State Prison and went to work as an investigator for Fenco—cases like this excited him. Busting scammers was fun, and uncovering evidence that a suspicious individual really was honest was unexpectedly satisfying. He would have gotten a real boot out of the Crunch & Munch bartender, would have laughed about it and captured the video with relish. He would've almost wet his pants showing it to the bartender's attorney.

He had solved all sorts of cases for Fenco. There was the

infrared–aerial work he'd done to show that a pea grower could not have lost a crop to drought because he had not planted one in the first place; there was the disabled-vet disguise he'd donned to find out that a man who claimed to be paralyzed indeed was, he just had a crappy doctor; there was the plain old waiting-in-the-dark-on-a-hunch work he'd done to bust up a jet fuel swindle at a private airstrip at Lake Tahoe.

Yes, he would've been challenged and gratified by this stupid bartender's opportunism. And that was the thing about fraud: so often somebody without the brains to cook up a well-organized scam will be tempted by happenstance to defraud an insurance company. Such people were usually easy to catch, with tricks and bribes.

But now such stuff was hollow. Too easy. Stakes not high enough. George Rowe had become addicted to the chase. He needed a greater challenge, or his work was going to stop being fun.

He said to his boss, "Yeah, Avery, but an orangutang could do what I do. You know the case I want to go back to." He gazed at his whiteboards.

"Yeah," said Avery, who knew Rowe was the best investigator he'd ever worked with. "The Jeweler in the Jungle. Well, let's talk about it after you wrap this one up."

SEVEN

I pulled into the parking lot on the west side of Rodeo Drive at Santa Monica and backed into a space.

I was not here to shop.

At Ann Taylor in the Beverly Center I'd just bought, with some of the money Gary had handed me that morning, two neutral skirted outfits like you see on lawyers on Trial TV, plus a decent pair of closed pumps at Banana Republic. I had a slightly-beat-up-but-dignified Coach purse at home that would work, but I didn't know if I needed a briefcase. I let that go for now. I was OK for pantyhose as well. The new stuff was in the cargo hold of my Honda.

I shut off the engine and rolled down my window. The ambience of Santa Monica Boulevard instantly filled the car: four flowing lanes of traffic plus left turn, the sound like metallic surf, accented by the chug of an unmuffled tailpipe, the hasty skid of tires. The light turns red and the traffic-surf ebbs, the waiting cars sigh anxiously, then the cross-current of cars on Rodeo begins, a much smaller stream, their engines and tires almost individually distinct. Then the green light comes for Santa Monica and the relieved surge begins and builds to that metallic surf again. I closed my eyes and listened and breathed.

The air quality here was what you'd expect in the heart of Beverly Hills, which is, if not the heart of Los Angeles, then one of the major organs, L.A. itself being the heart of American car culture, with California being the conflicted nerve center of American popular culture. In short, the air here was lousy.

And yet the air here was rarefied and desirable. Anyone can come and breathe it, of course. But few belong to the shopping class of this part of Rodeo Drive, where a sweater might cost you six hundred dollars—or even six thousand—and a luncheon plate fifty. Not everybody can afford to pay money just to park a car, especially when you can park for free in front of the houses on Rodeo Drive on the other side of Santa Monica.

One day, shortly after Petey was born and I was still going full-time to UCLA for my theater degree, I realized I had to get out of my marriage. When you get hit in the eye, the shiner takes about thirty-six hours to look its worst, whether you've applied ice or not. I'd gone to class with a thirty-six-hour-old black eye, and although I'd gained enough makeup skills to reduce its obviousness, people could tell. My partner in improvisation that day, a gentle stud named Daniel Clements, bought me a coffee after class and said only, "That wedding ring is costing you a lot to keep, isn't it?"

It was like being hit in the other eye, only a good hit. I had to think, and after I left campus I drove aimlessly for a couple of hours, not caring that Jeff, who was in Torrance feeding Petey from the bottle of pumped milk I'd left in the fridge, would be furious that I hadn't come straight home. Let him fume, I thought for the first time. Do you believe it? For the first time. I was driving along in a state of deep confusion when I found myself turning into this parking lot at Rodeo and Santa Monica. All I wanted was to take my foot off the gas for a while. I call it a lot, but it's actually a two-level structure, with the first level underground and the top one raised just slightly above street grade. It gives you a little bit of a view, a little bit of elevation. Which is nice, for a parking lot.

As soon as I'd turned off the engine, a feeling came over me, a mystical type of feeling. The feeling felt like Gramma Gladys. I had the strong sense she was there with me, right in that parking lot.

I even said, cautiously, "Gramma?"

The feeling stayed.

I began to talk to her, pouring out my troubles. I cried about Jeff's drinking and horrible temper, the affair I suspected he'd been having with some bimbo at work. I told her how scared I was to be a mother, how I should have known better than to get pregnant, how stupid my dream of being an actress must be.

In spite of—or perhaps because of—having been dead a decade, Gramma Gladys was able to help me. She listened. I felt her say, in her all-exclamation-points-all-the-time voice, *Of course you have to leave him! Next time he'll put you in the hospital! Time after that he'll kill you! He'll kill the boy!*

You're too smart for this!

Gramma Gladys, my mother's mother, dug a life out of the apathetic soil of a Wisconsin alfalfa farm and the family of uncommunicative weirdos she came from. After giving birth to four kids

57

in six years, she talked my grandfather into buying her an adding machine and a typewriter, with which she started a business doing bookkeeping for neighboring farmers and the storekeepers in town. The town's name is Durability, chosen by early homesteaders who didn't want to tempt fate by calling their town anything remotely cheerful or grand. Even today doggedness is a valuable trait in those parts. She branched into tax preparation, then began giving business advice for money, and in this way eventually pulled the family into the middle class.

This was not a small achievement.

When I was little and Gramma Gladys came to visit, she was the brainiest, most glamorous person I knew. She wore pearls and the best clothes she could afford or sew for herself. She looked like a lady, cussed like a sailor, and her love was usually misinterpreted as hostility. But she and I understood each other.

It was clear to me, even at a young age, that she'd fought harder for what she had than anybody gave her credit for. And she realized the problems I would face, a little honey-haired cutie who got away with everything. I didn't know it was because pretty people always get away with more.

Pretty pretty pretty. I actually grew to hate that word. It was intended as praise, but I understood it as a fetter.

Pretty pretty pretty.

Gramma Gladys sought to elbow that shit out of the way by never agreeing with anyone that I was pretty.

"The kid's got brains, that's what counts!" I once heard her yell to my father. "Christ almighty, buy her a chemistry set!"

I never received a chemistry set and I never made it into honors math, but I got A's in history and psychology, as well as the leads in the school plays.

It became my habit to drop in on that parking lot whenever I was troubled. Miraculously, Gramma Gladys was always there, and I always had a little money for the meter in case I saw an enforcement officer coming. There was no explaining it—Gramma Gladys had never been to California. Her bones rested in the churchyard near the farm back in Wisconsin.

So this afternoon, after buying new clothes, I turned into that parking lot to commune for just a sec with my beloved spiritual advisor.

I breathed in the gas fumes and looked across the boulevard to the swell mansions of Beverly Hills and said, "Gramma, I took the bird in the hand."

A stiff breeze blew my hair into my eyes.

"I have a kid to take care of," I went on, "and I've got to do it alone. What are the odds I'd get that Oatberger job anyway?"

I felt Gramma Gladys say, *Go home!*

I STOPPED AT Plummer Park and found Petey and Daniel there. I took a bag of apples out of the trunk and strolled toward the monkey bars where Daniel was demonstrating how to hang sideways from a pole, which Petey found awesome. I had to laugh, watching Daniel try to give a tutorial in the physics of gymnastics to a four-year-old.

"I'll show you again. You gotta use your muscles." Daniel seized the pole, braced his elbow into his stomach, and swung his legs to horizontal and held them there rigidly, his body perfectly parallel with the ground, a startling and ridiculous thing to see.

"Wow!" said Petey.

I thanked the universe for Daniel.

He saw me first and murmured something to Petey, who raced over to me. "Mommy!" He wrapped himself around my legs, and my heart swelled as it always did when I was reunited with my boy, no matter how brief the separation. His little hands, lined with the clean dirt of the park, clutched my slacks. You could blindfold me and let a thousand little kids wrap themselves around my legs, and I'd know which one was Petey. Put them all in wool coats and mittens, and I'd still know.

He pulled away. "Watch me, Mommy!"

"Wait, honey, I've got apples!" The juicy Braeburn was ripped out of my hand and half demolished before Daniel and I took bites from ours.

We sat at a picnic table eating our apples, watching Petey try and try to duplicate Daniel's trick. His brown hair swung and caught the light like umber silk. Little-boy hair, cut in the cutest of bowl cuts. When Petey's cheeks were red with exertion, he looked like a small circus man.

"He's not strong enough yet," Daniel commented.

"Maybe you shouldn't have shown him that, then."

Daniel had grown up in some Carolina or other, and his voice still retained a touch of that soft southern hominy. "Rita, my gosh. It's something for him to work toward. A goal, you know?"

"But he's only four years old!"

"Old enough to have goals."

"Daniel, you're right. What a dunce I am."

He sighed. "Don't call yourself that."

"You know, I'm sitting here thinking how much more actually masculine you are than Jeff is."

He laughed, his proud square jaw jutting skyward, his hair fluttering in the afternoon breeze. I could tell by his posture he was relaxed and pleasantly tired. He snapped off a big bite of apple. The air in the park smelled green from all the different species of trees breathing in and out, plus all the shrubs and grass. I watched a small red beetle encounter a crack in a plank in the picnic table and try to decide what to do.

"I mean," I explained, "by the prevalent standard, Jeff's deemed a real man because he likes to screw chicks, and you're deemed a pervert because you like to do it with men. Yet the amount of manly leadership you provide for Petey compared with how half-assed Jeff is with him—uff. The amount of *daddy-ship*. Petey loves you, you know."

Daniel was silent, and I realized he'd gotten misty. He swallowed and said, "And I love him. You know, I doubt I'll ever father a child. And yet there's something in me that I feel opening up, somehow, when I'm with Petey. I admit, half the time he's a little asshole, but the other half—he's so sweet and original. He sees possibilities when we're climbing a tree that I don't see."

Petey called out, "Daniel, show me again how to do it!"

"In a minute, boyo. Meanwhile, do the overhead ladder twice back and forth without stopping. Can you?"

Petey ran to do it.

Daniel turned his spark-blue eyes on me and said, "Well?"

I met his gaze. "I took an acting job. It's an unusual role, and I can't talk about it with anybody—yet, anyway, and I know you're going to sit there and guess and try to tease it out of me, but—"

"No. I won't."

"*Thank* you."

"I can see it's a big deal."

"Thank you."

We gnawed our apples. The beetle stood back from the crevasse in the plank, thinking. It put a feeler out to the crack, then turned sideways and moved along until the crack stopped, then it turned and kept going the way it wanted to. "Did you guys get lunch?" I asked.

"Yeah, we went to my place for sandwiches."

"Another thank you."

Petey ran over to a couple of kids who sharingly gave him a sand shovel and allowed him to help them dig a hole "to Colorado."

"Colorado?" murmured Daniel.

"Anyplace," I remarked, "is the other side of the world from Los Angeles."

Daniel sighed mightily.

" 'Smatter?" I asked.

"Oh, the usual."

"Anything on the horizon?"

"I wish I didn't need a guy, you know?"

"Do I ever." The sum total of guys I'd dated since leaving Jeff was two, and only one of them had I felt OK about sleeping with. Then he turned out to be still stuck on his ex-wife. He actually asked me to help him write a letter to her in Milan where she'd gone to study design.

Daniel said, "I really should stop dating Hollywood guys. Definitely no more directors or actors. They're all black holes of need."

"Yeah, I guess they are, except you. So the profile of your dream guy has changed slightly?"

"I want a guy who's neither impressed that *I'm on a TV show!*, nor looks down on me because *I'm only a TV actor!*"

I laughed.

"I want a guy who's smart," Daniel went on, "you know, with a serious job or career. A guy who's so damn busy he doesn't have *time* to be neurotic."

"Yeah."

"I want never again to go out for coffee with another thirty-year-old child whose every thought comes out of his mouth, when, that is, he's not absorbed in looking at his own reflection in the Starbucks window." He looked down at himself. "And here I am in muddy pants, playing in the park. But—"

"I know what you mean."

"Course, there're plenty of old guys who hit on me, but I don't want Santa Claus either. Oh, listen to me whine. I have no right to feel sorry for myself. Although I do, really: my cleaner quit again."

"The same one?"

"Yeah, Connie. She went back to Colombia again."

"Oh."

"She was really good. Now there's grime everywhere."

"Why don't you try cleaning your own apartment? You might just—"

"Rita! You need professionals for these things."

Regular work on television is the holy career grail of everybody in Hollywood. I know I've said that starring in a Serge Oatberger film is the ultimate, and it is. The difference is this: being chosen by Oatberger is like winning the lottery, which is wondrous and giddy and if you're smart with the money you'll never have to do anything you don't really want to do. But finding yourself in the cast of a hit TV series is like getting in on the ground floor of a new business. If you handle yourself well, you'll be offered lots more opportunities. A multiseason hit show is to die for—or kill for, depending on the show and how you feel about your costars.

"You're just yearning," I told him. "Hasn't there ever been a Mr. Right in your life?"

"Hmmm." Daniel closed his eyes and inhaled as if smelling a fine wine, or a steak hot off the grill. "One time. He was the complete package. I guess I judge every guy I meet by him. Cute, but he didn't know it. That is such a godsend I can't tell you. Tough in public, very—and he did have a bit of a public profile. But tender in private. Bright, thoughtful. Not thoughtful in the way of being considerate, though he was that, but he was a man of thoughts, a guy who'd listen and read and come up with his own ideas."

"So what happened?"

Daniel's eyes clouded. "He wasn't—ready. He drew back."

"Oh."

"I still think of him."

Petey swung up into the branches of a tree.

"Not so high!" I shouted. He ignored me.

"He'll be OK," said Daniel. "That's our safe tree. He knows every move on it. Why don't you relax? I'm watching him."

"But what if he falls out? How are you gonna catch him if you're—"

"Rita, I hate to break this to you, but Petey *has* fallen out of that tree."

"Daniel! When?"

He looked at me with amused guy-smugness. "Lots of times! Rita, Rita, calm down, OK? He got the wind knocked out of him, that's all. He survived. That's how you learn to climb trees. You fall out a couple of times, and you learn quick what works and what doesn't."

"Oh, God."

"Metaphor for life and all that."

"Right, right. You must think I'm such a wuss."

"You're no wuss, you're my best girl. Look at your little pixie face! I'd say you're feeling upbeat this afternoon."

He drew a cigarette from a pack in his shirt pocket and lit up. The smoke drifted in the breeze. I didn't like it, but all I said was, "You and your lung candy." Huge numbers of people in show business smoke. We're all supposed to be so into health and fitness, and we are, but we're also obsessed with weight control, and the cigarettes help with that, plus we're stressed out half the time, ditto.

I said, "I am feeling upbeat." I mused aloud about growing up pretty, and wanting to do the things smart people did, and Gramma Gladys, and how people used to value me for miming and pretending, and tell me I had instinct. "I don't even know what instinct is, really."

Daniel listened quietly.

I said, "When I got married, Jeff, who had known me since before I got hips if not breasts, told me I wasn't smart enough to have any career but acting. He agreed with all of them. *Instinct's all you've got, baby*."

"He said that?"

"Yeah, and I believed him. And he was right, really. But I haven't even been successful at that. I've been relying on unemployment and child support for way too long now."

"Supporting a child takes other than money." He ashed his cigarette over the dirt.

"Yeah. Lately Jeff's been hostile when he comes to pick up Petey."

"Hostile how?"

"Well, belligerent. I suspect he's back to drinking, but I haven't smelled it on him. Last weekend he said he's thinking of challenging my custody because my income's been so low."

"Oh, what a prick."

"He is the biggest prick in the world. He's good at making me lose sleep. But you know what? I think—I hope—things are about to turn around for me."

I thought some more. "Seems like there are different kinds of intelligence. Maybe I'm not a genius. But I think I have a—a kind of emotional intelligence."

"You're smarter than you think." Daniel took a last hit from his cigarette, stubbed it out on the ground, then carried the butt over to a trash can. That's L.A. for you.

I wanted to be a success, and most of all I wanted to be a star. If I achieved that, I thought everything else would follow: a nice house, a college fund for Petey. Fame! Goddamn it, I wanted fame. I wanted love and support from audiences worldwide. I loved to hear applause, even the spattering of it around the set of a commercial when I flipped my hair and smiled in astonishment at my clean laundry. I loved to hear a director say, *Good work, Rita*. I loved the camaraderie of being in a cast. Frankly, I loved to show off.

EIGHT

One of the things they must teach very thoroughly in deputy school is door-slamming. Either that or it's a huge part of on-the-job training: "*Don't* turn the handle or knob, close the door, then release the handle or knob. This demonstrates weakness. *Do* pull the door firmly, creating maximum acceleration and, finally, full metal-to-metal contact between bolt and jamb. This demonstrates power and authority."

The sound of just one steel door slamming behind us as Gary and I walked through the jail to meet with Eileen brought home the This Is It feeling of incarceration.

The Century Regional Detention Facility sits just off the Century Freeway in one of those urban Gaza Strips where everything is bleak and mistrustful. The rents must be cheap for the scrap dealers and warehouses, then there's this building that looks like a concrete shopping mall where they keep the accused and the convicted, and the freeway noise pounds over it like an endless hail of bullets.

I had never been arrested and never visited anyone in jail, except for bailing out Jeff from the drunk tank in Green Bay once after we were engaged. (Talk about ignoring warning signs.) Television shows cannot convey the feeling of that sound of slamming prison doors. It's like getting a soft blow to the sternum from a crowbar. Surround-sound movies do a better job, but nothing is the same as feeling the actual vibes when thick steel strikes thick steel. And we weren't even on a cellblock.

Technology is great, you know, what with cameras and electric locks (with their eerie zapping clicks) and super-tempered glass, but in the end there's no substitute for brute solidity. In the days to come I would notice that other attorneys and outside people, who would be joking and laughing on the bright jacaranda-shaded plaza outside, stopped smiling as they passed into this building. Their voices, however, remained bluff in affirmation: *I'm not staying here! May the grace of God keep me safe from a place like this.*

Gary had scored a special interview room, private except for a window in the door. He tossed down his leather briefcase. Same as everything else in the jail, the table and chairs were overbuilt and ugly, like Soviet furniture.

The air smelled of disinfectant, sweat, and fear. Gary rubbed his eyes. It was early, barely seven o'clock, on the Tuesday after we'd met. We'd be permitted an hour to spend with Eileen, then go back to jury selection in court. This too was a special break: the other lawyers had to wait until nine-thirty to see their clients.

As we waited for the female deputy to retrieve Eileen Tenaway,

Gary said, "Now, you'll have carte blanche with her, except for one ground rule."

"Yes?"

"You're not to ask her about the night of Gabriella's death."

I dropped my hands.

"She doesn't want to discuss it."

"But Gary, how'm I supposed to—"

"Rita, that's it." His voice was hard right then, and I realized I sort of liked it. I liked that he felt he could be tough on me.

When she passed through the door, which was held by a deputy who couldn't wait to slam it, Eileen squinted like a mole, and Gary said her name in a hearty voice.

She was not shackled. The deputy watched from the window. "The officer can't hear us unless we shout," Gary said. Eileen shook Gary's hand and turned to me, still squinting. Gary introduced us and I grasped her hand with as much warmth as I could, even though my heart was pounding and my hands clammy. The fluorescent light bounced around greenishly to illuminate every line in our faces, every scratch on the table, every grain of grit on the floor.

Gary had spoken to her yesterday about me, he'd said, so I asked, "Are you into Gary's plan, Eileen?"

Ignoring me, she said to Gary, "I bet you forgot to bring what I asked you for, didn't you?"

He flipped open his briefcase. "No, I didn't forget. Here it is." He drew out a framed photograph, which I hadn't noticed when the deputies were searching our stuff and us. "The studio still had the negatives," he added.

Jail time is a type of anti-cosmetic, I realized: a jail is an anti-spa. You go there and your looks coarsen, your body slackens.

Eileen Tenaway had suffered its effects now for several months, and it showed. Yet she'd started with such a surplus of beauty, at age thirty-four and behind bars she was still caviar to most other women's ground chuck.

Eileen Tenaway took the photo from Gary and as she looked at it, I looked at her and thought about her public image. She'd always been more of an East Coast beauty than a West Coast one. You know, she dyed her hair blond, but not too light, and she wore it sleek and symmetrical, often in upswept knots. Her makeup had been more subtle than startling, her wardrobe more Beacon Hill than Beverly Hills, though that's where the Tenaways lived. She'd had an expensive, understated look that actually drew more attention than if she'd been a Hollywood clone wife.

I realized that that look was a better backdrop for all the jewelry. An emerald necklace, for instance, is going to pop against a cream-colored silk evening shell much more effectively than against some sequined piece of frou-frou.

However, the woman who had smiled out at us envious peons from the pages of the *Los Angeles Times* now stared dully, without makeup, her brown roots showing, her body scrawny and curveless in the orange prison outfit. She'd gathered her hair with a rubber band and fashioned it into a semblance of a French twist with another rubber band. I'm sure prisoners weren't allowed to have hairpins. I don't know how she achieved it.

All of which is to say, you can take the woman out of the Chanel, but you can't take the Chanel out of the woman.

Eileen Tenaway's eyes were widely spaced—another East Coast, Jackie-Kennedy-like trait—and poised over a straight, thin nose. Her mouth had a slight downturn just before the corners, followed by a tiny upturn—a double cupid's bow, doubtless highly attractive to a young Richard Tenaway at whatever fancy party had brought them together years ago.

Her jawline swept upward from the point of her chin to her ears with incredible youthfulness, and I wondered whether she'd already had face work—perhaps an under-chin touch-up. I strained to tell; if she'd had any, she'd had the best. Her skin color was pale and fairly even.

I silently moved to where I could see the picture over her shoulder.

It was a studio portrait of a baby girl. An expensive job, a beautiful job. The baby was sitting up in front of a burgundy brocade drape. Her hair was white-blond, curled about her tiny ears, and she was smiling simply and freshly, showing stubby baby teeth and the tip of a pink tongue. Her dress was a simple design of cerulean velvet, and her little feet wore chamois booties.

Over Eileen's head Gary mouthed to me, *First birthday*.

The child's healthy fat hands clutched at a miniature necklace made, it took no Ph.D. to realize, of fine topaz beads, the stones varying in color from light gold at the back of the neck to deep orange, almost brown, at the center. Absolutely arresting.

She could have been painted by Sargent, one of those children-versus-the-dark pictures he was so good at. Because in spite of her smile, there was a somberness about the child, an expression in the eyes of—what? Anxiety? Sadness? Wistfulness?

The picture was so terribly poignant, and Eileen Tenaway's spine slumped so dreadfully as she held it and gazed, that tears sprang to my eyes. I blinked them back.

At last she looked up. "I was starting to forget what she looked like," she said.

That was the agony she carried inside.

"I want my baby back." She had cried all she could cry, and all she could do now was talk, but that hurt too. At this moment I saw she was real. Not a name in a gossip column, not a white-fang smile at a charity ball. A woman who had gone through the thing every parent dreads more than death itself: the loss of a child.

Gathering myself, I said, "I'm so sorry, Eileen."

Gary looked at me helplessly.

I took a chair at the table at right angles to her and laid my hands flat. "Eileen, here's what I know," I said. "Somebody fed your baby enough pills to kill her. They think you did it."

She peered at me, but still did not really acknowledge me.

I hardened my voice and leaned into her face. "So do I, you bitch."

She gasped and then, when all I did was stare back at her, looked to Gary. He glanced sideways at me. I watched Eileen carefully, looking for a flush to come up her neck, or a vein to pop at her temple, or her hands to clench.

Nothing. It was as if her insides had been ripped out and re-placed with cold meat.

"I thought you were supposed to be on my side," she said.

She didn't talk East Coast, though. She talked California, maybe Marin County, or Walnut Creek. Yes, that was it, a cool Walnut Creek tone, locus of suburban San Francisco conservatism and wealth.

"All right," I said.

"All right what?" asked Gary.

"I am on your side," I told Eileen. "But I'm not here to be your new best friend. I'm here to make the *jury* want to be your best friend. You and I need to talk. Gary, can you excuse us for a while?"

"Uh," he said, surprised, and I thought a little hurt. Fine. "Uh, sure."

Before he walked out he said to his client, "The one silver lining to your talking to the police that day was I was able to show the tape to our jury focus groups. Based on their feedback, I decided to hire Rita. You need her."

"Yes, Daddy," she said, as the door slammed behind him.

When the gust died away, I said, "I'm new at this."

"Me too."

I smiled at that, but she just looked at me warily. I said, "Look, Eileen, I don't know what Gary told you about me, but I'm twenty-nine years old, mother of one, and fighting like hell to be the best actress in Hollywood. Maybe he saw that in me and that's why he approached me. I don't know."

"Well, I've never heard of you." She looked me up and down for the first time, and I knew what she was assessing: Does she look younger than me? Thinner? Prettier? Smarter?

It's exactly what goes on in casting waiting rooms.

"You will, Eileen. You will." I sat back in my chair diagonally like a hoody girl pretending she doesn't care if anyone likes her. I had determined not to be deferential to Eileen. I was the high-status one here: I was free. Moreover, the only way this was going to work was if I could inspire deference in *her*.

"It's no sprinkles off my ice cream if you don't get acquitted," I added. "But wouldn't it be a kick if you did?"

She just watched me, her lips a little open, trying to figure me out. Her body was tense, especially in the shoulders and eyelids, as if trying to keep me from looking too far in.

"Eileen, what was the name of your best friend when you were little?"

Her eyes opened in real confusion, and I saw they were a terrific color of hazel.

I said, "We're just talking here."

"Well," she said, "her name was Beatrice Rhinegold."

"Why did you like her?"

"Why did I like her? She lived on my street and she was nice to me. One time when I had the chicken pox she brought her dog to the lawn under my bedroom window and taught it to do tricks while I watched. She did that for days."

I could see the memory in her eyes. "Well, I like Beatrice Rhinegold too," I said.

"Yeah. We made popcorn balls every Halloween."

"Did you keep in touch with her?"

"No, she moved away."

I massaged Gary's leather briefcase with my hand, then looked up. "At some point, Eileen, you're going to tell the jury your side of things, and when you do it you're going to be talking to Beatrice as if she's sitting in the middle of the jury box."

"I don't want to think about it."

"You should think about it. You should look forward to it, because your story is going to set you free."

"I really don't want, uh, can't you just—"

I let my voice off the leash a bit. "What you want or don't want is totally irrelevant, Eileen. Do you get that? You want this horrible thing never to have happened. You want things you did in the past to be erased from the world. You want other people to come up to you and say they're sorry. I can only help you if you talk to me about that night. Otherwise I'll walk out and you can not think about it all you want in prison for the rest of your—"

"All right all right all *right*! *God!*"

She settled her butt deeper into the hard chair and heaved a sigh they must have heard at the front desk. "I put Gabriella to bed at eight o'clock. We read a story and she went to sleep. I didn't give her any ice cream that night. They said they found some in her stomach. I went to bed around eleven. When I got up to go to the bathroom in the middle of the night, I thought I heard something. I turned on some lights, but I didn't see anything. Gabriella was sleeping. I didn't hear anything else. When I woke up in the morning—it took me a long time to wake up. I felt sick. When I woke up, I could tell"—she paused—"something was wrong." Eileen's face was like carved wood; she was controlling it as hard as she could. Her hands trembled on the tabletop. I noticed her fingernails were neatly shaped and not too long. "I always heard Gabriella stirring when I went down the hall to her room. But that morning she was quiet. I went in and—found her." Another pause. "She was face-down outside the covers, and I thought, *Oh, she must be cold.* But before I even touched her I knew. I turned her over and she was purple. They say the blood pools when—you know. And she was cold. She looked so . . . gone."

We sat in silence for a while.

Eileen cleared her throat and continued, "It wasn't until the ambulance and police came that I realized the house had been burglarized."

"Yeah?"

"I hadn't seen it at all. The place was a mess, everything all over, every drawer dumped out, cushions cut open. The food from the refrigerator was all over the place. They'd even searched the room I slept in."

"Yes."

"I hadn't even noticed. They didn't get anything but some money I had in a tennis ball can, and a few small things—a jade figurine, a Louis Quinze inkwell, a clock. They couldn't figure out where the safe was." I expected to see a trace of triumph in her face but did not.

"Yes?"

"In Gabriella's room, set into an outside wall behind a flimsy poster."

"And how come you didn't wake up as early as usual?"

"I *couldn't* wake up. I had this terrible headache, I couldn't focus my eyes very well. I remember wobbling down the hall. When you're a parent, you sleep so lightly, you know? You always have this feeling of responsibility. I knew something had happened, and it was morning and I was struggling to become alert. It was like a nightmare."

"And why do you think—"

"I must have been drugged. Didn't you read the papers?"

"Drugged how?"

"I don't know. Maybe with some kind of gas mask over my face while I slept. I don't know how they did it," she went on, her voice solidifying like ice crystals. "You'd have to ask them."

"Who?"

She bit off the words. *"I don't know."*

At the moment, she was utterly unconvincing to me. The vibes she was giving off, plus her facial expressions, were a mix of real and fake. She was trying for total control, yet she couldn't help showing flashes of authentic emotion: I saw irritation, anger, and above all, fear.

Did Eileen Tenaway really know what had happened, or at least why it had happened? She was scared and confused and calculating.

And the grief was there beneath it all. She missed her baby. Was that the only footing for her life now? Maybe so.

As she talked she avoided eye contact with me, yet her eyes were overactive, roaming all around that harsh room as if looking for a chink in the masonry.

NINE

T hanks for making the time," said George Rowe, striding into a law office in a strip plaza in El Segundo.

"Sure," grunted the attorney. He knew what was coming, but he had to go through this exercise as he'd done on several unpleasant occasions before. Cost of doing business.

"Oh," Rowe said. "Good morning. Didn't expect to see you here."

"You know who I am?" The bartender rose from his chair.

"Of course. I'd recognize you anywhere, pants or no pants."

"What the fuck is this? Who the fuck. This fucker—"

"Shut up," said the attorney. He wore a cheap suit and a combover.

The bartender's mouth formed a tight slit.

Rowe carried only an electronic gadget the size of a paperback book. He opened it, pressing keys as he did so, and set it on the corner of the attorney's desk. The attorney did not ask him to sit, nor did Rowe care to; this was going to be quick.

The lawyer stood at Rowe's elbow looking at the liquid-crystal screen. The bartender crowded in, and Rowe stepped aside as the movie began. There was no sound, no need for it. The attorney and his client watched, the bartender breathing heavily.

Quietly, Rowe said, "It only lasts about four minutes." The attorney cut him a look, then bit his lip to keep from laughing. The bartender's eyes glazed over as he watched the video. His mouth fell open, then slowly closed into a tight slit again that got tighter still.

Rowe had chosen a slow fade-out to end the movie, a blackening of the final image of the bartender's white buttocks poised over the girlfriend's hips as they discussed, apparently, whether to do it again.

Los Angeles is a city of many movies.

Rowe shut the device.

He and the attorney looked at the bartender.

At last the bartender said, "That bitch."

Predictable, thought Rowe.

"And you bastard!" The bartender's face was a rich, interesting cranberry color all the way to his hairline. He stepped toward Rowe. "You're gonna—"

"Shut up," said his attorney again. "Do not make any threats."

The bartender lunged at Rowe, who moved quickly and obliquely in his hard-soled shoes to trip one of the bartender's legs backward, popping it out from under him.

"You fucking piece of fuck," the bartender said from the floor, holding his knee.

His lawyer said, "You're getting mad at the wrong people."

Rowe hooked his thumbs in his belt and said, "Look, fax us a letter within an hour and we'll consider not going after him."

The attorney said to his client, "Did you bring that two hundred and fifty dollars I told you to?"

"Yeah."

"Give it to me and get the hell out of here. I'll send the letter for you."

Rowe picked up his video player and said, "Your girlfriend doesn't live there anymore. Don't go looking for her."

"You shit fuck motherfucking fucker."

Rowe reached down and, with a move so quick it was almost invisible, slapped the bartender's ear, hard. "Understand?"

The bartender yelped, then gritted his teeth and muttered, "Yeah."

Rowe said to the attorney, "I can't help asking. Why did you take this one?"

The lawyer hated Rowe's flat stomach and unstained tie. But he touched his comb-over in self-affirmation, then answered cheerfully enough, "I wasn't busy, and the odds seemed fair. But I didn't know he was that stupid."

AT HOME ROWE shucked his shirt and tie for shorts and T-shirt. He opened a can of American beer in celebration, took a gulp, then phoned his boss.

"Avery. Have you gotten a fax yet?" he asked.

"Yeah, Nita just put it on my desk. Crunch & Munch closed. Good work." His boss's voice was a poppa-bear growl.

"Thanks, and now let's talk about Tenaway."

"What do you think?"

Rowe stood with the phone to his ear, holding his beer with the other hand, and gazed at the whiteboards in his living room. He had the boards practically memorized, not that they were any good. On them he had written things like:

Minas Gerais.
Baby revenge?
Reverse bribe, find all principals.
Sister-girlfriend weak link?
Visa dates.

Rowe said, "I want all the files again."

"What for?"

"I want the paperwork the Brazilian police wrote up, and—"

"There's nothing new, George." Avery was smiling, but his voice didn't show it. He liked to challenge Rowe and he liked to be sold up the river by Rowe's passion for the game. "And you know the claims have been paid."

Rowe took a sip of beer from the can. He pressed his upper lip lightly against the sharp metal opening. "Yeah. But if we can prove fraud, we can probably get it back from the company. And who knows about the wife?"

"She's blowing through hers right now paying Gary Kwan to keep her ass out of prison. I think her luck might be running out."

"I wouldn't," remarked Rowe, "call it lucky to have your kid die."

Ignoring that, his boss said, "This one we'd prosecute forever."

"All the way," Rowe agreed. "We'd have automatic front-page coverage. You can't buy deterrence like that."

"But why, George? Just tell me *why* on this one."

"I don't think we were as thorough in Brazil as we should have been."

"You're still mad you didn't get to go."

"Damn right I am! Yes! Schaller and Contini don't know their ass from an outhouse. I can't believe you just accepted—" He caught himself. "I'm just respectfully saying I can do better."

"Yeah," said Avery, "the respect is just squirting out of the phone here."

Rowe ran his hand through his cinnamon crew cut. "Look, we've got this businessman, this prominent guy, he drops out of sight. Essentially he flees the country, OK? He flees the country successfully, for whatever reason. *Then* he turns up dead? He either screwed over his business partners or he owed somebody something he couldn't pay."

"Drugs."

"Drugs, I don't know. Maybe. It seems like drugs would be too dirty for this guy. Some other crime." Rowe's voice came from deep in his chest, like a singer's, but he didn't care much for singing. He liked drumming. In an alcove off the hall he'd placed his drum kit, a small stand-up set of maplewood and chrome. Once in a while he'd jam with a few other guys, horn players who liked to play jazz standards, some ragtime. Drumming like that required steadiness, taste, and patience. He liked the precision of it. Sometimes when the music came together just right, tears sprang to his eyes.

Other things that moved him were pictures of racing yachts cutting through the ocean, the patch of purple irises that came up every year from a damp dirt corner near a laundromat in his neighborhood, and people who pursued principle at the expense of comfort.

He continued talking to his boss. "Offshore money, maybe. Political influence, maybe. I think political influence has potential with this guy. Or there's something about the woman, this Norah Mintz. Anyhow, he goes to the place where the gems come out of the ground, he goes to a place he's been to on business many times. You'd think he'd pick a different country, or at least a different region. Was he starting up a new business? Did he *want* his supposed body to be found? It's all so ambiguous. That autopsy report looked like a ten-year-old wrote it, and the anatomical—"

"We don't even require an autopsy, you know that. And she comes back with this photograph, the wife does."

"Yeah, that thing gave me the creeps. I gotta see it again. I gotta have the original, OK? Make a copy for you guys."

Rowe wandered to the window, talking. From it he had an unspoiled view of a chicken shack, a billboard with an ad for the DVD of *Fingershredder,* and the backside of a strip plaza anchored by a teriyaki carryout restaurant and a Vietnamese manicure salon, all topped by a jagged row of greenery. Eucalyptus and palm trees swayed like a dark crown over the tough little neighborhood. It was one of the last tough little ones in Culver City. He sighed with satisfaction. "She comes home with that picture and a jar of ashes. She just sits there on the money. Doesn't go out, doesn't do anything. Three months later—barely three months—she's up for the murder of her own child. That doesn't smell good either. See, what I'm saying is, if she didn't kill the kid, then the kid's death is related to Tenaway's disappearance. It just is. Then there's the sister-in-law thing, not to mention McGower, the business partner. He's got to have something. The fact that the company's not public is a hindrance to us, because—"

"Yeah, but they showed us their last audit!"

"That thing's a piece of crap, it's a hologram. Avery, you gotta take my word for it. You gotta."

"How much budget do you need?"

Rowe stopped, surprised. He collected himself and plunged on. "Well, the policies were ten million each, right? Ten to the widow and ten to the company."

"Right. But they've been paid."

"Yeah, OK. Fifty. I need fifty thousand."

"Thirty."

"Fifty."

"Forty."

"Fifty."

"Goddamn it, George."

"Thank you, Avery. Thank you very much. I'll stop in for everything in the morning."

By way of tidying his apartment, Rowe took digital photographs of his whiteboards, then erased them. He packed a pair of pants, two shirts, a change of underwear and socks, his cherry rubber flip-flops, a bottle of insect repellent, and his toilet kit into a rough canvas bag he had defaced with random strokes of permanent black marker to make it look dirty and poor. He buried his digital camera and a handful of batteries in the bag. He stood in his shorts and bare feet and considered, then went to a drawer and got out a small paper kite kit, a ball of string, a miniature chess set, six brand-new Duncan Avenger yo-yos, and a collapsible plastic drinking cup that made a satisfying sound when opened and closed. He put those things in too.

He found his passport. He went to his computer and bought an airline ticket to São Paulo.

TEN

"You know," I told Gary on the way to court after we left Eileen Tenaway at the jail, "I'm going to have about a fifteen-minute grace period with your team when they're going to believe I'm a paralegal. I can scribble on yellow pads and look intelligent, thus convincing any onlooker I know what I'm doing, but your real law people are going to ask me something about some motion or use some acronym and I'm going to look blank and they're going to know. You really should tell them something that won't instantly undermine my credibility. And yours."

"You're right," he said, knuckling his chin as he checked his mirrors for a lane change. "I'll tell them you're my mistress and I'm hiding you in plain sight."

I spewed coffee all over the dashboard of his Mercedes.

"Easy, Rita."

I blotted my skirt and the dash with a clump of napkins.

"Relax," he said, with a rough edge that sent a thrill through me. "Just whistle a happy tune. You're a special assistant to me, and you do only what I tell you. Look, the law is no mystery, it's mostly common sense."

"But . . . you must admit there's a lot of specialized knowledge involved!"

"Paralegals prepare documents, they look up stuff. And they prepare witnesses, so this is all very ordinary. Look, it's just not that hard. I told my team I brought you into this case mostly for show, because I wanted a woman at the table. My real paralegal gets too nervous to sit at the defense table, so that made sense. You don't have much trial experience, but you're good at reading people. You help defendants relax, and you help your team. OK?"

"I actually studied psychology."

"I sensed that."

"I'm really nervous."

"Be nervous, then. You don't have to reveal your pathetic lack of confidence unless you want to."

I sat there fuming. And I realized he was right. He and I were running a con, and the point of a con is not fooling people who don't know any better. The point is fooling people who do know better. That I was capable of. My whole career was a con. My whole life, for God's sake.

THE REST OF the defense team consisted of a young India-born lawyer named Mark Sharma who was cute and tried to walk with a swagger, a doddering white-beard lawyer in cowboy boots named Steve Calhoun, and the real paralegal, a round-shouldered thing in a beige cardigan sweater named Lisa Feltenberger.

"That's it?" I said, remembering the cast of thousands he'd hired to help defend Roscoe Jamison.

"You have to understand," Gary explained, "Roscoe wanted and expected a huge team. An ego thing. I made sure everybody had a job to do. It worked, for him, in spite of the problems it caused—the infighting, the resentments. I tend to feel too much hoeing ruins the rice crop."

"Yeah?"

"Old Japanese proverb."

Watching Gary handle the final stages of voir dire, or jury selection, I marveled at his ability to transform himself into whatever the instant demanded. Half the time he was an inexorable machine that flattened all obstacles without mercy, the other half a social worker dressed in a teddy bear suit.

Gary, unsure how to categorize a particular prospective juror, probing: "So your mother was arrested for shoplifting, but they realized they were mistaken and let her go?"

Prospective juror, a white man who said he was a short-order cook: "Yes."

Gary, head cocked to one side: "And you say this has made you distrust the United States justice system?"

Prospective juror, enunciating extra clearly: "It's more of a constitutional objection that I have."

Gary, puzzled: "But they realized they were wrong and let her go."

Prospective juror: "I took it very personal."

Gary, coaxingly: "It seems to me you could also view it as an affirmation of the American justice system."

Prospective juror: "All I know is they made my mother cry."

Gary, on his side now, gently: "Did anyone ever pay for that mistake?"

Prospective juror: "No, sir. No way!"

Gary, with quiet sympathy: "Thank you."

To me, he muttered, "Keeper."

The courtroom, the Honorable Gerald S. Davenport presiding, was in the Los Angeles Superior Court system, Airport Courthouse. I had never heard of this place. Gary told me it had been built to handle the burgeoning caseloads of West Los Angeles, which included Beverly Hills, where Eileen Tenaway allegedly committed murder. It was shiny and clean and up to the latest seismic code, which is good to know when you're six stories above street grade in Southern California.

There is an Old Los Angeles and a New Los Angeles, and the definitions of those terms vary by individual. While the La Brea Tar Pits and the oil field along south La Cienega are all parts of everybody's Old Los Angeles, Bergamot Station's art galleries, for instance, could fall into either category. In Old Los Angeles buildings were interesting, if unsafe in an earthquake. And there was never enough parking.

This courthouse rose from a tract of land just south of LAX, one of those baked wastes worth millions. The building stuck up from the barren dirt cool and handsome, and its green glass and buff stone, its fine wood paneling, plentiful restrooms, and ergonomic seating made me feel like a *citizen*. You could view the whole city from the broad windows, glimpse the HOLLYWOOD sign on a clear day, follow, at eye level, the approach of jet after jet as they glided down into the teeth of the prevailing westerlies.

The feeling of command over space was unmistakable, yet as I stood at the windows at recesses and watched cars circling the absurdly small parking lots hoping for spaces to open, I realized the place was as classically underparked as if they'd situated the building in the median strip of the I-5.

This was everybody's New Los Angeles.

AFTER THAT FIRST day, my life settled into a chaotic rhythm: jump out of bed at five and do my stretches before Petey woke, fix, eat, and clean up breakfast, throw the boy in the car, zoom to preschool thanking God for whoever invented preschool, plow over to the lockup to meet with Eileen for an hour, then off to court, where I would sit and take a deep breath, look at my watch, and be amazed that it was only nine o'clock. It was a straight shot across the 105 from the CRDF to the courthouse.

The money was already making a huge difference in my life, mostly because it made me feel calm no matter how hurry-up things had become. I had almost no time to shop, but managed to splurge on some new sneakers and toys for Petey—I got him a Slinky and an Etch A Sketch in defiance of the damn electronics, which caused him no little puzzlement. He'd play with them, but always with an expression like, *There's got to be more here, I've got to figure out how to turn this thing on.*

I bought a spring-green sweater set for myself. I admit it: I like sweater sets, the fine-gauge kind that show off my breasts, with sleeves on the cardigan I can push up. They make me feel respectable yet sporty.

Perhaps needless to say, I'd redeemed Gramma Gladys's brooch as soon as I could. Mr. puppy-shirt gladly took my $433—the four hundred plus interest—and I loved the sound of his door whispering shut behind me. I put the brooch back in the safe-deposit box for the next bad spell which I hoped would never come.

I briefly tormented myself with the memory of having gone to the ABC Mission down in South Central to ask for help with my utilities bill once, just before I'd defaulted on my credit card and hocked that brooch. They'd paid off my $246 debt to PG&E, thus forestalling our electricity getting cut off. The square-shooting black lady who runs that place was so good and kind to me, this desperate white chick. I sent a check for $500 to the mission and resolved never to lean on charity again.

The focus of my life became Eileen. With her, in the lockup, I began with simple relaxation—arm circles, leg swings, melt-into-the-chair—then progressed to basic concentration and elimination of distractions. Everything was a struggle.

I'd make small talk to try to relax her, which would work briefly. She seemed to enjoy talking about jail. She shared a cell with a pregnant African-American who had not been quick enough on the flush when the police raided her boyfriend's apartment for methamphetamine.

"She's twenty-two and she wears these incredibly thick glasses," Eileen told me the second morning. "Her lawyer gave her a pen and a yellow pad and she's writing a long letter to the Pope."

"The Pope—as in, the Pope in Rome?"

"Yeah, she picked up some Catholic tract somewhere. She's hoping he'll send her personal advice and baby clothes. 'He's been through a lot too,' she says." Eileen cupped her chin for a moment. "She hasn't asked me for advice. Hell, maybe I should write to the Pope."

On the third morning I told Eileen, "You're not working with me. You have to learn to manage your emotions, which doesn't just mean keeping them bottled up. When I called you a baby-killer and a bitch at our first meeting, you barely reacted. Listen, acting is a social art, and it's play. But we're not even going to talk about acting. Because what the jury needs to see is the real you, the one they want to root for."

"They'll want to root for me?" Her eyes looked oppressed.

"Yes! That's what actors always forget! Eileen, it's death to be afraid of an audience. They're not bacteria. They're humans who want to see a good show, they want to be absorbed by a show. They want *you* to tell them the story they want to believe."

I realized right then my whole paradigm. "A jury is a herd," I explained, "but you win them over one by one. We're going to tailor a manipulation plan for them."

She smiled slightly.

"You don't want to show tension," I told her. "You're in court, and you're confused as to why you're there. But you're secure in yourself. You're secure in your innocence. People are attracted to that quality. Before you can lay confusion and grief over that, you've got to be relaxed and easy."

I noticed her chest was tight, she was taking short, constricted breaths from her upper lungs.

"I know you know what I mean," I said. I was talking her language. "Now, I really don't have to keep doing this with you, because you're probably—"

She put her hand toward me and inclined her chin in a gesture of acceptance. Gary, who had come with me this morning and stood watching us from a corner, licked his lips and remained silent.

"OK, let's just try something," I said, scooting my chair nearer.

"I don't like meditation," she warned.

People who appear dull or angry are always tense. If you get rid of the tension, you have a chance to see the real person.

"We won't do any, then," I assured her. "All I'm talking about is breathing. We're only going to count our breaths. You know, breathing is very underrated in our society."

Gary grunt-laughed.

Eileen looked at me as if she disliked me for making her like me.

"Gary, you join in too," I urged. He smiled, crossed his arms, and remained standing.

I went on, "We're just going to release our breath, just focus on breathing out, and let the in-breath take care of itself. We'll let the universe feed us a little air, OK? Breathe all the way out now, all the way."

Eileen did, and immediately took a half breath and held it. Her chest seemed tight as ever. I talked to her about slackening her stomach and letting her back widen so more air could come in.

After a few minutes I thought she was getting the hang of it. Her breathing became somewhat deeper both in and out.

"Eileen, next I'd like to do an improvisation Audrey Hepburn used to love to do."

She looked at me with a spark. The spark had two parts, the first being an attraction to the word *improvisation,* the second being an interest in Audrey Hepburn.

She said, "Did you—"

"No, but I worked with her drama coach during a summer stock thing in Majorca." The side of my face felt Gary's incredulous stare. "Back when I was a kid," I added.

"Yeah?" said Eileen.

Duh, I said to myself, *I should have been dropping names from the start.* "Yes, Dennis Hopper was part of that group as well. OK, we do this one standing up. Come here. I'm going to stand behind you. You stand upright. Now you're going to feel my hands." I placed my palms on her shoulder blades and felt her back muscles go rigid. "Now lean back a little on my hands."

She remained upright.

"Just lean back very slightly. I'll hold you up. Come on, it's all right," I coaxed, in the supergentle tone I used with Petey when he woke from a nightmare.

Still she stood.

"What are you feeling, Eileen?"

The deputy opened the door and ordered, "No touching!"

I backed off, saying "OK, let's just talk some more."

Looking impatient, Gary left the room. She sat with me, relieved. When she flexed her body to sit I saw how sharp her hipbones were, through that dreadful orange suit. I said, "How's the food in here?"

She snorted. "It's not food, it's garbage."

"Maybe I can bring you something good. What would you like?"

"Oh, I'm getting my granola and some eggs and things delivered. Gary set that up first thing."

"Oh, so you're not getting any Gift Packs."

"What are those?"

I told her about the sign in the waiting area that pictured clumps of junk food and toiletries: INMATE GIFT PACK. IF YOU ARE LOOKING FOR A WAY TO SHOW YOUR LOVED ONE YOU MISS THEM. CANTEEN CORRECTIONAL SERVICES HAS THE ANSWER. ORDER AN INMATE GIFT PACK. SELECT ONE OF THE PACKS BELOW AND IT WILL BE DELIVERED DIRECTLY TO YOUR LOVED ONE. THIS IS A GOOD ALTERNATIVE WAY TO DEMONSTRATE

YOUR AFFECTION FOR THAT SPECIAL PERSON. BARE NECESSI-
TIES PACK, COMFORT PACK, MEAT & CHEESE PACK, HOT & SPICY
PACK, CHOCOLATE LOVER PACK, MEGA PACK.

"The prices start at ten dollars, I think. I could—"

"No, it doesn't matter. Mostly I give the stuff to the other girls
anyway. Tawny's discovered flaxseed bread. She loves it."

"Is there anyone from your family who visits?"

"I have no family."

"Are your parents dead?"

"My mother died five years ago, and my dad lives, if you can
call it that, in a nursing home in Palo Alto. He had a stroke and
he's pretty much a vegetable."

"Oh, I'm sorry."

"It doesn't matter."

I slammed the table. "If you're so indifferent to everything,
how come you didn't just plead guilty and let them put you away
in jail forever? What's the difference?"

She stared at the wall, but her gaze went much farther. "I do
want to be free, Rita," she said in a quiet voice. "I want to work
with you. I do. I do. It's just hard. I can't cry in front of other
people. The thought of being on trial. The thought of them all
thinking . . . But I know it'll pass. Everything does. I hope I'll be
able to—to have some kind of life."

With no window to the outside, the light in the little interview
room was unvarying, and I found it disturbing that the shadows
never changed, even slightly, as they would with a bit of daylight
coming in.

I breathed, and realized there was even more depth to Eileen
Tenaway than I'd thought. Searching for common ground, I said,

"You know, my older sister and I took ballet when we were little. I wasn't very good at it, but I liked it. My sister was the real dancer between us."

Eileen looked at me as if surprised that I would speak about myself.

I continued, "One time we had a quarrel about our ballet outfits. Our mother came in to break it up, and I remember yelling, *I want two tutus too!*"

She laughed genuinely, with a lingering smile. "My sister always wanted what I had."

I said, "We've sort of grown apart, my sister and me. Yet if she wasn't there, I'd miss her terribly, you know?"

She nodded, somber again.

"Tell me about your sister," I suggested.

Her face snapped shut as if a metal plate had dropped over it. *Doomed,* I thought, *we're doomed.* Then suddenly it opened again, wide as could be, all her features quivering and raw, like the face of an adolescent in some tribal ritual that's been going on for three days.

She uttered a gush of despair and fury so fierce that my neck tightened. She laid her head on the table and sobbed.

I touched her back and when she didn't flinch I stroked it once, twice, then left my hand there. This close, I could smell her. She wore, I guessed, prison-issue deodorant, which gave off a Listerine-like odor. Or else it was the jumpsuit. Too bad. I wouldn't want to smell like that.

The deputy opened the door again. I took my hand away.

At last Eileen looked up. I handed her a Kleenex.

"Norah's gone," she said emptily.

"You two were close once?"

"I—I tried to look after her. She was my little sister. She came to me whenever she got in trouble, which was a *lot*. The trouble she'd get into! But the more I helped her, the more she asked from me."

"Uh-huh?" I coaxed softly. Her voice was cool and measured, in perfect keeping with her looks. It was a flexible voice, I thought, a possible asset.

"One time I helped her out of a very bad situation. It was bad. I put myself in jeopardy to do it."

"Yeah?"

"I wish to God I'd turned my back instead." She fell silent.

I waited. Finally I asked, "Well, how come?"

Eileen opened her mouth and said, "Because if I had . . ." She didn't finish.

The metal sheet came down again and she said nothing more. After a time of sitting with her in silence, I left.

Gary met me in the corridor. "How did it go?"

I told him.

"You moved too fast."

Defensively, I said, "Well, hell, we don't have much time, do we?"

"No," he agreed. "Keep going."

"By the way," I said, "how many men are you trying to get on this jury?"

"Six," he said firmly. "I think half-and-half will be ideal."

"I disagree. It'd be better to have more men than women, seven and five. Eight and four would be better, but maybe too obvious."

"What do you mean?"

"Most men are going to find it impossible to believe that a mother could kill her own child, versus women who know only too well."

He looked at me, shocked.

I felt a surge of power.

He stammered, "That's what our jury consultant said, but I didn't believe him."

Amid all this intensity my eyes and brain still registered Gary's attractiveness. Actually, things were going beyond the liking-to-look-at-him stage. In the ongoing self-chatter that flowed endlessly through my brain, I had to admit the process was beginning, in spite of the fact that he was married, and often mentioned his wife, Jacqueline. Because I'd never met her, the wife was not concrete for me.

When I fall for a guy I first notice his way of holding himself, which has a real effect on his looks. He could be rough logger-jack handsome or slim sophisticated magnetic or boyish winsome, but his body language always grabs me first. Gary, I realized, was a combo of slim sophisticated magnetic and boyish winsome. His body language was like good wine: assertive yet not domineering.

Then the next thing occurs in my arms and legs, where I get a watery feeling when he crosses my mind or I see him. By now I've realized what a perfect person he is. Virile, intelligent, sensitive, protective, funny, appreciative, and loves kids.

Then he just steps into the crosswalk of my mind and stays, standing there commandingly, thrillingly, as all other traffic flows around him. I get annoyed at this stage, as you get annoyed when your upstairs neighbor plays her Eagles records over and over with the windows open.

Then I give in to the obsession and fall asleep and wake up to him, my pulse racing, and then when I see him my heart flies up on a songbird's back and I grasp for the nearest support.

Well, I'd certainly impressed him by my analysis of the jury-gender issue. "Huh," he said wonderingly. He touched my elbow almost respectfully and we walked down the corridor side by side. I considered turning my ankle and falling into him, but that would have been cheap, so I held myself in rigid control. Right-left-right-left.

Falling in love is such a pain in the ass.

ELEVEN

Something began to change in me the day the trial began.

I wondered how Eileen would handle the stress. I'd been working with her for a week, Tuesday to Tuesday, and now it was Wednesday, go-day for everybody. I sat beside her at the defense table, watching and making notes. She appeared calm, which was good, and detached, which was bad. I wanted her to be fully present. I wanted her to be able to become distraught at times. It wouldn't be realistic for her to be distraught the whole time, nor even possible, but I wanted her to have distraught handy, and she didn't.

I watched the jurors watching her. I could see them trying to make up their minds right away, because being undecided is stressful in and of itself. I mean, think about it: You encounter a stranger. Friend or foe? You want to figure that out immediately.

For the jurors, breathless in their box, this would be one of the hugest experiences of their lives: deciding guilt or innocence in a murder case.

Gary had managed a ratio of seven men to five women, along the lines of my advice.

They were a working-class bunch, plus a few retirees. A couple were unemployed actors (none of whom knew me, fortunately), the rest were mostly people who have the sorts of jobs that pay you to go to jury duty. There was not an entrepreneur in the bunch, not a millionaire society matron in the bunch. To call this a jury of Eileen's peers was a real stretch. "That doesn't matter," Gary told me. "I'd almost be more afraid of her peers anyway. Pack of dogs."

"Wouldn't you," I asked, "count as one of her peers?"

He just smiled.

Have I mentioned there were press all over the place? In the gallery, in the hallways, restrooms, cafeteria. There were only about fifty gallery seats for the press and other spectators in the courtroom, and they were all full. The reporters, lots from the Los Angeles media plus New York and even Europe, all shared a certain facial expression, a mix of tension and resentment: they were attentive, yet quick to boredom. Perhaps they didn't think much of this assignment. After all, this was not like the Roscoe Jamison trial where they could hope for a race riot at the end.

During voir dire I'd gotten to know the rest of the team. I liked Steve Calhoun, the prophet-bearded old lawyer Gary had brought on the team. I learned that Steve, with decades of experience defending hopeless cases in the L.A. system, had become this Yoda who could craft an alternate-theory defense for anybody, depending on which way the prosecution's spear aimed. His chin was deeply cleft, and he had an impressive scar on his neck, which he told me was "a souvenir from the VC."

So he had fought in Vietnam. In other circumstances I would've asked him about it.

Steve loved to talk law. "You can use a collateral fatality from a police chase to your advantage if you know how to spin it," he told me over a chicken Caesar at lunch one day. "Never be afraid of blood. The bloodier the better, that's my motto."

Then there was the boy lawyer Mark Sharma, who specialized in physical evidence. His parents back in India were waiting for him to come home and marry the girl they'd picked out for him when he was five. He had a moppish head of black hair and these hypnotic black eyes, and he spoke with an appealing Bombay lilt. He immediately saw that Gary's and my relationship was close, and tried to make the best of it in spite of his natural jealousy. I was impressed.

The paralegal, Lisa Feltenberger, also seemed to realize I was on a special track with Gary. However, this made her defer to me more, which was fine.

Fascinated by everything from the bailiff's gun belt to the prosecutor's feline smile, I watched and watched. What happened in this room was real. What happened in this room was life, and it was death. I couldn't get over it. Does that sound like the dumbest thing ever? It was so goddamned real.

The prosecutor, Tracy Beck-Rubin, was as formidable as she was unfashionable. She stood a thick-waisted five feet ten or so in her chunky heels, but violin-string straight, with an attitude of respect and calculation toward everyone. Her hair was a blown-out brown halo and her cheeks were fuzzy. She looked like a hungry comic-strip cat dressed in a lumpy suit and those scuffed Natural-izers. Her eyes missed nothing.

Looking down at my own much more perfect and expensive outfit, I felt unsettled—and fascinated. I was this little accessory to the proceedings, while she was a main player and could give a damn that her carnelian lipstick clashed with her gold silk blouse which clashed with her shell-pink nail polish. I couldn't get enough of her.

Gary had mentioned to me that he'd often felt, as a non-Jew, an outsider in the L.A. legal system. "A Jewish lawyer never loses that hunger," he said, when we talked about Tracy, "no matter if they've made it, no matter if they've made it ten times over. They look after each other, and I admire that. I've had to work double hard to earn my place here. Come to think of it, Tracy doesn't fit the stereotype either—she didn't go to Harvard or Columbia or UCLA, she put herself through some crap law school by deliver-ing pizzas and walking dogs, and she washed out of Lewis & Rossberg and nobody thought she'd make a name for herself, but she has. She went over to the DA's office and they saw she could work a jury. I was lucky to beat her on Roscoe Jamison. Trouble is, she's got it in for me now."

And indeed, when Tracy Beck-Rubin glanced toward the de-fense table, she aimed her gaze at Gary with teasing contempt. She was, I realized, the kind of girl I would have avoided in high school, a girl so frankly herself and so uninterested in pleasing others she seemed almost menopausal.

In her opening statement she welcomed the jury with a warm smile, then hit immediately and hard on the evidence against Eileen: *her* house, *her* child, *her* pills.

Gary had wondered which offensive strategy she'd take: Lazy

Mom Who Gave Kid Pills to Shut Her Up, or Selfish Mom Who Wanted Rid of Kid to Attract New Mate. She went with Selfish Mom right off the bat:

"Yes!" Beck-Rubin said, with an open-handed gesture from her heart to waist level, a graceful yet decisive gesture, "For a woman like Eileen Tenaway, once the gravy train stopped—that is, once her husband was found mysteriously dead!—she wanted to find another one. She wanted to hitch herself to another rich, exciting man. Look at her, ladies and gentlemen. A very pretty woman— lucky to be so pretty—and she'd used her beauty to capture a top-level businessman, and she enjoyed the ride, oh, yes!" Then, softer, "Who wouldn't? But enjoying the ride doesn't entitle you to commit murder. We will show you, ladies and gentlemen, that Eileen Tenaway enjoyed that ride so much—the jewels, ladies and gentlemen! the first-class tickets! the champagne receptions with *celebrities*!—that she would do anything to have it again."

Beck-Rubin settled her gaze into the jury box. "Well, we might ask, what's wrong with that? Nothing! *Unless* she decides she'd be better off childless. *Unless* she decides a high-class man won't look at her twice if he sees a baby in the background, no matter how far into the shadows she tries to push her! Little Gabriella!"

Tenderly, the prosecutor picked up a photograph from the defense table and held it before the jury. It was the same shot, mounted on posterboard, that Gary had brought to Eileen. "Gabriella Elizabeth Tenaway. We could try to imagine what the fullness of her life might have been like. But there will be no *life* for little Gabriella." She held the photograph as if it were alive. "Never to learn her colors. Never to ride a bicycle. Never to kiss a boy. Never to win a scholarship. Never to play the guitar nor plant a tree nor graduate with honors nor negotiate a labor contract nor run for office nor give birth! Nor lay a cool cloth on the brow of her dying mother someday." The jury gasped.

"Ladies and gentlemen. For Gabriella, *everything* is never."

This speech pressed incredible sadness into the faces of the jurors, it bent their shoulders. A couple of the women and one of the actors blinked back tears. The others swallowed.

"But there is one thing Gabriella can have. Only one thing, and you are here, ladies and gentlemen, to give it to her. Justice."

The prosecutor belittled the scant evidence of an intruder: the ransacked house, a Starbucks coffee cup found by police on the little girl's dresser, and a dirty baseball cap caught in the bushes outside. She talked about the effects of tranquilizers on an infant's body, and she hinted certain things about Eileen's social life—at least as far as she could between objections from Gary. The fingerprints and DNA on the items did not match each other, nor did they match Eileen's, nor Richard's DNA, which was harvested from a pathology sample from minor surgery he'd had not long before his disappearance from L.A.

"The defense will speculate that this so-called evidence came from somewhere. Somewhere. Right. Like from a garbage can on Sunset Strip! There are no other suspects, ladies and gentlemen, because there is no other murderer. She sits, charged with her crime, before you."

Eileen sat quietly through all this. At times she shook her head no. We naturally knew that Tracy Beck-Rubin wanted to stir the jury's emotions against her. But Eileen needed to have her emotions ready too, and she simply didn't. If only *I* could have acted Eileen's role for her. I sat there twisting a fingerful of hair in frustration.

Yesterday I'd told her, "Here's who you are in the courtroom: a proud woman, but a sensitive one. You're a woman who had it all and now has nothing—nothing *except your dignity and your honesty*. You don't understand why you're here. You're devastated that your daughter is dead. You almost don't care anything about yourself—but what you want is to know who the hell did it? This should be in your heart all the time, because then it'll show on your face. See the difference between being focused on *Who the hell killed my baby?* versus *I hope I can convince them I didn't do it*. See the difference?"

Eileen said she did.

But she could not focus and carry it out. She looked miserable and cold sitting there, her beauty up front, dullness behind her eyes. Gary had wisely given the job of bringing clothes for Eileen to Steve Calhoun, who knew to pick dark, conservative dresses. Eileen had been strictly forbidden to spice up her hair or use any cosmetic but a little lipstick. She obeyed, but she would have had to wear a bucket over her head to conceal her God-given skin and bones and flesh.

I could tell the jury wanted to like her, but her beauty was off-putting, at least to the women. I could see them thinking, *She must have brought this on herself somehow.*

The rich and beautiful are not allowed to have problems.

Gary's opening statement struck a gentle tone, a tone of reason.

"A terrible thing happened the night Gabriella Tenaway died," he began. "Those of us who are parents can begin to imagine how Eileen Tenaway felt when she found her daughter lying still in her crib. But none of us can *know* what it's like to lose a child, unless it has happened to us. To lose a child to murder. And certainly we cannot know how it feels to then be accused of being the murderer. Yes, a terrible thing happened. And then a second terrible thing happened, when the police decided to charge that little girl's mother with the crime. During this trial I will show you what a cruel mistake that was."

He went into almost as much detail about the evidence as Tracy Beck-Rubin had, only with a different slant: an intruder killed that child, and Gary promised to make it plain as day.

He held up his own photograph of Gabriella, this one a candid of her in a playground swing, laughing to the sky. "My colleague told us about all the *nevers* for Gabriella. And there are more nevers. Yes. The nevers are for that baby's mother. Eileen Tenaway will never hold her child in her arms again." He tolled his words slowly. "She will never comfort her again. Never bathe her. Never buy school shoes for her. Never sit in the audience watching her in the fifth-grade play. Never ground her for staying out too late. Never cry at her wedding."

Every single juror exhaled in wistful sympathy, matching Gary's sad, small smile. He knew that if they didn't warm up to Eileen herself, he sure as hell would make them like *him*. And he did.

I sat there trying, via ESP, to get Eileen to cry, but it didn't work. She sat, head slightly bowed, eyes veiled. The jury stared at her.

Gary's voice intensified; he spoke not faster but more sharply. "The truth is, ladies and gentlemen of the jury, that Eileen Tenaway did not murder her own baby. It is an abomination beyond words that she stands accused, hauled into jail by the police, who found evidence of at least one intruder. But after the crime, the intruder was nowhere to be found. Eileen Tenaway, on the other hand, was right there. She herself called the police. Goodness, how convenient. The police came, they looked around, then a short time later, they came back and clapped her in handcuffs."

He ran his hand behind his neck and slouched slightly. "Then on top of it, we have the district attorney swallowing the police's theory like an oversized hamburger."

The jurors smiled at the image, glancing at the robust figure of Tracy Beck-Rubin. At that moment I hated and loved Gary equally ferociously.

"Unfortunately," Gary said, now back to a restrained, reasonable tone, "in this case a *theory* just isn't good enough." He talked about time frame, police reports, forensic tests. He moved his body powerfully as he spoke, his shoulders and hips square, his hands emphasizing the points he made. "So we naturally ask: If Eileen Tenaway did not administer a fatal dose of drugs to her daughter, who did? We would all like to know, none more than Eileen Tenaway. Well, my job is to prove to you there is reasonable doubt in the state's case against Eileen. And I will. Ladies and gentlemen, there is enough doubt to fill the Grand Canyon. But perhaps also we'll uncover the real truth in this trial."

He glared at Tracy Beck-Rubin and sat down.

All the movies I'd seen, all the television I'd watched, all the improvisations I'd done pretending to be in a courtroom—they were nothing compared to actually being present—feeling the vibes, seeing the players writhe and fight. The trial wasn't so much a show, I realized, as a chess match, or a political campaign. Yes, that was it: who are the voters going to like more: Eileen Tenaway or Tracy Beck-Rubin? And who understands the voters better: Tracy Beck-Rubin or Gary Kwan?

I found myself thinking hard.

That first week, every night after putting Petey to bed I got on the Internet and reviewed famous murder trials, reading transcripts I downloaded from law school archives. I read about Tracy

Beck-Rubin's cases. How does she operate? Could her moves be predicted? I brewed coffee and downloaded newspaper accounts and magazine analyses of the Roscoe Jamison trial and read those too.

During a recess a few days in, I asked Gary again about the ball cap in the bushes. "Isn't there some way we can try to find out whose cap it was? I mean, the DNA from the hair—"

"The DNA on the cap is only relevant to us because it suggests a stranger was around that night. Remember, Rita, we don't have to prove anything. It's not up to us to solve this case."

"But if we *could*—"

"Our job is to represent Eileen's interests."

As far as keeping a low profile, I was aware of the reporters, and quickly walked away, eyes down, whenever one approached me. They were always trying to get close to the principals. All of us had to dodge the press. "It's hard to hit a moving target," quipped Steve Calhoun.

At least half of what went on zoomed over my head: reasons for certain objections, the little huddled conferences with Judge Davenport, the threats to make some motion or other.

But I liked it. And as the trial went on I got better at understanding things.

I realized that a trial is the tip of the iceberg, bobbing up from the ocean depths. There was much more ice beneath the surface. And the jury would never see it. As I read and thought and watched and tried to coach Eileen, I began to want to know about that big hunk of ice down there.

TWELVE

For his guide George Rowe wanted an old person because old people tend to be better at keeping their mouths shut, and they tend to be inconspicuous. The old person had to be agile, because Rowe might want to do some walking in the hilly countryside of Minas Gerais, the France-sized mining region of Brazil. He had spent several unsuccessful days in São Paulo trying to get information from various ministries of records and certificates. The old person had to be male, because this was after all rural Third World.

Rowe did not know Portuguese or even Spanish, but he learned the words for *good day, please,* and *thank you,* and this served him all right. The guide would translate everything else for him.

He avoided the tourist-bureau guides who approached him as

soon as he got off the bus in Ouro Prêto, which would be his base. He walked into town and ate a meal of sausages and grilled bananas at a café. The food smelled and tasted good. He watched the people in the café and on the street without staring. Portuguese, its vowels sandwiched tightly between hunks of consonants, sounded different from the more liquid Spanish. He enjoyed the strangeness of the steep old colonial town, all blocky buildings and wavy tile roofs. The buses that clanked by were quaint in the sense of being mechanically obsolete but with good paint jobs. He enjoyed the forthright sounds of the language, the flash of a smile beneath a businessman's Panama hat, the switch of the waitress's bright-pink skirt over her wonderful calypso hips. He had never realized how much he liked the color bright pink.

Rowe left the café and went to the Escola de Minas, the mining college. There were several colleges in Ouro Prêto, and at this one he expected to find English speakers with common sense and current knowledge of the mining scene. After walking around and talking with a few people, he found himself having coffee with a middle-aged professor of mathematics who spoke English well.

Rowe introduced himself frankly as an investigator from America looking into the death of an American mining businessman. He made it clear he was eager to pay good money for the right guide.

The professor, a thin-waisted man with upsticking salt-and-pepper hair, was named Tony Ferré. He knew instantly who Rowe was talking about, since the discovery of Richard Tenaway's body had occurred near Ouro Prêto and had been big news there—rich American run afoul of something, who knew what? He said he would like to be Rowe's guide himself since he had lived in Minas Gerais all his life, but due to his teaching obligations he could not. However, he knew just the man.

As a token of goodwill, Rowe gave Tony Ferré two hundred reals—about a hundred dollars. Money is a very easy way to make your way around. In a city this size, about sixty thousand people, Rowe knew he could give money to people and even if they talked about it he would not attract too much attention for a while.

That night, Rowe went to Tony Ferré's house for dinner. The professor lived in a small house on a slope that overlooked the town. The house was tidy, the table set. The professor introduced him to his wife and teenage daughter, who spoke only a little English. A chicken was stewing on the stove. Then he led Rowe outside to a chicken coop the size of a small cabin. Rowe noticed a chopping block with a patch of recent blood, and a pair of contented-looking cats lounging near it.

The professor rattled the coop's wire door. An explosion of clucking. From the darkness burst a flurry of feathers and stinking guano dust, then a cloud of tobacco smoke and a little man. He was about a head shorter than Tony and had the same tiny waist and upsticking hair, only his was pure white. His face was seamed and very dark brown. He smoked a short cigar. His eyes were quick and candid and somewhat crazy.

Tony said, "This is Raimundo Ferré, my father."

They waited while the old man set down his cigar and washed at a spigot.

Over dinner, Rowe did not talk much. He gathered that Raimundo generally preferred the company of chickens to humans, but lately he'd been bored. When young, Raimundo had been a laundryman and a *garimpeiro,* or independent miner, and these days he raised chickens and sometimes drove a taxi on the streets that were not too steep to drive on. Tourists with good lungs loved Ouro Prêto because you had the upper and lower cobblestone streets to yourself, and it was pleasant to hike around the clean, interesting neighborhoods.

THIS PART OF Brazil was hot now. The high grasslands had been made more arid by logging and strip-mining. Of course, this had been, for the Portuguese explorers, El Dorado. They had found gold here, and they arranged for slaves to dig it up for them. The minerals had been replaced by blood and bones. Warm brooding fogs often wrapped the land and made everyplace feel secret.

Rowe told Raimundo he wanted to talk to some of the garimpeiros, the hardscrabble miners who worked ditches in the countryside looking for imperial topaz. He might also want to go to Itabira, where emeralds were excavated from deep shafts in the bedrock.

As his son had done, Raimundo nodded when Rowe mentioned the American businessman who had met his death around here half a year ago. "Yes," he said, in a raked-gravel voice, "all the people, they knew of it."

"Knew of what: the man going missing," Rowe asked, "or the man turning up dead?"

"Turning up dead."

The old man was perfect for George Rowe. Lean and quick, with tough hands and feet, good English because he had wanted to be a smart trader with the North Americans, and a sense of humor. Nothing funny had been said, but Rowe perceived this. He had learned that if you choose your associates with care and keep your own counsel, you'll be all right.

THE NEXT MORNING Rowe and Raimundo walked out of town, on the road north into the hills. Their short-sleeved cotton shirts soon became soaked with sweat. Rowe carried two bottles of water and some other things in a paper sack.

Raimundo's mood was buoyant. He had strapped a leather-sheathed hunting knife to his belt and put on a canvas sun hat. As they walked he told Rowe about Ouro Prêto, the town named for gold, the town that existed solely for the purpose of extracting gold from the mountains, so much gold that King Asshole of Portugal had to build a whole fleet to carry it away. That was the term he used, "King Asshole." Rowe laughed when he heard it, and that gratified Raimundo.

Rowe felt good today too. The clean mountain air filled his lungs with optimism.

Raimundo asked Rowe, "Do you have interest in sexual tourism?"

Rowe walked along, his hands in his pockets, his sack beneath his arm. He thought about his last girlfriend. She was cute but difficult, always finding fault with herself and depending on him to cheer her up. At first he could improve her mood by complimenting her petite figure or her gentleness, but over time she required more and more cheering up, involving gifts. At first a bottle of perfume would do it, but over time the only thing that would work was a new outfit from some boutique, or a trip to Las Vegas.

It was too bad, but he'd had to get away from her.

He thought about the pink-skirted waitress in the café. He would like a simple, romantic relationship with a woman. Bawdiness was OK, but the crudeness of being a john turned him off.

"I don't think so," he said. "Business first, anyway."

"Yes, yes," agreed Raimundo.

In half an hour they came upon a couple of men digging a trench next to the road on a government right-of-way. The road itself was red dirt.

The garimpeiros showed Raimundo and Rowe how they scraped away the gravel and washed it in wooden trays, hauling water in buckets from a nearby creek.

Raimundo said, "They only find a few crystals a week, but it is enough for feeding themselves and their families. They give a little to the state agent so they can mine here."

The men's bodies were as hard and fat-free as the rocks they dug. They wore the kind of motley clothes you'd find in an Ozark storm shelter. One man's T-shirt said BALLOU FAMILY REUNION beneath two donkeys wearing boxing gloves. Rowe didn't like it that such clothes were all that these fine-looking men could afford.

He squatted and removed a photograph from his paper sack. It was of Richard Tenaway at a charity ball, smiling smugly into the camera, glass of champagne in hand. The men looked blank. Rowe took out another photograph, a larger one, of a man lying on a mortuary table. The picture showed just the naked upper body. The man's eyes were half open and empty, his skin white and thick-looking. Stubble covered his jaw. The central fact of the photo appeared to be a purple gash in the middle of his forehead. He looked a little damp, as if he'd just been carried in from outdoors. His hair lay in greasy tendrils.

"Ah," said the men when they saw it, and he could see they now realized it was the same man in both pictures. Raimundo translated, and Rowe learned that they had sold stones to Gemini's local representative in town. The oldest of the garimpeiros had sold stones to Tenaway himself, but that was a long time ago. They also sold stones to another buyer, a big mining company.

Raimundo himself had never met Tenaway. He explained there were several mining corporations in the area: they sank shafts into rock and stripped dirt from hillsides to extract bulk minerals like kaolin and feldspar as well as the vastly more valuable emerald, topaz, and tourmaline.

The miners had heard of the unusual death of Richard Tenaway—an American of the sort who stayed out of real trouble.

Rowe would have liked to solve every aspect of this Tenaway thing, but he only had time now to focus on whether Tenaway had faked his death.

Granted, a death certificate had been produced, as well as the morbid photo of the dead body. Eileen Tenaway had returned from here with those things, as well as Tenaway's ashes.

An expert at Fenco had told Rowe the photo was an actual color print, not digital, and it had not been manipulated.

Rowe asked the garimpeiros if they knew who found the body, but they did not. They suggested the police might know, since they had handled the situation. All the men shared a shrug at the mention of police.

Also visible in the picture was part of a floor, tiled in a complicated black-and-white pattern, as well as the corner of a device that looked perhaps like a heart-lung machine or an oxygen apparatus. Rowe had found out, though, that it was an embalming pump.

So the picture definitely had been taken in a mortuary. It

didn't matter which mortuary, really, but he wanted to know who had made the photo.

The two other investigators Fenco had sent over to look into the claim in the first place had simply walked around Ouro Prêto like adolescents, asking questions randomly of the police and whoever else they bumped into. They wrote things down and believed so much in their superiority to these backward people they thought if there had been a conspiracy it would be sitting there in the wide open.

Eileen Tenaway might have taken the photo (hence been in on the scam from the get-go) but Rowe felt she had not. She and her husband would have needed local help in staging it, and Rowe's gut said it was not the kind of job Richard would entrust to his wife anyway.

Rowe bought three topaz crystals from each of the garimpeiros for thirty reals apiece, which Raimundo thought a fair price. The men were happy and urged Rowe to come see them again at their small camp.

The crystals were dry and only faintly amber-colored. He rolled the largest one back and forth in his palm. It was oblong, and even though rough, its planes showed the mineral's natural order. Imperial topaz, he had learned, was called that because of its golden-orange hue, rare and unlike ordinary topaz, which is commonly yellow or blue. Rowe understood that when cut— when the outer rough bits were chipped off and the stone was faceted—it would be a tongue of flame.

Rowe and Raimundo returned to town and ate lunch in a different café than the one with the pink-skirted waitress, but this one also had a beautiful waitress. There was one plain one as well, who clearly disliked the beautiful one. Raimundo reached out and pinched the beautiful one's ass through her skirt, which was blue stretch denim. She slapped his hand and uttered an insult. Rowe would have liked to be slapped by that waitress too, but he kept his hands to himself.

"THANKS FOR MAKING the time," he said when the buyer at Gemini Imports opened the office door. "This is Raimundo, my guide. He found these stones and thinks they're worth something." Of the six stones he'd bought from the garimpeiros, he only drew five from his pocket, having decided to keep the biggest one.

The gem buyer was a tall young Brazilian who spoke reasonable English. His name was Esteban and he was so happy to have educated company that he slobbered all over them. "Yes! Please be seated! What may I do for you? Would you like a snack, some coffee?"

Rowe had introduced himself on the phone as Tom Webber, a Canadian tourist. He smiled at Esteban's use of the American word *snack,* with just a tiny hesitation, but then a going-ahead with it, a plunge into the word. *Snack!*

Rowe was here to take his measure.

Esteban looked at the crystals under a stereo microscope and said he would buy them, but they were not worth more than ten reals apiece.

"Never mind, then," said Rowe, "I'll buy them from him myself, for souvenirs. I'll pay him more than that."

Esteban offered twenty reals apiece.

Raimundo shook his head.

"It's all right," Rowe said. "Never mind."

Raimundo suggested, "Forty reals."

"OK," said Esteban.

Raimundo was quietly beside himself with joy at Rowe's profit.

After the sale, which Esteban paid with a note from a local bank, the men talked, and Rowe learned that Esteban was tired of Ouro Prêto and wanted to go to America, "or at least Miami."

Rowe laughed so hard that Raimundo reached over and pounded him on the back. He asked Esteban if he'd like to have a drink sometime. Esteban said he would.

When Rowe and Raimundo got back out on the street, Rowe asked, "Where do the delinquents hang out?"

Raimundo supposed they hung out where he had hung out as a delinquent.

"Take me there," Rowe said.

They walked to a grotto below town where, Raimundo said, plans were laid, rendezvous kept, and alcohol drunk. He would not expect drug dealers, in the main, to hang out there, because they were grown-ups and had their own apartments.

Three hostile-looking boys about thirteen years old were sprawled on the cool rock of the grotto, smoking Marlboro cigarettes.

Raimundo immediately began talking Portuguese and laughing. The boys looked irritated, but what few brain cells of respect they possessed began firing, and they listened to old Raimundo. He launched into a story, fast and loud, which clearly had to do with dirty sex.

When it was over the boys smirked politely and looked at the two adult men questioningly.

Rowe pulled the miniature chess set he had packed in his luggage from his paper sack and opened it on a rock. The boys' eyes opened wider, but they tossed their heads back and the one who appeared to be the leader—the one who took up the most space and held his belly most relaxed—said something roughly to Raimundo.

Raimundo said, "What do we want? And do you have any electric music pods?"

Taking a deep blue Duncan yo-yo out of his pocket, Rowe said, "Who makes up fake IDs around here?"

Raimundo translated as the boys watched the yo-yo.

Rowe slipped the loop on his finger and began limbering the ancient toy. The two subordinate boys looked at the leader to see if yo-yos were beneath them. The leader remained neutral, and Rowe began to forcefully snap the yo-yo out and back, out and back, and they watched him. He snapped it straight down and made it sleep. He did half a dozen Around the Worlds, then five or six Rock the Babys. He would have done Walk the Dog, but you need a smooth floor for that.

He did Eiffel Tower and Split the Atom, and the boys, still trying to appear affronted, gleamed out smiles, and, finally, laughter. Their fingers twitched.

ROWE AND RAIMUNDO returned to the grotto the next day to meet the principal teenage forger in Ouro Prêto. Rowe brought wads of ten-real notes.

He was surprised to see a girl of about fifteen hanging out with the boys, all of whom were working on their yo-yo tricks.

Raimundo said, "This girl, she makes identifications card for the kids."

"Do the police," asked Rowe, "really enforce the drinking age? What is it, eighteen?"

"They don't care very much," Raimundo conceded.

"But kids like having fake IDs," Rowe said.

"Yes. Her name is Maria Helena."

Rowe handed Maria Helena a wad of reals. She put the money down the front of her blouse and stared at Rowe. She wore a tight red skirt and red sandals, and her blouse was pale green with red trim. She looked like the other curvaceous girls who walked with their mothers or boyfriends in town, except she wore an expensive-looking pair of sunglasses pushed up on her head, which, along with the bright stylish clothes, gave her a distinct look—an L.A. look, Rowe thought. Her clothes were clean and her black hair lay in a thick coil over her shoulder. No matter how much eye shadow she applied, Rowe thought, she could not ruin those searching deep eyes.

Rowe said, "Ask her who makes IDs for the grown-ups."

Before Raimundo could speak, she said sharply, "I do!"

Rowe pretended to laugh at that. "You have a camera?"

Her English came slowly. "I have *three* cameras and darkroom and computer and printer." Her pronunciation wasn't bad, though. "I have more of thing. Things. I have friends of mine also."

Rowe said, "Look at this, please."

Maria Helena sidled to him as he removed the mortuary photo of Richard Tenaway from his bag.

He watched her face carefully as she looked at the photo. In an instant chaos broke out in the grotto.

Maria Helena made a sound in her throat and fled, and the boys dropped their yo-yos and jumped George Rowe and Raimundo.

Rowe fought quickly and carefully, using enough force to throw off the two boys who attacked him but not enough to hurt them badly. He cursed when one of them picked up a rock. He ducked, but the rock caught him on the shoulder.

Raimundo held his own with the smallest boy, flurrying his fists in his face, until Rowe pulled the boy off and flung him down the hillside.

THIRTEEN

Relying heavily on Daniel and my friend Yvonne, I was able to juggle Petey's schedule and mine through the course of the murder trial. Yvonne was a makeup artist I'd met at a shoot for the Bank of America ads I'd modeled for. Her workdays usually started ungodly early but ended midafternoon, so on days when I couldn't take a long enough lunch to transfer Petey from his preschool on Beverly Boulevard to afternoon daycare on Highland, she managed to.

After the first week, I started working evenings with Team Eileen at Gary's offices, and Daniel stepped in to pick up Petey from daycare (the fabulous Bear Care, in case you're looking for a really good place with only analog toys like blocks and modeling clay and pogo sticks, no electronic diversions at all), run him in the park, then hang out with him at my place.

I gave their incoming cell numbers distinctive tunes, which I listened for hyper-alertly when my phone was not on vibe, which it had to be in the courtroom. Yvonne's was "The Trolley Song" in honor of her addiction to romantic happenstance, and Daniel's was "Dancing Queen," a fun and totally gay song I'd loved since I'd first heard it on a seventies retrospective on public radio.

This tag-team setup barely worked, but it worked. Daniel and Yvonne were very good about not asking questions, and they both knew I'd make it up to them big time.

I'd expected this intense schedule to exhaust me, but surprisingly it didn't. I felt enlivened by the all the excitement and, I must again add, the money. Before the second week was out, my rent and bills were current, I had scored a new frying pan, and Petey had a new Spider-Man jacket for cool days.

Now that the trial was under way, the sheriff's department brought Eileen to the courthouse by bus every morning, along with whichever other female prisoners had court dates. They got them going early, around six, so now we met in her holding cell at the courthouse. It was a grim little chamber, with the obligatory deputy keeping an eye on us. I kept trying emotional-access techniques with Eileen and they kept not working. I started wondering about pure facial muscle control. We'd worked a little on body language, but in an organic, holistic way, not specifically. To think about abandoning the acting techniques I held in such reverence went against my grain, so more time passed than should have before I figured out a new way.

During the late-night prep sessions at Gary's offices, everyone talked over strategy, listened to the jury consultants who gave Gary a lot of commonsense insights, revised lists of questions for witnesses, drew what-if diagrams, speculated on the reactions of the judge and jury. Both Gary and Tracy Beck-Rubin respected Judge Davenport, whose job was legal referee, talk-show host, and papa figure all in one. He was like this little dark cloud up there on the bench, but when he said anything, it was like a cleansing rain. "No, Counsel, you're trying to oversimplify. I'm going to let him frame it another way and if he does it right, I'll allow it." He was solicitous of the jury, who were like a school of guppies, all heads pointing this way, then that.

I studied the snub-nosed Lisa Feltenberger and imitated her up to a point, but mostly I pretended to be a bit of a putz. "Oh, did we need that today? Yeah, I could go find it, probably, yeah. Hey, Lisa?" Vagueness worked.

Rapidly I became Gary's preferred sounding board. We found ourselves alone in the office after everyone else had gone home, talking, talking.

"OK, WELL, CALL me if you need me," said Mark Sharma as he backed toward Gary's office door Friday night at the end of the second week.

"Just take care of that pinched nerve," said Gary. Mark had been telling us all about his lumbar trouble.

"See you Monday," I said cheerfully.

Mark shot us a sweet look and left.

"Go do some yoga," Gary muttered as the door closed behind him.

I snickered, then felt bad. "He's such a little bonbon," I said. "Like he wants to be your puppy."

"He gets on my nerves," said Gary. "But he sure is good with chemistry—the toxicology and DNA."

"I keep thinking he should date Lisa."

"Oh, spare me an office romance. Can't you fix him up with one of your friends?" Gary looked at his watch. "Hey, it's nine o'clock and we haven't eaten. How about you call in something from Jerry's?"

"Mm," I said, picking up the phone. "I feel so wistful about their pastrami. But I'll have the chopped salad again."

"I know what you mean," said Gary. "I'm getting Greek."

We had discovered a common thread in our lives: dietary discipline.

After I phoned in our order, I said, "I can allow myself a pastrami sandwich or an order of fries like once every six months. Plus I love chocolate, *but*."

"Oh, I know. I'm exactly the same way. If I have whatever I want I get *so fat!*"

I laughed, he sounded so much like one of my girlfriends.

I said, "But you're so trim."

"Oh, no!" He laughed. "You're the skinny one!"

Music to my ears. "Oh, my BMI is eighteen-point-five," I shared casually, "which is more than Kym LaFevre's but less than Electra Stenhall's." (Kym being the supermodel and you've seen Electra in fifty percent of the decade's noir films.) "I'd like it to be lower, but I go insane if I give up my microwave popcorn."

"My BMI is twenty-five," Gary confided.

I was semi-amazed that he even knew what BMI was, let alone cared about his. "For a guy, that's quite low," I told him. "You're lower than Dirk Westaway, Chet Muldoon, and Hanson Krüg. They're all in the high twenties. Even Vince Devereaux, I think." I knew these statistics from Daniel, whose BMI was twenty-eight.

Gary was pleased.

We just clicked, that was all.

His phone buzzed and he glanced at the display, a smile lighting his face. "Hello, sweetheart." Pause. "She is? Oh, now, listen"—Pause. "Now, Jade, I have to disagree with you on this. Mommy is not the meanest person in the whole world. There are millions of mommies who are *much*"—Pause. "Oh, my goodness. That does sound bad. Put her on, OK? Love you, sweetheart."

He went to the window and stood against its glossy blackness, facing out, his arm up on the glass.

"And how's your evening going?" he said. "Sounds like a bit of a power struggle." Pause. "Well, you know enough not to let her win. Just tell her if she doesn't settle down with one book or one doll, the bunny doll for example, you're going to have to put the whole toy box away for a while. Then do it. She'll settle down." Pause. "Well, you have to follow through." Pause. "I know. I know. It's past her bedtime anyway." Pause. "Yes, I can hear her. Tooth-brushing is not negotiable, of course not."

I smiled at his tone and cadence, so similar to the way he talked in court: measured, unhurried, clear.

His back tensed. "I'm working." His back relaxed. "Oh, really? I did two interviews today, which one was that? Oh? You're being kind, I couldn't have looked that good, I need a haircut! OK." Pause. "Now, listen. Stop. Jacqueline. I—I can't talk now. On the cell phone, you know." His back tensed again. "I'll be home as soon as I—"

I saw my own face in the night-black window, looking strained. My cheekbones are alertly high, my chin small—though thank God not receding—and this really helps me look youthful. But strain looks bad on me. I composed my expression.

Finally he said, "OK. You too."

Goddamn. He's a loving, caring, smart dad, and his wife thinks he's a good lay.

My heart, instead of feeling squelched by this, only flamed higher with insane infatuation.

Our salads came.

As we ate we talked about how Tracy Beck-Rubin was going hard after Eileen's socializing. She was calling all these witnesses who testified to seeing Eileen drunk in public (signifying Bad Mom) and how distraught she was when Richard died (to show how man-clingy she was). Then she was contrasting that with witnesses who told how *calm* Eileen was when Gabriella died (French for Uncaring Bitch, variant of Bad Mom).

Looking at the prosecution's witness list, Gary said, "She's gonna call Samantha Jacobi next." Wife of studio head Jake Jacobi, famous for his fleet of seven Gulfstream jets, one for every day of the week.

"And Samantha Jacobi will say what good friends she used to be with Eileen."

"Right."

"And then she'll ladle out the same crap, and—"

"Exactly!" Gary said. "And I'm going to come back on cross with, uh, *How many times have you fed information to the celebrity columns?* And she'll say, *Why, what do you mean?* And I'll press her, and finally I'll let her know I've got that phone list from *LA BackChat*, and then we'll see what she says. I'll make her look like the queen of backstabbers, you know?"

"Excellent strategy, Gary."

"I think so." He munched the rye toast that came with his salad and rolled his desk chair in his habitual back-and-forth pattern on the rug.

"Want me to do any more research on that over the weekend? I have time." Jeff was being better about doing weekends with Petey, which I didn't know whether to be relieved or anxious about.

"No, we're set on that." He paused. "But actually, I would like to have another graphic. You know, like a thermometer graph showing the number of times Mimi Pappas quoted her, you know, and the number of times that guy from *BackChat* said she called him."

I pictured that. "I think some of the jurors might take that as overkill," I ventured. "Especially three and eleven." I'd learned to refer to the jurors by their numbers. It was fun. "I mean, it's—"

"It's a good idea, and we're going to do it. I'll get Lisa to put something together."

"But I was reading about *California v. Trask,* and the defense did something similar with the numbers of complaints against his subordinates, and it actually backfired."

Gary looked surprised, then irritated. He said, "Rita. Listen to me." There was that rough tone of his again. He said, "I am dismissing your suggestion. I want a graphic on Samantha Jacobi's big mouth. That's it."

We ate in silence for a while. I didn't mind that he didn't care for my opinion; after all, I'd had about as much experience in the legal scene as he'd had breast-feeding.

I started thinking about Jeff, because I was feeling for Gary the same feelings that used to course through me for Jeff when things were good. How long ago that seemed. If only the alcohol hadn't gotten hold of him.

He'd always blamed his drinking problem on his 'upbeat personality', which was bullshit, because in the first place his personality was not upbeat, but I could see how he rationalized that.

He'd come home all happy about something—anything—getting a word of praise from his boss, or having avoided running over a chipmunk. Then he'd get blasted on tequila in celebration, and then he'd remember he was angry about something. His mood would turn in a second, and then he'd take it out on me.

After we got to California I never felt safe when he was drinking. It was as if leaving our families in Wisconsin gave him license to forget himself. As if he knew my dad or brothers couldn't just pop over in fifteen minutes and break his nose if I called for them. Not that I ever had. But still.

Upbeat personality my ass.

And yet, the good parts of the whole goddamn thing would creep, unbidden, into my mind at any time. The way Jeff looked when he came dripping out of the shower, so ripply and relaxed. How he used to let me massage his head with rosemary oil and then his hair would be all Valentino-like. How we used to go down to the beach and find a cove just big enough for making love—until the tide crept up, then it was time to go get fried clams and cold beer at the shack off the Pacific Coast Highway and drive home so happy.

How bitterly and finally that was all gone.

But now, whenever I was with Gary, I felt that same security and happiness. Yes, it was insane. I was happy spending time with a solidly married guy who talked to me in a rough tone. I loved fantasizing about him, and I loved fantasizing about the possibility of Jacqueline getting a painless yet fast-acting tumor. Yes! Or what if he caught her cheating on him? Oh, he'd probably be understanding and give her another chance. I wondered how I might plant evidence of infidelity, like in her car or their bathroom. Can you believe how unprincipled I was? I didn't even know where they lived. I'd never met the woman. Love can make you evil.

Gary said, "Tracy thinks Detective Lahane"—the main cop in the case—"is all she needs, she thinks we're going to be terribly damaged by him. She thinks the jury's going to find him charismatic. A charismatic cop. Boy, she really hates me. She wants to break my—" He stopped, not wanting to finish the vulgarism.

"She couldn't," I said quickly. "They're too big!"

He looked at me, his lips open, eyes darting. What a wench I was! Flirting with a married man, a married man who was also my boss, and who had a perfect alibi to be unfaithful? A man who'd said nothing to indicate he was unhappy with his wife?

Except there was something.

I swear there was something there. In his posture when he stood at the window talking to Jacqueline. He held that arm up as if to ward off a blow, to protect himself, or perhaps to hide himself. Did they have some kind of reverse-domination thing going on, perchance?

The office building was very quiet at this hour. My words about his balls hung in the air, unaddressed.

After a few eons-long seconds, he cleared his throat and said, "So I think I'll focus in cross on Detective Lahane's outstanding skill at convincing the DA to bring capital charges on circumstantial evidence."

On the other hand, how horrible is it to have an affair? Was I just being too midwestern? I know you're not supposed to break up another person's marriage, especially when there's a kid involved. But really. It's not like I'd be committing murder.

I thought those thoughts, then hated myself. I had to get my brain away from them.

"Gary, I've been looking into Tracy's methods, you know?" When I'm freaked out I start talking like a Valley Girl. "Including talking to Deputy Scanlon at lunch sometimes?"

"Who's Deputy Scanlon?"

"Uh, one of the bailiffs? And he told me—this is a rumor, OK, but I'm seeing it on the Internet too—that she's been known to tamper with witnesses. The win-at-all-costs thing might be—"

He stabbed that away with his fork. "Oh, I've heard that too. They say she gave somebody a script once, but mainly she makes deals. That's not tampering. Let's say you've got this lowlife up for possession and assault, and you offer to drop the possession if he'll talk about his old cellmate you've picked up for rape. That's a deal. Now, if you somehow let that lowlife know what you're looking for—what you *wish* he might have seen or heard—that's wrong. That's tampering. But it's actually hard for a prosecutor to do that, because your opponent's going to grill the hell out of the guy on cross, and unless you've really done a *lot* of work—a lot of tampering!—you're gonna look bad, if not get busted for it. It's a huge risk to take."

He paused to eat some more salad. I chowed down mine. "I think with Tracy," he said, "maybe there's a finer line between dealing and tampering than there should be. I don't know. I don't know. In this case, what opportunity would she have had? To do what? There's no such witness. See?"

He was so damn smart. "Yeah."

"So that's it."

"Well," I ventured, "since we're on the topic of rumors . . ."

"Now what?"

"It was in Mimi Pappas's column that the Tenaway fortune isn't as big as most people thought."

"How would she know that?"

"Well, I don't know."

Impatiently, he said, "Well, Eileen made one payment to me when we got going, and I've seen her last Merrill Lynch statement. I think my bill's gonna be covered, anyway."

"OK."

"Rita, what is all this?"

I met his gaze. "I want to know what happened that night."

He looked at me disbelievingly. He opened his mouth to say something.

We heard a sound in the outer office.

My heartbeat, already in high gear from being alone with Gary, went into firebell mode.

Gary glanced at his watch. He rose without hurrying.

Dread surged through me. "There's someone out there," I said needlessly.

The door swung open and a woman in the prime of her beauty walked in. She wore Ralph Lauren and Gucci, and, I thought I detected in the air, Caron's Poivre. She carried a sleepy Jade in her arms.

"Jacqueline," said Gary.

"We couldn't sleep," she said in a friendly voice, staring a hole straight through my forehead.

Gary said, "This is Rita Farmer, the newest member of the Tenaway defense team. Rita, Jacqueline Kwan."

She was blonder than me, spritelier than me, and nervier than me.

Glancing at our empty salad boxes and scrawled notes, she said, "Looks like you were just wrapping up."

"That's a fact," said Gary.

FOURTEEN

As the trial moved into week three, I found myself more and more relaxed in the courtroom. Gary and Tracy Beck–Rubin went at it like a couple of elk with antlers trying to knock each other into the next county. Besides the press, most of whom because of their limited wardrobes and shared cynical facial expressions had quickly become familiar to me, I noticed other regular observers. There was Padraig McGower, former partner of Richard Tenaway, now sole boss of Gemini Imports. He was there, Gary told me, to support Eileen. Gary had originally thought to call him as a character witness for her, but he was too concerned about what Beck-Rubin might pull on cross.

"Was Eileen having an affair with him?" I asked Gary quietly during a recess.

"Both of them have told me no," Gary said, "but I would expect them to deny it. Tracy would probably grill him on his relationship with Richard. Practically everything about Gemini Imports would be fair game for her if I called McGower."

McGower stood out. He towered over everybody, even Steve Calhoun, who stood six-three in his cowboy boots. And McGower looked even taller because of his brilliant, copper-fire hair, a red explosion starting immediately above his eyebrows, which were the same color. You could tell he tried to rein in the hair by combing a waxy product into it, but you might as well hold up a sheet of typing paper to deflect a hurricane. With his broad back and sloping shoulders, McGower looked as powerful as a longshoreman. He wore perfectly cut suits—dark silk or pure featherweight wool, in deep cocoa browns or black, always matched with gleaming brogues. His tie tack was a white sapphire the size of a thimble. He looked purposeful even when he was just tugging at his pant cuff.

I wondered about him. Every time I glanced at the gallery, I saw him paying close attention, always focused on Eileen or Gary. Eileen watched for him every day, and when their eyes met they exchanged warmth. In the hallways at recesses I'd see him talking on his cell phone or standing patiently with his arms crossed. Being responsible for a multimillion-dollar company, how did he have time for all this?

One time I said to him, "Who's minding the store?"

We stood at the windows outside the courtroom. It had rained in the night, and the ocean wind was chasing the spent dirty clouds over the hills to the desert, where they would evaporate before they hit Palm Springs.

He smiled, surprised. "I am minding it."

I reported that to Gary and he said, "Uh-oh," but then refused to tell me what he meant.

Another courtroom regular was a compact guy who looked maybe like an ex-Marine, with quick eyes and a spiral notebook in his shirt pocket. He showed up about a week and a half into things. He must have developed his dark tan by accident, because it immediately began to fade back to what I guessed was his normal whiteness. I hate guys who work on their tans. He had a bruise on his cheek as well, that first day or so, which also faded away.

He was cute in an ugly sort of way—he had this army-corps face and a crew cut, he was this very serious-looking guy who wore short-sleeved white shirts and wasn't very tall, yet he carried himself in a relaxed, tension-free way. You'd look at a guy like that and expect him to give off rigidity, even suppressed anger, which is so common with military types. But this guy was just the opposite.

He looked happy.

I never saw him talk to anybody. Gary didn't know who he was.

There was a painful absence of family at this trial. Where were the uncles and aunts? Where was anybody, besides this redheaded businessman, who professed to care about Eileen Tenaway? Where was anybody who shared Gabriella's blood?

WHEN MARK SHARMA's back acted up it made him feel ornery, a word he'd learned from Steve Calhoun. Steve was trying to be a mentor to the wispy lapsed Hindu, and Mark did appreciate this, certainly, because he was a super-smart boy, all of Varanasi had thought that! Mark appreciated Steve's venerable wisdom, but Steve was not the one running the show.

Mark got down on his exercise mat, flexed his knees, and rolled his lower back from side to side as Lisa Feltenberger had showed him. Her brother was a chiropractor.

It was Gary's attention Mark craved. It was Gary Mark wanted to emulate, it was Gary Mark wanted to tell his troubles to. Needless to say, it was Gary, also, to whom he wanted to be indispensable. He wanted to ride in on a mustang and slay the dragon.

He stretched his back, winced, and tried to relax. Because he had taken no time to exercise during this trial, he had put on a little fat around his middle, which made him look more mature. That was fine. He unbuttoned his pants and sighed.

No one could have worked harder on the physical evidence in the Tenaway case. He had checked every single minute of chain of custody, he had researched the testing laboratories, he had found lapses in police procedure, he had reviewed similar cases and written out condensed reports suggesting possible tactics for Gary's use and amazement.

For Gary too was the son of brownish parents, or at least it could be said not standard white parents. Ethnic minority. And neither of them was Jewish. Gary had made it in the glamorous world of big-money legal defense in spite of that. How did he do it, Mark pondered incessantly. Certainly it had to do with bold action. Bold, independent action! Gary made people do what he wanted.

Mark Sharma wanted to come across well. He wanted to attract a wealthy American wife as Gary had. American wives look at you with more love if you are successful and televised. Lisa

Feltenberger liked him and kept offering to come over and help him with his back, but the thought of her hunching over him digging her skinny fingers into his muscles was too dreadful. He wanted to charge clients two million dollars. He did not want to go back to Varanasi as his parents were ever more loudly insisting, to marry the little girl for whom he had made a flower wreath when he was five. Dowry or no dowry. He wanted to step up to bat and throw a no-hitter.

Who was this damned new paralegal? Who was this Rita, always at Gary's side like a dog? What had been wrong with the original team? Rita did nothing. She acted like a mongrel to Gary and a duchess to everybody else. Why was Gary permitting her to spend so much time with him?

He lay on his exercise mat.

His back hurt like cotton-picking blazes.

AT LUNCHTIME WEDNESDAY of that third week my cell phone vibed and it was my agent. Marly said, "Sunshine, I know you haven't heard from me forever—it's just been a drought for your type—but OATBERGER WANTS TO SEE YOU FOR *THIRD CHANCE MOUNTAIN*! How's that for a long-time-no-hear-from? Huh? Be at his office at ten tomorrow. They're not giving pages in advance. As usual."

Can a heart simultaneously soar and crash?

"Marly, I can't."

"What, hon? You what?"

"Can't."

"I'm afraid I'm not hearing you properly, Rita. There must be something wrong with—"

"Marly, listen. Petey's in the hospital and he's having surgery tomorrow."

"Oh! Oh, my. Um, who's Petey again?"

"My son."

"Oh! Well, is it—"

"It's a heart operation. Open-heart surgery. He has to have it right away. I have to be there. I can't do this audition."

That night I sobbed my way through two pillowcases and half a box of Kleenex.

Petey wanted to know what was wrong.

"Mommy's sick, baby."

I remember the next day with crystal clarity.

I was in the courtroom, but in my mind I was being waved through Colonnade Studios' main gate, my hair and face perfect, my clothes neutral, as you never know what you'll be asked for: prairie maiden? gypsy crone? In my mind I strode into Serge Oatberger's conference room projecting poise and quiet power.

In my mind he nodded to me and I met his lackeys. In my mind Oatberger and I talked, and he suggested I improvise a scene with him based on his rough-out of act one.

In my mind I was incandescent.

In my mind I wanted to kill myself.

In reality Tracy Beck-Rubin asked a witness, "And exactly what signs did you see of the defendant's Valium dependency?"

"Objection!" shouted Gary.

Judge Davenport said nothing.

The whole courtroom looked at him. His face had gone gray and sweaty. He leaned forward on his elbows. "Uh, sustained," he said weakly.

The clerk rose uncertainly.

Judge Davenport cleared his throat and said, "I'm afraid I'm not feeling well. Recess. Half hour." He got to his feet and tottered into his chambers.

Half an hour later the clerk announced court was adjourned for the day. I looked at my watch. It was eleven o'clock.

I rushed to my car, flipping open my cell phone. I screamed to Marly, "I can audition for Oatberger! Call them and tell them I'm coming!"

"I'm on it."

She didn't even ask about Petey's heart operation. For all she knew, he'd died on the table and I was getting on with my life.

She called while I was on the 405 to tell me they wanted to see me at two. I headed for home, where I changed into a simple beige dress and one-inch heels, and made it to the Colonnade main gate at one-thirty.

And this time it was all for real.

My heart clattered in my chest as I identified myself to the guard. Colonnade Studios! All that history, all the stars and directors who'd come through these gates! The air thrummed with the very essence of moviemaking: the excitement, the heartbreak, the smashes, the flops. Legends swirled everywhere.

However, as I drove in, something caught my eye in my rearview mirror. It was a silver Mercedes just like Gary's. "Dear God," I muttered, pushing down panic, trying to see through the glare on the windshield. Who was inside? The Mercedes followed my Honda to the parking area, then pulled past, deeper into studio property. Now I could see the person inside and it was a young non-Asian guy in a livery cap. OK. The stab of fear went away and only the excitement remained.

My heart throbbed so hard I felt my pulse in my toes.

Oatberger was flanked by Mel Santoro, his cinematographer, and two murky-looking assistants, one of whom offered me a bottle of green Gatorade.

I hate Gatorade, but everybody knows Oatberger loves it, so I accepted the cold drink and took a couple of wretched sips.

Oatberger quizzed me to see how familiar I was with his films, then he stood up with me and asked me to talk to him as if I were a ranch wife whose husband had gone to fight Pancho Villa across the Rio Grande. "Your name is Emily Rounceville, you've just given birth to your fifth child," he said, "and I'm the rancher next door. I'm not a nice man."

Nice or not, he was thoroughly tanned, with that signature shaved head. You could almost take him for a Moroccan, or maybe a burly Egyptian, with the right headwear. He wore little silver glasses, which made him look in a constant state of narrow, intense focus.

He began the improvisation by telling me he was kicking me and the kids and old gramps off our ranch.

I avoided doing the clichéd weary country wife posture of bracing my back with my hands. Instead, as I worked the scene, I shifted my weight from side to side as if my feet hurt. I had some indignation ready, as I knew Oatberger liked his heroines indignant. I underplayed it, though, wanting to let my emotion build slowly.

I sensed he was trying to goad me into playing it obviously, trying to push me into a crying rage, so I resisted. I held my temper back, showing it was there, but holding it as if it were an unbroken horse. Right then I got the idea to metaphorically be a proud mare, and so I imagined equine feelings. I lifted my head warily and flared my nostrils, shifted my hips. I loosened my jaw.

I talked in short sentences about how our families, his and mine, were close. When you're close you don't expect news like this. When you get news like this you got to think about it. You got to think what to do.

I looked at him as if I were planning to kill him with my teeth as soon as he turned his back.

If you ask me, I was incandescent.

Oatberger merely muttered, "Thank you."

FIFTEEN

Judge Davenport felt better the next day, Friday, and the trial resumed. Marly left me a message saying Oatberger typically takes weeks and weeks deciding on his leads, which evidently was what I'd auditioned for. I couldn't imagine what the hell I'd do if he wanted me back for another look before the trial ended. Even though I had carefully trained myself to think positive after auditions, I knew my odds were slim; Oatberger typically met with dozens of hopefuls per lead before making up his mind.

Tracy Beck-Rubin brought forth a Montessori mom who testified that Eileen had once pointed to Gabriella and said bitterly, "If she's lucky, she'll die young!"

Gary objected all over the place, but this wasn't his day. Using witnesses as her colors and questions as her brushstrokes, the frumpy-cat prosecutor painted a picture of Eileen as Mom From

Hell. You almost started to be glad Gabriella was dead and spared the horror of growing up Eileen Tenaway's child. I watched the jurors gradually abandon their natural skepticism and start to climb into Beck-Rubin's pocket. She could see it and feel it too, and it felt mighty good.

That night, an exhausted Gary took it out on me, half rightly. "Rita, whatever you're doing with Eileen—it's not working." He paced his undersized office, the black dark shining in through the windows. I fidgeted at the conference table. "I'm busting my hump against Tracy every day here—*and* the judge!—and all we're doing is losing ground. It's obvious, I look at that jury and I see that they've totally gone with Tracy, they're not even glancing at Eileen anymore, and when they do they look at her like she's a toad." He stopped pacing. "Do you agree with me?"

I sighed, "I don't want to agree with you."

He did not smile. "What are you going to do? What are you going to change? You've got to start pulling more weight around here, or I'm going to have to—"

"Gary." I loved how the fury flashed from his eyes, but I didn't want to hear him threaten to fire me. "OK. Calm down." I toggled my pen in my fingers. "I admit I've been stalling. Afraid to try something different, maybe."

He began to speak again, but I said, "I have an idea."

ON MONDAY MORNING in the holding cell I said, "All right, Eileen, to hell with feelings. To hell with life story, to hell with emotional touchstones." *To hell with Method,* I'd decided over the weekend, *time now to devote ourselves to pure technique.*

"I agree heartily." Fear had taken over her eyes.

All along I'd thought everything would fall into place if only she could bring forth her deepest feelings. Huh. "Here's what you do," I said. "This is what's going on in your brain. Forget the grief. You'd been thinking all this time that because you're innocent, they can't frame you for it. You've been complacent that Gary would get you off. But now, to your alarm, you see the prosecution just might win!"

As I knew she would, Eileen agreed. "I'm frightened of exactly that."

We both glanced around the horrible little claustrophobic sun-deprived cell. The deputy's face hung in the window like a dark moon.

"All right," I went on. "You must communicate that to the jury. I want you to change the way you sit. No longer just passive in your chair, like a good girl. I want you to *move*. Like this." I brought my upper body forward, erect, and placed my relaxed hands on the table. "This is a good position to return to anytime you feel unsure what to do. Now watch." I rocked back with a look of shocked amazement. "But not all the way back; I don't want your shoulder blades to touch the chair ever again."

"I like that," Eileen said. "Gives me something to focus on."

"OK. I want you to breathe audibly, sometimes, like people do when they're upset. You're feeling the walls of a trap closing in. It's a trap!"

"Yes!"

"At times cup your chin in your hand, as if you're trying to listen patiently and understand the prosecution's case. Then, after Tracy Beck-Rubin thinks she's made some triumphal point, you shake your head firmly. You look at Gary like, *How can they get away with such a lie?* OK?"

She tried it, opening her eyes and mouth as wide as they could go.

"Too much," I said. "Too much head-waggle, too much eyes. You want to underplay it. Trust me, you'll be more convincing. You're holding back your story, see?"

My student tried again, subduing her expression.

"That's better. Obviously you can't say anything yet. You can't interject a word out loud. But let's talk vocal presence."

"Vocal presence?"

"Yeah, I learned this stuff from Meryl Streep. We did a scene together in one of Eastwood's films. It got totally cut from the final movie because of a prop failure. Anyway, here's what you do. You clear your throat from time to time, like you desperately want to speak, but then you remember you're not allowed to."

"Yeah! That's good." Eileen's energy was rising moment by moment. She was *getting* it.

"Try it now. That's fine. Good. And *gasp,* for God's sake. Take in your breath at some outrageous piece of testimony, like you're about to say, *Oh, my God!* But you catch yourself just in time. You swallow. In discomfort. Keep your hands visible, you're not hiding anything. Try gasping."

She gasped.

I said, "Softly. Remember, you don't need to be loud for the jury to hear you. You don't want the judge to think you're trying to call attention to yourself. This stuff is coming out in spite of yourself, right? Try it again."

She did, and came across perfectly. At last I'd hit on the right approach: not *drag forth* her emotions, but make her work to *hold them back.*

I told her that doing some of these things might bring sadness up, and if it did, let it. The jury would expect her moods to be changeable, since she was under tremendous stress. "So if you quietly start to cry, that's all right."

"I just can't cry in front of—"

"Try to suppress it, then, get what I'm saying? But that only makes it worse. If you let your mouth twist sideways, that'll suggest pain, and show you're trying to keep it under control."

"Yes."

"Try it. Good." Eileen's sideways mouth looked awesomely stricken.

"Let this happen when Gabriella comes up, but not when they're saying how evil you are, because crying might look guilty—or desperate—right then. You believe the jury won't let you down. It's all you can do to not let your emotions totally take over and destroy what sanity you've got left."

I paused to let all this sink in. Eileen looked at me gratefully. I watched her think.

After a while she said, "God, I miss my baby."

I nodded. "Yeah." We sat there missing Gabriella together.

After another while she said, "Should I look at the jury? I've sort of been trying not to stare at them."

"Yes, go ahead and make eye contact now and then. As if you're trying to see into their hearts. You're not asking for anything. You're not trying to appeal to them. You're just wondering about every single one of them, *Who are you? Do you have a just heart?*"

"My God, Rita, I can do this."

"Attagirl."

"It's paradoxical, isn't it?"

"Yes. Yes, it is."

For the first time since I'd met her, she breathed freely, as if relieved of a burden. I lingered, basking in it.

Eileen rather shocked me by saying, "Almost feels like after sex, doesn't it?"

"Um," I said. "Did you and Richard have a good sex life?"

"Yes, I'd say so. You know what we liked to do?" Seeing my face, she said, "No, I mean—I mean afterward. We'd talk."

"It's nice when a man talks to you after sex," I remarked.

"Talking was a tonic for us. We'd lie there, propped on our elbows drinking old cognac, and we'd speculate on how often our friends did it!" Relish crept into her tone.

I smiled.

She went on, "We'd talk about who was having an affair, and why. Richard always defended the guys. I rooted for the women, of course." She paused thoughtfully. "That made for some tension, but you know . . ."

"Tension can be good for sex," I said. "I'd think that in your set, the wives rarely leave the husbands because the money is too good."

"Boy, are you right." Eileen leaned forward confidentially. "If the guy's mentally cruel there's always a ski instructor at Klosters or a masseur at Cabo, you know? Or even, hell, the nanny. Who's uptight about things like that anymore?"

"Comfort's comfort," I agreed.

"Besides, if you let him have sexual adventures you can always use them for leverage later."

"True."

"We'd hash over stuff that happened to our friends, like *she* almost died from a tummy tuck, *his* kid got caught bribing a professor, *their* parents got conned out of a fortune by some stranger on the Internet."

"Schadenfreude can be fun," I said.

She knew the word. "We liked feeling happier than other people."

"Yes," I said. Knowing others were full-on miserable made you happier still. We talked some more, and I learned that Richard had been an exciting mate: athletic and bold, tall, with heavily muscled legs and back from rowing crew at college. Any man who rows crew you can assume is a disciplined man, and I found that interesting.

Eileen said, "You don't get up at five a.m. every day of the week and row your guts out unless you have discipline, unless you can do delayed gratification. Richard rowed for the medals and, once he had them, the knowledge that other men knew it. Deep down, if only to themselves, they acknowledged his superiority. That was what he lived for. That and sex."

Eileen understood all this about Richard. Nevertheless, she mused as we sat in that godawful interview room as the morning pressed forward all around us, invisibly, something had changed in him. She realized that one day. Was he less attentive? Yes, that was part of it. He hadn't given her a new piece of jewelry in six months. She tried not to let it bother her.

Richard would never get old. He was a perpetual boy, with a boy's enthusiasms for novelty, and a boy's talent for getting away with things, and for being forgiven things. No matter if his face showed a crease or two, his whole persona was naughty-boy ageless. She, of course, aged, and I understood how strongly she would have felt the dread all trophy wives eventually feel: the desperation borne of a nonrenewable resource that was starting to get tapped out—her own physical beauty.

Then Richard left her, and then Richard was dead. I wanted to hear more, but it was time to go.

Eileen, that day, came across differently in the courtroom. Not startlingly different, subtly so. She didn't use all the tricks we'd practiced, just a couple, once in a while. I could see the change, and most of all I could feel it.

So could the jury. She began to draw their attention. A few of them looked at her inquisitively, as if for the first time. Gary gave me a half hug in the corridor.

SIXTEEN

I had a lot of balls in the air, and one I kept dropping was Petey. I was leaning pretty hard on Daniel and Yvonne, but even when I *was* there for Petey I wasn't.

At home all I wanted to do was study trials on the Internet, think about how I could learn the truth of Gabriella's death, and fantasize ever more seriously on how I could begin a guilt-free affair with Gary. Some nights I'd open a bottle of Merlot with my Le Cork Weasel, the ingenious new corkscrew Daniel had given me. The thing was a real marvel of gears and levers and so on. I'd pour a glass, then use Le Cork Weasel to crack a few almonds in the shell left over from Christmas, because Petey had taken our real nutcracker to the park for some reason and lost it. The corkscrew worked great on the almonds, it was amazing. I'd munch the nuts, drink the wine, and brood.

In a weird way, the ever-present photographs of Gabriella Tenaway had begun to work on me. I wondered what kind of kid she'd have been if she hadn't died. I decided she would become the kind of extraordinary fourth-grader who would read about a terminally ill child in some distant place like Pennsylvania and galvanize all her classmates to raise money for a new iron lung and a birthday party for the kid. She'd be the kind of seventh-grader who makes the most points on the basketball team but sits down in the big game because the coach broke his promise to play all the kids on the team, thus forcing him to put in the weakest kid, who shoots the winning basket anyway. She'd be the kind of teenager who would stay out late, but then learn ancient lace-making skills and proceed to repair her grandma's wedding gown so she could wear it someday. I wanted a girl. Well, maybe someday.

As I say, even when I turned away from the Internet and played with Petey or read to him, he sensed my distance. And it pissed him off.

"I won't!" became his favorite sentence. Didn't matter what, I could give him two or three choices—because as a contemporary parent I knew the power of choice-giving—and he'd reject them all.

"I only eat chips!" he'd scream, dashing his chicken and lettuce to the floor. "I won't *go* to school!" His will was strong.

So was mine.

When he began hitting—kids at school, and sometimes me—I'd quiet him down, explain, "We don't hurt," then tell him guilt-tripping stories about little animals who victimized other little animals until they themselves were victimized. Then they sorrowfully saw the light. He'd listen skeptically.

I prevailed, but it wasn't fun. I found it harder and harder to keep my temper. I was starting to have abandonment fantasies: just drop the little bastard off with some sincere shepherd and *go*. Of course, his bad behavior was all my fault: I was a lazy, weak mom. Which I felt like shit about, but then it was just one of the many things in my life I felt like shit about. There was my failed marriage, the wound of which I pressed on regularly. Analyzing my relationship with Petey, the word *enabling* came to mind.

With Jeff, I'd certainly been an enabler, and in a really nasty way. Sometimes when his chips were down I'd pick a fight, knowing he'd probably go on a binge. Why did I do that? Maybe to feel superior to him. Maybe I was angry about his lack of respect for me. Over and over he told me I was too dumb to have a real career, that acting would probably be the only thing I could do. He thought actors were soulless pieces of meat. He tried to make this sound like witty teasing. These days I was temporarily making myself feel better about all this by fantasizing about Gary with my vibrator at night.

I was enabling Petey too. Whenever I'd snap in anger, my guilt, like a bottle of toxic slime, would spill all over the place. He could perceive that, and it pleased him, for reasons he didn't understand yet.

I was starting to fuck the kid up.

One evening after a particularly acrimonious struggle over television-watching which I'd won by seizing the remote control and taking it down to the car and locking it in the glove compartment, Petey washed up by himself and went to bed oddly docilely. I turned on the computer and settled down to read case files on Trial TV's Web site. This was now Tuesday night in the Tenaway trial's fourth week. After an hour I went into the bathroom to pee and lifted the lid to find that Petey had dropped all my cosmetics into the toilet.

All.

My.

Cosmetics.

Into.

The.

Toilet.

To achieve this, he had climbed from the toilet seat to the toilet tank to the windowsill to the top shelf of the cupboard where I kept them, somehow transported them to the floor without much noise, then gone ahead and placed them in the toilet bowl. He had peed in the bowl either before or after adding my compacts of powder and eye shadow, bottles of foundation, under-eye whitener, my mascara, liner pencils, lip pencils and lipsticks, my tubes of blush, pots of gloss, vials of nail polish, my emery boards and nail files and clippers, my eye creams, my Visine, well, that was just to start.

I went to his room.

He was sleeping soundly, splayed on his Spider-Man sheets, his breathing even and deep, his small body as relaxed as if I'd given him a fatal dose of Valium. I stood there looking at him, breathing in his clean little smell—it would be merciful years before the rankness of puberty would set in—when the phone rang.

I stood there another moment, feeling oddly detached from my temper, which was rampaging through my chest like a fire-spewing elephant. I could not allow myself to lose it. I closed my eyes, breathed out, then turned and closed the door.

I answered the phone.

A man with a deep voice introduced himself as George Rowe,

representing the Fenco Insurance Company. He addressed me as Ms. Farmer, and told me he'd been following the Tenaway trial. "I'd like to talk to you," he said.

"Uh, I'm afraid I can't," I said. "How did you get my—"

"I understand you're not to talk about the case, ma'am," said this George Rowe. Although his voice came from the baritone register, he didn't swallow his words, he spoke cleanly. "But," he went on, "I don't want to discuss Eileen Tenaway's situation."

"You don't?"

"I want to talk about her husband, Richard Tenaway."

"Oh?" A current of excitement zoomed into me, replacing the elephant rage.

"Give me an opportunity to tell you what's on my mind, then you can decide if you want to talk to me."

It dawned on me that this was the cute-ugly guy in the courtroom with the pocket notebook and crew cut. "Yes, but how," I demanded, "did you get my number?" My home phone was unlisted.

"I'm an investigator," he said.

My God, I thought. *The iceberg.*

"Ms. Farmer, my business is helping people separate right from wrong. Sometimes it's not so easy. Does that interest you?"

"Yeah. Yes, it does."

"I thought it might."

"How come? Have you been scrutinizing me?"

"Not in the way you think."

My pulse accelerated. "I cannot betray Gary Kwan."

"I'm not asking you to."

He gave me his boss's phone number if I wanted to check him out.

TWO NIGHTS LATER we met at the Hot-n-Tot, a diner down the PCH in Lomita. I'd worried vigorously about the ethics of this, but my curiosity about this George Rowe—and the iceberg—just barely overrode the worrying. His boss had assured me George was doing legitimate work for the insurance company, but still I was nervous.

I was charmed by George's suggestion of the Hot-n-Tot. Retro in the real sense, it'd been established in the forties and had not changed since. I parked in back and looked around carefully, guiltily, clandestinely. A robin rustled under a bush and I about jumped out of my dress.

The restaurant was plain and smelled good inside, and the waning light was L.A.-golden-gorgeous. Usually on days like that I felt a little depraved going indoors, but not in a nice bright diner like this.

George Rowe had gotten there first and stood to greet me. I had the feeling he would have held my chair for me had we not been given a booth. I asked him to call me Rita.

He ordered coffee and a grilled ham sandwich, and I decided on cinnamon toast. My mouth watered, not only for the toast, but at the prospect of learning more about the Tenaways. I smoothed my dress, a lemon-and-lime palm leaf print I'd scored at a thrift shop in North Hollywood. Perfect, I thought, for a mysterious meeting with a deep-voiced stranger at a retro diner in Southern California.

"You may be wondering why I picked you out," he began. "Why I'm trusting you with what I'm about to say."

"Uh, yes."

155

"In my business, hunches pay off." He sighed as if he knew that sounded lame, though I found it thrilling. He added, "But you have to weigh the strength of the hunch against the possible payoff. I haven't had a lot to go on. So here we are."

In straight, compact sentences, he told me that Richard Tenaway's life had been insured under a dual policy by Fenco, which had been obliged to pay $10 million to Gemini Imports and another $10 million to his widow, Eileen.

Fenco suspected a scam, but couldn't prove it before they had to cough up the money. After all, the circumstances were suspicious. The guy had disappeared, Eileen's sister Norah had disappeared, then the guy turns up dead and twenty million bucks spill out of Fenco's coffers.

Our food came, and George Rowe said, "But how dead is he, really?"

I liked his frankness. I smiled, fascinated.

He ate his sandwich in eager guy-bites, but used his napkin and chewed and swallowed before speaking.

"Since I came back from Brazil," he said, "I've been attending the trial. I guess you've seen me in the seats. It seems to me you have a special relationship with Eileen Tenaway. She trusts you. I believe Gary Kwan is using you to prepare her to testify."

A bite of cinnamon toast went sideways in my throat and I asked the waitress for water.

I asked him, "How would you know that?"

"Well," he said, "you're meeting with her in the lockup, and that's one of the things paralegals do, they prepare witnesses. You are spending quite a lot of time with her." He saw the look in my eyes and shrugged. "I wasn't spying on you, just looking into things."

"Well, yes, I am helping her prepare," was all I said.

He went on, "My investigation for Fenco is a whole separate thing, legally, from the murder trial. So it wouldn't be a conflict if you could help me know for sure if Richard Tenaway is really dead. If he's dead, I can go on to another case. If not, there's money in it."

"For you?"

"For Fenco, first, of course. I suppose I'd get a bonus. And there could be a reward for you."

"Not that I'm terribly interested in money, but how much?"

He smiled. "I can't say. It would be a percentage of anything recovered. Ten or twenty percent."

"I see." My mind, suddenly mathematically agile, calculated that ten percent of twenty million is two million.

"Usually," he added, "only a small fraction gets recovered."

"Oh."

He drank three cups of coffee during our meeting. I accepted one refill. We agreed that the mugs made the coffee taste better: thick porcelain, with the cheerful Hot-n-Tot logo splashed across them in red. I finished my buttery, fragrant toast.

George held himself easily but carefully, hands relaxed, fingers curled, like a boxer a little afraid of his own power to hurt.

We talked about Richard Tenaway. I said, "He must be, or have been, a man of great charisma."

"Oh, yes," said George Rowe. "Everyone fell in love with Richard—women, men. He was handsome, but most of all he knew how to manipulate people so they didn't even know he was doing it. I think he might have stolen money from his own company, but the people at Gemini are being very quiet about it. Even I can't find out exactly what went on."

157

I smiled in spite of being nervous, waiting for him to tell me what he wanted me to do.

He said, "All I know is, they're really mad at him over at Gemini."

I told him my main job was to work on Eileen's murder rap and asked, "Are you sure that's not connected with Richard's disappearance?"

He tipped his head back and looked at the ceiling for a while. He drank some coffee. "Might be. Padraig McGower won't talk to me anymore."

"Yeah? I wonder about him. Like, is he really a benign family friend? Maybe he's just faking being nice. Eileen seems to feel he's on her side, though."

George Rowe said nothing.

"Well," I asked, "how can I find anything out about Richard Tenaway? It's not like I can ask Eileen point-blank if she knows anything."

"Of course you can. If the opportunity presents itself."

"And you want me to create the opportunity."

"Yes. You're becoming girlfriends, right? She trusts you, right?"

"I don't think she trusts anyone. I'm useful to her, that's all."

He nodded. "There's got to be some way you can lean on her, or—"

"Trick her." This came out in spite of myself.

He quirked an eyebrow and smiled.

Suddenly I felt out of my depth. "I don't know about this, George. Really. I don't want to jeopardize my work with Eileen." It was fine for me to be curious about all this gnarly stuff below the surface, but now that I was supposed to actually be a player, I got scared. "I'm not sure I want to—"

"You know, it doesn't take much looking to find out certain things." He leaned forward, resting his arms lightly on the table. "I'm surprised nobody in the press has bothered to research you."

I looked at him. "Oh, God."

"I guess you're too uninteresting to them, just a paralegal."

Sweat sprang out on my palms. He knew I was a fake! I mustered indignation. "I can't believe you would threaten me. And Gary."

He sighed and looked down at the wood-grain tabletop. In a quiet voice he said, "This is nothing."

"Well. I see."

He looked up, alarmed. "That didn't come out right. I mean, oh, Rita. All I meant was, I don't consider this a threat. I'm so used to doing whatever is necessary to get the information I have to have that—ugh! Oh! I am a dunce. Not handling this well." He touched his cupped fingers to his forehead.

I said, "What blew my cover? I mean, how do you know I'm—" I stopped. Maybe he was just trying to bluff me.

"An actress."

God damn it.

He sat back on the leatherette seat as if to give me more space, but left his hands on the table, palms nonthreateningly up. "Nothing blew your cover," he said in a gentle voice. "When I want someone to cooperate with me, I begin by just asking. But beforehand, I do a little homework just in case I need some— leverage. Your name, conveniently for you, doesn't come up on an Internet search, because you haven't been in any feature films. But your occupation is stated in your divorce papers."

"What!"

He passed his hand over his coffee cup against the waitress's carafe. "I thought you were somebody who might be able to help me because of your proximity to Eileen Tenaway. But that's where I found it out. Before I go into a meeting with anybody, I do a few routine document checks."

"Document checks?"

"I have access to specialized databases."

"Oh."

"When I found out you were an actress and not a paralegal, I guessed what Gary hired you for." He smiled. "He's a smart lawyer."

"He is smart."

At last George Rowe said, "Look, here's a promise. Even if you don't help me, I promise I won't expose you. All right?" His eyes were hopeful. "I don't want to ruin my reputation."

"Or mine?"

"Or yours."

"Hm."

He looked down at the table again. "I guess I wanted to show off to you a little."

I suppressed a smile and made no comment. He licked his lips. The awkward moment passed, and I thought we were finished talking. But he took something out of an envelope he'd brought with him.

"Knowing your real line of work, I want to ask you something about this." He laid down a photograph of a man lying on a stretcher or table.

I picked it up and looked at it, then at him.

George said, "Is that man dead, or just acting like it? Can you tell?"

How strange. I picked up the picture. Then I almost dropped it. "Is this Richard Tenaway?"

"It's him. It's supposed to be proof that he's dead, besides a death certificate signed by a Brazilian doctor. I tried to talk to the person who took the picture, but, uh, had no luck." He glanced into the far distance, then returned his gaze to me.

I studied the picture. "Well, he sure looks dead." I held it up to the light and slanted it away from the glare. Even in that condition, Tenaway was strikingly handsome, with perfectly balanced features that stopped short of prettiness. "If he's not dead, that means he's got some makeup on. The gash looks real. But I suppose it could be real and still he wasn't dead. Somebody did something to his hair. His expression is good—the slack mouth, the eyes not quite closed."

I looked at George. "Why does this picture mean anything? Even if it's a fake, it's still not proof the guy's—"

"The picture is proof of nothing. But if you think it's faked, I'm going to go back and be more aggressive in finding and questioning the photographer. See, if Tenaway's alive, he's probably got at least one set of forged travel documents. And likely whoever took this shot did the documents too."

"Well—" I stopped and looked some more. As genuinely dead as Richard Tenaway seemed, there was something very slightly off about him. Not that I was an expert on corpses, but I did play Juliet in college. In case you haven't actually seen the play, she lies there for a really long time after she's dead.

What was the problem here? The pallor was right, the overall limpness was right. His eyes looked a little sunken, even. But—

I said, "May I show this picture to one friend?"

SEVENTEEN

When I got home it was close to ten o'clock and Daniel was asleep on the sofa in front of the TV. A new show about an autistic Salvadoran immigrant with a talent for stand-up comedy was on. The autism forces the Salvadoran to deliver his gags with his back to the audience, and that's what makes it so funny.

I muted the set and gently woke my best friend.

He sat up groggily and gave me a hug. "Hey, sweetie."

I got him a Diet Pepsi out of the fridge and started to tell him about a police chase I'd seen on Sepulveda on the way home, but he interrupted with the single most heartbreaking line an actor can deliver: "My show's been canceled."

"Oh, no, Daniel!"

He slumped against my new IKEA cushions, despondent. "For a second when you woke me I thought it was all a nightmare."

Not that it mattered, but I had to ask, "Did they give a reason?"

He rubbed his face. "What other reason is there? Ratings."

"But I thought—"

"No. They've been in the crapper for weeks now. That's all you get: weeks. *Abilene Cop Shop* is shut down as of this minute. No last episode, no goodbye party."

I squeezed his arm. "Those parties are miserable anyway."

"I know, but I can still complain about not getting one."

"I'm very sorry, Daniel."

He looked up. "Well, the bright side is I can give Yvonne a break and pick up Petey from daycare now. Preschool too, for that matter. At least until my agent lands me my next gig, which as you know could be never in this business."

"Hey," I cajoled, "be positive, huh? You'll be working again in no time. With all your experience?"

He punched a cushion, his jaw tight. "Rita, there comes a point when experience is a liability. There's so much fresh young chicken in this town! I see it every day!"

"OK, OK."

"And I don't even have a boyfriend to come home to!"

"OK, Daniel, honey, dear. Hey. Dear one."

He calmed down and drank his pop.

I said, "I have to say I'm a little surprised you'd want to spend yet *more* time with Petey. I was thinking I ought to try to hire—"

"Don't you dare." He gripped my shoulder. "I need him. I'm not kidding, Rita. He'll keep me occupied, between trips to the unemployment office. He'll keep me sane. I just hope *your* gig doesn't end soon, whatever the hell it is."

"Mm, yeah."

The muted TV showed the credits for the Salavadoran autist

163

show, then a news teaser about the Tenaway trial. Daniel's eyes caught the screen, which featured a snip of Gary Kwan talking earnestly into a picket fence of microphones. I feigned disinterest. Daniel, gazing at the screen, started to say something, then stopped himself. He sighed.

"What, hon?"

"Nothing," he said. "Not a damn thing."

We hugged tight, then he went home.

I peeked in on Petey and found him asleep. The blind was up and the window halfway open, and because there was no screen, a few bugs had strayed in from around the security light over the fire escape. You don't see many mid-rises with fire escapes, but I'd looked for one because of Petey. After all, you can't expect to jump from the fourth floor. In the dim light I saw a Starbucks cup on the windowsill. I picked it up, took it to the kitchen, and found two cigarette butts and a dead moth floating in the dregs of a latte.

I couldn't believe Daniel had been smoking in Petey's room. Granted, he'd been upset tonight, and nicotine helps. But I'd asked him not to smoke in my apartment.

I pictured him sitting on the bed reading *Goodnight Moon,* one arm holding Petey and the book, the other fanning smoke out the window.

As I carried the cup to the sink, something jiggled in the back of my mind. But I was tired, my head filled with George Rowe. I threw away the cup and phoned Yvonne.

As I waited for her to pick up, I glanced at this week's *LA BackChat,* which Daniel had left splayed on the footstool. A small headline said, "Bad stars for Gemini?" The item quoted an un-named (but terribly reliable!) source saying the company was on the verge of going into receivership, and wouldn't that put a crimp in Padraig McGower, the surviving founder and current chief executive?

I told Yvonne she was off the hook for picking up Petey, due to Daniel's misfortune, but I wanted another favor.

"Now what, babe?"

"Can I come over tomorrow before dinner?"

"Absolutely."

Don't you just love a friend like that?

GARY AND I met at the court lockup in the morning. Mostly he talked over strategy with Eileen in his thrillingly authoritative voice, which I could not get enough of hearing. I diligently worked with Eileen, giving her feedback about her appearance in court yesterday and making suggestions for today. When Gary and I left, I said, "I really think I'm getting through to her. I feel we're becoming . . . friends." As soon as I said this, I brushed past a woman who gave off a very angry vibe. We were coming out of the elevator in the parking garage. I didn't really see her face; her back was turned and she was looking away.

Gary gave me a reassuring smile, but said, "Watch your speech in public places."

I am so madly in love with you, said my brain waves.

MY FRIEND YVONNE was a big girl who dressed in flowing caftans which went with her flowing auburn tresses. "Flowing auburn tresses" was how her first boyfriend, age fourteen, had described her hair, and ever since she told me that, the words "flowing auburn tresses" went through my mind when I saw her. Today when she opened her door she had chosen a moss-green charmeuse caftan with some kind of magenta sash draped over her shoulders. I loved her style but would never have the guts to copy it. She had a booming, Brunhilde-style laugh, which created friends all over town. Her hands were pudgy yet delicate, with tapered fingers that worked miracles in the makeup studios of Hollywood.

Yvonne excelled in the business of making people prettier than they were, or uglier, or older than they were, or younger, lighter, darker, more Asian, less Irish, thinner-lipped, fuller-cheeked, sleepier, drunker, blotchier, bloodier, or all the way dead. Have you seen *Waterflame Bayou,* that up-from-the-grave flick with B. B. Ford and Cam Jeffers? Yvonne invented the makeup technique that gave the swamp zombies that convincing look of having their faces bitten by all those rattlesnakes.

She poured iced tea for us. Her tortoiseshell cat came in to meow hello. I laid the photo of Richard Tenaway on her breakfast counter. "I would be still more totally in your debt than I already am," I said, "if you would take a good long look at this."

She glanced at the photo, then at me.

"Isn't this that guy?"

"What guy?"

"The diamonds guy. Tenaway. Eileen Tenaway's husband."

"Yvonne, I'm not sure," I lied. "I just want you to look and tell me what your impressions are."

She put her iced tea on a coaster. "Wait a minute." She left the room and returned with a large fluorescent-ringed magnifier, the kind they mount with extension arms on walls in makeup rooms and toilet facilities at studios. She plugged it in next to her toaster oven, turned on the light, and slid the photo under it.

Details popped out as she focused the magnifying lens.

She scanned the entire photograph. She looked at the background, the embalming machine, the table, and the figure lying on it. Her cat, Robert, glided between the legs of our stools.

At last she looked up and said, "It's a fairly good job."

I set down my glass. "What do you mean?"

"Well, this guy's supposed to be dead, right? I mean, obviously this is a photo that's supposed to show us a corpse. The guy's lying on a morgue table and he looks like hell. Except for being so good-looking. Man, I could go for this guy in a big way."

I said nothing.

She pointed out various details. "He's got foundation on. His nose is in good focus as you can see, and that's how I know he's got foundation on, because I can't see the pores on his nose, they're filled with makeup. Whoever did the job didn't use stark white, they used about two shades paler than his skin—I'm guessing—and a finishing coat of white powder, which gives that true-to-death gray tone. Good job. They didn't stop at the jawline, they used it on his ears and neck and body as well—what we can see of it. The eyes are good, they darkened them not only beneath and on the lids, but all around—near the bridge of the nose and out beyond the corners. It looks pretty real. The lips, too, are well done, they're appropriately pale—don't they look cold?"

"Yes," I agreed.

"That's a good technique, most people don't realize how the blood leaves the lips after death."

I sighed heavily.

Yvonne looked at me. "What's the matter?"

"I just realized something. This guy could have makeup on, but he could actually be dead. You know what I mean? The plain fact that he's made up to look like a corpse doesn't mean he isn't one."

"Well," said Yvonne, her eyes gleaming above the magnifying lamp, "he might be a corpse now, I don't know. But he wasn't one when this photo was taken."

My pulse accelerated. "Why?"

She tucked a flowing auburn tress behind her ear. "When a person dies, their muscle tone goes away and the skin shrinks a little bit, hence the sunken-eye effect. We're seeing just the hint of beard stubble, but you'd expect pronounced stubble after death, at least before decomposition gets going. Once the maggots show up, all bets are off."

"Ew."

"Except here. See this?" She touched the tip of her pinkie fingernail to Richard Tenaway's upper lip. "See a little longer stubble?"

"Yeah."

"Yet it's not of a consistent length. But most of all look at this, see this sheen here, like a soft ridge just above his lip line?"

"Yeah?"

"There's a similar patch on his forehead." She looked at me. "Rita, his makeup is slipping."

"Well, so what?" I was thinking about the heat and humidity of Brazil. "It was really hot there," I said.

"Rita. What causes makeup to slip?"

It hit me. "Perspiration."

Yvonne handed me the picture and let out one of her operatic laughs. "No matter how hot it gets, corpses don't sweat."

EIGHTEEN

Daddy!" shouted Petey, accelerating fifteen feet across the living room, vaulting over our spanking Swedish sofa, to wrap himself around Jeff's legs.

It was nine-thirty Saturday morning, the beginning of Daddy weekend, and Jeff looked undrunk.

"Hey, big guy," he said in his fake hearty way that didn't fool Petey. However, the boy had no choice but to be crazy about him, given how boys want their dads, and especially given the treats and toys he invariably got showered with on Daddy weekends.

I looked at them. The contrast between the two couldn't have been starker: the energetic boy, every cell in his body living in the present moment, and the listless man, half of him focused resentfully on the past, the other half peering fearfully into the future.

Jeff's upper lip tightened with contempt—his signature

expression—as he glanced around the apartment. I was beginning to feel a shade more confident about being an independent human in this world, and he clearly sensed it and didn't like it.

"New furniture," he said.

"Yeah. IKEA." Besides the sofa, I'd gotten a new coffee table and two lamps. It had been a pleasure to drag the old stuff to the curb, where it sat for less than an hour before a scavenger loaded it into his truck. The Swedishness of the IKEA items coordinated nicely with my geometric rug and Daniel's paintings.

Jeff said, "I thought the credit card companies had cut you off."

Petey said, "Let's go!"

"Actually," I said calmly, "I paid cash for this stuff, and my credit card, singular, is paid off."

"Well, this place is still a dump." Right in front of the boy. Well, I was used to it.

In high school Jeff had been a baseball star and still looked it: solid body, broad nose, and wide-set blue eyes—he'd been handsome in a Kirk Gibson way, competitive and brash. But something was different. What was it? His good edge had been rounded while his bad edge had gotten sharper. He wore the same weekend clothes every thirtyish straight guy in L.A. wears, untucked polo shirt with the name of some resort in the Grand Tetons embroidered on the left breast, cargo shorts, sneakers.

I didn't respond to his comment, only made sure Petey had his backpack and Spider-Man jacket before he raced down the hall to the elevator and Jeff's waiting black Mustang.

I DRANK ANOTHER cup of coffee and ate some of the nutritious Swedish cereal I'd bought recently, I'm sure you can guess where.

Every time you buy something from IKEA, you have this pleasant Swedish feeling for a couple of weeks.

Last night, I called George Rowe as soon as I'd left Yvonne's. He was delighted to hear what she'd said. He came right over to pick up the picture and told me he'd be in touch. Before he left, he pulled a tiny windup dinosaur from his pocket and gave it to my son. Petey had never seen such a toy. The dinosaur ground its head up and down with a beensy fierce sound and waddled in a circle. I asked George how he happened to have a tiny windup dinosaur in his pocket.

"I knew you had a child, of course," he told me. "But I always carry toys." He looked shy and left.

Petey played with it for fifteen minutes, then put it in his backpack, where he kept his current favorites.

This Saturday morning, after seeing Petey safely off with Jeff, I went to meet with the defense team at Gary's offices. Gary and Mark Sharma were planning the cross-examination of one of the prosecution's expert witnesses, this one on toxicology. Mark was going to do the questioning. He said, in his liquid accent, "There's no way she can be certain as to what was in the baby's blood. I intend to be aggressive against her theories—all that drug half-life information, molecular bonding. I can confuse the jury by asking her about the percentage of Caucasians classified as poor metabolizers."

"Huh?" I said.

"What is your goal?" Gary asked, finger poised at his cheek.

"My goal is to get her to admit the test results could be evidence of two other drugs, bromazepam or chlordiazepoxide. The jury won't know what to think!" Mark drew in his cheeks to try to give the impression of dimples. Little chipmunk cheeks.

He had, I noticed, gotten his hair cut like Gary's—short on the sides, long and almost floppy on top, a boyish cut that made Gary look vigorous. But it only made Mark, with his chubby cheeks and poufy lips, look regressed. Also, he had bought loafers similar to the Allen-Edmonds pair Gary wore, only his weren't quite right. They were made of some exotic pebbled leather like manta ray or something, which was supposed to make him look individualistic. He didn't understand shoes.

Poor Mark. He wanted so badly to be like Gary, to show he had balls, to succeed. It was so clearly written all over him—the way he looked at Gary with those spaniel eyes, the way he knocked his ass out trying to please him.

He was so loyal and so clueless.

Gary sat thinking.

Almost without realizing it, I plunged in. "But Mark, that's just the problem: confusing the jury. We don't want to mix them up, we want them to know exactly what to think. They're looking to us to simplify and *tell* them what to think." I glanced at Gary, who had shifted his attention to me. "We should hit hard on the couple of shaky links in that chain of custody—the envelope seal, the fallibility of the lab—any lab—and that vial that got juggled around. And we should hit on the police not doing a toxicology on Eileen herself. If she seemed at all guilty, plus the fact that she told them she felt sick and sleepy when she got up, and they still didn't do a tox on her? All due respect, Mark, but we should leave the woman's theories alone. Drug dosage and toxicity—she's spent her entire professional life studying and developing those data tables, and she's going to be able to deflect our attacks fairly well. That just stands to reason. And the jury's going to think, well, hell, *she* didn't kill the kid, why are they giving her such a hard time? We'll look desperate."

Gary cleared this throat.

I finished, "But! If we focus on possible contamination or tampering, plus bad judgment by the police, that's something everybody understands. Everybody knows a simple mistake can change the course of history. The Watergate burglars left a piece of tape on the lock."

Gary and Mark were looking at me with totally different expressions. Gary's was a relaxed smile, while Mark had erased his self-satisfaction with that forced-blank expression people have when they're trying to hide disgust or fear. Mark so, so wanted to be a team player, but this was the best he could do. I pitied him, he was so harmless and transparent.

Gary said, "I'll handle the toxicology cross, Mark."

I watched Mark exhale and looked down at the tabletop, where he had untwisted a paper clip into a thin silver straight needlelike object. He rolled it on the table and looked up at me.

WHEN I OPENED the door for Petey that Sunday night, he was alone; I saw the elevator doors close in front of Jeff's impassive face at the end of the hall.

As I dumped Petey's dirty clothes from his backpack I asked him if he'd had a good weekend.

"Pretty good," he said, busy searching in the front pocket of his backpack. "We went to a lady's house. She has a pool and I went swimming with her dog."

"How nice."

"Her dog's name is Dolphin."

"She named her dog Dolphin?"

"They're a lot funner than you." He pulled out the windup

dinosaur George had given him, looked at it for a moment, touched its head with his forefinger, then put it down and drew out his ScoreLad to play the new superhero game Jeff had given him. With a look of satisfaction, he turned it on.

The device booped and *whick-whicked*.

I said, "Honey, that's not a nice thing to say. Wait a minute before you play with that. Did you stay overnight at the lady's house?"

He looked at me impatiently. "No, we came back to Daddy's with pizza. I had two Cokes!"

"My goodness, that's a lot of Coke. But you're a big boy. How did you sleep?"

"I don't know. I watched *Police Academy*. Daddy fell asleep on the floor."

"Oh? What did Daddy have to drink?"

"Barley soda!"

Barley soda. How creative.

"Bottles and bottles of it! They were lying *all over* the place."

Petey settled down to play his game and I unloaded the dishwasher and wished Jeff had approached life differently. He'd snowed the judge at the divorce, going to a two-week rehab and swearing he was clean for good. So on that basis he got Petey on weekends.

I thought about Jeff's capacity for beer and tequila, and I thought about his zooming black Mustang, and I tried not to think about the L.A. freeways and slamming metal and screams and blood and a cop snapping a sheet over a small corpse on the pavement.

VERY EARLY NEXT morning, I drove to the parking lot at Santa Monica and Rodeo where Gramma Gladys's spirit, or part of it, hung out.

174

"Gramma?" I asked, getting out of the car so I could feel any possible vibes better.

A man in a filthy rain jacket and bare feet wandered among the parked cars. I glanced around for one of Beverly Hills' plentiful security guards or cops, but saw none. The man veered toward the exit to Rodeo Drive.

After a minute a sparrow flew past my face, and I decided it was a sign Gramma Gladys was willing to listen, from deep within the spirit world.

To be polite, I made small talk about my parents and aunts in Wisconsin, then gushed out my worries.

"I'm doing the wrong thing in this weird job I took, I'm sure. What about the poor little dead girl at the center of it? But is she really at the center of it? All I want to do is make love to this guy, the main lawyer on the case. I told you about him. That's all I want to do—drink sake and go to bed with him. But moreover, oh, Gramma, it's so senseless. I'm in love with a married man, there's nobody else on the horizon, nobody else I want in the world, and Jeff's being a butthead. If anything happens to Petey, I'm going to have to kill Jeff *and* myself. Something bad's coming, I just know it. And I'm scared. Oatberger will never call me. I should go back to Durability and get community playhouse roles in *Blithe Spirit* and *Our Town*. And I'm mad, mad at myself. I feel sorry for Jeff because he's such a loser. Hah! A loser with a Mustang and a new girlfriend with a pool and a mermaid dog. I hate myself because I want to kick his ass, then wipe the blood off with a soft cloth. Maybe that makes me a loser too."

I stopped. The sounds of the cars flowing through the intersection swelled and crested and receded. I listened.

I felt Gramma say, *Just kick his ass and let him bleed! You gotta pro-tect the boy.*

"I know. But what if Petey turns out to be a butthead too? Think of some woman down the line, some son or daughter—"

Then you'll have to kick his ass too. How do you think your uncle Tim got straight? Because he wanted to? Hell no! I kicked his ass until he got it right! The turd-butt!

"You mean when he left Aunt Cecilia and the kids and went to Wyoming—"

Who do you think hunted him down and brought him back?

"Oh, my God."

I stopped at nothing!

"But I don't know exactly how to—"

Suddenly the filthy man was right behind me. He smelled as if he'd just climbed out of a bathtub filled with sewage and muscatel.

"Excuse me," he said, "but who are you talking to?"

I felt Gramma Gladys waft away.

"Myself," I told him angrily, "and you're interrupting."

"I beg your pardon," he said.

"Ah, the hell with it."

"Spare change?" He held out his hand, fingers slightly spread, as if he didn't expect any change to fall into it but might as well make the gesture.

As I dug a five-dollar bill from my purse I asked, "How did you get this way?"

He clenched the bill in his greasy sore-encrusted hand and an-swered, "What way?"

NINETEEN

The prosecution devoted that week, the trial's fifth, to the level of diazepam in Gabriella's body, as well as time-of-death estimates, the tedium of which I can't begin to describe. We were now nearing the end of February, and who knew how long Tracy Beck-Rubin was going to draw it out? I was amazed the jurors stayed awake, but I realized that Tracy Beck-Rubin must have figured that if she put a lot of juicy stuff out there first—like Eileen's supposedly scandalous lifestyle—they'd pay attention during the boring parts. However, when Gary got up to do the crosses, he was brilliant, impressing even the judge, who kept swatting down Beck-Rubin's objections.

Maybe Eileen really didn't kill her own daughter. Whether she did or didn't, there was something big in it for her if she kept her mouth shut. Did she know Richard had staged his death—did she help?—or was she handed, when she arrived in Ouro Prêto, the fake dead-Richard picture, a phony death certificate, and a closed casket she sent to the incinerator without opening? I wondered what George Rowe was up to.

Jeff came for Petey Saturday morning, and this time I could tell he'd been drinking from the look in his eyes (slight glaze plus avoidance of looking directly at me), plus I smelled gasoline on him. His same old stupid trick: he'd gas up the car and spill some on himself to mask booze or, when we were married, to cover up the bimbo at work's perfume.

I was furious. I accused him, he denied it, I refused to let Petey go with him, and then a dreadful thing happened.

He pushed past me, grabbed Petey around the waist, tucked him under his arm like a football, and stalked out.

I followed, yelling, "You are not—not!—going to do this!"

"Shut up!"

Petey yelled, "Wow!"

"Put him down, Jeff!"

"He's my son," he snarled, flinging open the stairwell door.

"Oh, yeah, what a loving father!" I shrieked.

Petey, at first amused by the whole thing, began to cry. I heard him wailing down the stairwell. None of the neighbors were dumb enough to come out of their apartments.

I was no match for Jeff in that state.

What would Gramma Gladys do? She would leave off shrieking, for one thing.

With a sudden calmness that amazed me, I returned to the apartment and called the police.

To make a long day short, Jeff got busted for drunk driving, I picked up Petey at the police station, and Jeff, I knew, would declare war.

PETEY WAS NOT in bed that Tuesday night when I got home. He and Daniel were busy in the living room, putting the finishing touches on a sort of Ewok village they'd built of furniture and beach towels. Daniel explained that it was Commander Butch Peterson's temporary quarters during the neutron wars. Petey was holed up in the command center, between the sofa and an armchair. Commander Butch Peterson was the name Petey, when under stress, liked to use as an alias. It was late, almost eleven, and something was wrong.

Daniel asked the commander to come out and meet with the emissary from the Teleflora System, but the chief wished the emissary to come to him. I looked at Daniel and received the cue to enter. The three of us huddled in the soft darkness, along with Benjamin Bunny, Petey's bedtime companion.

Daniel told me that when he picked up Petey after preschool, the police were there. Speaking quietly, he said, "The teachers took the class for an outing to the park, and one of the kids got grabbed by a stranger."

Petey said, "Ryan. Ryan. He's my friend."

"Ryan got grabbed?" Ryan was the same age as Petey to the month. When they played together they looked like brothers: same brown bowl haircut, same skinny-boy build.

"Yeah," said Daniel. "But fortunately one of the teachers and a guy who saw what was happening came running over and stopped it. They had to physically rip the kid away from this woman. His arm got dislocated, but they said he's going to be OK."

"Who was the woman?" I asked.

"I don't know," said Daniel. "It wasn't his mom or anybody he knew. Supposedly she drove off in a blue sports car. I couldn't find out anything more because the cops were talking to everybody. The teachers were calling all the parents, but it happened at the end of the day and I guess they hadn't gotten to you yet. This little guy here's fine."

Petey corrected, "Commander Peterson."

Daniel said, "I'm afraid Commander Peterson, although unhurt, got a little shook up by the incident."

Petey burst into tears and threw himself into my arms.

"Oh, honey, it's all right," I soothed, holding him close.

"I wish Ryan didn't come to school today," he sobbed. "Then it wouldn't of happened."

"Don't worry, honey, Ryan's arm will get better."

"But my Spider-Man jacket got torn."

"You tore your Spider-Man jacket? Where is it? Did you leave it at school?"

"I let Ryan wear it to the park and it got torn when the bad lady grabbed him."

It didn't strike Daniel, but my protective-mom adrenaline was surging and it rammed my gut like a paranoid rocket: the woman meant to snatch Petey! The boy in the Spider-Man jacket!

"Petey," I said, "did you know the bad lady?"

"No."

"Does Daddy's lady friend have a blue car?"

"I don't know."

I left the command center and called Petey's teacher at home, not caring what time it was. Moreover, as a mother herself I knew she'd be sleepless tonight anyway. Ms. Crayden told me the would-be abductress was white and wearing a headscarf and big sunglasses. One of the parents who saw the incident from across the park remembered seeing a similar blue sports car parked in front of the school that morning. "The police are looking into it," said Ms. Crayden in her reassuringly brisk voice. "Let's try not to worry."

I WAS SHOCKED, on Saturday morning, to hear a knock and see Jeff through the peephole.

I debated whether to open the door.

Jeff called, "Hey, Petey!" and pounded.

"Daddy!" cried Petey, scrambling for his backpack.

I opened the door. "I thought this weekend was canceled."

"Because of my arrest?" The curled lip.

"Yes." I figured he'd have gotten out on bail, but didn't expect him to have the gall to come here yet.

He slouched past me into the apartment and shut the door. I smelled neither liquor nor gasoline.

With smug triumph, Jeff explained that he'd called in a favor with a cop he knew and gotten the charge dropped.

"You can do that?" I asked like a naïve idiot.

"No, *you* can't do that," Jeff said, hitching up his cargo shorts. "Not everybody knows the right people. Come on, big guy."

I could only watch in horror as Petey raced to the door.

Jeff let him out to the corridor, where he thundered down to the elevator. Jeff said, "You have to let me take him. It's the law."

Venomously, I said, "If you let anything happen to him, I'll kill you."

Jeff laughed and slammed the door.

I wandered vaguely around the apartment, went for a walk, came back, drove to Gary's office, where only Mark Sharma and Steve Calhoun were working, went home, vacuumed, looked at Trial TV for a while. They were doing a full-saturation job on the Tenaway trial, in spite of not having video feed from the courtroom. Judge Davenport hated TV cameras in courtrooms and wasn't about to allow one in his, no matter how pruriently interested America was. It was odd to watch it all, occasionally catching a flash of myself in the background of a shot of Gary striding toward the press in the corridor or courtyard. I'd managed to keep my face away from the photographers, not that I cared all that much by this point. The whole thing was just so surreal. I turned the TV off.

I tried to read Nicola Glassmore's latest novel, this one about a twelve-year-old girl who runs away from an abusive poverty-stricken broken home and just as she's about to die from hypothermia gets adopted by a coven of crones in the woods who teach her the ancient ways of being kind to the earth. In turn, she uses her youthful agility to procure cliff-growing herbs for their healing potions. Usually I enjoy Nicola Glassmore's books—I love all those Empowerment Of The Weak themes she uses—but this one I couldn't get into.

The phone rang and I hoped it was Daniel, but I guess even he needed a break from Planet Petey-Rita. The person on the other end was a compassionate-sounding woman who said she knew who I was, whatever that meant. "My name is Janet," she said. "I want to see you."

"Uh, what about?" Holding the cordless, I hip-shoved the armchair, which hadn't quite gotten back into place after the dismantling of the command center.

"You and your little boy are in danger, and I can tell you why. And what to do about it," she added.

"Is this a joke?"

"No joke, Rita Farmer."

"Does this have something to do with Jeff? Is he there? Put him on."

"Meet me at the Starbucks on Santa Monica at La Brea."

"Well—oh, for God's sake!"

"Let's just be low-key."

Gramma Gladys would go find out what the hell this was about.

"OK," I said. "When?"

"I'm here now."

AT THE STARBUCKS a brunette in a flare-collared yellow top motioned to me and I joined her at her table on the plaza. She was smoking a cigarette in the sunshine and sipping from a frothy iced beverage, which competed for table space with her large pink purse. I wanted nothing to drink.

The main thing I noticed about Janet was her distracting amount of jewelry, which reminded me of the stuff Eileen had worn during her police interview. It had to be costume jewelry, though; this woman was no Tenaway. Janet, while pretty, looked hard-bitten and older than she probably was. Cheap, especially with that vinyl purse. A little thick in the body. Still, she hadn't lost all the juice of youth yet. You know how there's a litheness about a younger person that doesn't go away even if her face betrays time spent on the streets, or too many nights alone with a bottle or needle?

She told me a wild story.

"Eileen Tenaway is insane," she began bluntly. "She's got a friend trying to intimidate you and other people, including I myself." Her voice was one of those top-of-the-throat ones, not exactly high-pitched, but childlike and intense. It cut through the ambient clinks and fizzles and hipster music coming from the café, not to mention the engines zooming along Santa Monica. "You ask why? Because Eileen and Richard embezzled money and stuff from Gemini. They smuggled and stole and covered it up, and they cheated a bunch of people out of money, again including I myself." She tugged on the sleeve of her smooth yellow top, something from Ellen Tracy, I thought. It was nicer than the purse.

Trying to follow, I said, "Yeah, but what does—"

"Now she's afraid. She *wants* to be convicted of killing her child, that way she'll be in prison, safe from the people she's cheated." She looked at me from under her eyebrows as if daring me to believe her. "All of whom are very angry."

"Including you yourself."

"Yes."

A Starbucks employee came out to us and reluctantly said, "I have to ask you to stop smoking. We're no-smoking."

"But we're outdoors," Janet said. "I've smoked here before."

"It doesn't make any difference," said the black-aproned barista, clearly uncomfortable with the nicotine-squad thing.

"OK, I'll put it out," said Janet, not putting out her cigarette.

That was enough for the barista, who went back inside. Janet kept smoking and talking. This Starbucks is attached to the nicest Target shopping center you've ever seen. Dozens of Hollywood transsexuals are addicted to shopping here. I noticed one old grim one sitting in a purple dirndl skirt and a tight scoop-neck top with a Starbucks Venti and three teddy bears lined up facing him at his table. At first glance I thought he was trying to sell the bears, but then I realized they were keeping him company. A hard breeze eddied around the plaza, shifting, lashing the palms and baby jacarandas in their urban pots.

Janet was making no sense, but I listened. At one point she saw me looking at her gems and said, "Oh, this is nothing. You should see."

I asked, "Why did you call me and how did you get my number?"

"You're near to Eileen, and she's got something I want."

I studied her face. "Have I seen you in the courtroom?"

She didn't answer.

I said, "Well, if you want access to Eileen, why aren't you talking to Gary Kwan? Or just go to the jail and ask to see her."

"He won't return my calls. And she wouldn't see me, no way. Anyhow, it doesn't matter now that I've got you."

"You don't 'have me.' Who gave you my home number, anyway?"

"Just forget that, OK? For now, just forget that, OK?"

I shook my head. "What does this have to do with my son? This danger you're talking about."

Another customer, two tables away, got up and stood in front of us. We looked up.

"You're polluting my environment," he said with cold pissiness. He wore a polo shirt that said Coppermill Glen or something and cargo shorts. Considering the carbon monoxide engulfing us from La Brea and Santa Monica, I thought his anger amusing.

"Well, my friend, fuck off," said Janet in an elfin voice. His face flushed. He looked at me and I stopped smiling and stared at the brick pavement.

185

Janet shook out another Benson & Hedges from her pack on the table and lit it from the first.

"You stop smoking," the man commanded, as he might speak to an annoying dog. "It's against the law!"

"I have a personal arrangement with the government," said Janet.

"You do not!"

"Call a cop on me, then, Rambo," she said, flicking her little finger at the man as if he were a flake of pastry. "I'm sure one will come running."

The man looked as if he might try to snatch her cigarettes away, but he thought better of it and stomped away, saying loudly, "Rude bitch won't put her cigarette out." Other customers glanced over indifferently.

Janet turned back to me. "You have to understand there are forces beyond your scope. If you get to know me, you'll see that I'm a very deep thinker. I have certain connections. You are valuable to certain people. I've got a deal for you. Want to hear it?"

"Yeah, sure." A bad feeling crept into my stomach. *Connections.*

"Get Eileen to tell you where a certain key is. Then you tell me where it is, and if I find it, there will be no trouble for you and your boy."

I couldn't believe this. I managed to say, "That's not a deal, that's a threat. You're saying something will happen to Petey or me if I don't get some key for you, right? You're threatening me. What's this key to?"

Janet sipped her cold latte or whatever the hell it was. "Look, I'll cut you in and it'll be a real deal. The key is to a storage locker. Inside the locker's everything Richard Tenaway stole from Gemini. Stones and cash. There's millions of dollars' worth of stuff in there. I think about fifteen million's worth. You should see!" The look in her eyes was penetrating yet blurry, exactly like I'd seen in my uncle Fritz just before he burned the barn and got diagnosed schizophrenic.

I almost wanted to talk to her about her problems, whatever they really were. But at that point I had too many people with problems in my life.

"Well, have you seen it?" I asked.

"In a way," she responded, the same screwy look in her eyes.

So I got up, as Gramma Gladys would do right about now. "That's complete bullshit," I said, and walked away.

"Wait!" called Janet, following. "Think it over. It's just you and me, Rita." She seized my arm in a surprisingly strong grip.

I turned on her, flinging her arm away. She held her hand up beseechingly. "You're nuts," I told her. "You just made up the whole thing to try to get money from me somehow."

Janet's neck slumped and she stared at her shoes, a pair of sad sulfur-yellow Mary Janes. People walked by in their detached city way. I left her standing there in the sunshine and went to my car, which I'd parked two blocks down. Yet, just like my uncle, there was something sympathetic and lost about Janet. I almost liked her.

I circled the block to go the other way on Santa Monica. As I pulled up to the light I saw Janet unlock a royal-blue Audi parked on the side street. Blue sports car! I followed her, trying to see the license plate, but a bus cut me off. When I got around it she was gone.

TWENTY

Rita, I can hardly understand you, you're talking so fast," said Gary. "You're driving now? For God's sake hang up and come over to the office."

In the cool safety of Kwan & Associates, which this Saturday afternoon was deserted except for his dazzling presence, I did calm down. I started over about Ryan's near-abduction while wearing Petey's jacket, then my strange meeting with Janet.

"So should I call the police? I mean, they could look into . . . all this."

Gary set his square shoulders back on his little office sofa, his unlogoed silk polo shirt draping glossily over his muscles. I had the feeling he wouldn't wear cargo shorts if his life depended on it. He said, "You could call them, certainly, but I'm not sure exactly what you'd tell them, nor what you'd expect them to do.

You've already said this Janet didn't fit the description of the kidnapper—"

"Only in that the teacher said her hair was blond, and this Janet's hair was brown. There are wigs."

"OK, there are wigs but the point is this: Los Angeles is full of crazies, every city is. They come out of the woodwork when they smell excitement and money. You don't know how many screwballs have written letters to me—*and* to Eileen, *and* the police, *and* the DA. False tips, pleas for money, people wanting to get involved somehow. Psychics. Mind-readers. Lip-readers. Reward-seekers. Amateur detectives. They all watch Trial TV. As disturbing as it is, it's nothing to worry about. You should have just hung up on this woman in the first place."

"Except she knew my name and unlisted phone number."

"Rita, listen to me." He grasped my arm firmly, and my diaphragm, guts, and pelvic organs fibrillated as one. Looking into my eyes in an incredibly reassuring way, he said, "There is nothing to worry about. This incident in the park where the little boy's arm got hurt—you weren't there, you have no idea whether the woman was actually trying to abduct him or what. For all you know, there was a misunderstanding between that kid and her kid, or something, and the teachers blew it out of proportion. Even if it was an attempted abduction, *they didn't take your kid!* It was a coincidence."

I said, "But what about the blue sports car?"

"There are thousands of blue sports cars in Los Angeles. You don't even have a license number. Forget it. You'll never hear from her again. You were right to walk away. If Tenaway had stashed a bunch of loot from his company, do you think he'd talk about it to some nut wandering the streets? Do you think he'd put it in a storage locker instead of an offshore account?" Gary's powers of reason calmed me. He concluded, "But go ahead and ask Eileen, if you want to, about this storage locker key. I guarantee she won't know what the hell you're talking about."

"OK. OK."

He released my arm almost caressingly. "I too know the power of parental paranoia." He smiled, as did I.

We sat in silence for a minute, during which in my mind's eye I saw Gary and me coming home to our lovely home after a long day in court and on the soundstage, respectively. I envisioned us cooking a gourmet dinner of organic salmon and heirloom pasta while Petey and Jade read their schoolbooks and practiced their dulcimers or looked at plant specimens under their microscope which they share without quarrel. I saw us taking family vacations to offbeat yet beautiful places like the Gaspe Peninsula or Kiev. If hard times ever hit, we'd tough them out together.

Maybe it was the stress, or maybe my heart was fed up with being Miz Nice Guy, but at any rate I still can't believe what I did next, which was to start unbuttoning my blouse while holding Gary's eyes with mine.

Slowly, his jaw dropped. He turned his head toward the door. "Rita, please."

"Please what?" I let my blouse fall from my shoulders, revealing my cognac lace Victoria's Secret bra and my acreage of unblemished skin above it.

His profile was beautiful. "Stop this and pull your shirt back on."

I didn't. I knew I was making an irrevocable idiot of myself, but something propelled me forward. Something? Yeah, hormones, for God's sake. I hadn't had a man in so long I'd practically forgotten how intercourse felt. Gary was so achingly right for me that somehow, at this moment, I was able to smush down every bit of good sense I was born with. "But," I said in a smoky voice, trying to channel Ava Gardner in something like *Mogambo,* "I was just getting started. Don't you—"

"Rita, come on."

"Jacqueline doesn't have to find out."

"My God, Rita."

"Gary, admit it: you want to. Don't you?"

He scrubbed his face with an open hand. "Rita, there's something I—"

"No, Gary," I interrupted firmly. "This time I get to talk first."

"Oh, no."

"I love you, Gary."

"Rita, I—"

Goddamn it, when Gramma Gladys wanted something, she went after it.

"You've stolen my heart," I told him softly, "and it's time I said so. There is not one thing about you that's not perfect. You're attractive, you're brilliant, you're brave." I saw him shaking his head no, no. I pressed on, "You're a great daddy, yes, you are, Jade adores you—and I know I'm being insane here. I know it. I have no idea about yours and Jacqueline's intimate life, but—"

"Rita, I really need to—"

"And I'm sure she's wonderful and everything, but—"

"*Rita!*"

"Please, Gary! I'm not asking you to leave your family." My own lie stopped me for a millisecond. "To be honest, I *would* like you to leave Jacqueline. Take Jade and set up housekeeping with Petey and me. That's my dream, OK? But at the moment all I'm asking is for you to—well—let me love you too."

He took a deep breath. "Are you finished?"

I didn't want to stop, because I didn't want to hear what he was going to say. "You're what my Gramma Gladys would call a man of intuition."

"I'm—"

"You're kind."

"I'm—"

"You're generous."

"I'm—"

He paused, and so, at last, did I.

"I'm gay," he said.

WHEN I COULD speak again, I murmured, "You're kidding."

"No." His eyes met mine unflinchingly now, and his voice dropped. "I figured it out a long time ago. I got married anyway. Funny, I didn't think I wanted a child. But we had one, and she's wonderful. I really thought I could—you know. Make it work."

Slowly, looking at nothing, I buttoned my blouse.

"I'm sorry, Rita."

My chest felt like it had been kicked by a horse. "Gary, I can't believe it."

"It's true." He looked at me steadily.

"Well," I said, "you sure can drop the bomb."

"Well!" he replied. "I was under some fairly heavy fire, wasn't I?"

I laughed weakly.

"I considered lying, but I—I feel I can talk to you. Actually, I feel quite warmly toward you, I'm sure that's what you felt. If I were straight, you know—"

"OH, GOD, that hurts, Gary. *Missed by that much*." I gripped my temple. "I can't tell you how many times I've heard that."

"I'm just being honest, Rita. You feel safe with me, I feel safe with you. I don't really talk about this."

We paused, made coffee, and talked for more than an hour. The coffee aroma filled the air with comfort.

I was thunderstruck, of course, and more hideously embarrassed than I'd ever been in my life. Naturally I didn't blame myself. I wanted only to throw all the office furniture through the window, then go home and cry. I forced myself to be low-key and accepting. Somehow I was able to hold my temper and be a listening ear for Gary that afternoon without wanting to commit suicide.

He told me he was tremendously relieved to be able to talk about it. He said he trusted me completely, which, again, made me feel both great and horrible.

I said, "Well, I have to ask, what's the situation with Jacqueline? Is she in denial?"

"Totally. I've hinted at it, but she won't see it yet, and frankly, I don't want to be blunt about it. I know that's dishonest. I'm thinking of Jade. I'm living a double life."

"You mean you—"

"No, no, I'm not seeing anyone. Hell, I have no time these days. But as you saw when she dropped in the other evening, Jacqueline has a subsurface suspicion that something's wrong, but she can't bring herself to figure it out."

"Seems like you ought to just tell her and let the chips fall."

"I will. But . . . I'm . . . I'm afraid!" His eyes brimmed up and his splendid chest heaved with sorrow. "I fought it all my life. I fell in love with boys at school, but ran from them in shame. I dated girls. Japanese families aren't big on diversity. I feared my own culture. And I was warped by it. My ancestors ought to punish me for saying that so harshly. I was so glad to be in America. Still, I suppressed my feelings for years—quite successfully! When Jacqueline agreed to marry me, I thought I'd beaten it. How can a married man be gay?" He waited for me to comment.

"That was pretty dumb, Gary."

"Can you imagine I thought such a thing?"

He talked on, telling me that since Jade was born he'd only acted on his feelings with one wonderful guy. They'd met by chance, had a passionate affair, but the man couldn't take Gary's closeted lifestyle.

Because of course Gary's celebrity was a problem. How many big-time defendants want a known homosexual defending them in the courtroom? How many jurors would have a hidden prejudice against a fag attorney?

"When this trial is over, Rita, I swear I'll handle it with Jacqueline. I've been a deceitful bastard too long."

"Well jeez, Gary, you don't have to be St. Augustine about it."

"When you were telling me how wonderful I am, it made me sick to my stomach." He dropped his head into his hands. "I hate to break up my family," he almost sobbed. "I feel that I'd find the courage to do what I have to do if I could just meet up with a good man again."

I touched his shoulder, the shoulder I would never think of in the same way again. "You know, there are other options. Maybe Jacqueline wouldn't mind if you—"

"She'd mind. Believe me, she'd mind."

Well, it was a mighty fine fantasy while it lasted.

TWENTY-ONE

George Rowe carried toys wherever he went because everyone likes them. The sudden appearance of a toy makes people relax and smile. With a toy, a child can be bribed to stop crying and go away, or climb through a window and unlatch a door, or come back tomorrow with something from Daddy's workshop. Also, tossing a kite into the air and flying it can be a distraction, if you need one.

The yo-yos and chess set had, by the skin of their teeth, helped with the tough boys in the grotto. However, the schoolgirl forger, Maria Helena, was not a child anymore, especially given her line of work, and it was work.

"Her father, he taught her the business of false documents," explained Raimundo as he and Rowe hiked through the dark colonial town as night fell. "She is sixteen years old." Rowe had been away in America for more than a month, and now he was back. Raimundo had found out some things in the meantime.

Ouro Prêto was especially beautiful in the evening, when the wind turned soft and the houses and cantinas threw their sparks of light over the hills. It was as beautiful as San Francisco, Rowe thought, his favorite city. He liked to drive the six hours from Los Angeles to San Francisco just for overnight. He would hike the headlands, glorying in the cool breezes, then eat spaghetti in North Beach with a couple of bail bondsmen and their wives, old friends.

Raimundo, in his questioning Portuguese accent, said, "Her father, he is in the prison now because he hoped he would do better to counterfeit American money. But—he found too much competition. Too much big fishs." Raimundo said "hoped" in two soft syllables, *hope-et*.

"I see," said Rowe.

This evening Raimundo wore his canvas hat and carried a stout walking staff, swinging it along with only a tiny tap as it hit the road. "He has two sons, worthless bastards who suck the money Maria Helena makes."

"Two sons. They live there?"

"Yes, but they are drunks. Her mother, she sits in the wheelchair from polio."

"I see," said Rowe. "Dog?"

"No dog. Dogs are not a problem in any case." Raimundo pointed with his wiry brown arm. "There is the house."

"At the foot of the hill?"

"Soon the brothers will be drunk for the night. They have television. The mother, she can not go down steps. There is a room below the ground. If I made photography I would build the darkroom there."

"A cellar?"

"Yes. I have seen light come through a hole in the wall."

"How big is the hole?"

Raimundo held his thumb and forefinger a few inches apart and shook his head. "Small. Only for air."

"A vent?"

"A vent."

Rowe said, "You tried to get her to talk to you again?"

"Once. No good. She is very like wolf."

"You mean a fox?"

"No, I mean wolf."

They walked on.

Raimundo said, "I told my granddaughter where Maria Helena goes with her friends. I gave her one bottle of rum to take to there tonight, also DVD of American movie called *Shred the Finger*."

"Raimundo!" exclaimed Rowe, pleased at the ingenuity yet disconcerted, remembering the meek girl he'd met that first night at dinner. He didn't expect she'd fit in to the delinquent crowd.

"My granddaughter, she thinks she can keep Maria Helena away until eleven o'clock." He glanced sideways at Rowe. "She has my blood. More brave than you think."

Rowe didn't like to involve more people than absolutely necessary, but he didn't have much choice at this point.

"We will tunnel in," announced Raimundo.

"*What?*"

"Best way," said his companion confidently. "You will see."

"I thought we'd just knock on the door and do the police detective thing."

"The family, they are on guard. The mother will not open the door. Even if so, why let strangers in to look in her house? Too risky. The brothers? They will rise up if we make trouble. Who knows?"

Rowe had already told Raimundo he did not want to use force or terror on Maria Helena or her family. "They'll hear us," he said. "And we don't even have any tools."

"You will see."

Flanking Maria Helena's house on one side was a neighboring home, on the other a steep bank down to another street. The front windows glowed golden, spilling lamplight in a soft pool toward the road. Rowe saw a flickering TV screen behind the thin curtains. The windows were open.

They crept up to the side of the house next to the embankment. The walls were masonry, like all the other houses in town, painted white, with the same cheerful red tile roof. Raimundo chose a spot behind a bush and between the two windows— thankfully dark—that overlooked the bank. He began scraping the rocky soil away with his staff. Only now did Rowe notice how sharp the staff's point was. After Raimundo had loosened half a bushel's worth of dirt, he set down the staff and drew two pairs of leather work gloves from his pocket. He put on a pair and handed the other to Rowe.

"Help me," he directed in a whisper, and the two men got down on their knees and scraped the dirt away by hand. A half moon, which had begun to glow at sunset, helped them to see.

So it went: Raimundo would disrupt the dirt with his stick, and they would paw it away from the house's foundation. The work went fast. Raimundo manipulated the stick in the soil expertly, prying up rocks, lancing the sharp end down again into the dry hole, loosening dirt by the bucket's worth every few seconds.

Rowe marveled at the low-tech efficiency of it. Without metal tools striking rock, and with the night breeze riffling the trees, their work was almost noiseless. Raimundo whispered with a smile, "This is how a garimpeiro pays back another who has wronged him."

Rowe didn't know exactly what that meant, but Raimundo had the look of a hound on the scent of a rabbit. Rowe felt the same way, his breath coming deep, his nerves taut. More conversation would be foolish.

The predominant trees, whatever they were, gave off a resinous smell after the day's heat.

Rowe supposed the cellar would have a dirt floor, and he was right. Raimundo dug down about seven feet, came to the end of the stone block foundation, then started going horizontally. He filled his hat with dirt and rocks, which he tossed up to the surface. Rowe kept the opening clear. He wondered whether any of the stones they were digging up were topazes or emeralds.

At last Raimundo slithered feet-first into the tunnel. Just before his head disappeared, he whispered, "Wait."

Rowe strained his eyes trying to see the dark bottom of the hole. A rat or a night bird rustled leaf litter nearby. He paid no attention. His whole nervous system was attuned to that hole.

He wondered what he would find in Maria Helena's workroom. Practically anything would do, he thought. He would carry away some incriminating things, perhaps ID blanks or stolen passports, or perhaps spoiled pieces thrown into a bin, or computer disks. Then he would approach Maria Helena in some neutral public place for a quiet discussion. If he were to find copies of the documents she might have made for Tenaway, so much the better, but he judged she was probably too careful for that.

He felt a tap on his shoulder.

Biting back a grunt of panic he whirled, already calming himself, prepared to find Raimundo laughing at him silently, having magically found his way out some other way.

Instead he was confronted by the angry countenance of Maria Helena herself. She hissed at him in Portuguese, but did not scream. Though her eyes were in shadow, he could just make them out. He detected absolutely no fear in them. She seemed to want to be as quiet about this extraordinary intrusion as he did. He could tell she recognized him from the grotto.

He collected himself almost instantly. He kicked a spurt of dirt quickly into the hole to attract Raimundo's attention. He pointed to his chest, then to the hole, then further with the same finger, then held up one finger, to indicate an accomplice. He did not want her to be surprised by Raimundo.

The girl was fierce and amused in equal parts. Rowe saw something in her eyes, as if she were seeing the dawning of some special opportunity.

Raimundo appeared, said, "Euh!" then spoke to her in Portuguese. She stood in the deepening darkness with her hands on her hips, then spoke to Raimundo and walked into the house.

"Follow me," said Raimundo, sliding down the hole again.

Rowe's first instinct was not to go into a situation he could not quickly escape from. But he had perceived that amusement in Maria Helena's face, as well as in the way she tilted her hips, so he took the risk.

Inside the cellar they brushed themselves off. Raimundo found a light switch, and Maria Helena descended the steps, closing the upstairs door carefully behind her. They spoke in low voices.

The cellar, capable of being blacked out as a darkroom, was crammed with all sorts of equipment—scanners, a computer, a small hand-driven press, paper supplies, plastic film, a stereo microscope, bottles of dye, and a strongbox that looked like it fell off a pirate ship three hundred years ago. The place smelled of the sharp chemicals of photographic processing.

A few photographs had been clipped to a wire strung across a corner. They were pictures of people at a festival, middle-aged Brazilian moms and dads from the working class, you could tell from their clothing, who had gotten caught up in the spirit of celebration. They looked violent, almost feral, dancing or throwing back a drink, inadvertently baring their teeth and gums in uninhibited joy. Maria Helena, evidently, had an eye for the decisive moment.

The girl perched herself on a worktable, Raimundo threw a leg over the one straight chair in the place, and Rowe squatted in the center of the room beneath the bare bulb.

Maria Helena's face was classically oval, like the waitress Raimundo had pinched in the café, with a longish nose and peaked upper lip. The nose gave her face an arrogance beyond what showed in her eyes. Her body, Rowe perceived, was unspoiled by neurosis; no anorexia, no tight posture. She was one of those rare humans with unconditional self-confidence.

She spoke, and Raimundo said in English, "She understands what you want. She will tell you what *she* wants. We will find no thing here. She says if you threaten her you will not get what you want."

Rowe asked Raimundo, "Where is your granddaughter?"

"Maria Helena says she made her go home." He looked crest-fallen.

"Ask her what she wants."

He did, and as she spoke, Raimundo burst out laughing. "She wants to go to the film school in United States!"

Rowe did not smile.

"She wants to make film. Films," he corrected himself. "About the way people really are, deep in the heart!"

The girl spoke at angry length, swinging one sandal-clad foot in a short arc.

Raimundo, chastened, told Rowe, "She wants to get away from the black market. She is more smart, I see, than her father. She does not want to live like this, work in secret. Good pay, but dangerous. She has some money in the bank she wants to give to her mother. Then she wants to go to America with ten thousand new dollars. From you! Ha! Ten thousand dollars. My friend, you must not—"

The girl spoke again. "I am learning English. Not good yet."

"Oh," said Rowe.

"I have travel papers," said Maria Helena.

"I bet you do," said Rowe, glancing around her factory. "How come you use old photography—not digital?"

Slowly, she said, "Old . . . ? Ah! Because I can use thick paper. More thicker than for digital. Better for making emboss in pass-port." Lifting her head proudly, she added, "I do by hand, under microscope."

"I have to tell you, film school's going to cost more than ten thousand dollars."

She said, "I get to America, I get work. No problem." She ges-tured to one of her photographs of the revelers. "The world is in that eye. That mouth. That foot. I want to find it. All of time is in one thing."

"Your English is better than you think," Rowe told her.

THE NEXT MORNING the three met in town at the bank Maria Helena had named. She watched as Rowe wrote out directions for a wire transfer from his Fenco account. She would not agree to half now, half later. "All now," she said coolly, as if certain her luck had finally changed.

Rowe found himself helplessly charmed by this child racketeer. The money, though a huge chunk out of his expenses for this job, was all right. If he didn't spend it here and now, he might lose Tenaway entirely. Raimundo struggled to manage his shock that Rowe would hand over so much money to a little girl.

When the bank manager showed her the new balance in her account, they went to a café. The manager looked after them as they went out. Rowe had slipped him two hundred to keep his thoughts to himself. Rowe and Raimundo wore clean clothes and Raimundo had on a newer, city-type straw hat. At the café they ordered the sweet, boiling-hot coffee Brazilians love, bread, and soft white cheese that Raimundo said was a local specialty. It tasted good, but Rowe only took two bites; he was too keyed up.

Maria Helena spoke at length about Richard Tenaway, in Portuguese. The words poured out; she did not want to hesitate to find English ones, she explained through Raimundo.

Her story was as simple and heartbreaking as the landscape of Minas Gerais on a foggy morning.

"I am smart but this man, he made me stupid," she began, and Rowe saw that, for her, that was the alpha and the omega of it.

Tenaway, last summer, had found her through the seedy conduits of the town's after-hours taverns. He had wanted a new U.S. passport, and she agreed to supply it, for three thousand dollars.

Her method for American passports, which were next to impossible to forge from scratch, was to zero in on a tourist who resembled her client, and who planned to stay in Brazil for at least a week. She would get a look at the tourist's passport, briefly stealing it if need be to make a quick photocopy. She was good at lifting wallets from day bags, and she had an arrangement with maids at certain hotels. But she would return the passport so it wouldn't be missed. She would go to her studio and fabricate a replica of it that would fool neither a customs officer nor any government's computer system. That was not the point; once the replica was exchanged for the real—during another secret visit—the tourist would believe he had his passport up until the moment he tried to use it.

Meanwhile, the original, perfect passport would have been used by Maria Helena's client, then destroyed once past the border. This method guaranteed smooth transit for the client. But all this spying and thieving were risky. She was beginning to use some of the rough boys of Ouro Prêto to help her. But that was risky too.

When she delivered Tenaway's new passport to him, he rejected it—the owner of the passport was not nearly as handsome as he. He insisted Maria Helena take a photograph of him and replace it in the passport.

Maria Helena had had to explain to him how one ought to change one's appearance for a border crossing anyway—one should use hair coloring, new glasses, and makeup to alter the contours of the face. She teased him that he would have to make himself ugly to be successfully anonymous.

One thing led to another, and Tenaway took Maria Helena to a fine hotel in Belo Horizonte, where no one would know them. With an expressionlessness that Rowe recognized as buried agony, she told Rowe and Raimundo she had been a virgin. She had known enough to reject the dopey boys of Ouro Prêto for all the years of her life. Rowe felt a physical pang at that *all the years of her life*—for she would have been only fifteen then.

She gave herself to Tenaway, swept into bad judgment by his charm, his sophistication, his beauty, his promises. She called him Ricardo. They stayed at the hotel three nights in a row. She tried to explain that she had thought men's promises could only be believed if they could deliver on them, and Tenaway clearly had the means to do so. He had promised to enroll her in film school in the U.S. He had pledged her his body, there in the high-priced hotel room with chocolates and lilies.

There had been a woman around him at first, Maria Helena knew, because she could smell her on him, but the second night she could not, and she supposed the woman, whom she never saw, had gone away. That night she noticed bruises on Tenaway's knuckles but immediately forgot them as he told her about UCLA and Hollywood and sailboats and the rest of the horseshit a guy like that would ladle to an underage girl.

He was an important person, and he made her feel important too. He taught her about sex, though she had been studying it in magazines and on the Internet. She lowered her eyes as she talked about this, but seemed determined to get it all out. "Ricardo" had introduced her to light bondage, which she found to be intensely pleasurable.

Rowe wiped his face with his handkerchief.

Still not looking up, Maria Helena said in English, "For ten thousand dollars I tell you everything, I think. You are good men, I see now."

Rowe and Raimundo exchanged glances.

Resuming her narrative in Portuguese, she told them that on the fourth morning of their affair Tenaway asked her to bring her camera and go with him to a funeral home, where he had bribed a mortician's helper. There they staged the photo Eileen Tenaway had brought back from Brazil along with the pot of cremated ashes. The mortician's helper applied the makeup, laughing all the while at the reversal of making a live man look dead.

Wiping off the makeup, Tenaway explained that he would take Maria Helena away the next day. She packed her satchel, said goodbye to her family, and rode the bus to the São Paulo airport. He, of course, never showed.

Two days later she returned home, narrowly in time to stop her brothers from convincing their mother to empty the bank account Maria Helena had signed over to her. At the time there were seventy thousand reals in the account, equaling perhaps thirty thousand American dollars.

The brothers knew that Maria Helena's boyfriend, whoever he was, must have thrown her over, and they jeered at her. The mother had intuited everything and was already crying. She had not tried to prevent Maria Helena from leaving, because while she benefited from her daughter's work as a forger, she knew Maria Helena too would end up in jail unless she got away. At that point, Maria Helena had not the courage to go to America by herself. But now she was sixteen, a grown woman, ready to make her way in the big world.

She sipped her coffee and spread some more cheese on a round of bread. She ate the bread with the cheese.

Rowe spent a moment imagining how it would feel to knock Richard Tenaway to the ground, flip him onto his stomach, steady him by planting a shoe on his back, pull up his head by his wavy pretty hair, and slit his throat wide open.

Old Raimundo scraped his chair and ordered a brandy for himself. His eyes showed that he was mentally transposing his own granddaughter into Maria Helena's place. He gnawed his lips. Rowe asked for more coffee and watched the girl eat. Her table manners were nice.

Rowe took a Hacky Sack from his pocket and tossed it back and forth in his hands.

Maria Helena's eyes lit up.

He handed her the toy, and she jumped up from the table, dropped the little soft sphere, caught it with her foot, then with a hop tossed it to her other foot, kicked it up, caught it in her hand, and sat down again, laughing.

Rowe said, "Where do you think he went?"

TWENTY-TWO

I mourned Gary. I mourned the loss of the possibility of sex with him. I grieved for the stupid fantasy I'd built up about our lives and children merging. In the interstices, thoughts of tiny Gabriella kept coming at me. I wondered whether the dress she wore in the studio portraits had been her favorite garment, or whether perhaps she preferred a pair of red corduroy overalls. Sometimes, reading tales of unimaginable violence in the newspapers, I decided Gabriella had been a lucky child—she merely went to sleep—forever—had not been raped, strangled, mutilated. Could never be.

When Jeff brought Petey home Sunday night, he acted all confrontational, which meant puffed chest, lowered lids—you know that smug thing?—and theories as to why the world is not a perfect place.

"You're just a plain old traditional bad mother," he informed me as Petey dashed to his bedroom to play with whatever the hell new game Jeff had bought him for his ScoreLad. "He seems afraid of something. Maybe it's that fag you've got for a babysitter. And look at this neighborhood, huh? You call this safe?"

"Lay off Daniel. What the hell are you talking about?" Discreetly, I whiffed the air for tequila or petroleum. He seemed straight, but I couldn't be sure.

"Those characters hanging around the park."

"You mean the old guys?"

The elderly men who monopolized the picnic tables played checkers and cards for money and were supposed to be kingpins in the Russian mafia. People said so, but I didn't think it was a problem. Petey would one day be old enough to go there by himself. The men never talked to any kids. Once in a while you'd see a couple of druggies sitting in the dirt, but they kept to themselves.

Jeff scuffed the edge of his Nike sneaker on the rug, leaving a dirty line. "Obviously you can't even afford a decent apartment for my son, even with all the child support I pay. What happens to all my money, besides buying shitty furniture? Do you snort it up your nose?"

"Jeff, what?"

As I think I've mentioned, he was a high-level accountant (practically CFO!) for a fancy restaurant chain. So fancy, in fact, they don't even call it anything so vulgar as a *chain,* no, they call it a *collection* of restaurants.

He just stood there, so I said, "Your income is great, Jeff. And I'm glad you pay your child support on time. But guess what? I've been getting a little work. We're doing all right. Petey might be a little anxious right now," I conceded, "but—"

"Unlike your work," he interrupted, sarcastic air quotes around *work,* "my position with Continental Pavilions will keep paying me year in and year out. What're you going to do when your commercial for Joe Blow's Used Cars goes out of syndication? No, Rita"—he chuckled nastily—"you're a total, perfect failure. And I think Petey needs counseling. I'm setting up a date for him with Harold Saxby."

"Who's Harold Saxby?"

"That just goes to show, doesn't it?" he sneered. "Harold Saxby is the most prominent kids' psychiatrist in L.A."

There was something going on as dangerous as it was obvious: Jeff was laying serious groundwork to challenge our custody arrangement. I felt my spinal muscles tighten. I didn't know what to say or do. He added that he was taking Petey to San Diego for the Spider-Man World Convention two weekends from now, "to give him something to look forward to. I'm trying to get him centered."

Centered? That had to be girlfriend-speak. I said, "Oh, it sounds like a perfect venue for that." I could imagine how nice and calming a superhero festival, with its jumbo-trons and trinket-hawkers and sugared beverages, would be for a four-year-old.

Jeff added some more nasty comments and took off.

Later, Petey slammed his pre-bedtime snack of warm pudding to the floor and yelled, "I hate you! Daddy never makes me go to bed!"

As mildly as possible, I said, "I'll bet not."

He jumped up and yanked the electrical cord of one of our new Swedish lamps, toppling it to the floor, where to my astonishment he stomped on it with all his might, cracking it to pieces, from papyrus-style shade to geometric anodized-looking base.

"Petey!" Shocked not by the loss of the lamp but by the deliberateness of the destruction, I pulled him to me. His flushed little face was so appallingly full of malice, I could not speak. As if determined to push me over the brink, he socked me in the stomach. His sharp fist felt like an ice pick going into me.

"We don't hurt!" I roared.

Then I slapped him across the face.

I wish I could say I did it before I knew what I was doing, but that would be a lie. I meant to hurt him. My baby boy!

For a second he stood absolutely still, eyes wide, mouth slack. Then he took that first deep breath of anguish, and the world split when he began howling. And for the first time in his life when in tears, he ran away from me. He hid under his pillow and would not let me touch him for a long time.

I SPENT THAT long dreadful night sleepless, berating myself as only a guilt-ridden mother can. I could have given him a concussion. I could have killed him. I was a hypocrite. Jeff was right: I was a plain old traditional bad mother. If I killed myself, would it do any good? No, my punishment was living with this memory for the rest of my life. After Petey permitted me to tell him I'd done a terribly wrong thing, he fell asleep. I checked in on him and rechecked. His face, now, was that of the tenderest cherub Michelangelo ever painted.

I wanted Gary. I wanted the thought of Gary to soothe me, but it didn't, couldn't.

I tried to read *Heaven's Dose of Comfort,* which one of my aunts had sent me for my birthday the year before, but not even that collection of heartwarming stories could ease my agony.

It's hard not to make eye contact with yourself when you're applying mascara, but Monday morning I found it can be done.

When I met with Eileen I asked her about a woman named Janet and a storage locker key. She shrugged and shook her head.

"I don't know anyone named Janet," she said, meeting my eyes with the practiced, wide gaze we'd worked on in the lockup.

I did not feel comfortable with that.

Court came to order. During the brief moments I was able to get my mind off my horribleness, I watched the trial and brooded.

Eileen was doing well, doing the strategy we'd settled on, even adding her own touches. One gesture she'd perfected was what I called the high-duck shrug in which, in reaction to some dubious prosecutorial point, she'd shrug up her shoulders while simultaneously ducking her head, as if she'd been startled by a low-flying fruit bat. Then immediately she'd straighten and look at either Gary or me with a rueful quarter-smile. It was a wonderfully expressive move.

By now there wasn't much more actual work for me to do with her; my holding cell visits had dropped off, and I acted mostly as her quiet support. We didn't talk much.

I watched her and wondered. I wanted to find out more about Gabriella's death on my own. I wanted to skulk around looking for clues, I wanted to talk tough to shady characters. I'd vary my route home every night out of boredom, and as I'd pass through the ickier sections of Sunset or Pico, I'd wonder like a yokel, would any of these shuffling dirty characters know something? Would one of them recognize that ball cap from the bushes?

More rumors were cropping up about the financial difficulties of Gemini Imports, and I had to speculate yet again about Padraig McGower. Looking at his suave figure in the courtroom, it suddenly struck me that *he* might have killed Gabriella, as a way of getting back at Richard Tenaway for his embezzlement, if Tenaway did indeed siphon resources from the company. That crazy Janet may have been right about that, who knew?

It was possible McGower did it, or paid for it to be done. Yet he simply did not give off the creepy vibe you'd expect. If he *had* done it, that proved McGower knew Tenaway was alive somewhere, waiting for . . . what? Maybe nothing. Maybe he'd gotten away with everything. Except there were the life insurance millions, controlled by Eileen. I just couldn't rationalize McGower putting himself at risk for the sake of vengeance.

"Maybe," I suggested to Gary during a recess, "McGower's just pretending to be supportive of Eileen. Why would he want to help her?"

"Goodness of his heart," muttered Gary, reading a deposition on his laptop. We'd remained at the defense table as everybody else went to the bathroom or whatever. Eileen had been taken backstage to use the facilities in the lockup. It was the seventh week of the trial and it had begun to seem that we'd all be doing this forever, breaking only to get fitted for dentures and hearing aids and so on.

"Maybe," I persisted, "she's promised him some helpful information."

He looked up and sighed. "And maybe a fleet of swans is about to carry this courthouse to a serene mountaintop." His eyes were tired.

It was a beautiful image, but all I said was, "Never mind." I wondered if right now George Rowe might be grappling with Richard Tenaway on some serene mountaintop.

"Look," Gary said, "I have a little job for you."

I defensively thought, *Well, I am doing a job already, unless you've forgotten.*

He said, "I want you to rent a house for Eileen in case she gets acquitted. The prosecution's about to wrap up, and I really don't think I'm going to belabor our defense. So it won't be long, one way or the other. I have my plans, and I feel quite confident. Take the rest of the day."

"What about her own house?"

"The press'll be there like lice. She'll be better off with a quiet place to decompress for a while. Find a place up a canyon some-where. Or up the coast, but not too far. Private. Big. She can af-ford it. Sign a six-month lease. I'll write you a check." He went back to reading.

WHEN MONEY IS no object, things can happen *so fast.* In two phone calls I'd found a high-end rental agent with a good reputa-tion, and before night fell I'd seen four houses and shaken hands on one: a posh Mission-style place up Topanga Canyon with a heart-stopping view of the Pacific, five secluded acres of gardens, and a pool with a high dive, all for only seven thousand a month. I brushed my hands on my skirt as I walked back to the agent's Bentley, thinking, *There now, that's how you do business around here! Throw somebody else's money around!*

TRACY BECK-RUBIN BEGAN her summation on Thursday of that week, wearing her freshly pressed navy blue suit and, star-tlingly, a *brand-new* pair of navy Naturalizers. Puttin' on the dog there, Trace.

I felt like lead inside, still so dark and heavy about Petey, who had awakened talking of the upcoming Spider-Man convention. Jeff was trying to turn him against me, clearly. What the hell could I do about it? Stick it out all nicey-nice until the kid's eighteen?

I thought it was telling that Beck-Rubin spent so much time belittling the evidence she expected the defense to highlight: the forced lock, the Starbucks cup with a cigarette stubbed out in the dregs, the hat in the bushes—"nothing, really," said she. "What we do have is evidence that the night this innocent child was murdered in her bedroom, the defendant staged it all after the fact. It's been done before."

Innocent child was murdered.

Child was murdered.

Bedroom.

The Starbucks cup.

The Starbucks cup.

Something stirred deep within my medulla oblongata.

Wham! went my brain cells. *Slam!* went my gut as I remembered the Starbucks cup and cigarette butts in Petey's room the night Daniel's show got canceled. Dear God!

At that instant I knew that the night Gabriella Tenaway died, evidence of an intruder had indeed been planted—but not by Eileen. And certainly not by Padraig McGower. No, this one had a woman's touch all over it—a psychopathic woman's touch.

I don't know if I muttered anything to Gary; my heart was thundering out of my chest. I leaped from the defense table and tore out of the courtroom. I heard a shout behind me, but panic drove me and there was no pausing.

I don't remember starting my car, gunning it out of the underground garage, and flooring it up the 405. I don't remember anything until I pulled up at the preschool and stampeded to Petey's classroom.

Where is he? Where is my boy?

There in the corner! He was mixing paint in a bean can, clutching a stained brush, gazing dreamily at a sheet of white poster paper the teacher had just clipped to his easel.

As I snatched him into my arms, startling the living hell out of him, I saw that the paint was a gorgeous, beautiful, wonderful, perfect shade of summer green, and as it flew out of the can and splashed down Petey's blue sweatshirt and soaked into my toffee-brown suit jacket, it looked absolutely lovely.

"Wow!" he said. "Mommy!"

After making a nonsensical explanation to the teacher, I calmed down, stripped off Petey's sweatshirt (thankful I'd put a T-shirt on him as well), returned him to the peaceful sheepfold of the classroom, dabbed my suit with a paper towel, and called Daniel on my cell phone from the school steps.

"Did anyone ever," I asked, "come into the apartment while you were babysitting?"

He thought for a moment.

"Ever?" I pressed.

I heard his exercise video in the background. He owned the entire *Hurts So Good* series by that famous former POW, what's his name? The guy who makes guys feel like they're really in the army while they're trying to do their hundredth push-up. "Again, you pussy! And again! And—"

"Just a sec," said my friend, and the video went mute. "No, nobody ever came by. I mean, I never had any *company* over, if that's what you're wondering. Why?"

My throat eased. "OK. Good. I'm kind of embarrassed to tell you this, but I just made a fool of—"

"Oh, wait a minute, Rita, I mean nobody came over except that one night when the super stopped in."

"The super? You mean the property manager? When was that?"

A bird cheeped weakly in a bush next to the school steps. I glanced over. A baby had fallen—or been pushed—from a mud-daub nest beneath the eaves. Tiny and fuzzy, it was sitting on the ground uttering painful rapid cries. From the stone ledge two stories above, an adult swallow looked on in distress. The baby beat its beensy wings and rocked from side to side.

"Let's see," said Daniel. "It was the night my show got canceled. I was so busy feeling sorry for myself I guess I forgot to mention it."

"Oh. Well, what was that about?"

"She said she was the building supervisor, and she wanted to check the security light outside Petey's room, where the fire escape is. We chatted for a few minutes about acting and so on. She tested the light, it was fine, and she left."

"She?" With sickening slowness, my heart grew cold. "My building manager is a guy. Did she introduce herself?"

"Well, maybe it was his wife or something. Funny, I don't think she ever said her name."

"Was she black?"

"No, she was white."

"My building manager and his wife are black," I said grimly. "Was she holding a Starbucks cup when she came in, by any chance?"

"Uh, yes, as a matter of fact."

"Was she smoking?"

"Damn."

"Daniel, what?"

His voice took on his abashed confessional tone, which usually I found charming. "To be honest, Rita, she and I had a cigarette on the fire escape. She offered me one, and I thought what the hell. I know you asked me not—"

"Did you use the coffee cup for an ashtray?" I asked.

"Yes. I must have—"

"Left it on the windowsill."

"Yes."

"Oh, God, Daniel."

"If my littering was such a big deal, how come you didn't mention it before?"

I didn't answer, but made him describe the "super." As his voice projected her face, hair, and mannerisms, a picture coalesced on my mental movie screen of the only person it could possibly be: Janet. I tried to remember the pack of cigarettes that sat before her on the table at the Starbucks on Santa Monica. The butt left in the cup at Eileen's house was Benson & Hedges. When I asked Daniel if he could remember the brand the super offered him, he said, "I think it was Benson & Hedges."

"Did she say something like, 'I myself' am this or that?"

"Yeah! She used that exact expression."

"How about jewelry?"

"Well, she had these gigantic rhinestone earrings that looked like they were from my mom's dress-up box."

"Could they have been topazes? Or were they green? Emeralds?"

"They were amber-colored, I think. Plus she had this flashy faux-emerald pendant that was just too much."

"How did you know it was faux?"

"I don't know, you just don't wear real jewels like that to your job in an apartment house."

I made him promise to be extra-careful about Petey, our angelic little bastard. "Be sure to get there before school ends every day, OK?"

"I promise. But Rita, what's this all about?"

"I'll tell you soon. Just be careful with him."

"Relax. Who's going to mess with *me*?"

I looked up at the empty nest again. There was no way I could reach it to return the baby to it. As I stood watching the baby bird, it moved. With a burst of energy, it skittered into the bushes and was gone.

TWENTY-THREE

When I reached Gary on his cell he was driving to the office after court. I explained my sudden exit from the courtroom.

He listened, then simply said, "That is a little strange. Well, be careful. This will all be over soon."

I stared into the light well. "That's all I get?" I asked plaintively. " 'Be careful'?"

"Rita, what do you want from me?" Gary's voice was tired. "I'm trying to marshal my energy here. What I need is a goddamned night off from all this. Clear my mind. I'm sorry."

"No, I'm sorry." Then a brilliant idea occurred to me. "Come to my apartment tonight for dinner. I'll fix my Gramma Gladys's meatloaf. And—and—I have a friend I think you'll enjoy meeting."

"Oh?"

"We'll forbid talk of work. We'll forbid worrying. We'll have some wine. Come on, what say?"

"Hm."

"Gary, he's cute."

"Rita! Are you trying to fix me up?"

"Hell yes!"

"Well . . . all right!"

DANIEL WAS, TO my surprise, quite torn at the prospect of a blind semi-date with someone of my choosing.

"I totally trust your judgment," he said fervently, "but I've just been so burned lately."

I was scurrying around my apartment with the phone to my ear, doing the one-handed tidying dance. "It's just for fun," I told him. "Don't get too keyed up. But he is wonderful. I met him not long ago, and I'm embarrassed to say I fell for him until—"

"Oh, Rita, you didn't."

"Look, I don't have gaydar." I swept my dust cloth along the bookshelf, swagging it in and out along the book spines.

Daniel said, "But you do, at least you have it better than any straight person I know."

"I'm afraid I'm turning into a fag hag."

"Hm. I don't think so. You're not old enough yet. If you hit menopause before you get married again, I'd start to worry, but—"

"Do not even speak it. Hey, remember when you were telling me about your ideal guy? This one qualifies. He's handsome—though you're handsomer—smart, mature, accomplished—"

"So how come he's not claimed already?"

"Well—I'd say he'd be the best person to answer that."

"Hm."

Whew. Hotfooted it through that one. I flicked a dead fly off a windowsill. Daniel still seemed undecided, so I briefly changed the subject. "Hey, I bought a new cartridge for the kitchen faucet. I'll try to put it in this weekend so that drip'll stop. But being a guy, do you think I'll need any special tools? Because—"

"The only tool you need is a phone. Call a plumber. Or the landlord, for God's sake."

Daniel believed one hundred percent in summoning experts.

"He's out of town," I said. "But I like doing things myself. Or trying, anyway."

"Well, that's the key phrase, isn't it: *or trying*. Listen to me. Never do for yourself anything you can pay a professional to do. It's always cheaper in the long run. You'll try to fix it and screw it up and have to call somebody to come and fix not only the original problem, but the new problems you've caused."

I said, "I'll call a plumber if you'll come over for dinner."

He made a sound as if he'd just had a boil lanced. "All right. All right. Do you think I should wear my cashmere T-shirt, the periwinkle one?"

"Absolutely. You look gorgeous in it. And not too much hair gel."

"Rita, I *know* how to do my hair."

I BRIBED PETEY with McDonald's and unlimited Spider-Man on his ScoreLad until bedtime, which I moved up to seven-thirty, by which time his little peepers were so tired they rolled shut like doll eyes. I made sure his window was locked tight.

I lit some candles and chilled a good bottle of Chardonnay to go with the crab dip, and stationed the Cabernet on the counter for use with the meatloaf. Gramma Gladys really did know how to make a great meatloaf—moist but firm, no ketchup, plenty of onions.

I'm not that much of a chef, if you haven't noticed. I love good food, but I never learned to cook as well as I wanted. I never got that knack where you look in the cupboard, see what's there, and throw a few things together with that indefinable cooking intelligence some people have. So I generally follow recipes. My older sister has that cooking intelligence. I could live on nuts and chocolate and red wine.

When Gary walked through the door and saw Daniel, they both stopped in mid- "Hi." Their faces looked like they'd hit cold air. Frozen, stunned.

They stared at each other. I didn't know what to do.

Finally Gary opened his mouth. Slowly, he said, "Whiskers on kittens."

"Schnitzel with noodles!" exclaimed Daniel.

"Huh?" I said.

They looked at me. Daniel began to laugh. For a few horrible seconds I couldn't tell if it was real or fake, like one of those nauseating sitcom moments when one person starts laughing and then everybody joins in.

But he kept laughing, delightedly, and then Gary laughed too. "Heh-heh ha!"

"Guys, please. What have I just done?"

They ignored me. Daniel, smiling wide as a river, opened his arms, and Gary practically fell into them, still laughing.

There was a what-the-hell feeling in the air.

Whiskers on kittens.

Schnitzel with noodles.

Even I finally figured out the unbelieveable. "Oh, don't tell me."

"It's true," Gary said, wiping his eyes. "We met at Sing-a-long-a *Sound of Music*."

"In San Francisco," added Daniel. "Castro Theater. Popcorn line."

Gary said, "He wore little whiskers under his nose, that was all. Simple. Eloquent."

My God, they were kindred Rodgers and Hammerstein buffs. I'd known it of Daniel, but only at this instant did I realize Gary was one too. Suddenly I remembered little moments when he'd quoted bits of lyrics—from *The King and I, South Pacific, Carousel*. I'd gotten used to discovering unexpected connections between people in L.A.—it's a much smaller town than people think—but this was extreme.

As they broke their semi clinch, "How," I asked, "did Gary make himself look like schnitzel with noodles?"

Daniel looked at me kindly. "Sometimes it's best not to learn certain details." Then he stepped back, hands on hips, and said, "I've known for a long time where you've been going every day, but never, like a dummy, did I connect it with Gary. I thought you were doing something else at the courthouse."

"How did you know I was going there?"

"I followed you a couple of times. To the jail too. But I never saw you two together. I always lost sight of you going into the parking garage, and I never followed because I didn't want to be too obtrusive."

"Well—now you know."

Daniel laughed incredulously. "*Know what?* You're working for Gary, right? But what the hell are you doing—giving Eileen Tenaway tips on how to snow the jury?"

I looked at Gary, who said, "Um, yes."

"Really?"

Gary said, "I can explain it to you."

I withdrew to open wine. Whatever was about to happen, I wasn't going to make us all face it stone sober. From the quiet of the kitchen I heard Gary say, "I've missed you."

Softly, Daniel said, "I couldn't wait for you. You know?"

"Yes."

"I've regretted it."

"So have I."

TWENTY-FOUR

Joshua Tree again, Sally?" A woman in a kimono robe and tinfoil pincurls peeked from behind her apartment door. Her skin sagged, but her face was kind. "I see you got a new backpack."

"Yes, I was about to call and let you know," said her neighbor. "I'm leaving tonight. I'll be back in a week, I think."

It was now Wednesday of the Tenaway trial's eighth week, and Gary Kwan had that morning launched into the case for Eileen Tenaway's defense, sparking a new surge of press coverage. The woman named Sally carried a newspaper with Gary's picture on it.

The other woman said, "Well, it's getting dark now. You going soon?"

"Yes."

Sally Jacubiak, a slightly built young woman with eyes that took a little longer to focus than most people's, needed the desert. Her nerves were shot, just shot. She closed the door to her apartment, a gummy little place in a building on Crenshaw Avenue south of Olympic. If you opened the window for one second, oily black traffic dirt would settle on everything. One good thing the landlord had done was install tough security doors on every apartment last summer. There hadn't been a break-in since. She threw down the paper and her sunglasses.

Sally wore her chestnut hair in a Ukranian-style braid pinned around her head like a crown, and it was very becoming. Though her mother found many things to criticize about her, the hair was not one of them. "Our women know da best way to wear hair," her mother would assert in her guttural accent. "Whether they have a job or not."

Well, that was a fact: Sally was unemployed. She received disability payments because her shrink had convinced the state she couldn't work. She thought she would like to work, and she tried to attract job offers by sewing small magnets into her clothing and sometimes interweaving dried herbs into her braids, but no job ever materialized. *Couldn't* was such a subjective term, she thought. There were plenty of things she could do, certainly, but none of them happened to bring her any income.

After she'd filled her new pack with her stuff and tried it on, Sally Jacubiak changed into her hiking shoes, placed the pack next to the door, set her keys on it, and turned to look at the telephone in her dining nook. She glanced apprehensively at the door, then made a decision.

MARK SHARMA GAZED at his increasingly portly, full-length reflection in the night windows of Gary's office and asked briskly, "And your conclusion, Doctor?"

He shifted his weight, stepping one foot dynamically forward. He hooked a thumb into his belt loop, flipping his suit coat open in an assertive, comfortable gesture. "Please tell the jury exactly how your analysis showed the DNA from the ball cap came from a possible sex offender."

Gary had launched the case for the defense brilliantly today, and in one or two days' time, Sharma would be handling their witnesses on physical evidence.

Mark became aware of a phone ringing. Irritated, he ignored it, but it rang on. He strode to Gary's desk. "Yes?" he said into the receiver, Gary-style.

"Um," said a tense female voice. "I thought I'd get a machine. I wanted to leave a message for Gary Kwan."

Something in her voice, an extraordinary urgency, made Mark Sharma hesitate. On a hunch, he said, "This is Gary."

"Oh!" said the voice. "Well, I just want to tell you something that's been, uh, well, I'm not supposed to—"

"Just tell me," Mark interrupted.

"That little girl, Mr. Kwan? Her mother didn't kill her. I think."

Sharma inhaled slowly and deeply. He grabbed a pen and wrote the number showing on caller ID on a pad of sticky notes. "You mean Gabriella Tenaway? What do you know about it?" he asked.

"Norah Mintz knows something about it."

"Norah Mintz!"

"Gabriella's aunt. You know? She's been, uh, quote-unquote missing."

"Yes," said Mark, his midsection tense with excitement. "You've talked to her?"

"Yes. She's my friend."

"Where is she?"

"At the moment I don't know."

"Why do you think she knows something about this case?"

"She herself told me. We were watching TV and the trial came on the news. She said, 'That kid was a brat, but her mother didn't kill her.'"

Mark Sharma's eyes narrowed. "Have you called the police?"

Sally Jacubiak snorted. "They wouldn't be interested. I'm not stupid, you know. The police never like to be wrong. They come after you."

Hearing the instability in her voice, Sharma agreed, "Good point."

"Mr. Kwan, I knew you'd be the best person to tell this information to. See, I once had a dog I rescued from a homeless situation."

"Yes?"

"So you can see I feel strongly about injustice."

"Ah, yes."

"I'm taking my life in my hands telling you this."

"Why is that?"

"Norah used to be my housemate. She went away for a while, she never said where. I felt that rejection. I felt it terribly. I think she went with a man. She had boyfriends heck to breakfast."

"But now she's come back?"

"Just for a little while. I said she could room with me for a little while. I got a smaller place. I said why don't you get in touch with your sister, and she said no way. She made me promise not to tell anyone she's here. She went out, but she'll be back any—"

"Where are you?" asked the young lawyer.

"Look, just talk to her. But Mr. Kwan, be careful." The caller gave a number. "That's her cell phone. It's the best way to—"

Mark Sharma heard a click. "Hello?" he said. "Hello." He replaced the receiver.

Sweating, he began to calculate.

The information he had just received was astonishing, case-cracking, career-making.

If it was true.

For he had learned from Gary to be skeptical about anonymous tips in cases like this. Most nuts with tips were merely nuts. But this nut, he felt, was special. If he could run this one down himself and prove something, Gary would have no choice but to—

He heard the *ca-chick* of the outer door. He thrust the note pad into his pocket, leaped away from Gary's desk, and fell to his hands and knees. As Gary came in, Mark Sharma looked up and smiled, like a puppy caught chewing a slipper.

"Just stretching my back," he said. "How was the play?"

"What's wrong with the floor in your office?" Gary asked, throwing his keys on his desk.

Sharma kept smiling. "The floor is harder in there."

Gary said, "Huh?"

"How was the play?" Sharma asked again, getting to his feet.

"Oh, she was great in it." Gary pulled out his swivel chair. "She played a daffodil."

"She must have been very cute," Sharma said enthusiastically. "The best daffodil!" He flipped back his hair with the fingers of one hand and subtly adjusted his crotch with the other.

I'D PUT PETEY to bed and was drinking a glass of wine and cracking a few almonds in the gear teeth of my Le Cork Weasel when Daniel dropped in. He stood in my doorway, his arms stretched wide around an outer-space frenzy of dahlias, their bright blossoms bobbing like planetoids around the happy sun of his face. "Another small token of my thanks."

"You're insane," I protested. He'd been showering me with gifts since that meatloaf dinner last week.

He helped me arrange the flowers in my two biggest vases, chattering all the while about how totally wondrous Gary was. They'd met for coffee once since that night, and I gathered it had gone well.

"I think you guys might have a future," I commented.

"Yeah, but 'midst the ointment of my happiness 'tis a fly," Daniel said, pulling out a dry stem. He was taking a Shakespeare refresher at Karen Bell's acting studio.

"Oh, hell, their marriage has been dead for years."

"But the little girl. Jade."

I tried to take the positive. "Look, Daniel, for all you know Jacqueline's a heroin addict and Gary will get custody and you'll all live happily ever after. You love kids—you'll love Jade. She's like Gary with slightly less testosterone."

The phone rang and I let my machine get it. Jeff's voice, honking and drunk, spewed into the digital recorder.

"Hey, bitch, better line up your lawyer. And give your precious little boy a hug, because pretty soon—"

Daniel covered the speaker with his hand. "That bastard. Not even worth listening to."

GARY GLANCED AT the papers on his desk. "Where's that DNA comparison of the sex offenders and the ball cap?"

"I—it's almost finished." Sharma dropped his eyes.

"Mark, what?" Gary stared, hands open. "It's eight-thirty. What've you been doing? I'm tired. I want to go over that. We need it tomorrow."

Sharma turned. "I'll finish it right now. I'm sorry. It won't take long."

"Sorry? *Sorry?* In the middle of a trial like this?" Gary did not bother to hide the contempt in his eyes. "Get out of here."

This was a shock. "But don't you want me to—"

"No. Just give me your notes and go home. Give me what you've done so far."

The junior lawyer stumbled from the office and returned with two pages of handwritten notes.

"This is it?" Gary scanned the pages. "This is all you've got?" The ice in his voice changed to heat. "God *damn* it! I take one night off last week and two hours tonight to go to my daughter's play, and you drop your whole fish box!" Something, perhaps, his father used to say. "Steve gave me his analysis on final strategy this morning! Lisa took care of the PowerPoint by six-thirty tonight! Why can't you handle a simple fucking assignment? I have other things I need to do! I'm trying to figure out . . . my life."

"What?" said Sharma.

"Never mind. You've blown it, Mark."

Sharma squeezed his eyes shut and wished to cover his ears. He ventured, "There was another anonymous call—"

"Shut up! I thought you had balls. Go."

Sharma backed to the door. "See you . . . in the morning?" he nearly whimpered.

"Yeah, one of us ought to get some sleep." Gary turned away.

MARK SHARMA TRUDGED down the corridor. He punched the elevator button. All he wanted was to get outside, to breathe the night city air. Anything to get away from the toxicity of Gary's insults.

Why are the elevators so damn slow in this building?

He was angrier than he'd ever been, angrier even than when the president of his condominium association had accused him, in front of twenty-seven people at the annual meeting, of throwing garbage into the recycling bin.

As the elevator doors opened, he saw himself in a mirrored panel: chubby cheeks, wiry black hair flopping into his eyes. What a ridiculous haircut! Only a fool would wear a haircut like that.

He rode down to the lobby. The nights he'd sweated and worked over this trial! And here was one time—one time!—when he'd relaxed. He'd taken Gary's esteem for granted. But there never had been any esteem, he saw now.

What a fraud Gary had been, all along.

LISTENING TO JEFF'S muffled obscenities on my machine, I couldn't help crying with frustration and anxiety. After a few long minutes of raving, he hung up. Daniel encircled me with his arm. I felt his strong muscles and smelled his warmth through his linen guyabera. Why must so many gay guys be so damn perfect?

The phone rang again immediately, and we looked at it as if it were a snake. But when I heard Gary's voice I picked up.

"I hate to ask you this," he said, "but is there any way you can come to the office and help me finish Mark's work for him?" I could hear his fatigue.

"Right now?"

"I'll give you the day off tomorrow. If I do it alone, it'll be an all-nighter. I can't reach Steve or Lisa."

"What happened to Mark?"

"I fired him for the night."

I looked a question at Daniel. He nodded.

Smiling, I said into the receiver, "Luckily for you, Daniel just stopped over with a third of a ton of flowers, and he says he can stay with Petey. So hey, I'm on my way."

"Rita . . ." Gary said, then paused. "Let me talk to Daniel for a second."

Daniel took the phone and listened.

"I love you too," said my friend gently, tears filling his eyes.

TWENTY-FIVE

As Mark Sharma approached the glass lobby doors a woman rushed up from the night outside. She wore sunglasses and a melon-green T-shirt. Her mouth was frantic, as if she were talking to herself.

He pushed open the door.

She almost collided with him, but he stood firm in the doorway, sizing up this little situation.

"Is this Gary Kwan's office?" she said in a cold fast voice.

This was not an occasion to be rushed through.

Her tight shirt drew his eye to her breasts. He noticed drops of blood on the green fabric. The blood almost appeared to be a red decoration, a pattern. But it was a spatter of blood, yes, there at her breast line, and what's more there was a smudge of blood on her bare arm. The woman carried a shoulder bag; one hand was hidden in it.

"I have to see Mr. Kwan," she said.

Sharma looked into her eyes, but her sunglasses were in the way.

As if she were joining him in an act of rare honesty, she removed the glasses.

The moment was very brief.

He saw fury and humiliation in her eyes, and he knew his own eyes showed the same. For one moment, with someone—a woman!—he felt perfect harmony.

He knew exactly who she was and what she had come for.

And it was as if lightning struck and split the core of him. He felt charged with destructive energy, and he was no longer the same old Mark Sharma. He was exceptionally alive. He stepped into the street and held the self-locking door open for her.

"Suite 7A," he said.

LOS ANGELES IS a funny place, I mused as I drove down Santa Monica, then veered right on Wilshire. From high in an airplane, the city is an untidy mottled blot spilling from the desert and the mountains all the way to the sea, indeed reaching out into the sea with fingers of piers, breakwalls, and, down at Long Beach, the monstrous wharves.

Then, closer, say if you are looking down on the city from one of the stone parapets of the Getty, or from a deck in the Hollywood Hills, the whole thing appears much more orderly, like a circuit board. The buildings line up neatly by the block, their pediments toe the level concrete. You see the crisp squares of parking lots, the clean recognizable shapes of the downtown skyline and the arenas. Cars and trucks flow like electrons along the neural gridded pathways.

But up close again, at street level yourself, how narrow and nasty the avenues feel when you are merely trying to maintain the speed limit. You see and smell the garbage cans, you hear the jarring sounds of millions of lives meshing, clashing—the chock-ablock storefronts—Chaldean cell phone shop by Haitian fruit market by Colombian taco stand.

The crosstown boulevards make their motley journeys from the stink and grandeur of downtown through the cheap gauntlet of low-end Hollywood, then the out-of-body luxe of Beverly Hills, out through the quieter wealth of the farther west side, to Santa Monica's theme-park shopping streets, then, well, there's nothing more but the astonishing beach underlining the ocean with its painted ships and Hawaii just over there.

I let myself into the building with the keycard Gary had given me. A few other tenants up late; from outside I'd seen a spattering of lights around the different floors.

When I walked into the outer office of Kwan & Associates I always felt so excellent: glad to be doing something important, glad to be needed. Plus being with Gary always settled my nerves.

As I passed Lisa Feltenberger's deserted desk, I smelled an odor I wasn't expecting, thus I did not identify it consciously.

But my subconscious knew what it was.

Too, the place was silent, completely silent. Although the door to his office was standing open and his light was on, I heard no squeak from Gary's chair as he habitually rolled it back and forth in a three-inch pattern on the rug. I heard no throat-clearing, no finger-drumming, no paper-rustling.

I stood at the door for a moment, cherishing the world as it was. Then I walked in.

———

GARY LAY ON his side halfway between his desk and the door. A huge ghastly smear of blood trailed from him to a place next to his desk.

Blood pooled in the rug under and around him, a pool of it, it appeared to have depth, that was the most horrifying thing, the pool of blood was not a flat spill of blood but a pool, and even though I knew he was dead, I went to him, fell to my knees, and turned his face up.

My throat closed.

He was not cold yet, but he was no longer warm either. His eyes were open and his expression was a mix of bafflement and regret, as if he had spent himself trying to remain alive, then had met death with some measure of acceptance.

Somehow, a bluebottle fly had materialized—from thin air, it had to be, since I had never seen a bluebottle fly in that building, ever. It buzzed up from Gary's nose when I turned his head.

I remember the fly, but I don't remember recoiling.

The eternal message of the universe: this beautiful fit body was nothing but food for decay now. How quickly they work, the agents of rot, drawn by the rich powerful smell of blood. The smell filled the room, and I supposed more flies were on their way, hoping to lay eggs and have kids.

Gary's pale blue shirt was cruelly soaked with blood, dark red like a howl from hell, much of it having originated, it seemed, from his upper belly.

A numbness I had never felt before came over me, my whole body from spine out to skin, and I rose and stepped to his desk. I read what he had written on his legal pad—a to-do list for the rest of his life:

Tell Jacqueline—ask for understanding.
Give her everything—start over if I have to.
Be best dad to Jade.
Show him I love him.
Let the chips fall.

Somehow my heart was able to ache within its ache. I considered taking the pad away with me or hiding it somewhere in another office, but I saw a dot of blood on it, and left it alone. The chips would fall.

Poor Jacqueline, unless she did this. Poor little Jade. Poor Daniel.

It didn't enter my mind that the assailant or assailants might still be around. I felt totally, thoroughly, alone.

I walked to the outer office not feeling my legs under me. Lisa Feltenberger's desk. Her telephone. 911. "I need the police. A man is dead. I believe he's been murdered," I began, then followed the dispatcher's prompts.

"OK, stay where you are," she said to conclude our conversation. "And don't make any other calls on this phone."

I took out my cell phone and called Daniel.

I told him.

"No, Rita," he said, his voice small and brittle.

"It's true. He's lying in there bloody. Dead."

"For God's sake, give him CPR! You don't know he's dead! Go do it!"

"Daniel. Listen to me. Gary is dead. He is cold and dead and the flies are already coming."

I heard a groan of primal anguish, then another.

Lisa Feltenberger's desktop was very neat. Her pen mug said PARALEGALS DO IT WITH ALACRITY.

"Daniel," I said quietly, "I need you."

He managed to gather himself. "They'll be there in a minute," he said, his voice trembling. "What happened?"

"Daniel, I don't know!"

"Who was there?"

"Well, Mark Sharma, that other lawyer on the team. I guess they'd had an argument. But by the time Gary called me, Mark had gone home, I thought. It had to be someone with access to this building. The security guy locks the doors at six when he goes home. Or the person was already in the building."

"All right, don't speculate to the police. You could be their first suspect, you know, since you discovered—the scene. Be careful what you say."

I looked down at my hands. I hadn't gotten any blood on them. I looked at my knees, but I must have instinctively avoided plopping down in Gary's pond of blood. I was clean, I thought. Clean. What does that word mean, anyway?

Daniel's voice now was expressionless from the shock, yet he had gone into some kind of hyperfunctioning mode, as somehow I had done. "Rita, listen. Don't say too much."

"Yes," I said. "I should go down and let them in."

"Wait. Can you check the phone log right now? You guys have phone log software, right?"

"Yeah, I think so. Why?"

"He just called you. Your number will show up."

"What's wrong with that? Even if I wanted to hide it, I don't think I can erase numbers, so—"

"I want to know if any other calls came in."

"Well—"

"Just look. Can you look?"

I went to the cubicle Gary had assigned me, where I'd spent hardly any time. I turned the PC on and clicked on the phone log icon. The day's numbers popped up on a white-and-blue screen. Above my number, which Gary had called at 8:46 p.m., I saw Gary's home number, then three other numbers I didn't recognize. Mine had been the last one.

"Read them to me," said Daniel.

I did.

"But Daniel, why?"

"I'm good friends with our technical consultant—former technical consultant—and—"

"You mean from the show? *Abilene Cop Shop?*"

"Maybe it sounds silly to you. But he's a cop himself, and the stories he's told me about how things can go wrong when the police get there and find it's a VIP! They lose their minds. I want to protect you. He told me if anything heavy ever goes down to call him."

"Well, for God's sake, don't! I don't want a—"

"Rita, listen to me. Relax. Breathe. You've got to compartmentalize your emotions now. Put your shock in a box. Put your grief in a box. You'll open them up when the time is right. There's too much going on now. Too much danger. Hear me? Danger for you and for Petey. Your boy needs you, OK? I need you. Do you hear me? Whoever did this will not get away with it. I promise you. Now go down and meet the police. Do not call his wife. Do not talk to reporters. They'll be there, you know, they have police scanners. Call me again as soon as you can."

TWENTY-SIX

I remember things in shards.

The police asked me many questions, but not much about myself except what was on my driver's license. I told them I was a paralegal, but that was the only lie I told that night.

The place filled up with cop-vibes, all these cops with their gun belts and forearms and black tactical shoes.

Detectives came in and looked carefully at what Gary had written on the yellow pad, and I realized they were going to treat that list as something of a Rosetta stone. They stood talking to each other in neat sport coats of maroon and navy hopsack.

Fine, I thought. *Maybe that's exactly what it is.*

It appeared Gary had been stabbed to death. "Looks like he put up some resistance," a skinny-faced younger cop, high on the sight of a dead man, had said out loud in the corridor, "but the first strike incapacitated him to a large extent." He was addressing his boss, the detective who would interview me in a minute. "I bet it was a surprise to him."

I saw the eager servility in his face and thought, *Boy, the beat goes on.*

The detective shifted his weight toward the younger cop and said, "Be quiet."

When a parent dies, the children cling together even if they'd fought like dingoes before. So it was with Mark Sharma and me. Not that we'd been overtly hostile, but there had been a lack of warmth, that's for sure. He arrived about fifteen minutes after the police. A reporter had called him; Daniel had been right about that. We locked eyes and made a silent pact to talk later.

Up until tonight I'd thought he was a cute little thing, a guy who, if he'd been born American with big American muscles, would have excelled at college football then gone into industrial sales, where his commissions would be big enough to support a family and a country club lifestyle. I could see him hitting a four-iron or something to the green at Riviera.

I thought he lived to serve his master and role model, the gold-plated legal genius of L.A., but when I saw his face come through the door I realized he'd been a python all along. His lips were narrow and tight around his jaw. He moved smoothly and with more reptilian authority than I'd have thought possible. Even so, I felt relief. He would not have come if he were still somewhere washing off blood.

Insofar as the cops permitted him to, he took charge, organizing things in the corridor, thinking of logistics, thinking ahead. The police questioned each of us separately, around the corner and far down the next corridor. The detective who questioned me was bald with a sparse mustache and deep-sunken eyes, and he showed neither friendliness nor hostility. He jotted notes as I recalled the events of my evening.

Then he said, "Haven't I seen you somewhere?"

I looked at him with my full open face. "I don't know."

"I've seen you before."

When a cop says that to you, you go pale even if you haven't murdered anybody.

"Maybe so; I don't remember," I said. "Where?"

He wiggled his pen. His nostrils flared. "The library! You were telling a story to the kids at the library downtown!"

I smiled weakly.

He said, "Month or two ago. I took my kid."

"What's your kid's name?"

"Mike."

"I have a boy named Petey. Maybe they played together that day."

"Yeah." He watched me. "Gary Kwan was there with his kid too."

"Oh! Uh—yeah!"

Mark came out and used his cell phone to call Steve Calhoun. It was appropriate for Steve, being an actual friend of the family, to go over and stay with Jacqueline. A cop said another cop had already been dispatched to break the news to her. "Hurry up," said Mark into the phone, his Indian-homeland lilt a bit strained. "No, there's much to be sorted out."

I watched him work the situation, I watched him actually work the police personnel. Cops don't always feel real buddy-buddy with defense attorneys, who are usually pitted against them in court, and I saw Mark Sharma busily striving to ingratiate himself. He asked them if they wanted coffee and sandwiches, and they actually said yes they did, so he sent for some, which a uniformed officer brought up.

It didn't take the police long to be finished with us, maybe an hour.

Mark and I walked out together past the news trucks. He shooed the reporters away, "But I promise a press conference tomorrow!"

"When?" called out one.

"Two p.m."

Late enough in the day to have a game plan ready, early enough to make the evening news.

In the cool dimness of the parking garage we stopped and faced each other.

I said, "I guess now's as good a time as any."

"Yes," agreed Mark.

We stood at one of the fat concrete columns that held up everything. The garage smelled of rubber and old hamburger wrappers.

We evaluated each other narrowly, again like the orphaned dingoes. It was not necessary to go somewhere for a drink; that would have been vulgar, and moreover we were both tired and would have to get up very early tomorrow, if we could sleep at all. He was sweating. So, I guess, was I.

I didn't trust him, but felt it wise to act as if I did.

I told him how Gary and I had met, and exactly what I'd been hired to do for Eileen.

"I've been giving her acting lessons all along. Helping her appear more sympathetic to the jury."

"I knew it!" he exclaimed, but obviously he hadn't. "You are not a real paralegal."

"That's right."

He smiled. "I saw a difference in Eileen immediately. Yes, yes. She looked mean, at first. Juries are stupid. Gary understood this." He gazed off into the distance with an expression of respect on his face, as if Gary's ghost were standing in the shadows. "I admire that strategy," he said. "I am in charge of the case now."

"Mark, which case? Eileen's? Or Gary's?"

His confidence didn't waver. "The case on trial now. You must understand that—"

"Mark, what did you and Gary argue about tonight?"

"Oh, so that's how the lieutenant knew."

"Yes, I told him Gary called me in after firing you for the night, as he put it."

"That's what he said?"

"Yes."

"That's all he said about me?"

He was working me, just as he'd worked the police.

"But what did Gary and you—"

"We argued about whether to put Eileen on the stand."

"I thought you guys were in accord on that. That she's going to testify."

"Gary had doubts. But we will put her on the stand. I'll move for one day's recess only. We must keep this trial on track."

I half collapsed against the pillar. "Mark, *one day*? You've got to be out of—"

"Steve and I have already talked. He is—"

"You have?"

"—very supportive of me. I lead this team from now on. Rita, the murder of Gary will explode all over the city tomorrow. How long should I wait? We cannot make this jury wait. We cannot start all over again in three months with a new jury. We must act."

I took my keys out of my purse. "Well, I guess it's a good career move for you."

For nonnative speakers of American English, sarcasm is the last thing they pick up. "Yes," agreed Mark Sharma. "We will resume the defense of Eileen Tenaway the day after tomorrow. I will work tonight." He patted his briefcase. "I have everything I need."

I stared at him. How can I explain it? I'm always searching for the motive in people, always trying to peel them back and look beneath the surface. And that's served me well as an actress.

Mark said, "The police will find Gary's murderer. We will let them do their job. Your job, on the other hand, is finished. You may go back to your acting."

I stood for a second, absorbing that. He watched me closely with his large black eyes.

"All right." I turned to go, relief flooding me like cool water.

Hey, everybody, I just got my life back!

But what the hell am I going to do for rent money!

"Sure," I said over my shoulder. "Put her on the stand without me. She ought to be fine. Just fine, all by herself." I strode toward my car.

"Rita!" Mark said.

I turned back to him. "Don't bother asking her if she wants me, because I'm certain—"

"Perhaps you should stay on the team after all." He tugged at his Gary-style forelock. "Eileen and I will discuss it. But if you do stay to help us, I will not pay you one thousand dollars per day."

"I see. You snooped into Gary's employment records."

"He made me a partner in his firm. It is now my firm."

That was news to me. But irrelevant right then.

I said, "You will pay me a thousand a day. It's Eileen's money, anyway, right? You owe me three thousand so far this week."

"I'll pay five hundred."

I turned. "So long, Mark. It's been good working with—"

"All right!" he shouted.

Once again I turned to his face, flushed dark with blood. "Mark, who do you think murdered Gary? Who could have come in like that, so quickly in between your leaving and my arriving? And why, for God's sake?"

He fixed me with the kind of look I remembered from high school debate class, a best-defense-is-a-good-offense look.

"Who do *you* think did it?" he asked with a little upturn in his voice.

Fuck you.

I said, "Well, Mark, someone who doesn't want him to defend Eileen. Someone who would benefit from him suddenly being out of the picture."

He smiled. "Or someone who was angry that he would not cheat on his wife."

Oh, fuck you, buddy.

"Or," I suggested, "someone who lost his temper in an argument."

The reptilian smile did not waver.

"Or," he said, "someone with a completely different problem."

My mind was like an oven with too much stuff trying to bake in it.

I wanted to talk it all over with Gary.

248

"Dear God," I muttered.

Standing there with Mark Sharma in the dead of night discussing savagery and blood and cops and impenetrable mystery—this was the Los Angeles I never thought I'd get to know.

TWENTY-SEVEN

U h-uh-uh! was the sound Esteban, the gem buyer, made when George Rowe's fists snapped into his upper gut, left–right–left.

Rowe punched him five times. The last two times Esteban made no sound because the first three had driven all the air out of him.

He toppled heavily to the floor of his office in the building on Ouro Prêto's main drag and lay gasping. Rowe said, "If you yell, I'll kill you." He had brought no toys with him today.

A moment ago Esteban was certain he'd had the upper hand. He had figured out that this man who had introduced himself as Tom Webber from Canada had some money at his disposal, and he had figured out that Webber was not really a tourist. He had learned what Mr. Webber was after. And given that he would very much like to leave Ouro Prêto and settle in the Miami region near America, possibly with one of the fashion models who lived there, he had laced his thick fingers behind his head as he had seen his boss Richard Tenaway do, leaned back in his fine leather chair, and said, "I never said one thousand, I said fifty thousand."

Rowe, sitting across the desk, had looked at him and sighed. He had, for this next meeting with Esteban, brought a thousand U.S. dollars in an envelope because he had been directed back to Ouro Prêto by someone in Berlin. He was getting tired.

In the past ten days he had journeyed to São Paulo, he had flown to Berlin, Helsinki, and Madrid, because the young Maria Helena had listened to Tenaway talking about all of those cities. He had promised to show them to her.

But Rowe had had nothing more than that to go on, and his contacts in those places had been of little help. They weren't very good contacts. His gut had been uncomfortable the whole time, because it had told him Tenaway hadn't gone to Europe in the first place. If Rowe had been Tenaway he would not have gone to Europe.

However, a gem dealer in Berlin had cheerfully shared the fact that young Esteban, the gem buyer in Brazil for Tenaway's company, Gemini Imports, had accompanied Tenaway to Berlin on several business trips just before Tenaway had disappeared. The German and Tenaway met alone and he would not say what Tenaway had discussed with him.

For lack of anything better Rowe asked, "Did you like Richard Tenaway?"

"Oh, yes!" answered the dealer, an apple-cheeked multimillionaire. "Herr Tenaway was a most pleasant man. He possessed— charisma. Women liked him very much, I tell you! Like a little boy. He always looked like a boy ready to steal some chocolate!"

Herr Gem Dealer laughed a Bavarian belly laugh.

So Rowe had returned to Ouro Prêto to talk to Esteban. Rowe had come to see Esteban alone, without Raimundo, because Esteban spoke fairly good English.

With the promise of a bit of money, Esteban revealed that before Tenaway "turned up dead"—with American-style air quotes around that—he had shown a special interest in Esteban, the only full-time Gemini employee in Ouro Prêto. Esteban had become Tenaway's buffer in acquiring copies of ownership documents to mines that had been locked up in local disputes—bad blood between families, or arguments between local authorities, the ecology people, and legitimate companies. Esteban had been the one to fill out the paperwork requesting these documents from local clerks in the various jurisdictions.

With these documents Tenaway analyzed the strengths and weaknesses of every player. He would step in with offers to the irresolute ones, getting them to relinquish their property or mineral rights to him, with all proper legal papers, then he would visit the stronger players and make them a deal, which always included something for Tenaway.

This went on until the Ministry of Mines wised up and put a stop to it.

Esteban gathered that the profit margin in these deals had been low, anyway. The main outcome seemed to be that one of the mine owners north of town had become quite indebted to Richard Tenaway. Esteban sensed Tenaway was holding this owner, a man named Pedro Rocha Grana, in reserve for some special role in the future.

Esteban thought he would, for this special work, receive extra money from Richard Tenaway, but he had gotten none.

He was angry at Tenaway and angrier at himself. So after this Tom Webber approached him to talk about Tenaway and promised him a thousand U.S. dollars, he decided he would not be taken advantage of again. He would be the one to take advantage. This little Tom Webber from Canada was amusing. The money, in an envelope, crossed Esteban's desk, and they began talking, but then Esteban said he wanted fifty thousand, if Tom Webber really wanted to know something.

When Webber stepped around the desk, Esteban rose to meet him, thinking he would easily block a blow, but the shorter man had thrust his arms right through Esteban's and gotten at his solar plexus.

After he had finished hitting Esteban, Rowe said, "You don't know anything, do you?"

George Rowe did not like to beat up men stupider than himself. There was no pleasure in it, even if the man was bigger and stronger, like Esteban. The Brazilian was a smooth, heavy young thing with no clear idea how to protect himself, let alone land a hard punch in Rowe's face.

That was how it was, though. Intelligent men tend not to get into fisticuffs with other intelligent men.

It was a pity Rowe could fight so well, could neutralize a man with a fast combination of traditional punches, or, if he felt it wiser, with an eye-gouge and a hard-soled shoe to the side of the knee, blowing out the joint like a Twinkie. If you did that you had to be prepared for screaming, because that's what you'd get a whole lot of, until you got out of there. It was a pity he had developed those skills so well but rarely liked to use them. His drumming had helped with the fighting skills, the all-four-limbs coordination, as well as, of course, the rhythm.

When a demand is made with no commensurate offer placed on the table, that is extortion. Extortion requires direct action.

But Esteban did have something for this Mr. Webber.

Lying on the floor, he raised his hands like kitten paws. "I have an address."

One day perhaps nine months ago, Esteban had photocopied one of a sheaf of shipping receipts he had found in Tenaway's briefcase. He had snooped while Tenaway was in the men's room. The receipts were unusual, showing a series of packages sent to an address in Tijuana, Mexico. Esteban had thought the photocopy might come in useful someday. But Tenaway had vanished before he'd had the chance to use it.

Rowe left the office with the photocopy of the shipping slip. It didn't take a long night in front of a crystal ball for him to be fairly sure the packages had contained gems, possibly some cash, Euros perhaps. They would have been transferred from Tijuana to Los Angeles easily. It also stood to reason that somehow this Pedro Rocha Grana, a Brazilian mine owner with international connections, was going to help Tenaway resell the gems once he was ready to start that process. That was the beauty of it—with the gems out of Brazil, so much was possible: bulk sales in the U.S. or Mexico, or more-profitable small-batch sales through a dummy company.

All this fit Rowe's feeling all along, that Tenaway would wait at the border until he could know whether it would be worth his while to return for the resources he had secured in Los Angeles.

TWENTY-EIGHT

A rancid haze settled over me the next day, which was Thursday. It was as if the whole city had turned poisonous—as if micro-bubbles of toxin were raining down on the city, green in color, the exact chartreuse of the mittens of the tiny bully in my first-grade class who had used them to mash snow into my dumb pretty little face that winter, over and over. When the snow melted, she used mud.

As Mark had foretold, news of Gary's murder detonated in the city. The morning announcers shouted it over and over, their voices so glad that something really dreadful had happened last night, and I supposed everyone was talking about it over their coffee and muffins. I expected to look up and see skywriting: *KWAN MURDERED. SURRENDER RITA.*

Daniel and I had held each other and cried all night.

This morning I found myself composed: I felt strong, curious, willful. Nothing was a game. Nothing would be there for me if I crumpled.

Crumpling was a luxury you could have if there was a safety net for you.

I felt very unsafe.

True, I had Daniel, but he had his own shit to deal with. His ideal man had been returned to him, then snatched away. He was unemployed. He loved me like a brother, but he could not make life different for me. He could not manipulate my world as I needed it to be done.

In the wake of something like this I expected total chaos. Just last week, Steve Calhoun had said, "Only Mount Rushmore has a higher profile than this trial."

But I learned this day a valuable lesson: when chaos comes, you carve it into chunks and address them one at a time. In this way all the parts are carried away and dealt with. By the police, the evidence-gatherers and -analyzers. By the coroner with his bone saws and microscope slides. By the widow in seclusion with her rage, bafflement, and little kid whose permanent footnote would be *Daughter of Murdered Lawyer Gary Kwan*. By family in Japan, the friends, the broker, the barber. By the media, of course. We are all audience for the Spaceship Media. It chews you up and spits you out, then makes you watch.

When I dropped Petey off at preschool at seven o'clock, a man with a friendly face stopped us outside on the steps. "Ms. Farmer?"

He sported one of those straw porkpie hats that suburban dads used to wear to barbecues. Now they were in style with handsome black guys at Dodgers games.

"Yes?" I gripped Petey's hand tighter, friendly face or no.

He handed me an envelope, tipped his hat—quaint gesture!—and said, "Thank you."

I hoped the envelope would be full of payola—*I* don't know—but I had a bad feeling this fellow was a process server.

The other moms and dads hurried past. Petey tugged against my antilock grip. I'd dressed him in a sweater for this cool morning, having mended his Spider-Man jacket but left it, for now, in my sewing drawer. I released him into the school and went to my car holding the envelope.

As I unlocked the door, quick footsteps pounded behind me. I whirled.

"I'm sorry I didn't catch you," said Ms. Crayden, a large, Birkenstock-wearing woman, "but I wanted to talk about Petey for a minute. I'm afraid he's gone back to hitting the other kids." She angled her eyebrows apologetically, but her gaze was pretty direct.

"Oh!" I cleared my throat, "Well—"

"Rather a lot." Ms. Crayden had been in this preschool racket for at least a decade and did not shrink from difficult facts. "It's become an issue."

"I see. Well—"

"Is there any trouble at home?"

"Oh, no. Things are fine at home, but you know his dad and I are divorced, and maybe he's, um, feeling a little, uh—"

Dominantly, she set her hip against the fender of my car. "I've tried to work with him on it, but he hasn't been cooperative. The other parents aren't happy. Would you talk to him, please?"

"Yes, of course."

"Because otherwise—"

"Yes! Of course!"

I went with her into the school and took Petey aside. I squatted down, gripped his little tan sweater, and got in his face. "Ms. Crayden tells me you've been hitting."

He opened his eyes and mouth wide, the signal for an oncoming lie, so I quickly said, "We don't hurt. OK? Remember we've talked about that?"

He hung his head.

I felt for him, because he didn't have a little brother or sister to beat up. He had to go through this on his own: learning the exhilaration of hitting, the feeling of mastery hitting brings, then making the dismaying discovery that you can't keep doing it.

"We'll talk some more later, OK? Have I ever told you the story of the little panda bear who liked to hit other little pandas?"

"No," he mumbled to the floor.

"Well, you'll hear it tonight," I promised grimly.

He brightened. "I'm going to Spider Con with Daddy tonight!" His eyes danced, and I could see he was already forgetting this scolding.

"No, honey, that's tomorrow night." I wished I could threaten him with not going, but no way would Jeff back me up. "Remember, honey, we don't hurt." I gave him a squeeze and left.

Outside in the car I opened the envelope. Legal papers spilled out—an attorney's letterhead, *Dear Ms. Farmer*—Jeff was suing me for exclusive custody of Petey on the outrageous grounds of "risk of substantial harm."

I pictured myself throwing the whole goddamned packet down a sewer.

I pictured myself cramming the papers down Jeff's surly alcoholic throat.

I pictured myself blowing Jeff's head off with a shotgun.

After I'd made him swallow the papers.

We don't hurt.

Yeah, my ass.

WITH GRAVE SADNESS, Judge Davenport took the bench. He'd known Gary for ages. The jury's faces all showed one degree or other of freak-outedness.

Tracy Beck-Rubin looked gray but determinedly unemotional.

The usual media huddled about, plus a bunch more in the farther corridors and the ground-floor lobby. Padraig McGower occupied his customary seat, towering tall even sitting down. As usual, he and Eileen met eyes. I watched.

The judge sent the jury out while he and the lawyers had a discussion in open court. Mark entered a motion to adjourn for one day.

"Don't you want more time than that?" asked the judge, surprised. "Don't you think it would be appropriate to show some respect to your boss?"

"I respect his memory," answered Mark. "We will show respect by defending this client who has been promised a speedy trial. We are ready."

And I guess we were. He and I had met with Eileen earlier, and I felt my bones chill as I stood by and listened to them.

Eileen, calm and perfectly dressed for court, had been told the news. Her expression was neutral when Mark walked into the holding cell, then it grew a little hard when she saw me. She focused her attention on Mark.

They discussed the pros and cons of waiting a decent interval, but there really was nothing that would change about the defense strategy. Gary's murder had nothing to do with the question of whether Eileen had fed tranquilizers to her baby girl one night six months ago.

"But wait," I said. "Aren't we even going to talk about—"

Mark interrupted, "There's no time to sit and speculate. We have work to do."

He wore a fresh gray suit with a light gray shirt, and a silver tie like a sword blade down his shirtfront. He held his shoulders square and his head back. His small feet in their exotic shoes tapped with impatience and energy.

The arrogance had come over him. *Yes,* I thought, *this guy's got what it takes. He'd been the little follower, the cupcake-eater, and now he's the king of the jungle.*

Later I showed the custody-suit papers to Steve Calhoun. He was in the conference room that had been put aside for us, eating his twentieth roast beef sandwich of the trial, having hours ago come out of his initial shock about Gary. As Gary's associates we would all be under suspicion at first. Until we were cleared. If we were cleared. He ate his sandwich steadily. Smelling it, I felt a bit sick.

For a few minutes we talked about Gary, then I showed him the papers. He looked at them and said, "Man, this guy hates you. How did you break his balls?"

"It's a complicated web of bullshit, Steve."

"Who did your divorce?"

I told him, and he said Jim was a good lawyer. "Just forward all this crap to him and forget about it for now. If your ex really thought your son was in danger, he would have had Protective Services on your rear already."

My cell phone played "Fame."

I thanked Steve, flipped open the phone, and left the room.

"Hi, Marly."

"Hey, sunshine, it's closing in, just like I told you it would."

I rested my head on a cool steel seismic beam. "What's closing in?"

"*Fame, baby!* No more scream auditions for you, I'll bet the farm! Oatberger wants to see you again!"

TWO POLICE OFFICERS, one with a slight hitch in his walk from having been bitten by a Doberman during a wife-beating call the previous night, climbed the stairs to the third floor of an apartment building on Crenshaw Avenue near Olympic. The beater and wife lived in a house just a block away. He wondered if the guy had made bail. He wondered if the Doberman would pass quarantine.

Consulting her notebook, the other officer said, "This is it," and stopped before a door. She knocked briskly and called, "Police." She didn't call with an exclamation point from deep in her chest, since this was not a warrant situation, merely a question-and-look-around situation. A phone call had been placed from this address to Gary Kwan's office last night. "Ms. Jacubiak? Police."

The next-door neighbor popped out and, touching her hairdo, which had come out of the tinfoil pincurls nicely this morning, touching it automatically in the presence of the male cop because he was a total hunk, said, "She's out of town."

She explained about Joshua Tree and next Tuesday, which was when Sally had said she'd be back. The cops stared at the locked apartment door. "But if you need to get in, Mr. Lee will let you in, I'm sure, you being the police and all."

"Who's Mr. Lee?" asked the male cop, rubbing the sore place on his arm from the tetanus shot.

"The landlord, he's in—"

"Thank you, ma'am," they said, and went away because they didn't have cause to request a warrant.

In the patrol car they got in touch with the park service and asked them to look for Sally Jacubiak's car. They wanted to talk to her and any possible companions. It was a blue Audi, they said, and read off the plate number.

TWENTY-NINE

Twilight settled on Los Angeles, the great swath of sun moving west and away. I crammed my Honda into the parking lot at Santa Monica and Rodeo and got out. There was no breeze; traffic surged and ebbed beyond the railing; fumes; more fumes. A heavy haze was solidifying into dark clouds. Gary had not been dead twenty-four hours.

"Gramma?"

I waited.

Rain is the castor oil of weather in Los Angeles. Everybody whines when it rains, they crash their cars on the suddenly slick roads, but they know it's good for them. Rain replenishes the reservoirs and wets down the eager-to-burn undergrowth in the hills and wherever else the ground isn't paved over.

Moreover, winter's grip on the city is always deceptive—in

spite of the desert factor, no one ever feels safe from the sudden storms lashing in from the Pacific, carrying over the cold beaches into the city like a foretaste of old age or sickness. Spring was fighting hard to take hold.

The first drops of a shower fell. A bit of a west wind kicked up. I remained where I was, feeling the rain on my face.

"Well, Gramma, if that's the way you feel, so do I. The wheels are coming off my life. I'm trying to be like you. I don't know. I feel like I ought to be in a modicum of control here. But every time I think I am, somebody gets murdered."

I didn't waste time whining about the man I loved and all that.

"Should I just pack up my son and run away? I'm not a sissy, but I don't want to be stupid. Maybe I've made a whole row of bad decisions without even knowing it."

Gramma Gladys's voice came with a brisk gust, *Hell no! Don't you dare run away. Stand and fight. You've got to take them all!*

"But fight how? I mean, I can't imagine myself—"

To the death, Rita.

The wind blew the rain away. I waited, not wanting to leave. Not wanting to think about fighting to the death.

I felt a plop on my sleeve: birdshit. I peered up to see a flock of pigeons zooming gracefully away over the darkening rooftops of Rodeo Drive, chasing the rain. I reached into the Honda for a wad of McDonald's napkins I methodically accumulated in the console for juice box spills and the like. *Console.* That's such a nice word. I wiped off the oily crap and noted to self to get to the dry cleaner's with this fairly expensive jacket that Gramma Gladys would have really liked.

As I straightened up again to look at the sky, I heard a shuffle. A street guy rounded the car next to mine and came up to me, quite close, almost touching my sleeve. I pulled back. I hadn't seen him coming through the parked cars.

He ran his fingers through his greasy hair, then wiped them on his windbreaker. He jiggled one palm. "Spare change, lady, for me and my dog?"

I sighed and held out a dollar, expecting to be thanked. I saw no dog.

Folding the dollar, he said in a completely different voice, "What's wrong?"

"What?"

"You only gave me a dollar this time. Last time it was a five."

"What?"

"Wasn't I as convincing today?"

"What are you talking about?" I looked at him closer. It was the same bum I'd given money to before. Different coat. "Buddy, I'd like to be alone, OK?"

"I'm Vince Devereaux," he said.

I looked again. For Christ's sake, it was. As a member of the Screen Actors Guild I was entitled to vote for the Academy Awards, and I'd voted for him for best actor last year when he was in *Storm Surge*. He didn't happen to win that time. I said, "What the hell?"

"I'm preparing for a role in a picture," he explained. "Could you tell me exactly why you didn't think I was as convincing today as before? I've been panhandling on and off for two months, and I really thought I was getting better."

"Well," I said, "maybe you're trying too hard."

MY ANSWERING MACHINE was packed that night with messages from astonished friends who'd finally seen my face on TV or heard my name mentioned on the air as the person who had called the police to Gary's murder scene.

"I didn't know you'd given up acting!" said Yvonne in dismay. "Well, paralegal—paralegal, right?—'s a nice line of work, I guess. Call me if you want to talk. I mean, how terrible for you, last night. I'm kind of wondering, you know."

Marly said, "Whatever you're up to, it's working! Oatberger *himself* called me *again* after he saw the TV report with you in it. He acted mad! He said, 'This kind of actress I don't need.' But he wanted me to tell you he'll meet with you at eleven o'clock Saturday, just like you asked. Isn't that a kick? I played dumb about the Tenaway stuff. Which I am, because I had no idea. All I said was, 'Well, at least she's not sitting around the pool waiting for the phone to ring.'"

As I was deleting messages the phone rang again. I let the machine get it, but when I heard George Rowe's deep voice I picked up. "George, I'm here." I was so relieved I almost threw up.

He'd heard about Gary from his bosses at the insurance company. "I'd just made up my mind," he said, "that Richard Tenaway wasn't dangerous, then this happens. How—how are you doing?" I was touched by the concern in his voice.

"I'm OK. I guess I ought to be more scared than I am. My only worry, really, is Petey. I mean, if something happens to me." I didn't tell him about Ryan's attempted abduction and the Spider-Man jacket, and I didn't tell him what a little butthead Petey was being, and how guilty I felt about having slapped him, and the process server. But I did tell him about Janet, the strange threat she had made, and the even stranger request about the locker key.

He was silent, and I thought we'd gotten cut off.

"George?"

"Yeah. What did Kwan say about this Janet?"

"He told me not to worry about it, that the world is full of crazies."

"Well, that's true." He fell silent again.

"Uh, George?"

"I'm thinking."

I let him think. The kitchen clock, an old Sunbeam electric I'd gotten at a junk store, hummed. I smelled the fragrance of six pretty peaches I'd put in a basket. Petey was absorbed in looking under his bed with a flashlight for something.

George said, "Listen, Rita, as we already knew after your friend inspected that photograph, Tenaway didn't die in Brazil. He left the country under an assumed name—stolen passport, which I'm sure he ditched immediately. I believe he's in Tijuana, which is where I am at the moment. I'm very disturbed by the murder of Gary Kwan. It's possible Tenaway arranged for the hit. It's even possible he did it himself, but I just don't feel he's in California yet. He's on his way, though, I'm sure. If not him, though, who the hell killed Kwan?"

"It was a messy hit," I offered.

He spoke gently. "Yes, stabbing, right? You discovered the body?"

"It was terrible, George."

"You have a lawyer?"

"Steve Calhoun is advising me for now."

"OK."

"You remember the young attorney from the trial, Mark Sharma? He was with Gary just before it happened."

"Did he do it?"

"I don't think so. I think he thinks I did, though."

George Rowe sighed into the phone, a deep sigh that ended in almost a growl. "Well, the murderer was someone who wanted to disrupt Eileen's trial, someone who thought Gary Kwan was about to get her acquitted and didn't want that to happen. Or maybe Kwan had a mistress and she killed him, or maybe his wife did it, or maybe he had a gay lover or something, or somebody with an old grudge found him, or maybe it was the janitor."

"Yeah."

"Rita, you have to be very careful," he said steadily. "Tenaway is out there and he's doing business. I think he'll jump the border as soon as the trial is over. If you see anything, call me. When you call, I'll get to a landline and call you back on yours, OK? Do be careful."

I said, "George, what does that mean, be careful? Detectives are always saying it in the movies, but now I don't even know what it means. I can't just lock myself in my apartment."

"Essentially," he said, "it means don't take candy from strangers."

WATCHING, NEXT MORNING, Mark walk the jury through key pieces of the physical evidence from the point of view of the defense, I saw he'd learned more from Gary than I'd thought. Even vocally he had modeled himself after his mentor. His voice was calm and measured, yet he brought out emotion with inflections and pauses for effect. This was a Friday, and he wanted to impress the jury so they could think about it over the weekend.

He hit heavily on the fact that no toxicology test was done on Eileen that awful morning, in spite of her having told the police she felt unwell, sleepy, peculiar. Of course, evidence of a strange drug could have done harm to the defense's case as much as it might have done good. But in the absence of proof, Sharma could and did imply police negligence. He implied that a tox test could have proved Eileen was victimized that night, along with her daughter.

"So the only difference," he said to a witness, flipping his coat back in a confident, Gary-like gesture, "was Eileen survived the attack, and Gabriella did not, isn't that right?"

Tracy Beck-Rubin objected, but he'd made his point.

He cast delicious doubt on the police evidence with short, tight testimony from three expert witnesses, called to the box bam-bam-bam.

Beck-Rubin couldn't achieve much in her cross-examinations, and realizing she was in trouble she kept her questions brief. She tried for maximum contempt effect, flipping her eyes heaven-ward, shaking her head in disgust, the whole can-you-believe-this-bullshit thing. It was a little too obvious for the jury, though; they only glanced at her dismissively. I could have given her some pointers.

Mark figured we'd probably only need two more days for the defense. "Fast and hard, like a good boxing match," he said to the team in the conference room that afternoon. A two- or three-day defense would certainly contrast astonishingly with the belabored eight weeks of prosecution we'd endured.

The police were investigating all of us the same way, fast and hard. They interviewed Daniel, they talked to my neighbors in the building, and I'm sure Jeff was on their list too.

I HAD MANAGED to pack Petey's suitcase for Spider Con that morning. I made sure to get home with a few groceries in time to fix him an early dinner of a grilled-cheese sandwich, carrot sticks, and a large mug of hot cocoa, his favorite beverage. A tummyful of love. He was so excited about Spider-Man World Con he could hardly eat, but I cajoled him.

"Spider-Man never goes on a mission on an empty stomach. He needs the energy from good food."

"Mmph," said Petey, who was losing the last of his baby fat before my eyes. His arms and legs were so thin—little pipestems sticking out from his shirts and shorts. Watching him eat, I had one of those mommy moments where you're alone with your child and a nameless wistfulness comes over you. What would occupy those little hands someday? A surgeon's scalpel? A carpenter's plane? An ice ax and loop of rope? I supposed the likeliest thing would be a computer keyboard, but I rejected that notion. His natural inclination toward climbing and jumping boded better for a future of conquering peaks, exploring oceans, well, who the hell knew, Olympic gold, why not?

I came back to the present thinking of Jeff. He'd served me papers trying to take away my boy—for no reason but to hurt and spite me. Steve Calhoun had called Jeff's challenge a nuisance suit, but I thought of it more as a hate crime.

To be frank, however, I was still feeling sort of schizophrenic about Petey. I begrudged him going away for the weekend, but I did need a break. He hadn't yet many friends who could come over and play, so he still depended on me a great deal for amusement. There was the hitting thing, but above all that, with a small child around, you're never alone; you never have a scrap of total peace because as a mother your senses are always on alert, to one degree or another, even when the kid's asleep. I badly wanted a couple of nights off.

Jeff had said he'd come for him at six-thirty.

I would have to be civil to him now and forever, tied as we were by the blood flowing through Petey's veins. And even when our boy would be a man and all custody battles finished, he would marry and have children (fingers crossed for that order) and Jeff and I would be tied by their blood as well.

It's really shocking, the long-term effects of the simple act of fucking. Moms and dads have learned this over and over through the ages. How smart we all are by now.

I pictured Jeff glaring at me across the aisle at Petey's ball games, his commencements, his wedding.

Six-thirty came and went, then seven.

"He'll prob'ly be here any minute," Petey crowed anxiously.

I agreed. "He's probably stuck in a traffic jam."

"Daddy'll just blast through that traffic jam! I wish I had a blaster, I'd just blast that traffic jam!"

"Into a jillion pieces," I suggested.

"Jillion pieces!"

I popped a Mickey Mouse DVD into the player, but Petey insisted, "No! Spider-Man! The first one!" I knew every word of those movies. But I put it on, and he settled down to watch, one ear cocked toward the door.

Which remained silent.

At seven-thirty, I phoned Jeff's office and condo and left voice mails, then tried his cell phone. No answer.

If Petey had been only three, I'd have been able to distract him, make up an interesting story, create some special fun that would have delighted him. But he was four and had developed the single-minded focus on an adult promise I'd hoped wouldn't happen for a few more years.

His small dimpled face searched mine for reassurance.

That was a long night, during which I witnessed the six phases of juvenile disillusionment:

1. Giddy excitement.
2. Buoyant optimism.
3. Steadfast hope.
4. Creeping desperation.
5. Full-on desperation.
6. Sobbing despair.

The final phase lasts longest, approximately two hours or until loss of consciousness occurs, whichever is latest. Tonight it was midnight.

He came to at about six-thirty in the morning and brought an optimistic attitude to the breakfast table, then remembered Spider Con.

"Oh, Spidey," he wailed. "Oh, Daddy."

He'd begun grieving for Jeff. Good.

Daniel came to the rescue, brushing aside my almost incoherent gratitude. He swept Petey off in his turbocharged Porsche to the lovely boulder fields in the San Gabriels, to scramble around and later eat enormous chickenburgers at some hippie bar he knew.

"YOU BASTARD!" I let my anger flare just a little higher. "You think you can kill with money. Choke off the life in this valley."

I listened to Serge Oatberger sputter a denial, my head turned away toward the dark line of trees at the edge of the open range, far beyond the walls of the conference room at Colonnade Studios.

I brought my anger down now from fire to frost, like water freezing on a pond, crystallizing so swiftly you can't believe it or stop it. "I know it was you bought up all the heart medicine in the county so I couldn't get any for Paw. Well, now he's dead, just like you wanted."

We went on with the scene, improvising as we had the first time. Appropriately, the conference room was as gloomy as the inside of a pine shed in the rain.

Sometimes you just know it's the right moment to take a risk.

I craved this role of Emily Rounceville in *Third Chance Mountain*. Hell, if for no other reason I'd need work after the Tenaway trial.

In my first audition I'd been loose enough to let ideas come to me during the improvisation, and I'd used them. But I'd worked carefully; there had been a dab of *don't blow it* in there, and afterward I'd wondered whether Oatberger had seen it.

Today I felt differently. Maybe I'd finally lived long enough to understand that caution has its drawbacks.

His lackeys were there, and once again I'd been offered Gatorade. I declined it. The blond-tipped bootlicker who'd offered it to me gasped slightly. Then Oatberger stumbled over a chair, and another tight-jeans had said, "I'm sorry."

Honestly.

Oatberger was a good actor. I perceived the equal parts evil and fear in his eyes, as the selfish rancher who long ago learned that money wasn't good enough to buy an honest woman. Now he'd used it as a weapon, and it still didn't work.

The lines in his forehead deepened, but his lips stretched into a smile. "You'll think different," he said, "once you've got used to my ways."

I drew up the saliva in my mouth and fired it straight into his face.

THIRTY

Jeff never called or showed that whole weekend. After returning from my audition I cleaned the bathroom, made pizza
dough, and crafted recriminations. "How could you break
his heart like that?" I muttered viciously, jabbing the toilet brush
under the rim. "You're not a daddy, you're a shit cloud."

I didn't think much about Oatberger. I was glad I'd jolted the
hell out of him. The significance of that—being glad about it—
escaped me at the moment. I figured, if spitting in his face doesn't
get me the job, nothing can. He'd sent me away with one of his
signature scowls.

Back to Jeff. I pictured him on a bender with the new
girlfriend—she'd probably convinced him to abandon Petey in favor of partying at her house with the pool and the dog named Tuna
or whatever. They were clinking glasses and laughing maniacally.

Then, of course, I imagined him dead somewhere—perhaps at the bottom of that very pool with all the dog turds. Or perhaps he'd driven off the PCH, his last thought before hitting the rocks being, *Let's see, how many hours has it been since I last got laid?*

"How could you be such a self-indulgent jackass?" I snarled, slamming the pizza dough around the kitchen. "Excuse? A reason? No. There's no way you're ever gonna get redemption from this one, asshole."

When Daniel brought my boy home that night, all of Petey's grief had been drained away, replaced by the relaxed happiness that always came over him when he was with Daniel. I'd pretty much gotten it out of my system too. Daniel looked like he'd worked off some of his torrential grief over Gary. We ate pizza and I heard all about the boulders and lizards and picker bushes.

On Sunday morning Daniel returned with the newspaper and an armful of comic books, and I went to the lockup to work with Mark Sharma and Eileen. (Weekend visiting for lawyers was another special privilege quietly scored by Gary, way in the beginning.) We went over her testimony for about two hours. She wanted to take the stand. It would happen this week.

Juries, you know, hardly ever get to hear the accused testify in major trials. Too risky, defense lawyers say. Well, let's face it—any defense attorney will admit that most of the people they represent are in fact guilty. So it stands to reason a good prosecutor would make pâté of a defendant on the stand, even if the defendant's story is well rehearsed. Gary Kwan had not permitted Roscoe Jamison to testify, even though Roscoe's friends all insisted in public that he was dying to tell the truth. Roscoe had a good PR department, you gotta hand him that.

Moreover, even an innocent person can be made to look shifty or foolish by a skillful prosecutor.

Eileen seemed both weary of this whole show and supremely confident. Her back was straight.

When Mark left the room for a moment, she asked, "Do you think I've got it?"

Right then I saw something extra in her. I guess I'd call it a sort of forward gaze, an intentness, as if she were already feeling the heft of the trophy in her hands. There was secrecy in her look, though, as well. I found her just a little spooky.

I said, "Do you mean do I think you're ready for the jury—and Tracy Beck-Rubin?"

"Oh, her."

"Well, with that attitude, yes. You've got it. But just in case, we'll be going over questions she's likely to ask you. And I want to work with you on your voice."

"Oh. I don't want a lot of homework right now."

"Look, missy." I scraped my chair closer to hers. Cold fluorescent photons rained down on us. "The jury's on your side now, clearly. Or at least they're *ready* to be on your side. They can't wait for you to talk to them. They really want to believe you. Remember Beatrice Rhinegold?"

Eileen looked at me quickly, a faint smile breaking on her lips.

I said, "Whenever you take the stand—maybe Tuesday or Wednesday—your best friend from the old neighborhood will be sitting today in the middle of the jury box. Place your voice to her."

THE CIRCUS STARTED up again Monday morning. The clangor of the media, the clench in my gut, my ongoing fascination with that chunk of the iceberg there below the surface. That iceberg was getting bigger by the day.

Gary's funeral was today. Jacqueline, we were told, wanted only family members there.

"Where's Padraig?" asked Eileen as soon as she joined us at the defense table.

I shrugged, looking. No sky-scraping red head in the gallery. This was the first morning he'd been absent. Not auspicious.

Eileen heaved a long sigh of distress. Firmly, I said, "We need you to be up. Focus ahead." She nodded and gave herself a shake. She sat relaxed and erect.

Through skillful questioning of his witnesses, Mark presented the defense's alternate theory of what had happened that night, developed by Steve Calhoun at a cost of roughly a hundred fifty thousand dollars (at least that was Lisa Feltenberger's whispered estimate). An intruder or intruders had broken into the Tenaway house with larceny in their hearts. Eileen had awakened at the noise, naturally, but they sedated her with a date-rape drug like Rohypnol.

"Isn't this type of drug especially useful," a friendly Mark suggested to a witness, "because it doesn't merely render the victim helpless, but it causes her to lose her memory of what happened to her?"

"Yes," answered the forensic toxicologist.

Mark pestered his next witness, the detective lieutenant in charge, on why the police had not requested a toxicology test for her. He'd been thumping on that since he began on Friday.

"I can't speculate on why no tox test was ordered," answered the beefy homicide lieutenant reluctantly. He'd been good-humored with Mark at first, but quickly became guarded. His forehead shone with sweat.

"Any of several people could have requested it, right?"

"Yes."

"But it was not done?"

"I've already said that."

"Therefore," speculated Mark, "we don't know exactly *why* Eileen Tenaway neither heard nor saw any intruder."

Tracy Beck-Rubin objected. "Is there a question here?"

Judge Davenport sustained.

But Mark, once again, had made his point. "No bruises or obvious marks on her, to indicate a struggle?" he resumed in his let's-suppose voice. "Wouldn't she have struggled?"

Beck-Rubin kept objecting, but every time she did, Mark simply backed off and tried again differently.

He called a witness, this one a martial-arts expert, who testified how easy it would be for two people to subdue the small-statured Eileen merely by pinning her arms to her sides in a bear hug from behind, then forcing a drugged liquid down her throat. Or they may have given her an injection.

Several jurors nodded, an excellent sign.

Mark then called up a psychiatrist, who, answering Mark's skilled questions, painted the rest of the picture the defense wanted: *Naturally, Gabriella wakes up crying. The neighbors may or may not hear her unconsoled shrieking—there is shrubbery between the houses, but why take the chance? Gabriella must be silenced.*

But wouldn't intruders have simply used the same mysterious drug on Gabriella they'd used on her mother? Well, we know criminals are not particularly intelligent life-forms. If they were, they wouldn't be criminals.

If they only brought one dose of a drug along and they used it on the one competent adult they knew to be in the house, what would they do? They could smother the child, killing her outright, or, not seeing themselves as murderers, look for something handy to use.

They find the Valium, bury it in some ice cream from the kitchen, and feed it to the little one. How easy. How simple.

"Perhaps," Mark continued, "whoever gave Gabriella the tranquilizer did not intend to kill her. We do not know." That had become his mantra: *We do not know.* Brilliant to identify himself with the authorities. With all of us citizens. *We. We do not know. We wish we did. If we did, we could put the correct individuals on trial.*

"Then," he said at one point, "they carried on with their plot to rob the house, didn't they?"

"Objection, Your Honor!" shrieked Beck-Rubin.

Judge Davenport sustained.

Mark pondered. A calm flip of the coat. A stroke of the jaw.

"They *might* have carried on with their plot to rob the house."

The judge almost laughed, and Mark kept going, conjuring the picture he wanted through his witnesses, one by one. *The intruders were sloppy. They left behind clues—the coffee cup, the cigarette butt, the hat in the juniper bush.*

Patiently, Mark fired his affable questions.

Now, this scenario fits the facts, doesn't it?

Home invasions happen in Los Angeles almost every day, unfortunately, don't they?

I ask you, does this fit the facts: that a stable, well-balanced mother would murder her own child, then clumsily try to blame it on strangers?

He got a witness, a police psychiatrist, to say it: "No, that does not fit. It does not fit at all."

"It does not fit at all," Mark repeated, taking a wide, nothing-to-hide stance. "That's what you said, correct? It does not fit." Just brilliant. Gary would have been proud. Beck-Rubin was able to achieve next to nothing on her crosses.

At lunch recess I got on the phone with Jeff's employer, Continental Pavilions. His secretary told me he hadn't come into work. She acted fishy, though, not directly answering me as to whether she'd heard from him.

"Well, this is kind of confusing," I said, "so if you'd—"

"I understand," she interrupted. "Goodbye."

So that was how it was. Next I tried his lawyer. He took my call, but said he had no idea where Jeff was. Which I'd basically expected—confidentiality and all—but I wanted him to know Jeff had gone AWOL, in case he didn't.

"Well," I suggested, "maybe we'd better file a missing-persons report, then."

"I wouldn't," said the attorney.

I hung up.

Fuck it, then. In seven years I'll have him declared dead and Petey can get his hands on his 401(k) for college.

"HOW ARE YOU feeling?" Mark asked Eileen as court convened the next morning.

"Fine." Her eyes were determined.

"Then we'll swear you immediately. You're our last witness."

"Mark," I suggested, "would it be all right if I moved the chart easel to the other side of the witness box? Then when Eileen turns her head to look at it she'll still be in line with the jury, and they'll see her face better. In case you use it, I mean, because—"

"Yes, yes, do it. If you have a good idea, act on it. I shouldn't have to babysit you."

Five minutes later Eileen took the oath.

Our star witness seated herself gracefully, wearing a caramel-brown dress of light wool, ordinary pantyhose, and gorgeous calf-skin shoes, neat and spare, but very quietly elegant with that dress. The dress was new for the day; she'd told me Steve Calhoun's wife had picked it out for her. It was perfect, giving her a warm, soft, yet substantial look. She wore plain gold ball studs in her ears, no other jewelry except her wedding set. She'd done the semi-French twist with her hair, and it looked pretty good. She'd gotten her roots touched up somehow—a smuggled box of L'Oréal, no doubt—and had on a bare sheen of lipstick.

She appeared rested, alert, and concerned.

I'd have hired her as prime-time anchor in a minute. I thought a strand of pearls would have completed the look, but then again it might have been overkill. What did I feel for her now? Only hopefulness and excitement. The thrill of taking the stage, as if I were taking it myself, striding out from the wings full of confidence. Guilty? Innocent? At this moment *I did not care.*

Mark set right off on the plan Gary had been considering, which was to merely ask Eileen to tell the jury what had happened that evening, "starting around dinnertime." No speculating, no leading other than an occasional prompt for direction.

The instant Eileen began to speak, the little ambient sounds of the courtroom stopped. Her throaty voice sounded clean and calm.

"We went into the kitchen together," she began simply. "I fed Gabriella some noodles and peas, and she drank some milk. I ate some chicken, but she didn't want any. Some roasted chicken."

Eileen was a mother, and she related the plain details of the last evening she'd spent with her child. Bath time, story time, bedtime. And yes, she was definitely projecting her voice, her *self,* to Beatrice Rhinegold there in the jury box. I could almost see Beatrice myself—a pudgy thing in glasses and a pullover sweater.

"I put her pink sleeper on her," Eileen went on. "She seemed a little restless, trying to get comfortable, so I sat in the rocker next to her crib for a while. She settled down." Eileen paused, and Mark asked softly, "What was the last thing you did before leaving her bedroom?"

"I kissed her."

After that came the dreadful time, the time when time itself stands still and the things people convince themselves to do are things that only nighttime can accept.

Eileen had no narration for that time, and so in her testimony there was just a dark blank as Mark Sharma paused.

Then he asked, "And what did you do when you woke up in the morning?"

Still poised, she began. Her voice trembled, but bravely she kept her eyes lifted, and I saw her instinctively and slowly shift her gaze to different faces in the jury box. Any cabaret performer learns that if you fix on one person, everyone surrounding that person will feel spoken to or sung to as well. I hadn't tried to teach Eileen that, feeling it might have been one too many things to remember. Plus often an amateur, trying that trick, will move her eyes around too much and look unnatural.

But she was doing it, all on her own, and it came off beautifully.

I pulled for my protégé, pulled hard for her.

Eileen's voice broke, and as she spoke about finding the dead body of her daughter, she wept softly. The judge asked if she wanted a moment.

"No, thank you," she said gently, managing to keep just enough composure not to break the spell. "I'd like to finish."

The jury had stopped breathing, everybody had stopped breathing.

"I felt the whole world had come to an end," said Eileen. "I knew if she was cold and stiff, she was dead, but I tried to pretend when the ambulance came she was still alive. I know it doesn't make any sense, but I thought if I told them she was alive, she'd be alive."

After a pause, Mark asked his final question. "Eileen Tenaway, did you give your baby that Valium?"

She lifted her head a notch higher.

Gazing over the top of Mark Sharma's haircut, her profile to the jury, noble and sad, she said, "No, I did not."

She was incandescent.

THIRTY-ONE

Daniel Clements's own incoming ringtone was "Sixteen Going on Seventeen." He identified with Liesl von Trapp in that he all too willingly believed the blandishments of the older men who hit on him. Trouble was, he wanted neither a daddy nor a boy toy. Meeting up with Gary Kwan again had been too good to be true. He couldn't think about that anymore. Except, of course, that's all he could think about.

Daniel had never been a vengeful fellow; even when badly wronged he'd preferred to walk away from it. But now he saw that some wrongs were different.

He wanted to participate in what was left of Gary Kwan: his memory, his justice. Daniel used to believe in letting an expert do it. But now he would find out some things for himself.

And the point was this: his phone played the song, and he

answered it to find Olin, the police consultant from *Abilene Cop Shop* on the line. Daniel pulled his grocery cart over to the oranges.

"So I checked those phone numbers, right?" said Olin. "One of them was for Steven Calhoun, and one of them was Lisa Feltenberger. Those are people on Kwan's defense team for Eileen Tenaway, right?"

"Right. What about the third number?"

"That's the unusual one. It belongs to a Sally Jacubiak," and he spelled it. "Do you know her?"

"No."

"Well, they're looking into her."

"Yeah, OK. I don't know if it means anything. It could even have been a wrong number."

"The guys on the case know the duration of the call, so I'd say it wasn't."

"OK. Uh, do you have an address for this Sally Jacubiak?"

"What for?"

"Olin, do you still want to go out with me?"

"You know I do."

"Then give me the address."

AN HOUR LATER Daniel, carrying a mixed bouquet from the Safeway, followed an elderly man into an apartment building on Crenshaw Avenue. He took the stairs to the third floor and knocked on the door of 3E. No one answered it.

Next door, 3G, flew open.

"I have a delivery for Sally Jacubiak," he said politely, holding the flowers over his lower face in case she had been a fan of *Abilene Cop Shop*.

The woman, hair once again in the tinfoil pincurls, told him about Sally's trip to Joshua Tree. She looked as if she'd like to eat up Daniel with a spoon. He gave her the flowers and turned away. As she thanked him, he heard someone throwing security bolts inside the door to Sally Jacubiak's apartment.

I CAME HOME that night late and tired, having reviewed with the defense team all of our files and notes, making sure we'd done as much for Eileen as we could. We'd met at Steve Calhoun's private office in Burbank, none of us eager to open the door again at Kwan & Associates. We helped Mark Sharma craft his closing statement.

It was almost midnight when I walked into my apartment.

Daniel was asleep on the sofa.

Just as I was about to peek in on Petey, the phone rang. I answered, expecting it to be Jeff.

"Hey, it's Janet," said Janet brightly. " 'Member?"

"Yes," I said, sweat springing out on my palms.

"Just wanted to warn you about something. They're after you again."

"Who's after me?"

"You know."

"No, I don't, damn you. Who?"

Daniel stirred.

Janet suggested, "Better check on your boy."

I rushed into Petey's room, holding the cordless to my ear.

His bed was empty. The curtain fluttered at the open window. Cool, peaceful night air filled the room.

"Oh, my God."

Down the rabbit hole.

"Daniel!" I called. Into the phone I said, "He's gone. I have to call the police. Tell me—"

"Calm down," said Janet.

Daniel stood in the room in his socks, his face bloodless, eyes huge. He crossed to the window and thrust his upper body out, then back in. "Shit, shit," he said. A large vein popped out on his forehead as his color came back. "Who is that?" he demanded.

"Shut up!" I said.

"Hey, girl," said Janet, "don't worry. Petey's safe!"

"What!"

"He's with me! Surprise!" Carefree intensity.

I couldn't speak.

Janet said, "Yeah, yeah, everything's OK! Had you going, there. He's fine. For now."

I willed myself to remain sane. I couldn't feel my body at all. Every cell was focused on the voice on the other end of that phone line.

Off to the side, she said, "Hey, Commander Peterson," and I knew she really had him. "Wanna say hi to Mommy? No?"

"Petey!" I shouted.

Daniel gripped my arm and put his ear close to the phone.

"I guess he doesn't want to talk to you," said Janet with a sympathetic inflection. "That's kids for you. He's busy watching fifty thousand shows on cable. You don't have cable, do you?" Her voice went too fast. "Look, hon, whatever you do, don't call the police. 'Kay? If you do, he'll—well, it'll be a real long time before you see him again. And when you do, he won't be like you remembered. 'Kay? At all."

"Right," I said.

"I promise I'll do it. You're being watched, so don't even consider the police. Don't even brain-wave the word. And keep your lunky dumb boyfriend out of this too."

"Right."

"Because what this is, Rita, is a fantastic opportunity for you."

I stood looking at nothing. "What do you want?"

"All right. Remember that storage-locker key we talked about? 'Member that?"

"Yes."

"Get it."

"But—"

"Find out from Eileen where it is. She knows, believe me. Go get it. Then wait for me to call tomorrow after court. Give me your cell number too, I don't have it."

"How did you get my home number?"

"Memorized it while I was talking to Mr. Pepsodent. It's on your phone. Cell number now."

I gave it to her.

"Thanks," she said. "You'll have your little guy back in a jiffy. All right, then?"

Desperately, I said, "He likes pizza."

"Oh, I know that already. We're great friends. We got some Frosted Flakes in here too, which I myself like. Potato chips, new DVDs—I've even got *Fingershredder,* kids are supposed to like that movie—oh, we're having a ball. I just hope he doesn't start crying too much. I've been a little weepy myself off and on. Well, he's pretty happy for now."

My throat tightened so hard my breaths grew ragged.

Janet said, "Rita, Rita, don't make this such a big deal! Very little for you to remember: Key. No police."

I'll never know the number of years off my life that night took.

When the phone went silent I spun on Daniel. "How could you have let somebody take him! What the hell happened?"

Tautly, he told me he'd let Petey play his ScoreLad in his room, loud, after dinner. Daniel had managed to fall asleep on the sofa, lulled by the relentless beeping and crashing noises, which, as I well knew, blended into a horrid white noise after a while.

We inspected the window. Whoever had come for Petey had climbed up the fire escape and convinced him to open the window latch. Or—

"Have you been smoking?" I grabbed Daniel's shirt and smelled it. "Did you—did you—"

Sinking under my grip, he said, "Yes. I sneaked out there to smoke while Petey was in the tub. I must have left the latch open."

The outside safety light had no bulb in it.

"Rita, I'm—"

"Don't even talk! Don't say anything!"

I could barely gasp enough air into my lungs.

"Call 911," said Daniel.

"No!"

"Are you crazy? We need the police!" He got his cell phone out. Then my wind came back. I attacked him like a leopard. We struggled there in Petey's bedroom, then when it became clear I would hurt myself in order to stop him, he gave up.

"He's my son," I panted, "and I'm not crazy. I'm not too distraught to think clearly. The woman is serious."

"All the more reason to—"

"Shut up, Daniel! I know what she wants, and I'm going to get it for her. I know I'm supposed to call the police. They tell you to do that. But I know she'll do what she said. I feel it and I know it."

"But—"

"God damn it! The Lindberghs went to the police and look what it got them. The Gettys went to the police and they got their kid's ear in the mail. The Hearsts went to the police and it only encouraged the kidnappers to ask for more and more."

He looked at me. "How do you know all that?"

"When you're a mother you make it your business to learn this shit."

"All right, Rita. I'm going now. There's no apologizing for what happened tonight, so I'm not going to try. I know Petey will come back to you."

"If you tell your cop advisor pal about this, I will kill you, Daniel."

He looked at me as if he believed me.

And I meant it.

He left without another word.

In cold anger, I paced the apartment. I went to Petey's room to look for his Benjamin Bunny that he slept with, but it too was gone. Oddly, that gave me some solace, because it meant Janet knew something about children.

The phone rang at two o'clock, and I grabbed it, my heart in my mouth. It was Daniel, sounding determined.

"Rita, I'm working on it."

"Well, don't, oh Daniel, for the love of God. Don't fuck this up."

"I just want you to know I haven't abandoned you."

"Goddamn it, abandon me! Please! And abandon Petey! You played a desk sergeant on a police show and now you think you're supercop. I'm handling this. Stay out of it!" I hung up on him.

I paced and was angry. Then I paced and thought. I thought harder than I ever had in my life. Then I began to plan.

AT SEVEN A.M. I was in Eileen's holding cell, ahead of Mark. Sitting at the little table, Eileen met my cold fury with a determinedly neutral attitude, as if she'd been expecting something like this and wasn't going to give any more than she had to—or wanted to.

I remained standing and said simply, "My son Petey has been abducted. I haven't called the police. She wants the key to the storage locker. Where is it?"

Eileen looked up at me. She had on a wine-colored dress, which she'd worn earlier in the trial. It brought out her hazel eyes, sharpened them. She sat on that one for a moment. I watched her think, I watched her weigh pros and cons. Then she said, "She would do something like that."

I leaned in. "Who? Who is she?"

She shook her head.

"Eileen, she's got some hold on you. What is it?"

"I know what she wants. She can have it. Yep, she can have everything that's in that locker."

"So there is a locker. Why did you pretend not to know what I was talking about before?"

"Rita, it was none of your business."

"Well, now it is."

"Yes. Yes." She tapped the table. "Rita, try to bear with me here."

I almost slugged her. "Bear with *you*!" I hissed so the deputy wouldn't hear, "My son has been kidnapped! Bear with—"

She sighed. "I'm trying to—I've made mistakes on several levels. I've had to bury my rage about Gabriella, or I would have died too, I'm sure of it. I guess you can really understand that now." She gazed at her hands on the tabletop. She looked up. "I don't think we can stop them."

"Them who?"

"But if I really do get out of here—then maybe. Maybe. I don't know about your little boy. Maybe he'll be all right. But the point is, you and your son are not the last people they're going to try to screw with. There's no end to what they want. I'd like to stop them from hurting anyone else."

"All right. Mark's going to be here any minute. What's in the locker, Eileen?"

"I guess you're going to find out."

"Where's the key?"

"At the house."

"Where at the house?"

"You'll have to get Mark or the police involved, because Gary had my keys. I don't know where they are now."

"Fuck that." I'd buy a chain saw and cut my way in, if I had to.

Eileen, seeing "chain saw" in my face, continued quickly, "It's in the garage. There's a car under a blue cloth cover. Go in the backseat behind the driver's seat. There's a string lying on the seat. Pull it. The key's on the other end. Did she ask you to find out where the locker is?"

"No."

Eileen shook her head again, then lowered it almost to her chest. She looked up at me with forced brightness, tears streaming from her eyes. "That bitch. That stone bitch."

THIRTY-TWO

Tracy Beck-Rubin had, by the looks of her, gone without sleep last night to work on the questions she wanted to put to Eileen on cross-examination. Her cartoon-cat face with its blurry corona of hair was pouchy and anxious. It was clear to everyone she'd been put at a disadvantage by Eileen's testimony.

Eileen sat with her head level, her body straight and balanced, symmetrical in the chair, her spine poised in space. Her face was relaxed yet with an exquisite wariness rooted in the corners of her eyes, a wariness meant clearly for Beck-Rubin. I watched the jury respond to Eileen, adopting wariness toward the prosecutor themselves. It was incredible.

This, the cross-examination—the unscripted, reactive challenge—was improv day for Eileen.

That morning, everything in the courtroom went on below

the surface. I mean, Beck-Rubin went on the attack against Eileen, and Eileen withstood it, but heavy, heavy feelings ran through her; everybody perceived it. I tried hard to quell my natural hysteria about Petey, to steel myself to focus on the trial since I could do nothing for him except wait tonight for Janet's call. Emotion coursed beneath everything that day like groundwater flowing from the mountains to the sea.

Eileen answered the prosecutor's questions, showing her grief and pain just under the surface. Beck-Rubin bore in, holding in check her feelings of being one-upped, or trying to. She really didn't understand how this shift had occurred. The jury didn't understand. No one else did either, except me.

Eileen had taken everyone in that courtroom and massaged their cerebral cortexes with the same magic that makes us cry when Ingrid Bergman turns reluctantly into Paul Henreid's arms on the tarmac. The same magic that makes us writhe when Anthony Hopkins discusses the flavor of human flesh with Jodie Foster. The same magic that makes us laugh when Diane Keaton disses Woody Allen.

Man, she had it.

I was glad Oatberger wasn't there.

Beck-Rubin got going on Eileen's use of Valium: "This designer drug—"

"Objection!" from Mark Sharma.

Beck-Rubin: "OK, this drug we've heard described as 'designer'—you've testified you took it as needed. You needed it a lot, didn't you?"

Mark, on his feet: "Object!"

Beck-Rubin: "Your Honor, I'm pursuing a valid line of questioning here."

The exchange ended pointlessly with Eileen testifying that she used to take half a Valium tablet once or twice a month. She denied that she'd taken any the night Gabriella died. The prosecution had no one to say otherwise, no sheaf of prescriptions from ten different doctors to brandish, nothing like that.

In spite of my resolve, thoughts of Petey kept ramming through my brain. When I let myself feel too much, I heard a *wah-wah-wah* sound in my ears, like when a high wind buffets you. I think it was my blood pressure. Over and over again I forced myself into an approximation of calmness. I could only help Petey if I stayed sane and smart.

Next Beck-Rubin decided to hammer on Eileen's habit of truthfulness, or lack of it.

"Have you ever read *LA BackChat*?" she asked in a scornful tone.

"Oh, yes!" answered Eileen with warm enthusiasm. "I used to pick it up every week!"

The jury broke into laughter at Eileen's frank ardor for the trashy tabloid.

Irritated now, bitchy now, Beck-Rubin said, "But no more?"

"No."

"It's hard to run down to the corner store to get it when you're in jail, isn't it?"

Mark Sharma sat still. It cost him effort to do it, but he could see Eileen was taking care of herself.

"Now." Beck-Rubin paced in front of the witness box like a patient cougar sizing up a rabbit hole. "As we've heard, in the space of two years, *LA BackChat* has run fourteen items mentioning you. And we've heard testimony that showed you yourself placed calls to their columnists."

"Yes," agreed Eileen patiently.

"So you don't deny making those calls, feeding gossip to this publication?"

Eileen looked at her. "I don't call it gossip."

Beck-Rubin stopped pacing, the toe of one pump touching the carpet. "What do you call it, Mrs. Tenaway?"

"Shaming the devil."

The jury got it, and loved it. Tracy Beck-Rubin almost staggered from the impact of Eileen's gentle wit. I expected a referee in a white shirt and bow tie to run in and throw a standing count in front of her eyes.

But she kept her fists up, wanting victory, now bearing in on something Eileen had said about Gabriella. That, at bedtime, she had seemed "restless."

"When a child is restless, sometimes it gets annoying, doesn't it?" prompted Beck-Rubin.

"Objection," said Mark Sharma, crisply and instantly.

"Sustained," said Judge Davenport. "Come on, Tracy."

Beck-Rubin touched her hands to her hips and paused. Then she said, "Had you ever found yourself irritated by Gabriella's restlessness?"

Mark looked anxious, but Eileen stared down Tracy Beck-Rubin as if she pitied her for her cluelessness and said, "She wasn't alive in this world long enough for me to have ever been irritated by her."

Collectively, again, the jury exhaled with satisfaction.

It was, of course, a barefaced lie—any mother will tell you that—but Eileen made it sound like the most beautiful truth ever spoken.

In Tracy Beck-Rubin's hour of desperation I found her no less fascinating than ever. I sat there trying to put myself in her position. How would I handle it? The momentum has shifted to the other side, but it ain't over. You gotta gather your guts and do the best you can.

She did, question after question, insinuation after insinuation, but Eileen held her own.

I was proud.

The defense rested.

JANET CALLED AT nine that night.

"First, let me talk to Petey," I said, my vocal cords tight.

"Sorry, he's sleeping. Wasn't easy to get him there, and I'm not about to wake him up."

"God damn you."

"Whatever. So?"

I said, "I have directions to where the key is."

She grunted in impatience. "I told you to get the *key*."

"Well, I'm scared," I said. "Plus you said this was an opportunity for me. You meant you're going to cut me in, right?"

Cautiously, Janet said, "Yes."

"For half, right?"

She paused. "Whoa. Whoa."

"A third, then. Because without me tonight, you're nothing."

"Whoa. Still." Then, clearly, she got smart; I could practically hear it over the line. "How 'bout ten percent?" she said slyly.

"Well, OK. Yeah."

Obviously she had no intention of giving me anything. Maybe she even thought she'd kill me once we uncovered the treasure. My aim was simply to exert a measure of control over her: I wanted her to get used to negotiating with me.

"So," I said, "we're going to get that key together, and we're

298

going over to the locker, wherever it is, together. I'm your insurance, and you're mine. See? It's better for both of us this way."

"But what if—"

"Look, Janet, you don't want to hurt my boy, right, you just want your rightful property. Right?"

"Essentially."

"Then drive over to that Starbucks right now, the one where we met before."

I hung up without waiting for a response.

She'd ditched the blue Audi for a beige Toyota. The streetlights, pushing back the city darkness, helped me make out drivers' faces. As soon as I saw her I ran over and jumped into the passenger seat. "Let's go," I said in a TV-cop voice.

Surprised, she stepped on it, and we peeled out east on Santa Monica.

"Turn around," I said, "and go to Eileen and Richard's house."

She did it. Her eyes scanned the road like cat eyes, back and forth. I could smell the nervousness in her, there beneath her phony, insane coolness.

She was taking direction from me.

"My boy OK?" I asked.

"He's fine, he's fine." She braked for a wheelchair person waiting in a crosswalk.

Coldly, I said, "I'm getting warped by all this stress. Janet, just swear to me my baby's going to be all right."

"Well, hon, that's gonna be up to—"

"When I get stressed," I interrupted, "I tend to start puking all over the place." This was not true, but I wanted her to tell me more about where Petey was and who was with him. "In fact—oh, God!—right now I think—"

299

"Whoa!" cried Janet. "Hang on, girlfriend. I need you, OK? I guarantee your boy's OK. OK? He's *fine*."

"But to think of him all alone, it makes me want to cut my throat." I drummed my hands wildly on the dashboard. I wanted her to think I was unpredictable.

"Well, that one I can—I mean—he's not alone, OK?" Janet maneuvered the car through the night traffic on Santa Monica.

"He's not? Who's with him?"

"Uh . . ."

"You just said he's not alone."

"Well, he is and he isn't."

What the hell does that mean? I said, "I know you can't tell me exactly where Petey is, OK, but just—I mean, but if he's under some bridge with a bunch of drug addicts, because he has a phobia about filth and bugs and strangers—"

"Well, this person won't bother him. I do not hang out with drug addicts. He's not under a *bridge,* Rita, come on. He's not in a particularly ghettoey area, it's really a fairly nice neighborhood. And it's quite a clean place, actually. I've been doing a lot of cleaning lately, actually." She gave a short laugh. "Hey, I'm doing everything I can to make Petey comfortable."

"Then would you do me the courtesy of calling there and letting me speak to whatever person is looking after him tonight? Because Petey has a—he has a heart condition where he needs to sleep with his feet elevated. And it's way past his bedtime. Would you? Please?"

Janet let out a tense little sigh. "I can't, really. I mean, I would if I could. But this person isn't exactly able to talk to anyone."

"You mean—"

"They're really not in any shape."

"You mean they're drunk?"

"Uh . . ."

"Or stoned or something?"

"Uh . . ."

"Or deaf-mute? or *what*?"

"Mm, it's a little more serious than that. I don't want to *lie* to you, Rita, yet—"

"Oh, my God."

"Just relax, Rita, 'kay?"

"You mean somebody's there but that somebody isn't alive."

Janet sighed with relief. "Yeah, yeah. I must admit. But it was an accident."

Now I really felt like throwing up. "An *accident*? You're storing a corpse in the same place you've got my son? What kind of—"

"Goddamn it, Rita, it's not what you think! Don't go to pieces on me." She braked emphatically to a stop at a red light. "Look, sometimes it's necessary to hide a certain situation. Right?"

"Oh, my God. Oh, my God. Oh, my God." *Be rational, be rational. Be rational.*

"Look! Let me be clear. The body—this person—is not just sitting out on display. I'm not a sicko, OK? I'm being methodical, which is what you have to be when you're trying to accomplish something. And what works in a case like this is Pine-Sol. Many bottles of Pine-Sol." The light changed, but Janet didn't notice. "I came upon that fact by chance."

Be rational. "You have the green."

"Oh, thank you. I've been running all over town buying more Pine-Sol. Original. I mean, the dumpster is the first place they always look—they never think of the bathtub! So I've been thinking

301

I need to wait awhile. You've never needed to dispose of—uh—have you?"

"Of a dead body?"

"Yeah."

"No, I can't say I ever have."

We glided past the restaurants and wine shops of West Hollywood.

Janet said, "Plus I'm such a procrastinator anyway. But I've got the shower curtain drawn, I mean, so everything's fine. Petey only needs to go in there to use the toilet. So as long as he doesn't pull back that shower curtain, he's in quite a wholesome environment, overall."

For the first time, I could smell the evil. This woman knew what she was doing. She really did. Order, for her, simply translated into chaos for everybody else.

"So," I asked, "who is it?"

"Oh! It's irrelevant. I mean, that person is not relevant to our situation."

"I see. I feel calmer now." Anything she blurted I might be able to use against her, if not now, then in the future. "Nice car," I commented, in a changing-the-subject tone. "How's the gas mileage?"

"Uh, it's a rental." She tapped out a Benson & Hedges and lit it with a purple plastic lighter. I noticed that the car lighter had been removed, indicating a nonsmoking vehicle. As if she'd give a shit.

"By any chance," I asked, "are you dating a guy named Jeff?"

"No, why?"

"Just wondering. Say, I can't wait to get some of that money and stuff. You said—what—fifteen million's worth in there?"

"Probably a lot more. Yep, I think so. Oh, it's gonna be great,

Rita!" She bopped along, driving. The cigarette was warming her up. She took a long drag, then exhaled into the windshield. The smoke kicked back into our faces.

"Is it all in, like, boxes, or what?" I asked eagerly.

"The stones are in plastic bags, heavy ones. Body-bag-weight plastic bags, then cardboard boxes."

"How do you know how thick body bags are?"

"Just guessing, just making conversation. I myself do not know. I mean, they have to be thick so the body doesn't fall out. I could've used one."

"What's the first thing you'll do," I asked, "once you get your hands on it all?"

Janet laughed as if I'd told a good dirty joke, then said, "Oh, I'm sorry. Like one?" She offered me the pack.

I could have grabbed the wheel and crashed us into any of hundreds of pairs of oncoming headlights. I could have brained her with the sixteen-inch pry bar I'd brought in my New Yorker tote bag. I could have jumped out and waved down a police car.

I took a cigarette. "Thanks."

Up to then, I'd smoked about four cigarettes in my life, all in a stall in the girls' room of my high school. I managed to puff this one down too. It was a communal act.

I was operating purely on instinct. I would not be a sniveling victim. I would not.

We got to the house around ten. The residents of Beverly Hills enjoy fine police protection as well as private security patrols. "Park on the next street," I directed.

We walked along the sidewalk, shadowed by grand trees. I'd worn a sweater; it was just cool enough for it. The air smelled dark-night green, automatic sprinklers clicked and hissed. Close though we were to Santa Monica—just more than a long block away—we could barely hear the traffic. A beautiful night for a walk.

"The people here just *shit* money," Janet whispered.

"I'll bet," I whispered back.

"I mean, I had a pony when I was a kid, but *these* people?"

The mansions in this part of town sit back from the street behind broad lawns, some behind garden walls. All the showbiz big shots were indoors watching their plasma screens or, in fairness, helping their kids with their homework. Or figuring out where their next mortgage payment of $21,000 was going to come from.

The Tenaway house, which I'd driven past out of curiosity when I began working with Eileen, had that upper-crust Tudor look, with half-timbers on the gables and all that. Fortunately, those Brits like to make hedges do for fencing.

We darted up the driveway and avoided the wrought-iron gate, finding a path to the garage right through the tall box hedge. In Beverly Hills you don't really get acreage for your four million bucks, just a whole lot of location. The hedge sheltered the garage fairly well.

A breeze came up, tossing the trees and skittering the odd piece of litter.

We came to a doorway on the side of the garage toward the house. It was a very large garage, for six cars.

The sturdy wooden door was windowless and locked. I simply attacked it at the bolt with my pry bar. I'd never broken open a door before, but the molding at the latch splintered, and after a couple of shoves, Janet and I were inside. I'd brought a flashlight, and Janet had a tiny LED one on her key chain.

We flipped our lights around. The place smelled of grease and mold. Four cars, draped with heavy cloth covers, hunkered in the stalls like shrouded horses. One end of the garage was a little shop, with a bench and vise and red tool chests.

"Did they have a chauffeur to deal with all this?" I wondered aloud.

"Oh, no, Richard just did it all himself very half-assed."

I pointed with my light. "This car here."

We tugged at the elastic binding and the dustcover slipped off the fenders, raising puffs of dust as it went. I threw it on the floor and we stood looking at a gorgeous Jaguar sedan with an almost flawless emerald-green paint job. I say almost flawless because a dent the size of a cantaloupe marred the right front fender. Janet went silent, and I glanced at her. She was staring at that dent in pure horror.

"Oh, my God," she breathed.

I noticed some scroungy stuff adhering to the dent. Bits of fluff, interspersed with dark crustiness.

There was a mighty *ca-chunk* inside my head as I understood something suddenly and strongly, albeit partially.

I looked at her, and she kept looking at the dent.

"You're Eileen's little sister," I said. "You're Norah."

She kept looking at the dent.

"And this is your car, isn't it?"

Instantly I saw it all, the mannerisms—the lost-girl aura of her—the arched brows, the tilt of the head, the curve of the lips— she *did* resemble Eileen. Not to mention the jewelry. Which was badda-bing authentic, not costume. I remembered the moment weeks ago—years ago?—when I'd asked Eileen about her sister. I remembered what she'd said: *One time I helped her out of a very bad*

situation . . . I put myself in jeopardy to do it . . . I wish to God I'd
turned my back instead.

This Jaguar, I realized, had been involved in a hit-and-run, some time ago.

"Did you know this car was here?" I asked.

"Shit." Her voice sounded as if steam were escaping her throat with every word. "I thought he'd gotten rid of it. I fucking can't believe it."

"Who? Richard?"

A tight smile spread over her face and she nodded. "I guess he wasn't looking out for me like he said."

Deep down in my chest, I exulted. I was getting closer to figuring it out—the connections, the grudges, the petty shit between people that grows into holocaust.

I opened the rear door, leaned in, and retrieved the key just as Eileen had instructed. The air in the car smelled of leather and stale panic.

"Where to next?" I said.

We turned to leave. Norah, stewing over the car, was slow to get going, and I glanced around the garage again, noticing for the first time something looming overhead: a speedboat, perhaps twenty feet long, its wooden hull shining sleekly brown, like the belly of an animal just out of the water. Thick canvas loops from a hoist suspended it conveniently above the garage floor. Curlicue script on the stern said *Little Gem*.

"Is this their yacht?" I asked as Norah finally turned from the Jaguar. She had decided to cover it up again.

"Oh, no!" I think she would have found that question funny under other circumstances. "They had a real one down in Marina del Rey. Eileen sold that. This was just a little toy."

The beautiful vessel gleamed there in the darkness.

We left the property.

"Oh, wait," I said as we neared the street. "I left the pry bar. Fingerprints. You go on, I'll just run back real quick."

A few cars passed as I walked, but I looked as if I belonged in the neighborhood, no problem.

In fact, I had replaced the pry bar in my tote bag. I stole up to the house's dark front door and slipped a small envelope through the mail slot. I had printed RICHARD on it, and inside, on a piece of notepaper, I'd written the address of the Topanga Canyon house I'd rented for Eileen.

George Rowe had speculated that Tenaway would return to Los Angeles after the trial, but I felt him coming closer now.

THIRTY-THREE

The storage locker was in Florence, off Central somewhere—I was starting to glaze over. En route, Norah's and my conversation flagged. I ached for Petey. Was he asleep? Warm enough? Terrified? Had he drawn back the shower curtain?

I couldn't believe I was trying to comfort myself by thinking, *Well, at least a dead body can't really hurt Petey. At least he's not being babysat by a pit bull or something.*

Norah fished a box of Jujubes from her purse and offered me some.

"Uh, no, thanks," I said. A cigarette was one thing, but taking candy from a stranger?

"I love these," said Norah, sucking.

Florence, one of South Central's border towns, is never included in any maps to movie stars' homes or anything like that.

Around midnight, street activity increases. Tonight the avenues buzzed with cruising crap cars like my Honda, plus the awesome metal-flake custom cars that crack built. It began to drizzle.

Norah turned off Central and followed an alley to a blind pig of a storage facility: rusted fence, new razor wire on top, some guy's name on the sign. In one place the razor wire sagged, sprung as if someone had actually tried to storm it with brute force. There was no tidy guy in a clip-on tie checking IDs. Norah drove straight up to a junk-strewn yard where three old black guys were feeding wood from broken pallets into a fire in an oil drum. They squinted into Norah's headlights unwelcomingly. Gravel crunched under the tires.

"Cut your lights," I suggested.

She did so. She got out. I rolled down my window and watched from the darkness of the car. The leaping orange flames hypnotized us both for a second. They looked so evolutionary and beautiful in the misty night. How long ago had I last seen an open fire?

I heard her say, "I have a key for eleven."

One of the guys, looking away from us, said, "Go ahead."

She got back in and said, "I tried to bribe that guy twice. Bastard pretends not to remember me. Well, that's good. I think Richard made a very, very special deal with him." She eased the car around to the rear of a long cinder-block shed. "The trunk in this thing's pretty big," she said. "I can practically back in. To, you know, load up."

I allowed myself a taste of hopeful relief. The show was almost over. In the time it would take to drive to wherever he was, Petey would be back in my arms. His dimpled smile, his fair-skies blue eyes.

The building had evidently served as a kind of preschool for vandals. Every surface was covered with the jumbled scrawls of taggers; there were no interesting drawings or scripts like you see in more prominent ghetto areas. Further, it appeared someone had tried to bash in the door to every one of these five or six lockers at one time or other; in the dim light I saw nickel-sized angry pits in the metal doors.

"Doesn't seem like a terribly secure place," I remarked.

"Look closer," grunted Norah, throwing the car into park.

She was right. Whoever had built that shed had built a bunker. Even the roof was concrete. Maybe a stick of dynamite would've busted into it. Maybe.

"Oh, boy," murmured Norah, actually licking her chops.

She held out her hand for the key, but I retained possession. As I stepped around her and fitted it into the lock, her breathing quickened; I practically felt it on my neck. I glanced at her. Her upper lip quivered, and sweat glistened on her scalp beneath the nesting material of her hair. Her lids were low, and she wet her lips over and over, like a woman about to have an orgasm.

I paused, the key still in the lock. "So this was the depot for the cash and gemstones Richard stole from Gemini, right?" I said.

"Right," she panted.

"How did you know about it?"

"I helped him." She clutched my arm in a talonlike grip. "Open the *door*!"

I waited.

She said, "I caught him at it—I opened a carton by mistake. He was about to bring it over here. So he cut me in on it if I kept my mouth shut. I did. But then it went to hell. Took a while, though."

Someone had pasted stickers for two goth-type bands on the

door at eye level. In jagged black typefaces, one said BRASS POPOVERS. The other said RELAPSE.

The concrete room was bare except for a lightbulb overhead and a steel chest against the back wall. The chest was the kind they store life jackets in on ferryboats, or stretchers and avalanche supplies at mountain camps. A large welded hasp hung without a padlock.

"What's that smell?" I said.

"Help me, this lid's heavy."

I found a fingerhold and together we heaved it open.

And I learned that the odor I'd detected a second ago had been but a molecule or two's worth that had escaped the chest.

Norah recoiled as the harsh light fell on what was inside. The body was tall, troublesomely so; someone had had to bend him at the knees to fit. His face was a mottled poufy mess, like a melting ice-cream cake.

But his wardrobe was impeccable as always, fine wool suit, silk tie—and the neat barbering of his thick red head of hair suggested the fastidiousness that wealth so often encourages.

Even as his flesh decomposed, Padraig McGower's presence was commanding.

Where were the flies? As soon as I thought that, one zoomed past my nose.

And McGower's odor was beyond commanding.

Could Pine-Sol have helped?

I staggered backward out of the concrete cell, vomiting before I knew I was going to. As it came up, I managed to bend over so it hit the ground instead of my shoes.

Norah wasn't as fast getting out. Conveniently, she upchucked right on top of McGower. Which would be an improvement, because now I knew that the smell of vomit, compared with that of a rotting human corpse, is perfume.

She let the door slam shut behind her.

We stood in the drizzle gasping. Neither of us screamed. I'm sure neither of us could have gotten enough wind.

"So that's his message," Norah said with hot bitterness, her body rigid with fury. "Quite a fuck you, don't you agree?"

"Quite one."

"Well." She cleaned her teeth with her tongue and spat in the dirt. "You've got a job now, don't you?"

"I guess I do," I said, trying to ignore the stake of anguish that was piercing my heart. I would not see Petey tonight.

We got in the car. She adjusted her seat belt. "I'll call you now and then for the next twenty-four hours. By then I'm gonna be sick of that kid. Find the loot."

"*How?*"

"I don't care. Do I look like I care?"

GEORGE ROWE HAD left a message on my machine, giving a landline number to call him back. Standing in the kitchen I punched it in immediately.

"Rita!"

His baritone voice steadied me. I pictured his crew-cut self on the other end, sturdy and earnest and competent.

I plunged right in. "Petey's been kidnapped by Janet who is Norah Mintz, Eileen's sister and Richard's former mistress, as I think you suspected already, and I got the key to the storage place and we went there but the only thing in it was Padraig McGower who's been dead since at least Monday which was the first day he

312

didn't show up in court, and now I have to find the treasure for her or she'll kill Petey because she's been trying to get her hands on that loot for the better part of a year."

I paused for breath, gazing out the kitchen window. The light well caught stray rays from the streetlights; they bounced around silvery in the narrow space.

After a moment, he said, "And it looks like Richard just beat her to it."

I said, "No, I'm not sure he did."

"You haven't called the police?"

"Not yet."

"Rita. Your *child*—"

"No, George."

"Well then—"

"Richard's here in L.A., all right. I thought he'd get moving before the trial was over."

Rowe said, "I've been back and forth to Brazil from Tijuana."

"Are you in Tijuana now?"

"Yes, but I'm going to drive back to L.A. as soon as we're finished talking. There's no question he was embezzling from Gemini. The company never did reach actual solvency, in spite of all the showing off. Obviously McGower found out at some point, then he got involved in covering it up. They owe money to a couple of government guys in a town called Ouro Prêto, and to another mining commissioner in São Paulo."

The gears of my mind meshed and clanked. "How did Tenaway's scam work, George?"

He blew a sound of amazement into the phone. "I can't believe you even want to know. I can't believe you're not talking to the police right now."

"There are as many ways of being an angry mama bear as there are women in this world."

He was silent, but I thought I could hear him smile. "You've changed, haven't you?"

I said nothing.

"Strong experiences can do that," he said.

It was my turn to smile. Coldly.

He said, "Richard Tenaway bought gems from local miners in Brazil and Venezuela with funds from Gemini. Most of them got shipped to Los Angeles and elsewhere, like they were supposed to. But over time, in small batches, he diverted gems and reals—Gemini's cash—mostly from Ouro Prêto, to another import company here in Tijuana. He had a deal with them where they bought from him but turned around and couriered the stuff to him personally in Los Angeles. Essentially, the gems were laundered, and the cash disappeared as if it were their cut. But the bulk of the reals got converted to dollars and went to Tenaway somehow."

"How did you—"

"I impersonated a German gem buyer and was able to set up almost an exact duplicate of the system. I'd visited this guy in Berlin and copped a few of his cards. Then I came to Tijuana and presented myself as him and flashed a wad of cash in this company's boss's face. And I was able to, uh, review some of their records after-hours." He sounded pleased with himself. He added, "The Mexican police and customs have their hands full with more dangerous problems."

"What about American customs?"

"Tenaway tried to appear as open as possible about what he did. He went down and paid off the couriers with checks from his own company. That's how McGower found out about it. But then I wonder about the cash. Either it was well hidden in the packages, or it didn't go in the same packages. Or there was no cash. One of my sources here insists Tenaway must have put the money offshore. If he did that, he drew it out in the U.S. and stashed it in this locker you're talking about. In fact, I think that's the likeliest scenario."

"But why would he—"

"Only if he'd been planning to fake his death for a while. If you're dead you can't get your money, even if your bank is somebody's desk drawer in the Cayman Islands."

"Oh."

"The other Gemini managers were starting to catch on, and that's why Tenaway decided to get out of town last year."

"In a hurry," I added.

"They always do. They always think they'll get away with it for just a little longer. But it looks like they had a nosy Joe in accounting who got suspicious. I saw some letters. Since it hasn't blown open, I guess McGower must've bought him off."

"The iceberg emerges," I murmured.

"What?"

"Nothing. So since he left without the treasure, he must have cleaned out whatever money he and Eileen had together. Now I get it. That's what must have led to the faked death—he knew Eileen and Gabriella needed money. Even as he was sleeping with the sister in some rented villa in Rio."

"Right," said George Rowe.

I felt a stab of hunger and reached for an orange; I'd barely eaten anything since finding Petey's bed empty. But I saw a chain of three tiny ants on it, so I rolled it on the counter to crush them.

Then I saw other ants around the fruit bowl. I set the orange aside and began smushing ants with my index finger. Little bastards: Argentine ants, the bane of California pantries.

I said, "Norah was the loose cannon in the picture, right?"

"So stupid and typical. He falls in love with her, leaves the wife behind, then all it takes is one dumb argument—about the money, probably—and he dumps her. Woman scorned. Only now he's got two women scorned."

"He thought he could handle it. Still thinks he can."

Rowe went on, "McGower probably tried to take care of Eileen, but he's been busy trying to keep the embezzlement a secret all these months. It was a fair amount of money—between twenty and thirty million dollars, all told. McGower did a sword dance through the audit the other company officers instigated."

"Is that why he was hanging around the trial?" I crushed the crisp ants.

"I think he thought he might learn something."

"George, I don't think Tenaway has the loot."

"You don't?"

"I think Eileen's got it. Somewhere. If Norah and Padraig knew Richard was stealing from the company, Eileen did too. Had to have. Maybe she even disposed of it already."

"No, I think it'd make more sense for her to sit on it than try to liquidate it."

"You think? How come?"

"For somebody like her to sell off large batches of uncut gems? The execution would be difficult, not to mention the attention she'd risk attracting. At least for a while. Likelier she'd use the stash as a bargaining chip with Richard or McGower. Or both."

"Yeah," I said, remembering the day my bad credit shut me

out of buying groceries. I thought about Adil's Pawn America and Gramma Gladys's diamond brooch. Ant carcasses littered the countertop. "She's hiding something until the trial's over. When I talked to her this morning about the storage locker, she hinted that there's some kind of cartel controlling things. She said she wants to stop them before they hurt anybody else."

"Look, Rita, if you'd just get the police involved—"

"If I got the police involved they would eventually locate Petey's body. George, I'm going to talk to Eileen in the morning. I can stall Norah if I have to, but I've got a strong feeling it won't be necessary. The jury's going to take the case today. And I think by this afternoon—I think—I hope—we'll know a lot."

"I'd have bet Tenaway would have stayed out of the country until the trial was over."

"McGower tried to fake him out. Told him he'd help him if Richard would come and open that locker. They all needed—wanted—that treasure. Richard wouldn't have left the only key with Eileen. He'd have kept one."

THIRTY-FOUR

A few sleepless hours later, I showered and dressed in my taupe suit with the maroon flecks, which worked with my coloring. I remembered thinking that when I bought it: *This works well with my coloring!* Now I was living in a different world.

The rain had stopped overnight, and the morning broke out in eighteen-carat sunshine. The Los Angeles I looked on as I drove to the lockup was different still than any I'd seen before. A city where, beneath Miramax and Sony and gas prices and guys trimming dead fronds off palm trees with knives on sticks, lives were bargained for and appointments with death were kept. My life. My appointments.

I said nothing to Eileen, simply sat down in the chair across the interview table and held her eyes. Actually, I drilled in just above her eyes as if I intended to extract coconut juice from her forehead.

She looked away. "I had to keep you busy."

I gripped the seat of my chair. If I stayed in it, I could not pick it up and slam it across her tired, wily face. Which would have been counterproductive.

"So you moved the goods after Richard ran away," I said.

"Yes."

"Where?"

No answer.

"Eileen, your baby sister is holding my boy." My eyes felt dead. "All for some pretty rocks and wads of paper with oval pictures on them."

"Rita, I'm sorry."

"Fuck you. We went to get the key together," I added.

She cut me a sharp sideways smile. "Did she react when she saw the car?"

"Yes, she did. Like she was seeing a ghost."

The smile widened slightly as she hooked an arm over the back of her chair. "I hadn't planned that. Too bad it didn't give her a fatal heart attack."

"Would've been a nice coincidence."

"Make no mistake: It wasn't that she gave a damn about the victim," said Eileen. "That car's a huge piece of evidence against her."

"Yes, I understood that."

"And that's when you figured it out—you realized she was Norah?"

"Yes. Tell me about the car."

And she told me about a fucked-up night about a year ago, the night when everything changed.

"It was the middle of the night. I woke up to—there was this pounding on the front door, this slow *pounding*. Richard grabbed

319

his pants and went down, and I followed. I was scared because you never know, people get shot by some asshole, you know?

"It was my sister standing there in her white mink coat—it was November—her face is all crooked, she's drunk. She stumbles through the door, crying and talking about some party in Los Feliz she'd been to. She was on her way home—she had a condo in Brentwood—and she'd hit something on Franklin. The way she said it, I tell you, my blood ran cold. I go, 'You hit . . . something?' She nods and I can tell she's going to throw up, and she does, all over my Kilim entry mat.

"Richard thought she'd hit another car, but I knew it was a person, I just knew it. We go into the kitchen and I make coffee and she tells us she'd been driving her Jaguar 'in a perfectly straight line' down Franklin toward Cahuenga when she felt a thud and someone in a down jacket and boots flew over the windshield."

The down jacket explained the bits of fluff I'd seen still sticking to the dent. "Oh, my God," I said. "So she didn't—"

"She panicked and floored it out of there. Then she ran out of gas on Santa Monica."

"Oh my God."

"That was Norah. A fuckup from the word go. She's there at my kitchen counter, drunk on her ass, and she's telling us she just ran somebody over and she strokes the countertop and says, 'I myself would like a kitchen like this.' Always wanting what I had. Yeah!"

Including Richard, I thought. *Including Gabriella?*

"Richard asked how she got here, and she said she walked up from Santa Monica." Eileen stopped and looked searchingly into the middle distance. "She always projected this *appeal,* that I could never figure out. Not exactly babe in the woods, not exactly wounded puppy. There was always a good-time aura about Norah. She tried to act so delicate. Which was a charade, when you think about it."

"A party girl?" I suggested.

"With a smart mouth and a soft heart. Except when she gets in trouble. Then it's number one all the way."

"Yeah."

"The car, by the way, had been a gift from Richard. He says, 'Where is it?' I noticed she still had her stiletto heels on, so it couldn't be far. We're all sitting there looking at each other. Nobody's saying it! Finally I do. 'We have to call the police.' She starts shrieking no no no, then she passes out. Richard carries her to the sofa and says, 'We have to get the car.' I'm like, Richard, do you realize how many times we've bailed her out of a mess? There was the lawsuit with the renter, then that crazy boyfriend—oh," Eileen swooped her hand in a gesture of infinity, "and before all that was the shoplifting. All my life I've covered for her. I even used to take the blame, if I thought nothing else would work. When was it going to end?

"We argue and argue, and finally he tells *me* to go get the car! And I do! He siphons some gas from his Land Rover into a can and hands it to me and says, 'Unless we're lucky enough that it's been stolen already, pour the gas in and drive it here. Leave your car wherever, we'll get it tomorrow.' And I went, and my nerves almost killed me. I found it in front of a cleaner's, with that dent in the fender and some scrape marks on the roof. I got it home and drove it into the garage. It was three in the morning, nobody saw me. Richard put one of those covers on it and that was it." Eileen looked at me, although her eyes were still on that night.

"All these thoughts went through my head: Why did he want to put us both at risk like that, without any discussion? He'd seen what a nutbag Norah was, he'd picked up the phone at all hours too. The next day we learn a student from USC was killed in a crosswalk on Franklin Avenue last night. An attractive young girl, Korean, I think. There was her picture in the paper. Nobody had seen the car."

"How," I asked, "did Richard react to that?"

"Good. He said *good,* with real relief in his voice. Student killed, no suspects. *Good.* That's when I realized they were having an affair. And what's more, they'd been at it for quite some time."

I observed, "You've done an awful lot to protect your sister."

"I sure have." If I've ever heard a rueful sentence, that was it.

All the facts I'd gleaned, all the gut-level sensations I'd felt for weeks now—all of it made me decide this was the time to take the leap.

"She planted that half-assed evidence the night Gabriella died, didn't she?"

Eileen paused. Then she said, "She put me here, you know."

"Tell me about that night."

"I can't—yet. But I think, Rita, you and I might have a chance to . . . do something about her."

"Yes?"

"But we have to wait."

"Depending on what the jury says?"

"Yes."

"Eileen, do you know where Padraig McGower is?"

I heard her catch her breath. Fucking fine.

After a moment, she said, cautiously, "No."

I drew it out. "Would you like to know?"

She nodded, searching my face for something good, but knowing no good could possibly be there.

I thought about cute ways to put it, like, *He's occupying a very small sublet in Florence,* or *He sleeps with the fishes,* but I finally just said, "He's in that gray chest."

She gulped and dropped her head. She mumbled into her hands, "Oh, my God. Padraig. Padraig." She looked up. "I had a feeling."

I reached across and took her wrist, then dropped it, remembering the vigilant deputy. *Fuck Padraig McGower, and I bet you did. Richard's back. Fuck Richard. We'll deal with him. But first, but first— this:* "Eileen, you're a mother. Your child is dead, but you're still a mother who gave birth and nursed your baby and watched the umbilical stub fall off. We are mothers. We have unity, you and I. You've got to help me."

She lifted her head and cleared her throat. "Don't mistake Norah. She's not motivated by greed, she's motivated by hate. Rita, I want to help you."

Was that actual warmth coming from her? Actual sincerity? I wanted to think so. Maybe it was. I smoothed my sleeves, comforted by the fine feel of the silk-rayon blend. "Why," I asked, "did Richard do this embezzling thing anyway? You two had it all."

She watched me touch my clothing, and I saw she appreciated the fabric. "It looked like we had it all," she said, "but really we didn't. Nobody does." She paused, thinking about that. "Richard was a good-looking bull, and he was a persuasive guy, but he was an atrocious businessman. He and Padraig became highly skilled at judging stones and bribing South American bureaucrats, but that only goes so far. They never had the guts to get into the business in Africa or Asia, where guys'll kill you over ten feet of dirt. He and Padraig discovered that you can fool a lot of people by how you look. And"—she smiled crookedly—"by who you owe."

"Yes," I said. "Yes."

"We piled up material things, few of them paid for. The guys kept borrowing to build the business, they posted losses all the time, but all the while they're drawing huge paychecks for themselves. People advised them to take the company public, but they knew it couldn't stand up to that kind of scrutiny."

I said, "So Richard decided to stock up a lifeboat."

She glanced at me sidelong. "Yes, that's a good way of putting it. And stocking the lifeboat caused the ship to sink!"

We both smiled at that witticism, but it felt uncomfortable.

Eileen said, "Do the police know about Padraig?"

"Not yet, as far as I know."

"He was never a match for Richard."

I decided to go for the present tense and see what happened. Bit of a trick. "What motivates Richard?"

"What motivates Richard," she repeated. "Well"—and the last of her pretenses fell away as she unconsciously lifted her arms to adjust her hair, which told me that he still moved her sexually— "if you ever meet him you'll immediately see that he's not a deep thinker. He's a schemer. He likes sex, lots of it, and he was starting to like it younger and younger. Get it?"

I had eased her into it.

"Yeah," I said. "Your little sister, then young girls."

"I even started to be afraid for Gabriella. Isn't that unspeakable? He liked luxury and he liked sex. Not much more there, other than arrogance, which he kept fairly well hidden. He was so good with people. A smile from him bought a year's worth of loyalty from some people, I'm not kidding. If he'd been a politician, I'm sure he'd have been president by now. He loved to get away with things. Deceit came so naturally to him."

That was all good to know. At last I said, "Eileen, you're going to be acquitted. I know it down in my gut: You could be free as early as today. I could tip off the police about what's in that garage. I could do all sorts of things to fuck you up once you're free. You've said you want to help me. Well?"

She looked startled, gazed at me intently, evidently did not find the hidden meaning she suspected, and relaxed with a touch of bitterness. "He tried to hold things over me too. He didn't think I'd hide his retirement fund—that's what he called that pile of stuff—from him, given my collusion in everything. He tried to hold that over me."

"Where is it?"

"Just wait. Just wait."

"I can't wait," I said in a hard voice. "It has to be today. When you're acquitted—Gary told you about the house I rented for you, right?"

She glinted with amusement at my use of *when,* not *if.* "Yes, I'd rather go there than . . . home."

"Today, Eileen."

She looked at me, and I couldn't tell if she was just putting me off for the moment, but she said, "All right, today."

By the looks of her I saw I wasn't going to get anything from her until she was damned ready. My child was still alive—I prayed—and her child was dead. Somehow that gave her the power to outstare me. I felt compassion for the pain she'd been through—would never finish going through—but that was beside the point today.

I said, "I want you to do something. When the trial's over, I want you to speak to the press just for a minute. Say you're glad to be free, but justice has not yet been done, blah-blah, OK? Then say you're leaving the country tomorrow for a much-needed rest."

"Where am I going?"

"Cayman Islands. Tell them that."

Her hazel eyes glinted into mine. "What are you up to, Rita?"

"Just please do that. All right?"

"You want the world to think I'm only going to be in Los Angeles for one more night. And that I might be going to arrange a financial thing or two."

"That's right."

"Could be good. Could be good."

THIRTY-FIVE

Unlike the police, Daniel Clements was not obliged to go on to another duty when Sally Jacubiak did not answer her door.

After his first reconnaissance with the flower bouquet, when he heard the locks rattling after his knock, he thought the nosy neighbor might be able to do him some good, somehow. Now that Petey had been snatched, he brought another bouquet and knocked, quite early in the morning, on the neighbor's door. But now she wasn't home either.

Last night, during the date he'd consented to go on with the former police advisor from *Abilene Cop Shop,* he'd gotten the guy talking about police work. He'd learned something important.

"Police work—investigative work, I mean," said Olin, placing a rawboned elbow on their cocktail table at the Chuckwagon, a gay club in Studio City, "is largely a matter of taking dots that look random and seeing if you can connect them. If you're looking for a line, you won't see it at first. All you get are dots. There's this dot here and that dot over there and you try to figure out the line. Sometimes there is no line, then you have to find more dots."

"So," said Daniel, "a fact is a dot?"

"Right."

"But if totally all you have is two dots—"

"Then you work like hell to find a line." Olin laughed. "'Cause what else're you going to do?" He stared at Daniel's chest hair peeping out from his orange Lycra bar shirt. "So, you want another mojito?"

DANIEL'S DOTS WERE:

1. The call from Sally Jacubiak's apartment to Gary Kwan just before his murder.
2. Petey's abduction.

Both Gary and Petey had a connection to Eileen Tenaway. Eileen was in custody. Gary was dead. Petey was somewhere. Sally's apartment seemed a reasonable place to look.

When the tinfoil-headed lady didn't answer, he knocked on Sally Jacubiak's door. No answer. He shouted, once, "Hello!" and put his ear to the door. Nothing. Or maybe there was a small sound, a bump or something, but he couldn't be sure. For the sake of thoroughness he tried the knob, then inspected the door more closely. Steel, in a steel frame. No way could he just kick it in.

He returned to the street and walked all around the building, looking at it. He got into his car. He watched the lobby doors, thinking.

IN THE COURTROOM I studied Tracy Beck-Rubin. She looked as if someone had tied her to a tree and left her there overnight. She had given her closing arguments for three hours yesterday afternoon, following her head-to-head with Eileen that morning. Prosecutors generally want time to prepare their remarks after the last of the testimony, but perhaps Tracy just wanted to get the damn thing over with. All she did was practically reiterate her opening arguments. Clearly this case had taken her to her limits. I took pleasure in her exhaustion. *You wanna know exhaustion, lady? Stand in my shoes for fifteen minutes.*

I wanted my boy back so bad I hurt all over, like the flu. *Focus, focus.*

Mark Sharma began the morning by making short work of his closing arguments, just as he'd pledged to. I was so intent on my plans, all of which hung by the merest of threads, that I hardly heard what he said. I thought about that house up Topanga Canyon, and about what might happen there later.

I can tell you Mark was forceful, precise, and passionate. The jury nodded madly. Eileen sat poised and brave. At last Mark stopped talking and sat down with sweat streaming down his neck, like a small, well-groomed horse. I looked at him sitting there so proud of himself. We were all so proud of ourselves, Team Eileen.

This was our triumph. Every member of the jury was looking at Eileen, openly and without anxiety. They appeared almost relaxed, yet clearly they wanted to get on with it and be the hell out of there.

Judge Davenport droned instructions to the jury, then it was time for an early lunch, only eleven-thirty.

I had a message from Daniel on my cell phone. "Just call me," said his buzzy electronic voice. "Please."

I phoned him back and he answered. I said, "Are you still try-ing to quote-unquote help?" I was in no mood.

"Yes, though you needn't be such a bitch."

People never understand. "Yes, I do need to be such a bitch." At this point, being a bitch was all I could cling to. "I might as well ask how you're doing, then."

A shame-filled sigh. "Not well, I'm afraid. But I'm—"

"Now I don't want to know."

"Will you be home tonight? That's why I called."

"Daniel, I don't know. I suppose I'll either be there or at the morgue identifying Petey's—"

"Rita, don't!"

"—his body, Daniel, or I may be at a house in Topanga Canyon trying to salvage what's left of my life and his."

He asked for the address, and I gave it to him.

After lunch the jury began its work, their absence from the courtroom as strong as a new presence.

Nobody left the building.

Mark Sharma and Steve Calhoun and Lisa Feltenberger specu-lated in low tones, their voices *rutabaga-rutabaga* in the hallway. I did not take part. The jury had already told me what they were going to do.

AFTER TWO HOURS Daniel felt foolish sitting in his car in front of Sally Jacubiak's apartment building. He started up the silver

Porsche and released the brake, but then froze because a woman walked out of the building, a woman wearing sunglasses and carrying a pink shoulder bag. Her jeweled pendant gave off sparks of sunshine. It was unmistakably her, the woman who had come to look at the light over Petey's window. The woman he'd shared an intimate smoke with on the fire escape.

THIRTY-SIX

Until the jury actually did what I knew they were going to do, there was this unbelievable suspense effervescing through my system, like one of those retro bubble Christmas tree lights, *bubble hot bubble red red*. No amount of lawyer shows on TV could have prepared me for it. You have to feel it to believe it.

At two o'clock we got word there was a verdict. Not as fast as Roscoe Jamison, but close.

At two-thirty everyone was in court.

At two-thirty-four Eileen Tenaway was a free woman.

She burst into tears of relief. Mark put his arm around her and murmured something very earnestly. Everybody shook hands and slapped backs.

I was pleased on several levels.

Using my cell phone I sent a discreet text message to George

Rowe, asking him to wait a few hours, then come to the Topanga Canyon address. I wasn't a hundred percent sure what would happen there, but I knew I'd want him.

The jury looked pleased with themselves. The judge thanked them.

Some of them inclined their bodies eagerly toward Eileen, as if they wanted to talk to her, or touch her, but she turned away from them, already dry-eyed. She looked at the bailiff as if to ask, *Really?* and the bailiff nodded, thinking about clocking out for the day. He too was pleased. She aimed her eyes at the exit, the one for free citizens.

The press clamored. They wanted Eileen, but Mark held her back, talking in her ear. My thoughts surged around Petey. *Maybe today. Maybe today.*

The jurors poured out and I stood in the sun-washed corridor and listened to what they blurted into the microphones.

"I just thought she was innocent," said Juror 2, a male middle school teacher who always wore little cap-toed sneakers to court in a futile attempt to be adorable. "I mean, at first I wasn't sure? But by the time she testified, I was convinced."

Juror 8, the guy who'd told Gary about his nonshoplifting mother during voir dire, said, "Yeah, me too. Those rotten cops better find out who killed her kid."

Another juror, a female film technician, said, "I *know* she didn't do it."

A reporter asked, "How do you know?"

"I just *know*."

Music to my ears. Dissonant music after all this, but music nevertheless.

The cap-toed juror broke in helpfully, "Well, they had this and that evidence, you know, but they didn't really show she did it. I mean, show me, don't tell me is how I've always felt about things like this. And I don't want to be small, but Tracy Beck-Rubin—ugh. It didn't look like she cared about Eileen at all. But Eileen, though—you could just feel what was going on inside her. You could . . ." He groped for words. "You could just *feel* she was innocent. It's hard to explain."

And there you are: the facts hardly count if you put on a good show. Does that make us all charlatans, then?

Mark bustled up, ready to talk, but the microphones wanted Eileen. Subtly, I took her elbow and pushed her forward. "I'll meet you in the garage. Lisa will take you down."

No one had spoken that day of Gary Kwan. For all I knew, no one had even thought of him.

I went back into the nearly empty courtroom. Tracy Beck-Rubin sat stiff and blank at the prosecution's table, gathering papers and tapping them on the tabletop. Her staff of two stood watching her carefully, not quite knowing what to do. Hypnotically, she tapped her papers, *dit-dit-dit*.

Seeing my hemline in her peripheral vision, she looked up.

I said, "I admire you."

She looked down at herself as if to check how much was left. When she looked up again, her pupils were small, her lids narrow.

"Who are you?" she said. "Who are you really?"

I should have been ready for that.

Her gaze held steady.

Then I thought, *What the hell.* "Mostly," I said, "I'm an actress."

That baffled her. Then she broke into a smile. "Ah! Ha-ha! I've always felt that way myself." Her assistants chuckled as the tension dissolved.

Then Tracy Beck-Rubin straightened, quickly stood up tall—the swivel chair went spinning away—and said, "Thank you. I love my job."

As I left the courtroom for the last time, I heard her begin speaking to her subordinates in a brisk tone.

Mark Sharma grabbed my arm as I walked toward the elevators. "What the hell is she going to the Cayman Islands for?"

The press had taken off to file their stories.

I kept striding. He trotted alongside me as I said, "You told me if I had a good idea to act on it. I had one, and I did."

"But what the hell—"

I stopped and faced him. "I know what happened the night Gary died."

His eyes receded. Then he remembered to demand, "What, then?" His mouth snapped into a razor-clam line.

Amazing. His reaction told me he knew something and was afraid of telling it. Or afraid of me.

My anger flared. "I'm going to nail your ass, Mark."

"I didn't do a thing, and you can't prove it." That sounded ridiculous and he knew it.

"Liar. If the police beat me to it, fine." The elevator opened. "But you're going to get what's coming to you, you treacherous piece of shit."

I stepped in, and the doors closed before he could think of something to say.

My cell phone vibed as I emerged into the parking level. The signal was poor, but Norah and I were able to communicate.

I ducked behind a pillar so Lisa and Eileen, who were waiting at my car, would not hear.

"So how goes it?" said Norah.

"Let me talk to my son."

"No can do, hon. What've you got for me?"

I hissed, "I want to talk to Petey!"

Norah sighed heavily into the phone. "He's *fine,* believe me. Believe me."

"God damn your soul to hell."

"No more cursing, OK? Because it gets on my—"

"Just let me hear his voice."

"Hey, kid! Say hey, OK?"

My boy's voice came faintly through the tiny phone's tiny speaker. "Hey!"

"Petey!"

"He's busy, OK? You satisfied?"

"All right," I said, forcing my brain—slicing it—into calmness. "What if I could do better than give you the treasure? What if I could give you Richard, too?"

"Don't play with me, he's—"

"I'll tell you where to find him. Today."

"I don't want to walk into—"

"Walk into it, Norah, you'll be glad you did. I'll have everything under control. Go up Topanga Canyon in about two hours." I gave her the address. "Leave your car at the foot of the road."

TOPANGA CANYON IS a gorgeous hassle, spilling in steep-walled glory mile after mile from practically the Ventura Freeway all the way to the ocean. Its only highway, a two-laner, twists you up and around the motliest properties in Los Angeles. Old hippies have established the canyon as their goal-line stand against the Pizza

Hut aesthetic, thus you will see wacky yurts with stained-glass cutouts of Jimi and Janis, hard by the herbal grocery stores which adjoin the pottery chimneys of the artisans which border the property lines of the movie people with their French Normandy horse stables and their natural-looking waterfalls, the waterfalls rarely visible from the road.

I'd always felt the word *Canyon* after anything makes it sound serious and mystical. The freeway signs abbreviate it CYN, without the period, which confuses nonlocals. "I'm looking for Laurel Sin Road?" they'll say. "I guess."

The house I'd leased for Eileen was a neo-Alamo with five bedrooms, killer views of the Pacific, and lots of privacy. She and I had dropped off Lisa at her health club in Santa Monica and stopped for a few groceries on the way.

I felt fairly calm at the moment, yet *Petey, Petey, Petey* throbbed through my heart. Helpless little fellow, only four years old. Please *God, let him live to see five.*

I flipped open the control pad next to the front door and punched in the code the lease agent had given me. The alarm lights switched from red to green. I made a deal of showing Eileen how to work it. Doing this technical thing made a sliver of thought come into my mind, of the film *Fail-Safe,* and then I thought of *On the Beach,* and then Serge Oatberger popped into my consciousness, surprisingly, like he'd been waiting behind all the heavy furniture to spring out. Oh, Sergy.

Eileen had tried to start a conversation in the car but I'd squelched it, not wanting to discuss anything of consequence while driving. I was feeling very tunnelly, like I could only do one thing at a time. And she was fine with that, lowering her window and breathing in all the smells she hadn't smelled in months. Her nose especially lifted when we hung our turn at the ocean and followed the PCH the few miles to the canyon road.

The day had really warmed up, into the seventies again. It wouldn't be stifling yet, even though now, in March, we were practically into what Californians call summer. Actually we call January spring, but I don't expect you to believe that unless you're one of us.

I showed Eileen around the swanky house. Outfitted in custom paint colors—three shades of cream in one bedroom—and a cool mix of Mission and modern furniture, plus lots of built-ins, the place was comfortable and sophisticated. I sighed enviously more than once.

Eileen seemed to relax completely once we were inside, though she seemed a little fragile. She stuck close to me. Waiting for cues? Maybe not. Maybe I was telegraphing something. I put some mental energy into being neutral and innocent. The place smelled stuffy like a closed house does, so I turned the temperature down to jump-start the air-conditioning. "As you can see, it's furnished and everything," I told her. Casually but carefully, I peeked into every closet as we went, prepared for Richard to pop out. Although the alarm system hadn't been disturbed, I wouldn't have put it past him to have defeated it somehow and been waiting for us inside.

I'd simply figured, as George Rowe did, that he'd come for Eileen as soon as the trial was over. If she was free, he could squeeze the insurance millions out of her, plus have some time to move his stash of loot out of the region, where, while liquidating it, he could wear a mild disguise and not be recognized.

If Eileen had been convicted, on the other hand, Richard

would have had to figure another way of finding his stash. A way to negotiate with Eileen behind bars somehow. Or perhaps he'd try to blackmail Gemini out of what fortunes it had left.

When I'd left the note at the Tenaway house with the address of this house in it, I was figuring he'd let himself in after Eileen's case went to jury but before a verdict. That way he'd be right there if she got acquitted, before she and the press and their cameras showed up at the house.

That's what I would have done if I were him.

So I expected him to find that note and make his way here as fast as he could. I wanted him to confront Eileen about the loot, and I wanted to hear them discuss its whereabouts. I thought if anybody could get that out of Eileen, it would be Richard. Then, of course, all I'd have to do would be introduce him to George Rowe.

I suppose I should have felt afraid, but I was focused and supremely angry. Rage flowed invisibly through my veins like hot wax. "Oh, the groceries," I said, remembering them. "Plus Steve's wife packed you a bag, did you see it in the trunk?"

"Yes, he told me she did that. I'll help you bring everything in."

That was uncharacteristic, I thought—she was the type to let a lackey do it.

We lugged the stuff into the kitchen, one of those quarter-million-dollar ones with granite and Sub-Zero and Viking and so forth. Plus tons of pots and gadgets—I even noticed a Le Cork Weasel, just like I had at home—all nicely stored in cabinets that gave an old-growth redwood feel to the place.

"I'll make some tea—would you like tea?" I asked, reaching for the kettle, which I found on a fix-it shelf loaded with screwdrivers, duct tape, scissors.

"Yes, please." My companion stood leaning against the refrigerator, hugging herself with one arm. "You know, Rita, I'm anxious to talk to you."

"Good." I saw purposefulness in her eyes.

And I turned, kettle in hand, and caught my own eyes in the black glass of the microwave. In that split second I had to admit something exhilarating: I wanted to kill someone today. Yes, I'd just about figured I'd have to do that, in order to get my boy back. And if I had to, I'd do it with a goddamn song in my heart.

"What would you like to talk about?" I said, filling the kettle at the tap.

"Well, I know you're worried to death about your son. Here's the thing. Well, first, I really have to bring you up to speed."

"Yes?"

The water began to roil above the blue gas flame.

"I've told you about Norah's hit-and-run and how Richard and I covered up for her. That . . . *incident* . . . seemed to break something loose inside her. It scared her, and she didn't drink as much after that, but it was like something was gone from deep inside her—like a barrier was broken. She took a life, even though she hadn't meant to. Then, everything went easier for her. As if she'd stopped being able to feel guilty about anything."

I took the kettle off and poured hot water over the Chinese black tea bags we'd bought at the grocery. The tea bloomed prettily in the white mugs I'd found.

"Let's take our tea into the garden," I suggested.

We walked slowly along the stone paths and breathed in the damp smells, this early garden with all the awakenings just getting going in all those juicy green plant hearts.

Surreptitiously, I looked everywhere for the son of a bitch,

340

even saying, "Oh, what an interesting little shed," and flinging it open to find only the pool machinery. The pool was pretty fabulous, twenty meters long at least, with a deep end, a springboard, and a small high-dive platform way up there. The high dive cast a gallowslike shadow over the water. It made me feel creepy and I turned away from it.

I checked my watch; it was about four o'clock now, and the sun was slanting through a few clouds to the west.

I said, "You know we're both in danger from Richard and Norah."

"Yes."

"We know too much."

"Yes."

Walking this way with Eileen suddenly felt pleasant, almost sisterly.

"So," I went on, "before they get their hands on us—"

She broke in, "We have to kill them."

THIRTY-SEVEN

The apartment building on plain-Jane Crenshaw Avenue, near the equally unprepossessing yet arterially essential Olympic Avenue, stood four stories, with six units per floor. Like most of the neighboring mid-rises, this building had no fire escapes. Flat roof, however, which could be the ticket. If Daniel could know for sure Petey was in Sally Jacubiak's place he'd get him out somehow, fuck it.

The apartment occupied the front corner, third floor, overlooking the street. The living room overlooked the street, anyway. Probably the other window was the bedroom. Quite exposed.

After the woman with the jeweled pendant disappeared from sight, Daniel drove quickly to a hardware store he'd noticed a few blocks away, bought a mason's hammer and a fifty-foot hank of double-braided nylon rope, and hurried back.

With the rope over his shoulder and the hammer in his belt loop, and wearing his navy blue twill shirt, he looked vaguely professional. Assuming a repairman's swagger, he walked briskly to the building's rear.

The roof access ladder ascended from the gaggingly smelly dumpster enclosure, starting about twelve feet up. Iron rungs, well anchored. He couldn't jump to it, and the dumpster was too full to drag over for a boost.

Other than bouldering, Daniel hadn't free-climbed in years. As a teenager he'd done a lot in the Smoky Mountains back home in North Carolina. Then he sold all of his gear to help pay for his leap to Hollywood.

Now he ran his hand over the crappy stucco wall. Cracked and weathered, it gave the impression of finger- and toeholds, but the stuff was as insubstantial as exfoliated greenstone. Using the chisel end of the mason's hammer, he chipped out bits of the wall, getting down to firmer stuff, holding his breath for the appearance of a manager or somebody. He chipped one-two-three as high as he could reach.

An elderly man shuffled into the dumpster enclosure carrying a plastic bag bulging with something disgusting. Without seeming to notice Daniel he poured the contents of his bag, which Daniel recognized as used cat litter, directly into the dumpster. Then he looked over and said, "Getting ready to paint?"

"Ah, sure am," replied Daniel with a smile.

The man carefully folded his empty plastic bag in quarters, tucked it beneath his arm for next use, and went away.

Daniel had worn a pair of sharp-toed lace-ups this day, which wouldn't do for gripping, so he kicked them off, shoved them inside his shirt, stripped off his lamb's-wool socks, and started up barefoot, the grainy stucco cold on his toes.

Once he grabbed the ladder's bottom rung he scaled it to the roof in seconds. Up top, the breeze tossed the surrounding oaks and sycamores. The neighborhood was heavily Korean, so he could see the tops of Korean business signs with their rectilinear characters. He saw in the distance a line of palms sticking up over some grocery lot on Olympic. Pigeons butted around in alarm. The rooftop had been graveled recently, so he put his shoes on and, skirting a narrow light well, strode to the front parapet.

This was a problem. He had thought to fix his rope to something on the roof and simply lower himself to the third-floor window, kick it in, and have a damn look. So what if it was broad daylight, people and traffic everywhere. He'd be risking getting stopped before he found Petey, but he couldn't think of a better course of action. Now, he saw, it couldn't work anyway, because the management had sunk thousands of bits of broken bottle glass into the mortar on top of the parapet, either to keep pigeons off (which it wasn't) or to discourage burglars.

"But what about us heroes?" he muttered. The broken glass would saw through his rope.

He returned to the chasmlike light well. The opening was only about ten feet by three. The ten feet was good, the three feet was bad, because also the shaft was home to one wall-unit air conditioner per apartment, which narrowed the situation even further. These mechanical obstacles hummed their locustlike song up into the sky. Nevertheless, Daniel anchored his rope to a nearby steel pipe, tied himself in, and descended. He was just able to squeeze past the first air conditioner, which luckily was smaller than the others. He reached a pygmy-sized window just above Sally Jacubiak's gurgling air conditioner.

Experimentally, he kicked the window, an eighteen-inch square of Plexi. It did not break. Was this the bathroom? No, you don't put an air conditioner in such a tiny space. The kitchen, then, or the bedroom.

"Hey!" he called. "Petey! Hey! It's Daniel!"

A few seconds later he heard a muffled voice. "Daniel! Hey!"

"Petey!" he shouted. A bolt of joy shot through him so hard he almost fell off the rope. He had sealed shut his emotions during the past thirty-six hours, not allowing himself to think *what if* about Petey, and now he felt the huge letting-go of that. He'd actually figured it out! Son of a goddang-gun. "Stand back," he yelled happily, "I'm gonna break the window!"

He could not reach down to the window with the hammer, unless he were to return to the top and lower himself upside down, which was too dangerous without having someone on belay. He braced himself with one hand on the opposite wall, rared back, and slammed his heel into the cloudy plastic. A corner gave way. The rest crumbled easily, like rotten ice. Now he could hear Petey's voice clearly, though he could not see him. He couldn't wedge himself any lower because of the air conditioner, and in any event the window was too small for him to get through.

"Hey, buddy, you OK?"

"Yeah," came the small reply.

"Good, stay that way. I'm gonna get you out of there and take you home. Wanna go home?"

"Yeah!"

"Can you reach this window?"

"No," said the boy. "It's too high."

"Is there anything you can climb on?" Daniel inhaled, then felt like he needed to spit. "Christ, did a cow die in there?"

"No, a lady."

"Oh, God. Look around you, boyo. Look around real good. Anything you can drag over to, you know, get up?"

"In the living room, but I can't 'cause it's locked, like."

"Oh. Well, hey. Pete. See that air conditioner?"

The weather-stripping around it was gray and gapped like bad denture adhesive.

"Yeah?"

"You're gonna push it out of the wall."

"Yeah?" said Petey dubiously.

EILEEN'S GAIT WAS tentative; it struck me that she probably hadn't walked this many steps all at once in months.

"Eileen," I said, "first tell me a few more basics. If we're going to plan a double murder, I really should be familiar with more facts. I get it that Richard and Norah started up an affair at some point, I guess before Norah's hit-and-run."

"Right."

"And I get it that they ran off together when the boom started to come down on Richard's embezzling, but they had to leave the goods behind." It felt so pulpish to say things like "the goods," but that was really the most useful expression in this case.

"Right."

"Then their relationship hit the rocks and she took off."

"He tried to have her killed."

With a sudden *burr* of wings, a house finch flew across the stone path into a seaside daisy bush.

Eileen and I both started at that, then smiled thinly at each other.

I said, "How do you know he tried to have her killed?"

"Oh, she was so stupid," she said, her voice heavy with remembered annoyance. "She thought they'd come back to the U.S. and set up housekeeping together in Los Angeles. She thought she'd have what I had. Fancy house, fancy guy. She thought he was going to *marry her,* for God's sake, and get her pregnant! When he told her he had no intention of returning to America, she couldn't believe it."

"She didn't like Brazil?"

"*Brazil* per se had nothing to do with it, it just wasn't in her game plan. He had the gall to get in touch with me and ask me to secretly sell off the gems he'd put away. He'd withdrawn everything from our joint accounts and taken it with him, but I had no idea he'd stockpiled cash as well as the stones in that locker."

We kept walking, slowly circling the acres-wide garden and the pool.

"All I wanted was to be Mrs. Beverly Hills," Eileen continued. She flipped a strand of hair that had gotten caught in a squint-line. In that gesture I caught a glimpse of the easy California-girl beauty that must have attracted the young Richard Tenaway. "I liked shopping and going to lunch. It was what I did, OK? I looked forward to fighting to get Gabriella into the top schools, you know, Wildwood, and Marlborough eventually, I think. I liked the parties. I liked flying into Tahoe for the weekend."

She stopped walking and touched my elbow. I turned.

"That's all I wanted," she said.

We resumed our stroll. "Not much to ask," I commented. Mercy, no. Simple little life.

Without irony she nodded in agreement.

"But back to Richard and Norah," I prompted.

"Yes. I hadn't known about his embezzling. I thought he was leaving on another business trip. He asked for my help packing. Then he essentially said, 'They're after me. I have to take you into my confidence.' He gave me a key and the name of the storage place in case something happened to him. He said, 'Honey, we're going to be tremendously rich, very soon, for real.' I said OK! Good! He said, 'Just tell me you'll do what I say, without questioning.' I said I would if he'd get rid of Norah. That was my deal: I keep my mouth shut about whatever's in that locker, and you quit your affair with my sister.

"He was surprised that I knew, like *duh,* you asshole, but he agreed. Well, Norah dropped out of sight, and I had no idea whether she'd taken off with him or he'd gone alone or what. Richard managed to get word to me to just sit tight and wait. So I did.

"Turns out they had left together after all, but after a few weeks Norah got on his nerves. He'd never really dealt consistently with her moods before. I didn't want him to kill her, for God's sake, but that's what he tried to do. The guy he hired botched it. He fell off the balcony before he got to her, and she figured out what the hell almost happened. She got out of there and came back to the States pretty mad."

"I'll bet. But how do you know all that?"

"Oh, I got it out of her in dribs and drabs."

"When?"

"That night."

"*What* fucking night?" I wanted to slap her so hard.

"When Gabriella died."

"Oh. Well, I wish you'd get to that, you know?"

"We're safe here," she said. "There's no hurry. No need for you to be impatient. You picked a wonderful spot for me. You know"—she smiled softly—"I guess I forgot to thank you for helping with my defense."

Like finally. "Think nothing of it," I said with a smile that tasted cold on the inside.

"Richard," she said, taking up her story again, "suddenly had all sorts of problems, even though he'd supposedly vanished! Mc-Gower was after him—the whole of Gemini wanted to get him, needless to say, but McGower was the only one who knew how much Richard had betrayed everyone."

"You mean how much he'd stolen?"

"Basically, yeah. So one day I get this call, Mrs. Tenaway, your husband has been found, and he's dead. I believed it! I go to Brazil and they hand me a death certificate and a picture. They stick me in some hotel to wait for the cremation, give me some song and dance about why I can't see the body. There was an autopsy, because of course Padraig wanted to make sure. The insurance company didn't require it, but he wanted it. He believed Richard was dead because he wanted to believe it. He was sick of the unpleasantness, and he was just as glad as anybody for Gemini to get the $10 million death benefit. I mean, he could cover a lot of Richard's tracks with that.

"I didn't want to bring his body back. But I did realize something was up. So I found the funeral place and slipped the guy some money to let me see it. Well, it wasn't Richard. Some doctor must have faked that autopsy report for a payoff."

"Good Lord."

"But you know what? I pretended it was him. On the spot, I realized what he was doing and why. I figured he'd stay in hiding until I got the insurance money, which was his way of saying he was

349

sorry. Then, I think, he hoped I'd split it with him, once everything had blown over. Unless, that is, I decided to take off with Gabriella and the gems myself. But the thought of fencing gems in Singapore or wherever, dragging Gabriella all over the world as a fugitive from the law—and from Richard—didn't appeal to me much."

"Do you still love him?"

She gave me an evaluating look, as if I were a nosy new hairstylist. "I would like to love him again," she said at last. "But that won't happen. I have tried to love him for a very long time."

"I see," I said.

We walked along the pretty stone path.

"Isn't that sad?" said Eileen.

DANIEL HAD BEEN perspiring heavily since he roped in. His right hand slipped on the rope, but he caught himself with his left. He dried his hands alternately on his pants and blinked sweat out of his eyes. How long before the kidnapper would return? Maybe Rita found the ransom stuff and this kidnapper chick had gone off to get it.

"Unplug the air conditioner, Pete, OK?"

"OK!" The machine went silent.

"Good job! Now find something like a stick or a tool. Something to poke with. See anything pointy?"

"Here's an umbrella."

"OK, take that and stab it around the air conditioner. You want to get it loose, see?"

If the unit was a good one, there would be a flange blocking him from doing that, Daniel thought, but it looked like a piece of crap, badly installed.

He thought of calling 911, but at this point that would likely use up more time than it would save.

A light went on in the corresponding window in the next apartment. Miz foil-head's place.

He heard Petey chipping at the caulking around the air conditioner. The kid was fairly coordinated, for a four-and-a-half-year-old. Mostly his blows made contact with the puttylike weather-stripping, only occasionally missing and striking the metal. The umbrella tip began to pop into view and out.

The foil-headed lady unlatched her window, pushed it open, and peeped out.

"Police, ma'am," said Daniel curtly, dangling from his rope. "Do you happen to have a key to this apartment?"

"I'm afraid not. Hey, aren't you—weren't you on, uh, that show with—"

"No, ma'am."

"Who's in there? Is Sally back?"

"Ma'am, for your safety I have to ask you to stay inside with your windows locked. Right now."

Petey kept at his chipping. After a few minutes Daniel called, "OK, Petey, now try pushing it."

An earnest little grunt came to his ears.

"I can't."

"Try some more."

More grunts, the last of which threatened to turn into a wail. "The lady said she'd be right back!"

"Be calm, Petey, I'm here. Can't budge it?"

"No."

THIRTY-EIGHT

It occurred to me that Eileen, probably innocent of murdering her own child, had yet been plotting a bloodbath for some time. That was why I'd found her demeanor so mixed, so puzzling: she was trying to cope with her daughter's death—by negligence or malice or both—but what was keeping her going were thoughts of murders she'd *like* to commit. With Richard and Norah dead, there would be no more conflict in Eileen's life. Nothing but an empty peacefulness.

By our third circuit around the grounds I started to really worry about Richard. Norah was on her way for certain, and I'd promised him to her. George Rowe would show soon but I wasn't sure he could make everything come out all right for me. My ears constantly attended to the cell phone at my waist, listening for

Daniel's song, "Dancing Queen." I knew better than to hope he would figure out where Petey was, but I couldn't help it.

There was only one thing I could do to try to ensure Petey's safety: find out where Eileen had stashed the goddamn loot and hook Norah up to it. An idea struck me—a crude idea, but it was an idea.

"Eileen, let's take our mugs inside," I suggested lightly. "I don't know about you, but I'm feeling a little tired."

I sort of guided us to taking seats on the thronelike barstools at the kitchen counter, placed so that guests could enjoy a drink and schmooze with the cook.

Such a pleasant room, this kitchen, all earth tones and granite, with those Spanish-style French doors leading out to the garden.

We'd left a bag of brown Bosc pears on the opposite counter, next to the sink. I got up, took a pear and bit into it, then said, "Hm, what shall we put these pears in, they're so pretty?" I scanned the glass-fronted cupboards.

"Who cares, Rita, we need to talk about how—"

"Here!" I put down my pear and took out a heavy stoneware bowl. As I moved toward the bag of fruit I seemed to stumble on something. The bowl fell from my hands.

Cruck! It lay on the floor in three or four pieces.

"Oh, no!" I stooped to pick them up. "Here, maybe it can be fixed." I laid the pieces on the counter. "In the meantime I'll just—" And I turned to the fix-it shelf, grabbing the duct tape.

"Well, duct tape won't—" Eileen began.

"No, I just want to keep the pieces together for when, you know—here, hold these pieces together, just nest them like that, and I'll just wrap them up in—"

Zeck-zeck-zeck.

And before she knew it—almost before *I* knew it—I'd bound her wrists firmly together.

"Hey!" She dropped the pieces.

I jumped to her side, drawing the tape as I went. I whipped it over her head, bringing the roll around her, binding her upper body to the barstool's back.

"Hey!" she cried again. "Rita! What are you doing?"

She struggled, kicking her feet. She tried to hop off the stool but only succeeded in knocking herself over. Thinking fast—I needed her conscious—I placed my foot at the spot I judged her head would hit the floor, and it cushioned the blow as she and the stool toppled to the tile. As she lay dazed I strapped her legs to the barstool's legs. I moved very fast through all this before I lost my nerve.

She was so shocked she could hardly talk. "Rita! What the— what the—"

"Look, babycakes," now talking still more like a pre-Code gun moll, "I have to know where you hid that loot. I'm not gonna fuck around with you anymore."

"Well, to hell with you!" she bluffed, searching my face. "I'll rot before I'll—"

"No, you won't rot, you're going to tell me because I will kill you slowly if you don't." I kicked her in the stomach.

Yes, I did, I kicked her in the stomach. The blunt toe of my Banana Republic business pump sank into her gut, then rebounded away with a live-rubber feeling.

She cried out in pain, her mouth drawn like a fish's on a hook, her eyes bulging. "Rita! I—I thought you were my friend!"

"Oh, you bet I am, just like Beatrice Rhinegold." I picked Le Cork Weasel from its drawer.

"What are you—what are you—"

I thought of Petey.

I could do this.

"Where is the goddamn stash, friend?"

"I—I don't know! It got stolen!"

I knelt to her. Very close. Burning, efficient anger coursed through me.

I drew deep on the spirit of Gramma Gladys.

I took one of her fingers—happened to be her right index—and, just as I'd cracked almonds with the sturdy gear teeth on my identical wine opener at home, I held the device upside down, inserted her fingertip, and squeezed the levers.

She shrieked, truly and horribly.

The hair on my arms stood up. I felt a sick rush of power.

"Goddamn you!" I yelled into her face. "Goddamn all of you!"

I bore down hard enough to make it really hurt. Then I stopped. She gasped for breath, and I saw a wet stain widening on her dress. Her urine ran to the floor. I'd scared the pee out of her, a wonderful accomplishment. She tried to head-butt me but couldn't reach.

I checked her fingertip, which had gone fairly flat and was beginning to ooze blood. Didn't look at all good.

"I will shred each and every one of your fingers unless you—"

"All right! All right! I'll tell you. It's in—"

A tremendous pounding on the front door shattered our special moment.

PETEY COULD NOT budge the air conditioner.

"OK," said Daniel, "I think I can sort of jump on it to loosen it. Wait a sec."

He reached up the rope, hauled himself vertically, then slammed down on the unit with both feet. He felt the shock into his hips. The unit rocked, almost free now.

"Petey, look, it's loose, but I can't pull it out for you. I can't get the leverage. You're gonna have to tip it out, OK? You can do it."

"Yeah."

"Take the umbrella and jam it under it. OK? Jam it in really hard. Super strong. Super strong. Now hammer it in with something."

"There's a frying pan."

"Yeah, hit it with that."

Sounds of banging.

"Got it? Is it firm in there?"

"Yeah."

"Now sit on the umbrella. Put your whole weight on it."

"OK. I'm—"

And with the most satisfying demolition noise, the air conditioner tore loose. It teetered a moment, plummeted silently, then crashed into the paved drainage zone thirty feet below. It sounded like the engines exploding on the *Titanic*.

Petey's head popped out and looked around.

"Wow!"

"HELP!" SCREAMED EILEEN, as the banging continued at the front door. "Help!" She struggled and squirmed, neck muscles popping. The banging ceased and footsteps spattered toward us, and Norah swept into the kitchen.

"What the hell? What are you doing here?" said Norah to her sister. She turned to me. "I thought—"

"What's *she* doing here?" cried Eileen. "Oh, God! Norah, she's trying to kill me. Help me!"

"You're wrong," I contradicted. "If that was the case I'd have finished stomping down your grave out there already."

I left Eileen to hyperventilate on the floor and stepped around the cook-top island to Norah, who looked stunned. Still clutching Le Cork Weasel, I told her, "I'm doing the best I can to find out where she stashed the gems and money. I'd sooner kill you both, frankly, but if I do that I won't know where to find Petey."

Norah looked at me as if I were insane. Which was odd since she was the insane one: a person who kidnapped and terrorized to get money, and perhaps for spite. All I was doing, by contrast, was torturing and terrorizing to preserve the life of my child.

My one comforting thought was this: *If Petey's alive now, he'll likely stay that way as long as Norah remains here.*

"Well, you're not gonna kill anybody," Norah told me. "If anything, I myself—"

"Help me!" Eileen grunted and struggled on the floor in her puddle of urine.

Norah said, "Where's Richard?"

"Richard!" exclaimed Eileen. "No!"

"Well, he's not here yet," I confessed. "See, I thought—"

Eileen said, "You told both of them where to find me?"

"I had no choice. Shut up. Is my boy all right?"

"Yeah, for fifteen million bucks he's fine, believe me. That kid sure can eat a lot of M&Ms."

Ridiculously, compulsively, I broke in, "They're his favorite, next to pizza and McDonald's."

". . . out of house and home," Norah was saying. "Yeah, we had some of that stuff too. You know, I sort of like the little bastard."

"Please just tell me where he is."

Norah said, "He's so cute. You know what he said? He puts his hands on his hips and he says, 'We don't hurt.' Very stern. Like he's telling me his rule. What a little *man*."

I closed my eyes. *Keep it together, hold on.*

"All I want is to get my property and get out of town." Norah reached into her Barbie-pink handbag.

"*Your* property?" yelled Eileen.

"I can hear you, I'm right here," said Norah. "You don't have to holler." She perched herself on the other barstool, extracted a Benson & Hedges from her purse, and lit it like Bette Davis, streaming the smoke sideways. "Well, sister of mine, we have all day to talk about this."

She flicked her ashes directly on the floor. Now that's a sociopath for you.

But before Norah had a chance to take a second drag on her cigarette, Eileen erupted from the floor, trailing duct tape like a George Romero zombie. She'd worked herself almost free, and she headed for the French doors to the garden, dragging the barstool by one foot.

She made it barely to the patio—Norah and I overtook her easily, but she, with the strength of desperation, managed to bash Norah in the mouth with her elbow, then turned, picked up the barstool, and rammed me in the chest with it.

I think she must have knocked me out for a moment, because when I got to my feet Eileen was free and the sisters were fighting like a couple of iguanas. Norah's purse was tossing on its shoulder strap and she seemed to be struggling to grab something from it, while slapping Eileen's face and neck with the other hand.

Eileen shouted, "You stay away from my money!"

"Oh, no, honey, you owe it to me!"

"You killed my baby! You go to hell!"

"I did not!"

Struggling there on the patio beneath the shadow of the high dive, they had forgotten me. I shook my head trying to clear it, fearing I'd faint, taking deep breaths, not knowing which sister to root for. Together like that, they showed those sisterly similarities you don't always notice when they're apart. For instance, Norah led with her left and so did Eileen. Each fortified her blows quite athletically, with power from the knees. They bared their teeth with the same hateful grimace. Very twinlike.

When I'd dropped down the rabbit hole after discovering Petey missing, I wondered what would be at the bottom.

This was it.

The sisters spewed recriminations as they fought. Norah shouted, "I sacrificed everything for Richard. He promised me that money."

"No, honey, he promised it to me!"

"You never wanted me to have anything nice!"

"All you ever wanted was exactly what *I* had!"

I saw something move, out of the corner of my eye. It was a shadow in the pool's shimmering water. A human shadow, the shadow of a man.

THIRTY-NINE

Seeing Petey's bowl of brown hair on his reedy little neck made Daniel so happy he couldn't find his voice for a second. He cleared his throat and told him, "Don't lean any farther out."

"Come get me," said Petey, reaching up one arm. He was still in his pajamas with duckies on them.

"Well, pal, see, I can't get any farther down than this."

The boy looked up to his friend's dangling figure and the square of blue sky beyond.

"I'll jump onto your legs and you pull us up, OK?" suggested Petey.

"No, Pete, that's not safe. I won't be able to control both you and the rope, see? Here's what we'll do. You're gonna be Spider-Man. For real this time. I'll show you what to do."

"For real?"

"Real as can be. You wait there."

With difficulty—his long legs in the cramped space worked against him, besides gravity—Daniel half hauled, half walked himself to the top. During this, he heard windows popping open and curious voices drawn by the smash of Sally Jacubiak's air conditioner.

He flung himself onto the roof, then scrambled to check his anchor, the iron pipe. It was fine.

He wished he'd taught Petey to make a bowline, that all-purpose, lifesaving knot of cliff and sea. He could not risk trying to talk him through tying one around himself now, sight unseen, because one mistake, an under instead of an over, would cause the knot to slip apart the instant it took any weight.

Instead, he tied a figure-eight knot to make a stationary loop just big enough, he judged, for Petey to slip himself into.

"OK, Spider-Man," he said cheerfully, "here comes the rope. Pull your head in."

The rope dangled in front of the hole and Petey's hand grabbed it.

"Now, Spidey, listen. Take that loop and step into it. Bring it up so it goes around your chest muscles."

"I'm doing it!" called Petey excitedly. "I got my sneakers on!"

"Ready?" Daniel wrapped his end behind and around himself in classic belay position.

"Ready!"

"Grab the rope with both hands. Not the loop, the rope above it."

"Like a loop?" Petey was suddenly baffled, his spatial circuits overloaded.

Daniel groaned softly. "OK, OK, just grab the rope and ease yourself out of the hole. I've got you." *Oh please oh please oh please.*

The boy clambered from the hole and swung into space, his little hands clutching the rope too high. Daniel's loop slithered off the boy's slender body and dangled below.

I LOOKED UP to the high dive and realized that the man had been hiding by lying flat on the platform, way above the blue dappled pool.

Amazing. I'd searched that whole damned house and garden and missed him.

"Stop!" he called, almost lazily.

Eileen and Norah froze in mid-eye-scratch. The three of us stood on the pebbled walk and shaded our eyes as the man looked down on us, spraddle-legged, hands outstretched like a pharaoh or Elvis, the sun flaring behind him. The pistol in his hand caught the late light like a molten chunk.

He laughed to see our faces squinting up at him.

"You bitches," he said, "would kill each other for a dead cat."

Handsomer, squarer-cut, and trimmer-hipped than even his pictures showed, Richard Tenaway stood above this clutch of agitated women in contemptuous amusement and evidently complete relaxation. He was wearing only a white T-shirt and a pair of slim black pants, as if he'd thrown off a coat and tie a minute ago.

He said, "I'm going to straighten you out. Everybody's going to get what they want."

Under her breath, Eileen said, "The hell you will." But she wanted to believe in him, it was there in her face, the longing to have some goddamn thing turn out solid today. He didn't catch

362

what she said. Norah looked at him fearfully. The breeze wafted the smell of pool chlorine.

He stood, crotch forward, and I saw that his crotch was absolutely central to him. In this moment, watching the man who had held such sway over so many lives, I understood everything.

For him to have sneaked onto the property—as I'd engineered and expected—and then waited, waited, listening as Eileen and I circled the gardens and pool—he didn't even really know who I was—how insidious and cool. Then hearing, as he must have, Eileen's screams from the kitchen—to have waited still, waited, to have known exactly what was going on—to know that if I murdered Eileen it would be for the money, then he would only have me to deal with.

And now to rise up above us as if he had created it all, like a grandiose puppeteer—he was pleased with himself and I could tell he'd been born pleased with himself, some men are. Women doing a fight dance below his feet! All we lacked were wet T-shirts and a mud pit.

There was, however, the question of his stash. The question of his murder of Padraig McGower. The question of his avoiding capture.

"So, you beat the rap," he said to Eileen.

His widow, bedraggled, urine-stained, sore-fingered, and furious, said, "You know what happened that night better than I do."

"No," he responded, "I don't." Now he held his gun pointing up, like a SWAT guy at ease. "Who would I have heard it from?"

"Richard, come down here so we can talk," said Eileen flatly.

He ignored that. "Norah, did you poison Gabby to hurt me? Were you trying to kill them both that night? Or Eileen, were you just taking the easy way out?"

What do you care? I wondered.

As if he'd heard my thought, he said, "I loved my little girl. I doted on her."

"That's what you used to call me," said Norah wistfully.

Eileen threw a hip forward. "*Doted* on her? Gabriella was just another piece of property to you, that's all."

He appeared to consider that. The sun slipped lower, behind his legs now. "Well, all I have to say is, no one fucks with my property. Least of all you two." He lowered his gun barrel so it pointed first at Norah, then Eileen. "I won't hesitate to shoot both of you. What happened that night? Tell the judge."

I couldn't believe it. He wanted to run his own little trial here. And the women obliged him, looking up at him, fearing him, fearing his gun, wanting him, wanting his gun. I watched, mesmerized.

Eileen said, "She came to the house, two months after you supposedly died. Fenco had just paid me my money. I was cordial enough, under the circumstances. I gave her a glass of wine. She told me what you'd tried to do to her, in order to get me on her side, I suppose, and—"

"What did I try to do to her?" Richard looked blank.

"The assassination attempt."

"*What?*"

"Oh, don't pretend, dear," said Norah nervously.

THE ONLY THINGS securing the boy to the rope were his own two hands.

Aghast, Daniel called, "Hold tight to the rope every second!" He forced a confident smile through his inner panic. "Use your leg muscles to walk up this wall, Spidey! Hold tight and just walk up, I'm taking in your slack."

Grinning, the boy obeyed. "Look at me!" he shouted. Then he decided to hand-over-hand it, like he'd seen movie heroes of all stripes do.

"No," said Daniel extremely calmly, "just hold tight with both hands and keep walking."

A shadow of strain crossed Petey's face. He faltered, his sneakers slipping on the wall's stucco facing, which was just as lousy here as on the outside. The boy gasped and looked down, one foot dangling.

Daniel deepened his voice to make himself sound calmer yet. "Don't look down, Spidey. Look at me."

Petey looked up desperately.

Daniel smiled. If he tried to haul him up, the boy might lose his grip entirely. "Spidey, you've got the muscles for this job. You're almost here. You can do it."

IT WAS *YOU* that tried to have *me* killed," Richard said to Norah. "That moron you hired, what a joke, as if I'd—"

"Oh, I see," I said. The words just popped out.

Richard turned to me.

"Who are you? The one in the trial? That left me the note?"

"I'm a mercenary for Fenco," I said.

"What?" said Eileen.

"Then I owe you one," said Richard. "But I'm afraid right now—"

Eileen broke in, "Norah came to try to get the stuff you embezzled. You were smart not to have given her access to it,

365

even though you were screwing her brains out every time my back was turned."

Richard made no reaction to that.

"She asked my forgiveness for having stolen you from me. She came crawling. I forgave her, all right. I did! But when I wouldn't agree to turn on you, she dropped something in my wine to put me to sleep. She knew there was a locker somewhere, and she thought she could find the key. She ransacked the house."

"No!" cried Norah, hands splayed anxiously.

"Shut up!" snarled Richard.

Caution to the winds, Norah wailed, "Richard, you never appreciated my mind! I tried to help you! I gave you lots of ideas!"

"Shut up!"

After a moment of silence, Eileen continued, "Gabriella must have woken up, and that's when she gave her the Valium in some ice cream."

"Auntie Norah," said Richard.

"I didn't do it! I didn't!"

"You were there." Eileen crossed her arms. "Who the hell else could have done it?"

Norah paused as if listening to something in the distant trees.

"Quit stalling," said Richard.

She looked up at him, and flung it in his face. "Padraig was there, and he did it."

Richard glared at her skeptically, but I thought, *Now I get it. At last I really get it.*

"Once I'd gotten Eileen to sleep," she said, "I started looking for the damn key. I couldn't find it. I looked everywhere. Padraig was waiting. Finally I called him."

"Wait a minute," said Richard, a terrible expression creeping across his face. "Back up. What was going on between you and him?"

"I can't believe it," whispered Eileen.

"I can." Addressing Norah, I said, "You seduced Padraig as soon as you came back from South America, right?"

Norah stood there trying to hold to some shred of honor. Hesitantly, she said, "How would you know that?"

"I put myself in your place. What would a screwed-up broad with good tits and no prospects naturally do? You'd whored yourself to Richard, then when that didn't work out you whored yourself to his best friend. You came back to the States and decided you loved him."

Everybody listened. "You told Padraig about Richard's stealing," I continued, "then the two of you joined forces."

With a grotesque primness, Norah said, "He was very interested in what I had to say."

"Fuck," spat Richard.

Norah peered up at him. "We decided the right thing to do would be to recover all that stolen property."

"How principled of you," commented Eileen.

The afternoon sun shone in everyone's hair, incongruent with the tenseness of their postures—Richard, thighs forward, Eileen with clenched arms—blood dripping from one fist—Norah in a half crouch, clutching her stupid purse like an Uzi.

"He must have been waiting for you that night, right?" I said. "The plan was for you to go over there, because you'd have a better chance with Eileen alone. Then when you couldn't find the key, you called him and he came over."

"So that's how that highboy got turned over," said Eileen. "That thing weighed a ton."

"Yeah," said Norah, "I thought I was being thorough, but I discovered I didn't know the first thing about ransacking a house."

"Good God," I said.

"There's almost a science to it. Gabriella woke up at that point. I couldn't calm her down." Norah's eyes drifted into the distance as she remembered the scene. I pictured it: the semidark bedroom, Gabriella in her big-butt overnight diaper standing up in her crib crying, clutching the top rail and shaking it with the full force of her little body, increasingly panicked the longer Mommy did not come. "The screaming was getting on Padraig's nerves. He came in and said, 'Let me try.' I suggested he look for some cough syrup, then I went downstairs." She threw up her hands. "Why didn't you have any cough syrup? That always works with kids."

Eileen had gone into some kind of fugue state. She stared at her sister.

Norah went on, "Well, like I say, I was in the kitchen opening all the canisters when Padraig came in looking for ice cream. He goes, 'This is for the baby,' and I thought how nice, he's going to give her a treat—why didn't I myself think of that? He didn't say anything about Valium at that point." Her voice dropped. "It was only later."

Richard said, "I can't hear you."

"I said Padraig McGower killed your goddamn daughter!"

Eileen's eyes looked like blank tiddlywinks. Norah added, "He didn't mean to. It was an accident! Don't you see?" she appealed to us belligerently, "An accident!" No one spoke. She went on. "Later, Padraig said, 'I only gave her a little more than what works for me. I didn't give her any overdose.' I go, 'Padraig, you're a two-hundred-pound man! She's this infant! It's like if you'd swallowed the whole bottleful.' And he gets this look on his face like, *Oh*."

Eileen spoke at last. "Why," she pleaded, "did you put me through . . . all this?"

Norah lit a cigarette and looked as if she wanted to sit down on one of the pool lounges. But she remained standing, most of her weight on one heel, grinding it into the paving stone. Same awful yellow Mary Janes. "I'd gone too far, frankly—there was no turning back that I could see. Padraig thought everything would turn out OK if we just kept our mouths shut."

She glanced at each of us in turn.

"So we did," she finished.

After a moment, Richard said, "If I'd known all that, I'd have made him suffer more."

"Well, it wouldn't have brought her back," said Norah.

"I can't believe you did that to me."

To him. There you go.

Eileen twisted her hands as if she'd tear them off.

Norah, holding her cigarette, looked at her hostilely. "What do you want me to say? I'm sorry? I'm sorry! OK? All better now?"

She stood there like a version of Eileen without a conscience, her life a wild mirror of her sister's.

Eileen said, "You and Padraig saw that Gabriella was dead, then you tried to make it look like a burglary. You didn't know how much of the evening I'd remember, did you?"

"I knew it'd be your word against mine," said Norah. "I made it look like a stranger did it so you'd know I tried to protect you. I'm smarter than you think. In fact, now that I've come this far in life . . . I feel . . . *empowered*."

Eileen spoke coldly to Norah. "Empowered, yeah. If I told the

369

police you'd been there that night, you'd have tried to pin every-thing on me. You'd have talked to the police, you'd have tried to implicate me, and you'd have helped them get us on the insurance trick. You worked it out very well."

The very air vibrated with craziness, danger, and the imminent death we were all trying to stare down in one form or another.

Eileen stopped and gazed at the treetops tossing so lightly in the late afternoon's golden breeze. "All this self-justification," she murmured. Then she turned to me. "Do you want to know the real reason I lost my baby?"

"Yes, Eileen."

"I let myself get sucked into the greed. It's that simple."

She'd come to it at last.

My cell phone played "Dancing Queen."

FORTY

utomatically, I grabbed the phone from my waistband.

My companions stood startled by the burbling dumb song.

"Are you in a safe place?" asked Daniel.

"Not really."

Norah drew something from her purse.

Daniel said, "Well, get out of there and tell whoever to go fuck themselves. I've got Petey and I'm bringing him home. He's all right, Rita."

A tsunami of relief broke over me. "Petey. Safe? Oh, safe."

As soon as the words were out of my mouth I saw, through my sudden tears, a look on Norah's face: the realization that she no longer had control over me. An instant later she lunged, a foot-long knife upraised in her fist, Norman-Bates's-mom-style.

And then I did something I hadn't done since the beginning of all this.

I screamed.

The quality of my scream resulted from, I'm quite sure, my emotional release about Petey combined with the sudden prospect of my heart being sliced open by this psycho twit. My anger spiked in a straight line skyward, no ramping up, just pure instant outrage. The sound that blasted from my throat was the most genuine, tooth-shattering scream I'd unleashed in my life.

My scream resounded in Topanga Canyon. I'm sure it stripped needles off the cacti growing up in the rocks. Made baby condors plummet from their nests. Set off car alarms at the herbal grocery store three miles away.

At that instant it hit me: if I did not die here, I would never act again.

Norah hesitated, driven back by the raw force of my cry.

Then, as if deciding to begin on an easier subject, she turned to Eileen, her knife still raised to strike.

Richard shouted a curse, set himself, and aimed his gun. *Krak!* One ugly sound, a punctuation mark at the end of the echo of my scream.

Norah collapsed like a sack of feed, the knife clattering off beneath a bush. She lay on her side, bleeding from her upper chest. One hand opened and closed spasmodically.

Eileen and I stood staring at each other in sudden we-are-fucked solidarity.

Then I looked up at Richard.

And an astonishing thing happened. He dropped his gun—it plummeted into the pool—silently grabbed his head, and tumbled from the diving platform. He hit the water headfirst.

The splash was tremendous.

Eileen and I stood stunned.

A noise like a bear scrambling through a thicket drew our attention to the garden wall, where after a second, a crew-cut head popped up. George Rowe's arms grasped the top of the wall and he hurled himself over, landing on his feet. He dashed through the Japanese maples and calla lilies and launched himself, his legs still churning at top speed, into the swimming pool.

He swam to the bottom. The surface roiled. George's head appeared, then Richard's, his eyes white crescents.

"Hold him up," George gasped. Eileen and I did so, by his arms, as George boosted himself out, spitting water. He hauled Richard out by the scruff of his shirt.

He knelt, listened for a heartbeat, turned Richard's head to the side, looked inside his mouth, then cocked his head back. His hand came away bloody from the back of Richard's head. He took a deep breath, sealed his lips to Richard's, and blew.

"You bastard," he panted, streaming water, "I want you alive."

He continued the artificial respiration.

Richard's eyelids fluttered.

"Goddamn cheating bastard!" George Rowe cried triumphantly.

Richard coughed.

"Jesus Christ," I commented to no one in particular.

Sirens shrieked up to the house.

And with the arrival of the police, the sorting out began.

George spoke to them, quickly outlining what had happened.

They called an ambulance for Richard and Norah, both of whom were breathing. Richard was actually coming to; a cop stood over him cautiously. One of the other cops worked on Norah with stuff from a medical kit.

The police were pleased to have an important situation here, one that was pretty much wrapped up for them already. They had cracked the whole Tenaway case, all the jagged ugly parts of it, even parts they didn't know anything about yet, right here in Topanga Canyon. They sorted and asked and jotted and called their bosses.

But who had called them?

I heard more car doors slamming. Daniel's voice. I dashed through the house.

Petey leaped at me and I enfolded him and kissed his face and his hair and his hands and he squirmed so happily in my arms like a one-man puppy pile and I cried so hard!

"Mommy loves you," I sobbed. "Oh, darling, Mommy loves you."

Daniel told me, "I heard you scream, and I called the police and changed course for here. Glad you trusted me enough to give me the address this morning."

I kissed Daniel and cried some more, then pulled myself together. Daniel told me he'd wait with Petey while I finished with the police. Petey clung to me, but I soothed him and Daniel wrapped him in a secure hug. Reluctantly, he let go of my sleeve.

I went back to the pool.

George Rowe was telling a detective, "You'll find a knife under that bush and a Wrist Rocket in the scrub behind that rock fence." He had taken off his shoes to let the water drain out. He stood in his wet socks. I wanted to put a blanket around him.

A Wrist Rocket, for God's sake. I remembered boys wanting those for Christmas. My brothers killed squirrels and the occasional slow-moving bird with them.

"Yeah?" said the detective.

"Yes, I watched the interaction between those four for about five

374

minutes. Tenaway had the women covered with that gun"—he pointed to the bottom of the pool, then to the high dive—"from up that tower. Norah Mintz pulled a knife and he shot her. At that point I shot him in the back of the head with a three-eighths-inch steel ball launched by my Wrist Rocket. I missed once before I hit him. The first pellet must have gone into those trees."

The cop said, "You carry a gun, too, right?"

"No, I don't, as a matter of fact."

"Why not? You're a PI, right?"

"It's against my employer's rules."

The cop laughed as one tough guy to another. "Are you kidding? You'd let a rule stop you?"

"It didn't stop me. I wanted Tenaway alive." George Rowe saw me listening and smiled a most becoming shy smile.

Eileen went away in handcuffs, her mashed finger wrapped up. But before she went, she wanted to speak to me.

I looked at this wreck of a woman, this Eileen Tenaway who had won every cakewalk she ever entered, except the last one. Back in custody after less than a day! They would charge her with insurance fraud, obstruction of justice, and God knew what else.

She said, "My life is over." Wisdom had come, late.

My heart breaking for her, I said, "No."

"But I don't hold it against you."

I never did figure her all the way out.

THE NEXT MORNING in the midst of everything else, I heard from Marly. She dispensed with hello and simply screamed into the phone, "You got it! Oatberger wants you! For the *lead*! Emily Rounceville!"

"How about that," I said, throwing my leg over the back of the sofa. I was tired even though I'd finally slept like a sow for nine hours last night.

"I knew it!" she yelled. "I knew he'd love you! I'll start negotiations for you as soon as—"

"Wait, Marly."

"What, hon?"

"I haven't said yes."

"Well—of course! We don't have a contract on the table yet, but it's just a matter of—"

"Look, I have to think about it."

"What's to think? Rita!"

"Tell him I'll make up my mind by tomorrow. I'll call you tomorrow. I've been through a lot lately."

Enunciating very clearly, Marly said, "Rita, what is the matter with you?"

"Tell Oatberger I'll consider taking the role if he'll give Daniel Clements an audition. He'd be perfect for the hunky mountain man who saves the blind slave's life. There's always one of those in an Oatberger picture. Get his agreement in writing. Mind you, I'm not insisting he give Daniel a role, only an audition."

Marly phoned back half an hour later. "He'll see Daniel, sure. But he's pissed that you're pulling this prima donna stuff already. Who's Daniel's agent, by the way? I should get—"

"Is his agreement to audition Daniel in writing?"

"*Yeah, Rita!* I faxed his assistant after I talked to him and he faxed me back! God in heaven!"

Faxes fly like lightning in L.A. when people on both ends want something.

"Good, thank you very much. Now, Marly, I don't know how

to tell you this, but I don't want that role. I do want to give you something for the work you just did for me."

Stunned silence.

"Marly," I said, "I'm quitting acting."

No sound.

"It's dawned on me"—speaking slowly so she could really hear—"that there's another destiny for me out there."

"Rita?"

"I'm not joking."

"Rita!" Her voice pitched upward. "What is this *destiny*?"

"I don't want to get into it now, Marly. I'm sorry."

"Oh God. Oh God. Oh God. I just put a deposit on three acres in Maui."

"Counting on your commission for this fat deal?"

"And beyond! And beyond, Rita!"

"I'm really sorry."

"Rita, he doesn't want anyone but you!" Her voice sounded like a thousand mice, on fire.

"Well, I'm sure he'll find—"

"No! Rita! Listen!"

I hung up.

DANIEL UNDERSTOOD. HE came over with sandwiches and cupcakes for lunch—I had no groceries in the house—and after we ate, Petey went to play Legos in his room. I told Daniel what had been building inside me. He listened quietly.

I said, "I've found out you were right, Daniel. Gramma Gladys was right. I'm smarter than a whole lot of people in this world. Smarter than I ever thought I was."

He finished the last bite of his ham panini. I'd only nibbled my sandwich. The herbs on it smelled good, though.

"That's my girl," said Daniel. "So what'll it be?"

I took a deep breath and said it aloud for the first time: "Law school."

He smiled. "Rock on, Rita, rock on."

"I'm going to spend the rest of my life nailing scumbags like the Tenaways and Norah Mintz. Not to mention Mark Sharma, that prick. And I'm going to keep my son and build a good life for us. No more auditions, scream or otherwise. From now on, the courtroom's the only stage I want to act on."

"I think you'll be a wonderful lawyer, if you can keep your temper in check."

"My temper?"

"Eat. I can tell you've lost weight from the stress."

"Daniel, I'm going to be a star."

We laughed together.

"You will," he agreed. "Insufferable bitch."

"Exactly."

"Speaking for myself," he said, "I'm thrilled Oatberger will see me. Thank you, Rita."

"I am so in your debt, I can never—"

"Stop. Have a cupcake."

THAT AFTERNOON WE all went to the Beverly Hills Police Department, where detectives from various jurisdictions talked to Petey as well as Daniel and me, at length. The homicide guys from downtown were there too. I asked the detective who interviewed my boy if he thought Petey ought to have some kind of trauma counseling, what with being abducted, having to hang out with Sally Jacubiak's dead body, narrowly missing plunging to his death, etc.

"Nah," he said, downing a paper cup of water in the corridor. "All that does is make 'em dwell on it. Let him deal with it his own way. I got kids too. Just be there for him, listen to him when he wants to talk. You know what I mean? He'll be all right."

And he was.

At home I cuddled him close and vowed to be the best mom I could be. I was wishing he had a halfway decent dad too when the doorbell rang. It was getting on to dinnertime and I thought I'd call for pizza, then replenish the groceries next morning.

Jeff stood in my doorway in a state of shaky but sober humility, accompanied by a scrawny, intelligent-looking guy wearing jeans and a USC sweatshirt.

"This is Manuel," said Jeff, "my AA counselor and new friend. May we come in?"

FORTY-ONE

Pleasantly shocked, I put some coffee on. Petey ran in to give his father a hug.

"I'm sorry about Spider Con," Jeff told him.

Petey stared at him briefly, unaccustomed, as children are, to being apologized to by an adult. Then he went to watch a DVD on rock climbing Daniel had left for him.

Jeff looked the worse for wear, mostly of the internal kind. He was clean-shaven but his skin sagged and his eyes brimmed with pain and regret. I have to say I was glad to see the regret.

Sitting at the kitchen table with the watchful Manuel, Jeff explained that he scared himself the last time he had Petey—he got drunk and mad and almost smacked the kid with a chair. Petey had not mentioned this. Besides, Jeff went on, his boss had caught him drinking at work. He had gone to a motel to try to dry out on his own, thus his mysterious dropping out of sight. But it hadn't worked, and his lawyer had guided him to Alcoholics Anonymous.

"And now," he said, "I'm on my way to check myself into rehab. Because"—he swallowed—"I keep backsliding."

"Are you going to rehab for Petey," I asked in a nice voice, "or because your boss's boot is up your ass?"

Holding my eyes as sincerely as he was capable of, he said, "For Petey."

Manuel said, "Jeff."

Jeff dropped his eyes. "Boss's boot."

He named a center in Malibu and said his company had arranged to pay for it. Moving his coffee mug in circles on the Formica, he apologized to me for the numerous wrongs he'd done me, carefully itemizing them, 12-step style. He told me he was dropping his custody suit as well. Finally I just said, "Everything's OK, Jeff. Don't worry about it." There's only so much of that kind of thing you can take.

He gathered himself and looked me in the eye. "Rita, I have to ask you something. Do you think, ah, you might be willing to give . . . us . . . another try when I come out?"

How did I know that was coming? "Oh, Jeff. I'm happy for you. I am tremendously happy that you're going to get straight. But"—I glanced at Manuel, who looked away—"I could never go back to you. I've gotten stronger."

"But—"

"No, Jeff. Our marriage is really over."

"I've never stopped loving you. All I want is one more chance."

"I gave you lots of chances before the divorce."

Manuel gave him an I-told-you-so look.

Desperately, my former batterer insisted, "But things are gonna be different."

"Maybe. And I hope someday you find a wonderful woman to share the rest of your life with."

Jeff drank his coffee and nodded slowly. "You were a good mother after all."

"Uh, well, I wouldn't overstate things," I replied. "Neither of us was a very fabulous parent. But it looks like we're both improving. Petey needs a good dad. You don't have to be married to me to be a good dad to him."

"Yeah," he agreed unhappily. "Yeah."

I ARRANGED TO see Tracy Beck-Rubin at the district attorney's the following Tuesday. "Yes, fine," she said, "I'd like to talk to you."

When we met in her office I told her my feelings about Mark Sharma and Gary's murder. "I just know he had something to do with it. I guess I don't have any real—"

"Were you aware," she interrupted, "that Gary Kwan taped his phone calls?"

"No!"

"He kept about a week's worth at a time, I guess for his own butt-covering. We have Mark Sharma on tape claiming to be Gary in a phone call a woman made that night. She wanted to warn Gary about Norah Mintz. You know that knife she pulled on you? They're running tests on it, and I'm betting—"

"Oh, my God. Norah. Oh, my God."

"She's not a very big girl. Do you think she'd had the strength to do it alone?"

"Hell, yes. She's this savage monkey who literally stopped at nothing. Richard had to shoot her to stop her. She'd have surprised Gary, I'm sure. Probably just walked into the office, walked right up to him, and stuck him under the ribs with that knife."

Tracy Beck-Rubin sighed and smiled cynically. "I wouldn't put it past Mark Sharma to have been involved somehow. Well, when she recovers from her injuries I'm sure she'll be ready to cooperate with us, given the situation she'll be facing."

"That is excellent, Ms. Beck-Rubin."

"Call me Tracy." She threw a foot up on her desk. Pantsuit today.

"Tracy. Thank you." I turned to go. I turned back. "You know Gary hired me to help Eileen win over the jury."

"Yes."

"That wasn't ethical, was it?"

"It's a moot point now." She saw I had something else to say, and waited.

I said, "Uh, if I were to, uh, apply to law school? And get accepted and study hard and graduate and pass the bar and want to become a prosecutor—"

She flashed her large teeth. "Come see me."

GEORGE ROWE SHOOK his head and made an admiring exhalation. "How," he asked, "did you get so many hunches that turned out right?"

We were having lunch at Dorsey's, this roadhouse-style place in Hollywood that forthrightly serves items like frogs' legs and liver-and-onions. I'd ordered the pot roast plate—I was just starving—while George requested spaghetti and meatballs.

I thought about George's question, and realized something.

383

"Well, I've trained myself to look for people's motivations, you know—to put myself in their place. I didn't just follow the money, I followed the heart."

The place smelled great, and it was dark and comfortable against the glare and concrete of the high-noon city outside. I think we were both tempted to have a beer, but we stuck to coffee, which tasted fine.

We talked a marathon brain-dump about all we'd been through, and boy did it feel good. We even ordered dessert (pound cake with strawberries).

I told him about my meeting with Tracy Beck-Rubin that morning, and about my plan to go to law school. "I'm going to stop and buy an LSAT book today as a first step."

"You'll be a great lawyer," he said. "With your intelligence and your . . . feeling for people." He smiled that shy smile again. His eyes were gray, I noticed for the first time. A clear, calm gray. As I passed him the sugar for his coffee, his hand touched mine. I liked his hands, so strong and good. I liked, I realized with surprise, George Rowe.

He mentioned playing the drums in his spare time. I was, again, surprised—he didn't have that animalistic look you'd expect in a drummer. Reading my mind, he explained, "Jazz and ragtime demand precise playing on the drums. You have to get your head into it. I like to get it right."

Looking at his arms and shoulders, I could see it—the energy, the competence. "I've been missing a lot of gigs," he said. "Maybe you'll come and hear me play sometime."

I found myself saying, "That would be . . . nice!"

He chewed some pound cake and swallowed. "How are you going to pay for law school?"

"Well. Yeah. Gary had promised me a bonus of fifty thou if Eileen got acquitted, but needless to say I'm not going to get it. I did save a lot of what he paid me." I perked my chin. "I'll work, and I'll apply for student loans. I know it'll cost a lot, but what the hell."

George tapped the tines of his fork lightly on his plate. He said, "I can't promise you anything right now, but remember I mentioned a possible reward from Fenco?"

"Oh!"

"Rewards are given at the discretion of the directors. You helped us break the biggest case I've ever investigated. I've talked to my bosses. Depending on how much we eventually recover, you could get—well, some tens of thousands, I'll put it that way."

"Eileen's acquittal be damned, then," I said.

"So where," said George, "do you think she hid the loot?"

"I have an idea, but of course we can't act on it. I'm sure the police—"

"What's your idea?" He leaned in, forearms on the table.

"It's got to be in that garage. The place was so dusty I'm sure the police couldn't have searched it thoroughly when they were investigating Gabriella's death. I mean, what for, if the crime took place in the house? And I'm sure by now—"

George clanked down his cup and threw fifty dollars on the table. "Let's go."

"But we can't—"

"We sure as hell can."

In the car on the way, he said, "Suddenly I'm understanding something about Richard Tenaway. You read this in cop stories all the time, but I never understood it before. It's the thrill that motivates him, just like it does me. The thrill of the hunt. He likes to be the one who gets away with something. It isn't about what he gets. It's the getting. Ordinary existence is too dull for him."

"For you, too?"

George smiled. "Depends on what you call ordinary."

"Well, *this* is certainly—"

"Here we are."

Bright daylight, quiet street. The Tenaway house hunkered lonely behind its hedges. I tagged behind as George strode up the driveway and shook the iron gate.

"Here," I said, "we can go through the hedge."

He held the branches for me. I crawled self-consciously through the greenery, my butt swerving like an ape's.

"Thank you," I said politely.

"You're welcome, ma'am."

The wooden door was closed as Norah and I had left it, but still broken, of course, so we walked right in.

A row of windows over the roll-up doors let in plenty of sunshine.

George paced around, getting initial impressions. I watched him raise dust as he moved.

And then, before I even glanced up, I knew it.

"The boat," I said. The *Little Gem*.

I'd remembered its gleaming hull, looking so sleek and athletic in the gloom.

"It's the only thing in here that's not dusty."

"You're right." George trotted over to the winch controls. "Oh. The electricity's off."

He clambered onto a tool chest and, nimbly using a broomstick to nudge the cables through the pulleys, jacked the boat down an inch at a time. "I think you might have it," he said. "Custom-made, I'd say. Beautiful."

He hummed faintly as he worked.

"What's that song?"

From his face, I could see he hadn't been conscious of humming. With an abashed smile at himself he said, " 'My Foolish Heart.' Victor Young and Ned Washington, 1949."

When the *Little Gem*'s keel touched the floor, we clambered aboard. George flung open the engine compartment, revealing only the engine. He pulled up the seat cushions and there, neat as could be, were cardboard cartons stacked, looking heavy, courier labels still on them with Richard Tenaway's name. The cartons measured perhaps a cubic foot apiece. There were ten of them per compartment, and there were four compartments, plus another, larger one in the bow.

George hefted a carton to his knee and cut it open with his pocketknife. He slit the plastic lining. I don't think he meant to spill it, but he was as excited as I was. A rush of colored stones poured onto the polished deck. There were so many, and they fell and rolled so smoothly they sounded like water. They lay in a square sunbeam on the deck.

We said nothing. The stones were irregular and dull, being raw from the earth. But catching the sunbeam in clefts here and there, flashes of pure color ranged from deep amber to almost burgundy.

"Imperial topazes," said George.

He opened another carton. This time—with a little smile—he spilled it on purpose, and a gout of green stones poured forth.

"Emeralds," I breathed.

"That's right."

"My God."

Impulsively, he opened another carton, then another. The stones piled up in the cockpit of the beautiful wooden speed-boat.

"Stop, George!"

We laughed like pirates.

"Look at that one." I pointed. "It's huge. It's—"

"Look," said George. "I believe these are sapphires." He kept opening cartons and spilling them.

Finally he stopped to wipe the sweat out of his eyes, and the spell ebbed.

"Too bad we can't keep any of these," I remarked.

He helped me down, his arm steady as a spar, and used his phone to call his bosses, then the police. "We'll wait for them," he said. "They'll secure everything. I guess it was all stones after all, unless they find cash in the bow."

I trailed my hand through the gorgeous riches and sighed, thinking of the women who would someday be adorned with these very gems, sparkling fire and ice.

George said, "Come here, please, Rita."

He had moved to another, clearer ray of sunshine next to the workbench. He drew something from his pocket.

"It's true we can't keep those," he said, "but look here." He held out his palm.

A single lovely stone lay in his gallant hand. Like the others, it was rough, but it too showed a flicker of fire. Blood-orange, clean and deep.

"This one is mine," George said. "I bought it from the man who dug it out of the ground." He took my hand. His eyes shone with hope. "Maybe it'll make a nice ring."

I gulped in surprise.

Softly, he said, "May I kiss you?"

"GRAMMA GLADYS?" I said. "I am, like, totally blind sometimes."

The traffic surged on Santa Monica.

"I don't think I'm ready. But it's awfully tempting."

I felt Gramma Gladys say, *Wait until you're finished with this college business! Then decide.*

I looked up to the dry blue Los Angeles sky. A flock of pigeons passed directly overhead. Not one of them pooped.

"Thank you, Gramma."

ON MY FIRST day at UCLA, I was about to mount the stone steps of the law building with my new briefcase in my hand and a flutter in my heart. A car honked very loud right at the curb, dual-tone horns that made everybody nearby jump. I looked, and Serge Oatberger leaned out of a glossy black limousine, which his driver had steered right onto campus. "Rita!" he called, smiling. He stepped out and held the door open like a bellboy. "I want to talk to you!" The sun glowed on his bald tanned head.

He shouted as if we were a long way apart, but it was really only about thirty feet. The students around me stopped and stared.

I shook my head, amazed at this coincidence. *Was* it a coincidence? Serge was a theatrical guy. "No, thank you," I said.

Oatberger's face reddened.

"Six hundred thousand dollars, Rita!"

"No!"

"You're throwing away an Academy Award!"

"No!"

"I'll give you a *two*-picture contract!"

"No!"

"You're turning your back on a marvelous career!"

"No!"

"None of the other actresses thought to spit in my face!"

"No!"

"You don't know what you're doing!"

At that I smiled.

The limousine idled like a giant black bug.

I said, "Yes, Serge, I do know what I'm doing." I flung my words high. "I damn well do know what I'm doing!"

Still smiling, I turned and ran up the steps. I stumbled, caught myself, and kept going, right on time for my first class.

ACKNOWLEDGMENTS

I'm grateful to my family and friends for their love, support, and belief, especially my mother, Carolyn Sims Davis, my brother, David Sims, and my sister, Kathleen Cristman.

Special thanks for excellent expert help to Jennifer Slimko, Philip and Monika Lenkowsky, Kate McNamara, Angela Brown, Margaret Baker, Ann Rosecrants, Solomon M. Cohen, and David Sims.

I'm indebted to my agent, Cameron McClure of the Donald Maass Literary Agency, and to my editor, Kelley Ragland.

Thank you to the Los Angeles Police Department; the Beverly Hills Police Department; the Los Angeles County Sheriff's Department; the Los Angeles District Attorney's office, especially Investigator Mel Wesson; the Los Angeles Central Library, especially the Children's Literature Department; and U.S. Customs and Border Protection.

Above all, thanks to Marcia, for everything.